PRAISE FOR ROBERT DUGONI'S TRACY CROSSWHITE SERIES

Praise for *A Steep Price*

"A beautiful narrative. What makes *A Steep Price* stand out is the authentic feel of how it feels to work as a police officer in a major city . . . another outstanding novel from one of the best crime writers in the business."

—Associated Press

"A riveting suspense novel . . . A gripping story."

—*Crimespree Magazine*

"Compelling and politically relevant, a perfect addition to this beloved series . . . Without a doubt one of the best books in the series . . ."

—Bookreporter

"Packed with suspense, drama, and raw emotion . . . A fine entry in a solid series."

—*Booklist*

"Fully developed characters and a fast-moving plot that builds to a shocker of an ending distinguish this crime novel."

—*Publishers Weekly*

Praise for *Close to Home*

"An immensely—almost compulsively—readable tale . . . A crackerjack mystery."

—*Booklist* (starred review)

"In bestseller Dugoni's nail-biting fifth Tracy Crosswhite mystery . . . [he] embellishes this clever procedural with well-developed characters and an interesting exploration of Navy criminal justice."

—*Publishers Weekly*

"*Close to Home* [is] another thrilling addition to Dugoni's Crosswhite series."

—Associated Press

"Dugoni's twisted tale is one of conspiracy and culpability . . . richly nuanced and entirely compelling."

—Criminal Element

Praise for *The Trapped Girl*

"In Dugoni's outstanding fourth Tracy Crosswhite mystery, the Seattle homicide detective investigates the death of Andrea Strickland, a young woman whose body a fisherman finds in a crab pot raised from the sea . . . In less deft hands this tale wouldn't hold water, but Dugoni presents his victim's life in discrete pieces, each revealing a bit more about Andrea and her struggle to find happiness. Tracy's quest to uncover the truth leads her into life-altering peril in this exceptional installment."

—*Publishers Weekly* (starred review)

Praise for *In the Clearing*

"Tracy displays ingenuity and bravery as she strives to figure out who killed Kimi."

—Publishers Weekly

"Dugoni's third 'Tracy Crosswhite' novel (after *Her Final Breath*) continues his series's standard of excellence with superb plotting and skillful balancing of the two story lines."

—Library Journal (starred review)

"Dugoni has become one of the best crime novelists in the business, and his latest featuring Seattle homicide detective Tracy Crosswhite will only draw more accolades."

—Romantic Times, Top Pick

"Robert Dugoni tops himself in the darkly brilliant and mesmerizing *In the Clearing*, an ironically apt title for a tale in which nothing at all is clear."

—Providence Journal

Praise for *Her Final Breath*

"A stunningly suspenseful exercise in terror that hits every note at the perfect pitch."

—Providence Journal

"Absorbing . . . Dugoni expertly ratchets up the suspense as Crosswhite becomes a target herself."

—Seattle Times

"Dugoni does a masterful job with this entertaining novel, as he has done in all his prior works. If you are not already reading his books, you should be!"

—Bookreporter

"Takes the stock items and reinvents them with crafty plotting and high energy . . . The revelations come in a wild finale."

—*Booklist*

"Another stellar story featuring homicide detective Tracy Crosswhite . . . Crosswhite is a sympathetic, well-drawn protagonist, and her next adventure can't come fast enough."

—*Library Journal* (starred review)

Praise for *My Sister's Grave*

"One of the best books I'll read this year."

—Lisa Gardner, bestselling author of *Touch & Go*

"Dugoni does a superior job of positioning [the plot elements] for maximum impact, especially in a climactic scene set in an abandoned mine during a blizzard."

—*Publishers Weekly*

"Yes, a conspiracy is revealed, but it's an unexpected one, as moving as it is startling . . . The ending is violent, suspenseful, even touching. A nice surprise for thriller fans."

—*Booklist*

A
COLD
TRAIL

ALSO BY ROBERT DUGONI

The Eighth Sister
The Extraordinary Life of Sam Hell
The 7th Canon
Damage Control

The Tracy Crosswhite Series

My Sister's Grave
Her Final Breath
In the Clearing
The Trapped Girl
Close to Home
A Steep Price
The Academy (a short story)
Third Watch (a short story)

The David Sloane Series

The Jury Master
Wrongful Death
Bodily Harm
Murder One
The Conviction

Nonfiction with Joseph Hilldorfer

The Cyanide Canary

A COLD TRAIL

ROBERT DUGONI

THOMAS & MERCER

Text copyright © 2020 by La Mesa Fiction, LLC
All rights reserved.

No part of this book may be reproduced, or stored in a retrieval system, or transmitted in any form or by any means, electronic, mechanical, photocopying, recording, or otherwise, without express written permission of the publisher.

Published by Thomas & Mercer, Seattle

www.apub.com

Amazon, the Amazon logo, and Thomas & Mercer are trademarks of Amazon.com, Inc., or its affiliates.

ISBN-13: 9781542093224
ISBN-10: 1542093228

Cover design by Damon Freeman

Printed in the United States of America

PROLOGUE

Cedar Grove, Washington
1993

Heather Johansen wiped her tears and the driving rain that blurred her vision and ran down her face. She walked the edge of the county road, with no street lamps or moonlight to guide her; the ink-black darkness rising from the asphalt beneath her feet to the heavy storm clouds gathered above the thick tree canopy in the North Cascades.

The tree limbs, leaden with water, let loose a shower spray with every gust of wind, and though she'd cinched tight the hood of her Gore-Tex jacket, the relentless rain continued to work its way through every seam and gap in her clothing. Her shirt collar and the cuffs of her long-sleeve shirt had become damp, and her blue jeans clung to her skin like leggings. Her boots, supposedly waterproof, were saturated. Worse, she could feel the temperature dropping, the rain progressing to sleet, and the ice clinging to her clothes. She could no longer feel the tips of her fingers, and her toes ached with each step.

She stopped and looked back in the direction she had walked. Again, she contemplated returning to Silver Spurs. But she'd become disoriented and could not deduce how far she'd walked—whether or not she'd passed the midpoint home to Cedar Grove. Besides, who could she call if she did turn back? She couldn't call her parents. She'd told them she was sleeping less than a mile from home, at Kimberly Robinson's house. She had no choice but to go forward.

She leaned into the wind and started walking again, each breath marking the darkness, each step filled with the same unanswered questions. What the hell was she going to tell her parents? What the hell was she going to do? Had she made the right decision, or was she just scared and being stupid? Was she just being stubborn?

Her stomach cramped from crying, and the pain caused her to double over. After a minute, when the pain lessened, she straightened and took deep breaths. The cramps eased, but not the weather. The howling wind caused the trees to sway and shimmer, and the sleet had now turned to snow.

From bad to worse.

She pushed on but got only a step or two farther before another thought stopped her. Where would she go when she got to Cedar Grove? She couldn't go home. What would she tell her parents? And she couldn't go to Kimberly's. That would place her best friend in an awkward position. It was the reason she had not told Kimberly in the first place. The Robinsons were strict. They attended the same church as her parents. They would push Kimberly to tell them what was going on. Heather couldn't do that to her best friend.

She thought of Sarah Crosswhite. They weren't good friends, but they were in the same class. And the Crosswhites' house was closer than her parents'. Maybe she could talk to Doc Crosswhite. He'd listen without judging her. He was a doctor. He'd know what to do.

A ghostly light flickered up ahead, a blue-gray radiance between the tree trunks—a car approaching the bend in the road. Heather felt a moment of relief. Then panic. She hesitated, uncertain whether to hide or to flag down the car. She couldn't take the cold any longer. Without further thought, she stepped onto the edge of the pavement and raised a hand, waving it.

The headlights blinded her and she lowered her hand to block the glare.

She heard the squeal of brakes above the gusting wind. The car had stopped in the middle of the road. Heather stepped forward, parallel to the hood, out of the glare of the headlights.

The driver's door opened.

"Heather? What the hell are you doing? You're going to freeze to death out here."

Her heart sank. *Shit.*

"Heather?"

She raised her voice to speak over the wind. "I need a ride to the Crosswhites' house."

"The Crosswhites?"

"Will you take me?"

"Why do you want to go to the Crosswhites'?"

"I just need to figure some things out. Please, will you take me?"

"What things?"

She started for the passenger's door. "It doesn't matter. It's personal. Can you please just take me there?"

"You need to let this go, Heather. This was an accident. A mistake."

The realization weighed on her, and she stopped moving.

"You need to think of the lives you're ruining, including your own."

"I am," she said. "One life in particular."

"No. You're just being stubborn . . . and emotional. I'll drive you to the hospital in Silver Spurs. We can all just move on."

"No. I'm not going back there. I'm going to Doc Crosswhite's house. If you won't take me, I'll walk." She started past the car, hearing the voice behind her.

"Get in the car, Heather! You want to ruin your life that's your business, but you have no right to ruin mine."

Heather heard the car engine rev, then the squeal of tires struggling to gain traction on the wet pavement. She glanced over her shoulder. The car had turned around. Headlights approached in the wind-whipped snowflakes.

She stepped from the pavement as the car sped past. For an instant she thought it would keep going, back to Cedar Grove, but the brake lights flared, red illuminating the falling snow. The driver's door flung open and the dome light flickered on, then off again when the door slammed shut.

"Just go!" Heather shouted as she walked quickly past the car. "Leave me alone!"

She heard a deep guttural sound—the noise her dog made when someone or something surprised them on the trail. She turned, uncertain, and looked into the headlights. She raised a hand to deflect the glare and saw a shadow in an aurora of color quickly approaching, something oblong raised high in the air.

It fell, like a logger's ax, hitting her in the head. The blow drove Heather to her knees. She pitched backward, her head striking the pavement.

Odd, she thought, looking up at the falling snow.

She no longer felt cold.

CHAPTER 1

Cedar Grove, Washington
Present Day

Tracy Crosswhite came down the stairs into the kitchen and put the bottle of freshly pumped breast milk in the refrigerator. Therese, the nanny she and Dan had hired on a trial basis, stood at the stainless steel sink, running her hand under the tap water, testing the temperature. Pop music emanated from speakers in the ceiling. On the granite counter beside the sink, Daniella lay in her rocker, stripped to her undershirt and diaper. Her belly protruded between the gap in her clothing, and the rocker shook each time Daniella batted the hanging toys—a blue elephant with red ears and a bright-yellow lion with an orange mane.

"Breast milk is in the fridge, Therese," Tracy said, shutting the door. "Hopefully that should hold her until we get home. We won't be late."

Therese spoke over her shoulder, her Irish brogue lyrical. "We'll be grand. You and Mr. O'Leary enjoy your night out. It's the first since she was born, isn't it? How long has it been?"

"Two months tomorrow," Tracy said. "And yes, first night out."

"Well then, you deserve it."

Dan had hired Therese upon the recommendation of a mutual friend—and after Tracy rejected seven other applicants. He urged Tracy to give Therese a chance, and Tracy had agreed, though she'd told him she'd make her own decision on Therese's competency. She had two months of maternity leave remaining before she had to return to the Seattle Police Department's Violent Crimes Section—if she returned. She hadn't yet made up her mind.

They'd moved to Cedar Grove while contractors demolished and remodeled their Redmond farmhouse. Dan had kept his parents' house in Cedar Grove as a weekend retreat from the city. The house was important to Dan, but coming home to Cedar Grove remained difficult for Tracy, whose own recollections of the town were far from positive—including the memory of her sister's disappearance. Each visit had been a little better, and Tracy did want Daniella to know where both her parents had been born and raised.

The timing of this trip had proved fortuitous. Dan had a motion to argue in Whatcom County Superior Court for Larry Kaufman, the owner of what had been Kaufman's Mercantile Store on Market Street. The time together in Cedar Grove would also give Tracy a chance to get to know and evaluate Therese—what Dan had called "a trial run." "Heck, the pound lets you try out a dog before you adopt it," he'd said. "What did Keanu Reeves say in *Parenthood*? 'You need a license to buy a dog, to drive a car. Hell, you even need a license to catch a fish!'"

"'But they'll let any butt-reaming asshole be a father,'" Tracy had said, finishing Dan's oft-mimicked line.

Tracy spied Sherlock's and Rex's empty bowls on the kitchen floor. The two dogs, 140-pound Rhodesian-mastiffs, weren't pleasant if forced to skip a meal. Dan had taken them on a run that afternoon, and from the looks of it, he'd succeeded in tiring them out. The dogs lay sprawled on round beds in the corner of the family room, fast asleep—a blessing. They pouted whenever Dan and Tracy left them at home.

"I better feed them before we head out," Tracy said.

"Don't you dare," Therese said, stopping her. "You'll get dog food all over your nice clothes. You look like a million bucks as it is."

Tracy moaned. "I feel like a million pounds, and most of it is up here." She pressed beneath her breasts.

"Well, I don't hear Mr. O'Leary complaining," Therese said. "Especially about the top half of ya."

"Complaining about what?" Dan entered the kitchen. "I never complain."

Dan rarely did. It was one of his many endearing qualities. Tracy sometimes called Dan "Mr. Optimism" because of his positive view of the world.

"Not about my wife, anyway." Dan wrapped his arms around Tracy's waist. "Doesn't she look like Charlize Theron? Am I a lucky guy or am I a lucky guy?"

"You're a lucky guy, Mr. O'Leary. No doubt about that," Therese said.

"Okay, you two eternal optimists, let's not overdo it," Tracy said. She'd put on forty pounds during the pregnancy and was still twenty-five pounds over her regular weight. Her doctor said she'd lose the weight more quickly if she breast-fed, and that breastfeeding was better for Daniella. Silently, Tracy envied Therese's slim figure. At twenty-six, Therese looked like Tracy once had—almost twenty years and one child ago—a cross-country runner with long legs and a slim waist.

"Do you think I should tuck my shirt in?" Dan wore the colorful button-down Tracy had bought him. It was not meant to be tucked in. She wanted Dan to have a little more style in his wardrobe. He either wore a suit, or baggy shorts and a T-shirt.

"It looks good," Tracy said. "I told you it's meant to be worn out."

"I feel like I should tuck it in. What do you think, Therese?"

"I think you look right styling," Therese said, turning off the faucet.

"*Right styling.* I like that."

Tracy rolled her eyes, then bent and nuzzled Daniella's cheek with the tip of her nose. "You be a good girl for Therese. Don't you get colicky and cry the entire time we're out."

Daniella cooed and kicked her legs. Her stubby fingers grabbed at Tracy's hair.

"Maybe I should feed her again before we go?" Tracy said to no one in particular.

"You feed her any more and Therese won't be able to lift her from that rocker," Dan said. "She's gonna look like the Goodyear Blimp."

"You go now," Therese said. "Daniella and I will be fine." She picked up the baby, talking to her in an animated tone. "You see, Daniella? She'll be the nighttime mommy, and I'll be the daytime mommy."

Tracy froze. She felt the heartstrings of motherhood wrenching her insides. No doubt sensing her angst, Dan quickly wrapped an arm around her shoulders and pivoted her to the door. "We better get moving if we want to make our reservation."

"We'll call when we get to the restaurant." Tracy grabbed her warm coat and scarf from the coatrack by the front door.

"No, we won't," Dan said, pulling open the door to a chilled wind. "That was the rule. No calls home on date night until we're on our way back."

"You have both our numbers," Tracy said to Therese.

"In my phone," Therese said.

"Put the alarm on," Tracy said.

"With those two dogs?" Therese jabbed a thumb in the direction of the two brutes dead asleep in their beds. "I'd like to see someone try to get in. It wouldn't be much of a row with the two of them at my side."

Outside, the brisk, cold air assaulted Tracy's cheeks and hands as she navigated the stone pavers in the grass. February had brought damp weather to the North Cascades, as well as occasional snow. Patches from an earlier weather system covered much of the ground and still dusted the tree branches. And more was expected. But tonight a full moon had turned the sky an indigo blue.

Tracy climbed in the passenger seat of her new Subaru Outback, Daniella's car seat prominently buckled in the back. She'd kept her father's 1973 Ford truck, rationalizing that someday Daniella might drive it, though Dan had expressed doubt that cars would still run on gasoline or even need a driver by then.

For now, the Outback was sensible and safe—a tank with airbags for the airbags, and all-wheel drive that could handle the worst Cedar Grove could throw at them. Every time Tracy drove it, she felt responsible and practical, and as old as dirt.

As Dan backed down the driveway using the camera screen, Tracy looked to the lights in the windows of the two-story house. Dan had his parents' one-story rambler remodeled to a Cape Cod–style home, architecture he had grown to love when he lived and practiced law in Boston.

Dan reached over and squeezed her hand. "She'll be fine."

A tear trickled down Tracy's cheek, and she wiped it away.

"Tracy, she'll be fine," Dan said. "It's only dinner. She's not off to college."

"Do you think that's how Daniella will consider me, as the nighttime mommy?"

Dan smiled. "You're not the nighttime mommy. You're the *only* mommy. Therese was just trying to give you some comfort so you wouldn't worry."

"I know." She took a breath and blew it out. "I'm just emotional. My hormones are all over the place. And I feel fat."

"You don't look fat."

"He says as he stares at my boobs."

"Hey, a guy can admire the mountains—can't he?"

She laughed. Dan could always make her laugh, as far back as grammar school when he had been the quintessential goober—pudgy with a crew cut and black-framed glasses. Never in a million years could she have foreseen them having a future together, but Dan had been there for Tracy in 2013 when she returned home to Cedar Grove to reopen the case of the man convicted of killing her sister. And she'd seen in Dan a good person carrying the baggage of an unfaithful spouse and a failed marriage, but who still possessed a kind heart and gentle soul.

"Let's go before we lose our reservation," she said.

"Lose our reservation? In Cedar Grove . . . on a weeknight?" He winked, put the car in drive, and headed for town.

They stopped at Cedar Grove's lone traffic light, dangling from a black wire strung across Market Street. The light swayed gently with each wind gust. Tracy marveled at how much Market Street had changed since their last visit. "You can't say Gary isn't getting results," Tracy said, referring to Gary Witherspoon, Cedar Grove's mayor. "New sidewalks, refurbished street lamps, new storefronts. Place is starting to look alive again."

"By stealing the businesses from the families that worked them for the past two generations," Dan said.

Dan would be in Whatcom County Superior Court in the morning to oppose a summary judgment motion filed by Cedar Grove's city attorney, Rav Patel. Patel filed the motion shortly after Dan entered suit against Cedar Grove on behalf of Larry Kaufman Jr., who contended Witherspoon and the city council had made misrepresentations to him and to the other business owners that the buildings needed expensive building code renovations that would cost more than the stores were worth. Kaufman claimed the representations had been intended to scare the owners into selling the buildings to the city. Most did. They saw the offer akin to manna from heaven—an opportunity to get a chunk of cash for a business that had either already failed or had been failing for a decade. Kaufman, whose grandfather started Kaufman's Mercantile Store, and whose father stayed in business by splitting the store and turning his half into a hardware store, refused to leave behind a seventy-five-year family legacy. He turned down the city's offer, and when the city moved to take back his store, he'd hired Dan.

The traffic light flickered on the refurbished iron sign that also stretched across the street.

WELCOME TO CEDAR GROVE
WASHINGTON'S MINING CAPITAL

There hadn't been any mining in Cedar Grove for one hundred years, and the city had never been Washington's mining capital, but Witherspoon had rationalized spending public funds by proclaiming it important for a city to remember its past . . . or to alter it.

Cedar Grove had sprung to life in the 1840s, when Christian Mattioli discovered gold, copper, and coal in the mountains and founded the Cedar Grove Mining Company. He'd built much of the town below the mine, and the business had been lucrative for several decades. But then the mine stopped producing, the new train route skirted Cedar Grove, and Mattioli, the mining company, and half the town went with the train. Those who stayed were hardy blue-collar workers without a lot of options. Tracy's father had been the exception. A general practitioner, Doc Crosswhite, as he'd been known, moved to Cedar Grove to be a country doctor, as well as to fish, hunt, and hike the outdoors. He bought the decrepit Mattioli mansion and renovated it to its original luster. The mountains, rivers, and lakes had been a bucolic place for Tracy and her sister, Sarah, to grow up, and Tracy had, at one time, every intention of spending her life in Cedar Grove.

Then Sarah disappeared. Everything changed.

When the light turned green, Dan drove past First National Bank, where he'd kept his law office when he returned to Cedar Grove following his divorce. The white stone had recently been cleaned, and the door and window frames painted. The refurbished building now housed Cedar Grove's city hall.

Dan parked down the street from Grandma Billie's Bistro. According to an article in the *Cedar Grove Towne Crier,* Grandma Billie's granddaughters, Elle and Hannah, had inherited Billie's recipes and her love for cooking. They'd taken out a small business loan to reopen the bistro.

"Looks like they also remodeled," Tracy said, stepping from the car into the spotlight beneath one of the newly furbished cast-iron light poles. A triangular-shaped banner hung like a sail from the pole, flapping in the breeze. It advertised the Cedar Grove Jazz Festival from the prior summer.

"Part of the downtown refurbishment, no doubt," Dan said.

"It does look great," Tracy said as they approached the gray awning over a pop-out façade. The storefront windows included written menus, and a slate chalkboard beside an iron bench advertised the evening specials.

Dan pulled open the door, causing bells to jingle, and they stepped inside. As they hung their coats and scarves on a coatrack, Elle personally greeted them and led them to a table near the window, handing them menus and pointing out the specials.

"You were just a baby last I saw you," Tracy said. "And your sister younger than that."

Elle smiled. "Speaking of babies, I heard you had a little girl."

"Daniella," Tracy said, fishing for her phone to show Elle pictures. "She's two months today."

"She's adorable," Elle said, looking at the photographs. "You two coming back here to live?"

"No," Dan said. "Just keeping my parents' home as a weekend retreat."

Tracy looked around the restaurant. "This place looks great."

"Things are changing around here."

"I've heard," Dan said. "You've remodeled. Was that expensive?"

"We took out a loan from the city to bring the building up to code and dust off decades of cobwebs. Then we applied for and got a grant from the Washington State Legislature to put on the new façade. We've been full just about every night."

Nearly every one of the dozen tables was occupied. The new interior looked like a country home, with white tablecloths and blood-red candles beneath a dim chandelier. A gas fireplace emitted a bluish-yellow flame, and mid-eighteenth-century mirrors hung on the walls beside assorted mining tools and made the room look more spacious.

"I hope you haven't changed your grandmother's cooking," Tracy said.

"Never," Elle said. "Still using Billie's recipes and added a few of our own. I'll get you some water and give you time to look over the menu."

"Don't," Tracy said to Dan after Elle departed.

"Don't what?" Dan said.

"You know what, Dan O'Leary. I can see by that look in your eye and the question you asked Elle that you're working on your case. The deal was no work, no cell phones, no stress."

"Just interested in the cost to remodel the building," Dan said.

"Uh-huh."

Elle returned with menus and filled their water glasses. As they looked over the menu, the bells on the door jingled, and Tracy looked up to see Roy Calloway and his wife, Nora. Calloway had been chief of police in Cedar Grove for more than thirty years. He'd retired in 2013 after the confrontation with Edmund House, the man who'd killed Sarah. Calloway now walked with a noticeable limp as a result of that ordeal, but no cane. He was too proud to use a cane. At six foot five, he had a barrel-shaped chest that still filled door frames, though he had to be in his late sixties.

Calloway removed a winter jacket, revealing a khaki-colored uniform and a gold star pinned to his chest. He smiled as he and Nora approached their table. "Can't stay away can you?" he said to them both.

Tracy nodded to the uniform and badge. "I could say the same about you," she said. "What's with the uniform? I thought you retired."

"He did," Nora said. "This is just temporary."

Calloway looked like he wanted to say something more, but the tone in Nora's voice clearly indicated work was not to be a topic of their conversation. "How long are you in town?" he asked.

"Probably a month," Tracy said. "We're remodeling our home in Redmond."

Calloway also seemed to give that some thought.

"Where's the baby?" Nora asked.

"Home with a nanny," Dan said.

"Then we won't intrude on your night out any more than we already have," Nora said. It sounded like a hint to her husband.

"I heard about Finlay's wife," Tracy said, wondering if the house fire that had killed Kimberly Armstrong was the reason Calloway was again acting chief of police. Finlay Armstrong had succeeded Calloway in 2013. "How's he doing?"

"He's on leave," Calloway said in a manner that made Tracy think the leave was not voluntary.

"Our first night out since Daniella was born," Dan said, not trying to be subtle.

"Enjoy your dinner," Nora said. "The food here is still great."

"Get the T-bone," Calloway said, and he gave Tracy a wink that made her smile. Calloway liked to tell people he was *tougher than a two-dollar steak*, though time appeared to have softened his rough edges. Tracy watched them sit at a table near the fireplace.

"Don't," Dan said, considering his menu.

Tracy turned to him. "Don't what?"

"You know what, Tracy Crosswhite. I can see by that look in your eye that you're wondering why Calloway is chief again."

"You're not even looking at me."

"Uh-huh. The deal was no work, no cell phones, no stress."

Tracy picked up her menu but sneaked another peek at Calloway.

"Don't," Dan said.

CHAPTER 2

Early the following morning, Dan left for Whatcom County Superior Court. The day had dawned with bright-blue skies and iridescent white clouds. Tracy took the opportunity to get outside and show Therese Cedar Grove. She bundled Daniella in a pink winter suit and pulled the hood tight, and together she and Therese sauntered along Market Street, sipping lattes from The Daily Perk, while Tracy pushed Daniella in the stroller.

"And I thought Seattle was cold in the winter," Therese said. "This is a wicked pissah, isn't it?"

Tracy remembered those clear, cold days from her youth, when the air was so crisp it almost crackled. "You think Daniella is warm enough?"

"She's loving it," Therese said. "Look at her taking everything in. I think you might have another detective on your hands."

Wide awake, Daniella did look to be absorbing everything around her.

So, too, was Tracy. Daylight had only further illuminated the changes happening to Market Street since Gary Witherspoon took over as mayor following the forty-year tenure of his father, Ed. In 2013, when Tracy had come home to bury her sister's discovered remains, Market Street had looked like a ghost town. The businesses had been boarded over, and stray papers blew down the sidewalks and gathered in the doorways. "For sale" and "For lease" signs littered storefront windows. Now, the signs in those storefront windows said things like, "Coming Soon" and "Grand Reopening." Cedar Grove would soon have another restaurant and microbrewery with twenty-four taps where once there had been a tin shop; a bakery where once there had been a thrift store; a hair salon instead of a barber shop; and a luncheonette and bookstore where once there'd been a five-and-dime. The corner drugstore remained, as did a refurbished Hutchins' Theater, as well as the large brick building—the name "Kaufman's Mercantile Store" in faded white lettering across the top. If Cedar Grove had its way, the building would soon become an outdoor recreation and apparel emporium catering to fishermen, bikers and hikers, campers, white-water rafters, downhill and cross-country skiers, and other outdoor enthusiasts.

The storefront windows had been fogged over, but behind them Tracy heard construction work—voices barking out instructions and the buzz and banging of hammers and circular saws.

When Tracy and Therese reached the corner of Second Avenue and Market Street, Tracy glanced at the entrance to the Cedar Grove Police Department. The one-story building of metal and glass wasn't part of any renovation project. She thought again of Roy Calloway and his return to chief.

"I'm going to check on an old friend," she said and asked Therese to take Daniella to the park. "I'll catch up. I won't be long."

"Take your time," Therese said, pushing the stroller to the crosswalk. "Daniella and I will be grand."

Inside the building, Tracy approached a female officer seated behind a pony wall. No bulletproof glass separated her from the lobby, as it would have in Seattle. Tracy pulled out her detective star and police ID and set them on the counter. "I'm here to see Roy Calloway. Is he in?"

"He is," the officer said, looking at the ID, then at Tracy. "Is he expecting you?"

Tracy considered the question and what she knew of Roy Calloway, who had been her father's best friend. "Yes," she said. "I think he might be."

Minutes later, Calloway pushed open a metal door and stuck his head out. "Tracy? This is a surprise."

"I was in the neighborhood and thought I'd stop by since we didn't get a chance to chat last night."

Calloway smiled. "Come on back."

She followed him down the hall, the worn linoleum glistening beneath white fluorescent lights. They stepped past what had been, for thirty-four years, Calloway's office. The colorful rainbow trout he'd caught on the Yakima River and mounted on a plaque no longer hung on the wall, though the wooden sign bearing Calloway's favorite saying did.

RULE #1: THE CHIEF IS ALWAYS RIGHT.
RULE #2: SEE RULE # 1.

"I let Finlay have the sign," Calloway said, turning back and noticing Tracy peering into the office. "But not the fish. That I had to work for."

"You gave him your desk too." Tracy recognized the nicks and scrapes in the burgundy-colored wood where Calloway had a habit of resting his size 13 boots. Calloway used to tell people they'd find his dead body behind that desk, because he wasn't leaving until then. That premonition had almost proved accurate in 2013. Calloway's limp reminded Tracy of that day in the mountains.

Calloway led her into the conference room with the pictorial history of Cedar Grove's chiefs of police dating back to the 1850s. Calloway's picture no longer hung last on the right, supplanted by

Finlay Armstrong's portrait. Finlay looked like a man unable to suppress a grin.

Calloway pulled out and sat in the chair at the head of the table and leaned back, folding his hands in his lap. "Can I get you anything? Coffee?"

Tracy set her jacket, gloves, and hat on a chair and sat to his right. She held up her paper cup. "Too much caffeine and Daniella won't sleep. Neither will I."

Calloway smiled. "I was happy to get the news. Thanks for sending us the announcement."

"Of course. You were my dad's best friend."

"I still miss him. I always thought retirement would be a lot of time spent fishing and hunting together. Even thought maybe I'd take up that pistol-shooting thing. What do you call it?"

"Single Action Shooting, though Sarah and I always called it 'cowboy shooting.'"

"Right."

"Young kids dominate the tournaments now," Tracy said. "It's the video games. They're quick as lightning. Much quicker than I ever was."

"Quicker than Sarah?"

"Maybe not." She smiled. Sarah had been called "The Kid" because she had been Tracy's kid sister, but when it came to shooting, Sarah was second to no one.

"I miss them both even more now that I have Daniella. My pop would have loved being a grandpa, and Sarah would have spoiled Daniella."

Tracy's father, James "Doc" Crosswhite, bereft over Sarah's disappearance and presumed murder, took his own life.

"Yes, he would have," Calloway said. "He helped so many. I still have trouble believing he couldn't help himself."

"How's the leg?" Tracy asked, changing from one painful subject to another.

"I get by."

"Still tougher than a two-dollar steak?"

Calloway grinned, as if hiding a secret. "I've become a little more tender with age."

"I won't tell anyone," she said. "And Finlay? How's he doing?" she asked, getting to the reason they were both in the building.

Calloway cleared his throat and sat forward. "Well, I'm sure he's been better."

Tracy waited.

He nodded. "Turns out the fire was arson. Someone used an accelerant, gasoline from a can Finlay kept in his toolshed at the back of the property."

She hadn't expected that news. "Really?"

"We just got the arson report. The fire started in Kimberly's office. Her body was burned beyond recognition."

When she'd heard the story Tracy wondered why Kimberly had not gotten out of the house. The fire had been at midday. "What did the medical examiner's report say?"

"That's exactly what I wanted to know. I called down to Bellingham and got the ME right away, though not the report. I got that about two weeks ago."

"She didn't die from the fire?"

"Maybe she did. But a blunt-force trauma to the back of her head is what prevented her from escaping the fire."

Tracy sat back. "Holy shit, Roy."

Calloway shook his head. "I know. The blow was hard enough to fracture her skull. Maybe hard enough to kill her. Strange that I would hope so, but I got a thing about fire . . . dying in it."

"You have any suspects?"

"You know how that goes."

"The husband is always a suspect. Is that why Finlay isn't here?"

Calloway started rocking a bit, then leaned forward and put his forearms on the table. They remained thick as woven rope. "Kimberly was writing a book. You know she wrote for the *Towne Crier*."

"Not sure I did."

Calloway nodded. "She was a reporter."

"What was the book about?"

"Heather Johansen's murder."

That name and incident gave Tracy pause. Heather Johansen had died several months before Sarah's disappearance. "I thought everyone wrote that off to Edmund House, a part of his killing spree."

"That conclusion was largely from a lack of evidence, and the fact that Heather's death was close in time to Sarah's disappearance, and other obvious similarities. House seemed likely."

"You ever ask him about it?"

"House?" Calloway nodded. "He denied it. But he denied killing Sarah too. Man was a psychopath. He was never going to admit anything."

Heather Johansen had been killed in February, six months prior to Sarah's disappearance that August. Both had been eighteen, and both disappeared along the county road. Johansen had disappeared on a snowy night, her body found in the woods four days after her parents reported her missing.

"Heather Johansen also died from a blow to the head," Tracy said.

"I know."

"And Heather was Finlay's high school girlfriend, wasn't she?"

"Yes, she was," Calloway said. "And you might remember that didn't end too well either."

Tracy did remember, though she had been four years older than Heather and away, in her last year of college. Sarah had told her. In a small town, everyone knew each other—and each other's business.

"Heather broke up with Finlay just before Christmas of his senior year," Calloway said. "He stalked her. It got pretty unpleasant. I put an end to it."

"I have a recollection he left Cedar Grove High," Tracy said.

"Finished up his requirements at the community college in Bellingham. Got a degree in criminal justice and came on board here with me."

Tracy gave that some thought. "What was the purpose of the book Kimberly was writing?"

Calloway sat back and rubbed a meaty hand over his face. He'd aged these past five years. They both had, though the ordeal in the mountains had taken more out of him. His silver hair no longer showed even a hint of the light-brown color it had once been, and his face sagged and looked weathered, even for a man who spent a great deal of his life outdoors. Tracy knew Calloway had not wanted to retire, likely because he was afraid he wouldn't know what to do with himself. Being chief in Cedar Grove hadn't just been a job. It had been his identity, and it had given him a daily purpose for more than three decades.

Tracy had a sense where this conversation was headed, but she decided to allow Calloway to ease into it.

"Kimberly was trying to determine who killed Heather," he said.

"She didn't think it was House?" Tracy asked, though she knew that answer. "Why not?"

"It's complicated."

"Start at the beginning, but give me the *Reader's Digest* version—I don't want my nanny or my baby to freeze out there."

"Okay. Until we caught House, after Sarah's disappearance, Finlay was our prime suspect. Kimberly, however, had a different theory that pointed to Ed Witherspoon."

"Ed?" Tracy said. "Why?"

"Heather worked part-time in Ed's real estate office, including the day she disappeared."

"Okay. So?"

"When Heather's parents called and reported her missing, they said the last time they'd talked to Heather was just before she left Ed's office late that afternoon. She told them she was spending the night at Kimberly's house, but Kimberly said she didn't know anything about that arrangement. We talked with Ed because we wanted to find out Heather's mental state when she left work. We wanted to know if Finlay had been coming around, if Heather had ever spoken about another relationship, if her personality noticeably changed. Those sorts of things."

"What'd Ed say?"

"He said Heather worked her usual shift, and he let her go an hour early to make sure she got home. There was a storm coming."

"Ed was the last to see her alive?"

"Last person we know of."

"Did he have an alibi?"

"He said he was at home. Barbara verified it. She said they stayed in all evening. It made sense. The meteorologist had predicted the first big storm of the winter that night, and it eventually dropped a foot of snow."

"So why then did Kimberly think it could be Ed?"

"She thought Barbara Witherspoon was lying."

"What was her basis for that?"

"A detail in the police report we had never made public but which Kimberly got through a public records request after we'd closed that file thinking Edmund House was the killer."

"What was the detail Kimberly found?"

"Eight inches of snow had fallen the previous night, but when we went to talk to Ed the next morning, there was only a couple inches of snow on the hood of his car. I put it in the report."

"Kimberly thought someone drove his car during the snowstorm."

"That was Kimberly's theory."

"What did Ed say?"

"He said he didn't know why he had less snow. He said the trees around his house might have protected the car."

Tracy gave that some thought. "Finlay have an alibi for the night?"

"Yes and no. He was taking a class at the community college in Bellingham, but the teacher also let the class out early due to the weather warnings. Finlay said he was driving home to Cedar Grove when the storm hit. Said it was slowgoing and he didn't get home until late."

"Did it check out?"

"That he made it home late? Yeah. His parents backed him up. And his teacher confirmed he was in class earlier that night."

"Okay, but did he have enough time to drive back to Cedar Grove and kill Heather?"

"It would have been tight, but yeah, he could have."

Tracy considered that. "Any other suspects?"

"Just Edmund House. We put everything to bed when we caught House."

"It was logical," Tracy said, "given the similarities. But House clearly didn't kill Kimberly."

"No, he clearly did not."

"Who knew Kimberly was writing the book?"

"Her editor at the *Towne Crier*. The Johansens, Finlay. And probably some others around town. Harder to keep a secret in Cedar Grove than in a college sorority. You know that."

She studied Calloway for a moment. "You don't honestly think Finlay killed his wife, do you, Roy?"

"I don't know what to believe anymore, Tracy. Not after what happened with Sarah and House's trial. What I know is, I'm getting too old for this job. It's gotten beyond me."

"Kimberly had to be asking questions around town. She had to have spoken with people, sought out documents."

"Likely she did. Here's another thing we never made public. The arson report says the fire started in her office, where she kept her computer and all her research materials. Finlay said she had binders on the

Johansen case, but it all went up in smoke. And there's something else that ties in here. Couldn't be certain before, but it seems likely now."

Tracy sat back. Waiting. Calloway let out a burst of air, like a whale breathing through its blowhole. Then he said, "Jason Mathews."

She shook her head. "Who's Jason Mathews?"

"You were gone by then. Moved to Seattle."

Tracy left Cedar Grove after Edmund House's first trial, which resulted in a conviction, but one she'd always questioned. Eventually people in town tired of her pursuing the matter. It drove a wedge between her and seemingly everyone else in Cedar Grove, including Roy Calloway and her mother. She'd moved to Seattle to get away—and to begin the process of becoming a Seattle police officer.

"Mathews was a criminal defense attorney from somewhere in Montana but retired here so his ex-wife couldn't take any more of his hide."

"When was this?" Tracy asked.

"This was right around 2013."

"Before or after I got House his retrial?"

"After. Eric Johansen did some work for Mathews on a remodel, and they got to talking about Heather's case. Given the doubts you had raised about whether House had killed Sarah, Eric thought it raised questions about whether House had killed Heather. He and Mathews worked out a deal. Mathews said he'd run things down in exchange for Eric doing carpentry work on his home."

"How far did this guy Mathews get?"

"He came in with a letter authorizing him to act on behalf of the Johansens and asked for the police file. I had him fill out a public disclosure request."

"He find anything?"

"We'll never know," Calloway said. "He's dead. Someone shot him."

Tracy considered Calloway. She sensed he'd set her up. Calloway knew Tracy—as well as or better than anyone in Cedar Grove. He knew she was stubborn like her father, and that when she latched onto something, she didn't easily let go. It had been why Tracy couldn't let Sarah's death go unexplained—it wasn't in her DNA to give up until she had answers, even if finding those answers nearly killed her.

"What happened to him?" she asked.

"Be easier to show you than to tell you."

She checked her watch. "Can't today. Daniella and the nanny are waiting for me. What about the Johansens? Did Mathews report back anything of interest to them?"

Calloway shook his head. "Not that I'm aware of."

Tracy again checked her watch. She needed to feed Daniella, or they were both going to be unhappy. It was time to cut to the chase.

"You want me to look into this, Roy?"

"I was thinking about it." He shrugged. "But you got the baby now and it wouldn't be fair. I'll find somebody else."

Which had always been Roy Calloway's way of asking, without asking.

"I'm on maternity leave," she said. "It's going to be another couple months before the remodel is to a point that we can move back in."

"You got the baby," he said. "That's your priority."

"Yes, she is. But I'm also working in a new nanny. Hard to tell how she's doing if I'm around all the time."

"You want to give this a look?" Calloway asked.

Tracy smiled. So like Roy to answer a question with a question—make it look like Tracy wanted the job. "Let me call Seattle and see if I can get approval. This pregnancy leave is all new to me, but I'm assuming they'll rubber-stamp it."

"What about Dan?"

Tracy almost said, *What about him?* She caught herself. "I'll talk it over with him."

"I appreciate it, Tracy." He gave her that hard stare that used to scare every kid in town. "I don't have to tell you that if my hunch is accurate and these deaths are all somehow interconnected, and word gets out you're looking into it . . ."

"I understand, Roy. I also know this job doesn't necessarily blend well with motherhood. I figure I better find out now whether I still want to do it."

"Talk it over with Dan. Take a couple days and think about it before you make a decision. If you decide you don't want to do it, I'll understand. No hard feelings."

CHAPTER 3

Whatcom County Superior Court
Bellingham, Washington

Dan O'Leary struggled very hard to look at ease. Sitting at counsel table, listening to Rav Patel argue Cedar Grove's motion for summary judgment, Dan appeared calm and undisturbed. His pen rested on his notepad, and his legs were crossed, as if to convey that what Patel had to say didn't warrant taking notes. In some respects, it didn't. The Cedar Grove city attorney argued that Larry Kaufman—who sat beside Dan at counsel table looking uncomfortable in a suit coat and tie—could not sue the city, Mayor Gary Witherspoon, or the city council members, that each was protected from a civil suit by the public duty doctrine.

Intelligent and clearly experienced in Judge Doug Harvey's courtroom, Patel had kept his legal brief short and his oral argument simple. He wanted to convince Judge Harvey a well-established legal basis existed to dismiss Kaufman's complaint. If Patel succeeded, Kaufman would be out of court before Dan even got started.

What Dan found even more interesting than Patel's legal argument, however, was that Patel was making it.

Like many cities, Cedar Grove had insurance to retain an outside law firm to represent the city's interests in litigation matters. Rather than tender this matter to their insurer and to that firm in Bellingham, however, Cedar Grove had chosen Patel to handle the motion for summary judgment. *Why?*

It was possible Patel would argue only this motion. If successful, there would be no need to pay an expensive law firm. If Patel lost the motion, he could still retain the Bellingham firm. But being an attorney, Dan saw conspiracies around every corner. He wondered if there was one here.

Dan's associate, Leah Battles, had discovered that Patel had become city attorney the same year Gary Witherspoon became mayor. She found that coincidence interesting, and rightfully so. It turned out Patel had also graduated from Washington State University in Pullman, and he and Witherspoon had been brothers in the Tau Kappa Epsilon fraternity. Dan wondered if Patel's decision to keep the matter in-house had anything to do with Kaufman's allegations of fraud against Witherspoon—Patel's fraternity brother—allegations they did not want to get out of Cedar Grove at a time when the city was seeking money for refurbishing the downtown.

"In all negligence actions, the threshold determination is whether the defendant owes the plaintiff a duty of care," Patel argued. He was a slight man with a heavy five-o'clock shadow. His suit hung on him as if he'd recently lost weight, and his voice had that monotone quality that could put insomniacs to sleep. Judge Harvey, however, looked attentive. And therein lay the problem.

Despite his physical demeanor, Dan was anything but confident. Patel's argument had merit, but only if one did not look deeper into the facts. Having not argued in Whatcom County in five years, and being unfamiliar with Judge Harvey, Dan had no idea whether the jurist would take the time to delve further—or take the easy road and bounce him from the courtroom.

"The courts of this state have long recognized the distinction between government duties that run to the public and those that run to the individual," Patel said. "The public duty doctrine prohibits the imposition of liability upon a governmental entity or its officers, unless the plaintiff can show the duty breached was owed to him as an individual. Stated another way, and as cited in our briefing, 'A duty to all is a duty to no one.'"

Patel allowed himself a smile, clearly pleased with the argument. He continued for another ten minutes. When he'd finished, Judge Harvey asked no questions, which meant Dan didn't know which way the jurist was leaning.

As Dan rose from his chair to replace Patel at the podium, Harvey leaned forward and spoke in a deep, gravelly voice that hinted at years of smoking. A deep wrinkle creased his brow, and equally grave crow's-feet shot out from the corners of his eyes. "Mr. O'Leary, the court tends to agree with counsel for Cedar Grove." This was not a good start. "The courts of this state have found that the intent of the public duty doctrine is to protect city employees doing their jobs. That includes the enforcement of state building codes. Why shouldn't we apply the doctrine here?"

Dan set his binder on the podium and, heeding Battles's warning that Judge Harvey didn't want to hear bullshit, he said, "The simple answer, Your Honor, is the state building codes never should have been enforced."

Judge Harvey raised his eyebrows.

"They are the red herring here," Dan said. "And they are the foundation of the fraud and misrepresentation perpetrated on my client. If I may explain?"

"I think you'd better." Judge Harvey sat back with an *impress me* expression.

"Counsel for Cedar Grove has correctly recited the public duty doctrine as well as the policy reasons for its existence. That doctrine, however, does not apply to these facts."

"Why not? To which of the four exceptions are you referring?" Harvey asked.

"None of them." Judge Harvey looked even more perplexed. Dan continued. "No exception is needed because the doctrine itself is not applicable. The doctrine does not apply when a government performs a proprietary function, in which case the government owes the same duty of care as a private individual engaged in the same activity. And a government performs a proprietary function when it engages in a businesslike venture."

"And what was the businesslike venture Cedar Grove engaged in?" Judge Harvey asked, not sounding convinced.

"The buying and selling of land from private individuals. If I may, the explanation requires a brief history of Cedar Grove."

Harvey grinned. "I'm a history buff, Counselor. Fire away. But let's be brief."

Dan placed the first of several poster-sized boards he'd brought to court on an easel. It looked a bit like a family tree. Moving to the top of the first board, Dan pointed to the name Christian Mattioli and recounted the history of Cedar Grove. "Soon after the discovery of precious metals, people moved to Cedar Grove either to work the mine, or to establish ancillary services such as selling mining equipment and clothing. My client's business was one of several that established what would subsequently be known as Market Street." Dan moved his pen along the rectangular businesses on the poster board as he spoke. "These storefronts included First National Bank and Western Union Telegraph, a pharmacy, a hotel and restaurant, and Kaufman's Mercantile Store. Now, pursuant to the Donation Land Claim Act of 1850, this land was free to applicants who resided on and worked the land. My client's grandfather purchased much of the acreage know as Market Street and

built the brick building that still exists today. Thereafter, he sold portions of the land to other business owners. Therefore, the owners of
those businesses on Market Street, and their descendants, owned the
land on which the businesses were built, not the City of Cedar Grove."

"Why does that matter?" Harvey said. "A city can still enforce
building codes."

"It matters precisely because, while for a time these businesses
flourished, with the depletion of the minerals and the closure of the
Cedar Grove Mining Company, a large percentage of the town left.
The businesses on Market Street began to fail. Some owners reinvented
themselves, but ultimately most shuttered their businesses and abandoned their buildings. Counsel is correct in his statement that *as to those
buildings*—abandoned for longer than a year—the city had the right to
enforce the newest version of the International Building Code before
those businesses could reopen—not that the owners showed any interest
in doing so. The city used this as the financial hammer to compel those
proprietors to sell their businesses, and the land, to the city. But—"
Dan put the final chart on the easel. "My client, Larry Kaufman, is the
grandson of Emmet Kaufman who established Kaufman's Mercantile
Store in the brick building that remains today. My client's father, Larry
Kaufman Sr., split the store down the middle and reinvented the business
as a hardware store. Unlike those other shuttered businesses, Kaufman's
Mercantile Store has remained open and in business since the 1850s."

Harvey eyed him, nodding ever so slightly. "You contend that the
original building codes remain the applicable building codes?"

"We do. And as such, in 2014, when Gary Witherspoon approached
Larry Kaufman and told him that his building would have to be brought
up to current building code standards, that statement was either igno-
rant or fraudulent."

"Let's assume it was fraudulent," Harvey said. Dan had a sense he
was playing chess with the jurist. "What reasonable basis did your client
have to believe the mayor?"

"Maybe none. But he did have reason to believe a building inspector sent on Cedar Grove's behalf. Attached as Exhibit D to our opposition is a report by the building inspector retained by Cedar Grove."

Judge Harvey shuffled through the exhibit tabs attached to Dan's motion and looked to be reading intently.

"When my client refused to leave the building, or to sell it for next to nothing, Mayor Witherspoon and the city council condemned the building as unsafe for the general public. That, too, was a sham. The condemnation was not done to protect the public. It was intended to drive my client out of business so Cedar Grove could own the largest building on Market Street and sell it to an established Northwest company that carries outdoor equipment, clothing, and supplies. Attached to our briefing, Your Honor, Exhibit E, you will find an expert report from a former building code inspector for the City of Seattle." Dan waited a beat for Judge Harvey to catch up, a good sign he hadn't lost him.

"That report states that Kaufman's Mercantile Store was not unsafe. In fact, as with many older brick buildings, the structure was overengineered by today's standards, and therefore, even if today's codes applied, the violations and the repairs were minimal and could have been readily made by my client."

Harvey sat back, rocking in his chair.

"In sum, Your Honor, the city acted as a private buyer of real estate, which is not a government function, and thereafter made false representations to pressure my client to sell. When he refused, the city fraudulently used the International Building Code to condemn the building as unsafe, shutting down my client's business and imposing onerous and expensive repairs. The public duty doctrine does not apply."

Patel got up to argue his reply, but Judge Harvey raised a hand. "I think I've heard enough from both counsel. Consider this matter taken under submission. You'll have my ruling tomorrow afternoon."

Dan left the courtroom feeling like a man crossing a river on a thin layer of ice, the reprieve could be short, and the consequences still dire.

CHAPTER 4

Cedar Grove, Washington

At home that night, Tracy provided vague answers to Dan's questions about her day, trying to find the right moment to bring up what she and Roy Calloway had discussed. Dan was focused on his morning hearing, and she was content to let him tell her all about it. After dinner, she put Daniella to bed, at least for the next few hours, and came downstairs to find Dan with legal papers scattered across the kitchen table. Therese had retired to her room to give them some privacy.

Tracy walked to the sink, ran a cloth under the faucet, and dabbed at breast milk Daniella had thrown up on her shirt.

Dan looked up at her. "If you're trying to excite me with a wet T-shirt, you're going to need a lot more water."

She smiled. "You wish. I do, however, feel like I'm carrying two Hindenburgs in my bra."

"Looks like one exploded."

"That would be your daughter."

"She still throwing up?"

"Doctor said not to worry about it. It's just an acid reflux." She nodded at the papers and briefs strewn on the table. "You don't look confident."

He explained to Tracy the ebb and flow of the hearing. "I should have argued CR56(f) and asked that the judge withhold his decision at least until we did some discovery, but this is a legal issue and I didn't want to confuse things. I'm looking into whether or not I can add a supplemental brief."

"Any idea when he's going to decide?"

"Tomorrow," Dan said.

"Therese and I took Daniella for a walk along Market Street," Tracy said, inching at the edges of the topic. "The downtown looks pretty good, Dan, better than it ever has. They're working on the sidewalks, remodeling the stores, revitalizing the storefronts. I'm not sure how Gary is doing it—federal and state funds according to the newspaper—but he's doing it."

"He's doing it by scaring business owners out of their buildings with bullshit threats and buying the buildings for pennies on the dollar. That's how he's doing it."

"Maybe, but . . ."

"But what?"

"Why would anyone think a new business is going to do any better than the one that failed?"

Dan sat back from the table. "I don't know, but his father never did anything unless there was something in it for him and, as your father liked to say, *that man was so crooked he couldn't put on a straight pair of pants.*"

Tracy smiled at the recollection. "I suppose it's possible there's something in it for Gary, but maybe he'd just like to see the city the way it once was. He was born here too. Maybe he has a soft spot for the way things were, like we do. Hutchins' Theater looks like the Hutchins' of old again. We had a lot of good memories there."

Dan set down his pen and gazed into the distance. "Saturday afternoons . . . making out in the back row of the theater. I remember it well."

She laughed. "In your dreams. You never laid a hand on me."

"I didn't say it was you."

"Really. Who was she?"

"Hey, they're my memories. Don't throw cold water on them. Save it for your shirt."

"Wet T-shirt again . . . making out in public. Are you horny Dan O'Leary?"

"As a red deer."

"And as the daughter of a hunter, I know exactly what that means. Maybe we can do something about it."

He stood. "I'm hoping."

"Something else," she said, stopping his departure from the table with what she really hoped to talk about.

Dan sat down again. "You realize it's dangerous to interrupt a red deer in rut."

"I got a sense at dinner last night that Roy Calloway had something he wanted to talk about."

"You and everyone else in the restaurant."

"I went to see him today at the police station. I wanted to know why he's back working."

"I'm betting he drove Nora crazy at home and she kicked him out."

"Actually, it has nothing to do with Nora. It's about Finlay."

"Finlay? Finlay Armstrong?"

Tracy explained the details of the conversation she'd had about the three murders and the thread tying them together.

"He wants you to take a look at it," Dan said.

She nodded. "He's too close to it, too close to Finlay. He needs someone outside the department."

"You told him no, though, right?"

His response surprised her. "I said I'd talk with you." Actually, Calloway had told her to talk to Dan, but she decided to leave that out.

"Do you need to?"

She could tell from the change in Dan's tone that the conversation had taken a turn. She didn't appreciate that Dan had assumed her answer would be no. "What does that mean?"

"Do you really need to talk to me?"

"I know what you said. I want to know what you're implying."

"I'm not implying anything. I'm just asking, do you really need to talk to me about it?" Dan repeated. "You're talking about three brutal murders, the last two likely committed to cover up the initial crime—if Calloway is right. What makes you think that person won't kill again?"

"That's exactly what I am thinking."

"Okay. Since you asked, let me be more specific. What makes you think the person won't kill *you* if you start asking questions?"

And therein was the question she'd been debating. She remained calm. "I'm a cop, Dan. I'm a homicide detective. This is what I do."

"No, this is *not* what you do. What you do is get a gang killing or drug killing or the-boyfriend-gets-mad-at-the-girlfriend-and-shoots-her killing, and you gather enough evidence to convict. That's not the same as poking around in a boiling pot and hoping not to get burned."

"If Calloway is right, this person has got away with killing an eighteen-year-old girl, and killing a wife. Who knows how much heartache this person has caused and gotten away with, Dan."

"And who knows how much more he's willing to inflict."

She hated arguing with a lawyer. "Someone used Sarah's death to hide the death of Heather Johansen for twenty-five years."

"That wasn't anything you did or did not do," he said. "Calloway decided it was House."

"Don't her parents have the right to see her killer brought to justice the way my family did?"

"Let's hope it goes a little better for them than it did for your family."

"Meaning what?"

"Meaning the obvious. Your father took his own life, and you nearly lost yours."

She wanted to get angry. Instead, she remained calm. "That's a low blow, Dan. That's beneath you."

"Those are the facts."

She tried another tack. "Then what about Finlay?"

"What about him?"

"Doesn't he have the right to have his name cleared and his wife's killer caught?"

"Of course he does. If he didn't do it."

"Finlay didn't do it."

"You once said Edmund House didn't kill your sister."

This time she couldn't tamp down her anger. "Are you seriously going to keep throwing that in my face?"

"I'm not trying to throw anything in your face, Tracy. I just don't want to see you get hurt . . . again. I'm worried about you, and I'm worried about our daughter. If you don't want to think about my feelings, think about her."

Tracy stood. "You know damn well I'd never do anything that I thought could hurt our daughter."

"But you're going to take this case, aren't you?"

"Why did you take Larry Kaufman's case?"

Dan also stood. "That is not the same thing. I'm not in danger of dying by representing Larry Kaufman."

"Why did you take his case, Dan? Why are you sitting at this table in Cedar Grove, late at night, looking for additional arguments? Why didn't you just sell this house when you had the chance?"

"This is what I do, Tracy. I'm an attorney. I help people who need my help."

"So do I," she said. "And you're avoiding answering my questions."

"No, I'm not."

"Don't tell me your decision to take Larry Kaufman's case wasn't at least in part influenced by the fact that it's Larry Kaufman, and he knew your father. I know how busy you are. You didn't need this case. You could have said no."

He shook his head. "It's not the same thing, Tracy."

"This was once my home too, Dan. And I hope someday it can mean something to Daniella. Something good and positive. Not the shit I had to live with. We've talked about Daniella knowing where her parents grew up. Is this what you want her to know? A city that cheats people out of businesses? A city where people die, and no one gives a damn to do anything about it? Do you want her to spend time here if there's someone out there killing people? Don't say I'm not thinking about our daughter, Dan. Don't you dare throw that in my face."

"Now you haven't answered my question."

"Do not cross-examine me," she said. "I am not on your witness chair."

"What's your answer?"

"I said, don't."

Dan nodded. "I thought so. You don't want my opinion. You want my approval." He shook his head. "Sorry, Tracy, but not this time. This time you have to make this decision on your own."

CHAPTER 5

Later that evening, Tracy pushed open the front door and let in a shower of snow on a gust of wind. She stepped inside carrying a storage box. Therese stood from her wooden stool—she was painting a landscape of the backyard—and helped close the door. Dan was working in his office, and the chill in the house from their disagreement was almost as cold as the temperature outside.

"Thanks," Tracy said. She set the box on the throw rug and kicked off her Sorels, which she hadn't laced for what she had thought would be a quick trip to the garage.

Outside, the wind howled, a ghostly wail that sounded like a freight train bearing down on the house. "It's really blowing, isn't it?" Therese asked.

Tracy pushed her shoes beneath the coatrack. "And the temperature is dropping."

She pulled tight her long down jacket and shuffled in her socks to the fireplace, standing with her back to the bright-red flames flickering behind the insert's glass window. Warm air blew out from the vent, heating the back of her legs.

"That is much better," Tracy said.

"The blower came on while you were in the garage," Therese said. "It's cracking warm in here now. I thought for a minute I was going to have to go out there to rescue you. You said you'd only be a minute. You're lucky you didn't freeze your knockers off. Then how would we have fed Daniella?"

Up until Therese's final sentence, Tracy wasn't sure she had knockers. Her chill passed, and she removed her coat and hung it on the coatrack. She knew exactly where to find the box she'd retrieved from the garage. What she hadn't considered was that movers had buried the box behind furniture from their home in Redmond.

Therese returned to the wooden stool Dan had found for her and picked up a palette on which she'd mixed tubes of different-colored paint. "It's really beautiful," she said, looking out the window before adding another stroke to the canvas. "We don't see snow often in Dublin. It reminds me of Christmas."

"It's beautiful when you're indoors," Tracy said. "It's a pain in the butt if you need to go outside for any reason, or to get anywhere."

As if to emphasize the point, the wind rattled the windows, a low rumble. Tree branches clicked and knocked together, causing dry snow to fall and catch on the wind gust—a temporary whiteout.

"I hope you don't mind me painting," Therese said, noticing Tracy's gaze on the canvas. "I'm using acrylic paint so there's no smell. I didn't want Daniella around paint fumes."

Tracy had indeed been staring at the canvas, and now saw, though it remained somewhat ethereal, the gazebo in the center of the snow-covered landscape. She stepped closer. "How long have you painted?"

"I started in Ireland when I was just a kid. My father painted. He taught me to just paint what I see."

"It's really good. Do you have others?"

"Here? You'd think I was shirking my responsibilities."

Tracy smiled. "I meant do you have photographs of your other paintings?"

Therese set down her brush and pulled up her phone. She scrolled through her pictures and showed Tracy some of her paintings.

"These are really beautiful. Have you ever shown them?"

"I'm showing them to you now."

"I mean have you ever shown them in public, for sale?"

"Get out," Therese said, smiling but shaking her head uncertainly. "You're joking."

"I'm serious. I'd buy one."

Therese gave her a stare—as if disbelieving. After a beat, she said, "I'd be too afraid to show them. What if nobody came?"

"Then you'd be no worse off than you are now."

"I'd be humiliated."

"Yes, but if no one came, no one would know."

Therese smiled. "That's one way to think about it."

Tracy looked down the hall. "Is Dan still in his office?"

"Mr. O'Leary is giving Daniella a bottle. I think you better pump. We've only one bottle left for the night."

"I'll do it before I go to bed," Tracy said.

She picked up the storage box, set it on the coffee table, and removed the lid, putting it aside. She'd kept several boxes of mementos from her years growing up—mostly the family photo albums and cards she'd received on birthdays and holidays. But what she'd really been after were the sweaters, mittens, scarves, and hats her mother had knit for her and Sarah. She'd always envisioned that someday her children and her nieces would wear them, but things had not worked out as she'd imagined. Not exactly. She did have Daniella now though, and the sweaters were a link to a grandmother her daughter would never know. They were also wool, which meant they were warm, perfect for the snow.

For years she'd kept the boxes in a cramped closet in her Seattle apartment, then in an unused room in the house she'd rented in West Seattle. The Redmond farmhouse had no storage space and barely enough room for her and Dan's necessities. She and Dan had brought the boxes to Cedar Grove and stored them on a shelf in the detached garage.

"Are those for Daniella?" Therese looked over Tracy's shoulder as she removed sealed plastic bags with the clothes.

"My mother knit them for me and my sister starting when we were infants."

"Get out," Therese said, sitting on a corner of the coffee table and picking up one of the bags. "You're serious?"

"My mother was a knitter." Tracy shrugged. "She knit all the time."

"A damn good one by the looks of it," Therese said. "They're gorgeous." The nanny held up a baggie with a white-and-yellow knit beanie with images of ducks. "Can I take it out?"

"Sure."

Therese did, twirling the beanie on her finger. "Daniella will be styling in these. You're lucky you kept them. I'm the oldest of seven. By the time my brother wore the hand-me-downs, they had to be thrown out, sometimes long before then."

Tracy had stored the sweaters in airtight bags to keep them safe from moths and mold. On more than one occasion, she'd thought of donating them to a shelter for abused women and their children. Better to put them to good use than keep them in a box.

"I wasn't sure I'd ever have a use for them."

Tracy worked her way through the box, showing each creation to Therese. The young woman reminded Tracy a bit of Sarah, who would perpetually be eighteen in Tracy's mind. It wasn't the years. It was Therese's unbridled enthusiasm for even the small things she came across. Sarah had been much the same way. Their mother called Sarah a Mexican jumping bean because she was constantly on the go.

Beneath the layers of knitted garments Tracy found a family photo album and flipped through the pages.

"Is that your sister?" Therese slid from the table onto the sofa beside Tracy. The picture was of Sarah in her cowboy action regalia—her well-worn cowboy hat, chaps, a plaid shirt, and a red neckerchief. Her leather holsters held her single-action revolvers snug against her hips. Sarah had posed for the picture, as if she were about to draw her pistols, and looking cocksure she'd beat whoever challenged her. By her teens, Sarah had established herself as one of the best shooters in the state of Washington.

"She was a pistol, my sister," Tracy said. "Everyone in Cedar Grove said that about her. She was the best shot in the county because she was cocky."

"She looks it. Is that you?" Therese pointed to a picture of Tracy inside the lobby of Hutchins' Theater, her hair in pigtails, her teeth in braces. The awkward years. On one side of her stood Dan, on the other, Sunnie Anderson—now Sunnie Witherspoon. Sarah and several other friends stood behind them, Sarah with a look of disgust. She was not happy Sunnie had taken what Sarah considered her rightful place beside Tracy.

"Do you recognize the guy with the crew cut and glasses?"

Therese bent down to look more closely. "No way. That is not Mr. O'Leary." She started to laugh and angled the album to better catch the light. "It looks nothing like him."

The only boy in the group of five girls, Dan had not yet gone through puberty. He was smaller than everyone except for Sarah, and he still had much of his baby fat.

"What are you two laughing at?" Dan walked into the room behind them.

"Your picture," Therese said. "You look like a nerd."

Therese held up the photo album so Dan could see the pictures. "Did Tracy tell you she was stalking me back then? I couldn't go anywhere without her following me."

"Get out," Therese said. "You're joshing me."

"It's true," Dan said. "I was quite the ladies' man. Check out those Clark Kent specs." Another wind gust blew against the house, drawing Dan's attention. "I'm glad we took down those trees along the side of the house last summer. These Northwest storms can be powerful." He turned to Tracy. "I'm going to read in bed. You coming soon?"

Dan had a principle he kept to even on nights like this one, in which they'd had a disagreement. He never went to bed angry.

She looked at her watch. "In a bit," she said. "I want to get out these sweaters and hats for Daniella."

"And don't forget you still have to pump," Therese said.

"And that."

Dan kissed Tracy atop the head. "Don't stay up late reminiscing," he said. "Night, Therese."

Therese checked her wristwatch. "Morning comes early around here," she said, standing. "I better clean these brushes and get ready for Lily White's party myself, as my mother used to say."

Tracy smiled. "Lily White's party? What does that mean?"

"It means I better get ready for bed."

"Is it Irish?"

"I don't know. Just something she used to say that stuck in my mind." She looked at the box filled with memories. "A bit like what's in that box." She grabbed her paintbrushes and departed down the hall, toward her room at the back of the house.

Tracy continued to rummage through the box. Near the bottom she found several flowered notebooks—her and Sarah's diaries. Tracy had kept diaries in her teens, hiding them to prevent Sarah from reading her teenage musings. No secret had been safe with her sister around. Sarah had always called Tracy's scribbles dumb, and given Sarah's inability to sit still, Tracy had no idea Sarah had also kept diaries until she'd cleaned out the family home after her mother passed. She was more than a little surprised. Sarah had apparently started her diary the year Tracy had left for college—or maybe *because* Tracy had left. When Tracy found them in a closet, it had been like finding razor blades. The first entry was Sarah's scribblings about how much she missed her sister, how everything had changed when Tracy left, and how nothing would ever again be the same. Looking back, Tracy wondered if Sarah had been clinically depressed, and scribbling in the diary was a form of therapy her father had prescribed. Typical doctor. He could diagnose everyone else's ailments but his own. Depression is what had led him to take his own life.

Each page Tracy had read had inflicted another painful cut, until it was simply too much to read them anymore. She'd put the diaries in the box, for what future purpose she didn't know. That thought caused her to pause. *Huh*, she wondered.

She took out the short stack, flipping each cover open, and setting them aside until she found the diary for 1992–1993, the year Sarah graduated from Cedar Grove High School.

Heather Johansen's body had been discovered by Vern Downie's hounds in February 1993, four months before graduation, and six months before Sarah had disappeared along the same stretch of the county road. Tracy opened the book, recalling that Sarah's entries seemed sporadic and disjointed, some written in black, others in blue and red, even one in purple. Sometimes she scribbled down thoughts, often just fragments or a piece of bad poetry. In others she drew pictures—trees, a road seemingly to nowhere, the moon on a cloudy night, what looked like a self-portrait. Rarely did she offer any deep insight into her feelings. Tracy thought the entries typified a young girl—likely one who, if she were a teenager today, would be diagnosed with ADD rather than described as a Mexican jumping bean.

Tracy flipped through the pages, glancing at, but not really reading the details, not certain, even now, about this invasion of her sister's privacy. In one passage Sarah admitted to being nervous about leaving Cedar Grove to attend college, leaving her home, her family, her friends. Tracy had never known Sarah to be nervous about anything. It's what had made her such a good shooter. She'd been daring and bold, often to the point of recklessness.

Tracy skimmed the passages.

> *Going to Oregon for Black Powder Championship this W/E. Wash. Wild Bunch Championship next W/E. Training hard w/ Dad. Tracy has too much work. Up to me to uphold family name. HAHA! Dad says Oregon has good shooters. Some guy named Jim Fick is best. I don't know, but kind of digging his cowboy name: "Cool Hand." Dad says he shoots a classic .32 Winchester and a Colt 45. Well, Cool Hand, you are about to get your ASS KICKED! 'cause The Kid is coming home with the medal!*

Tracy smiled at her sister's unbridled brashness. Tracy's cowboy name had been "Crossdraw," a play on her name and, like her father, her use of a cross-draw holster.

Tracy flipped the page, skimming entries, each word another prick drawing blood. She searched the dates and found an entry dated November 1992. Initials caught her attention.

> *Just heard about HJ and FA breaking up and FA apparently being a massive dickhead to her.*

HJ was Heather Johansen and FA was Finlay Armstrong. Tracy continued to read.

> *Heard he won't stop calling her and that he waits for her after school and calls her "Slut" and "Bitch." I'd shoot his ass!*

Tracy focused on her sister's description of Finlay Armstrong's actions, of the intensity of his words. Heather Johansen and Sarah

hadn't been close, at least not to Tracy's knowledge, so the fact that
Sarah was writing about it in her diary was an indication it had been
news at school.

Tracy flipped the diary page. Her eyes stopped again, this time on
a December entry when she saw the same initials.

> *Apparently Chief Roy talked to FA. D/K what Roy said, but*
> *he must have scared the shit out of Finlay! 'cause he's dropped*
> *out of school. Heard he's taking classes at community college.*

She flipped ahead several pages and came to the day they found
Heather Johansen's body. Sarah's writing was stilted and disjointed. The
blue ink looked to have smeared.

> *They found Heather. Found her body. She's dead. Police aren't*
> *saying anything and everyone around town is just real quiet.*
> *They sent us home from school. I asked my Dad if the police*
> *were talking to FA 'cause of him stalking HJ. He told me*
> *not to rush to judgment! But who else could it be? Has to be*
> *FA . . . Right? Has to be!*

The windows rattled, causing Tracy to startle. She looked around
the room and wished they'd put up curtains or blinds to at least cover
the windows looking into the backyard. Dan said there was no need,
that the trees provided a natural curtain. Heavy snowflakes drifted from
the sky, reflecting iridescent glimpses of moonlight. Tracy almost closed
the diary, then flipped the page and skimmed the next two entries.

> *Rumor going around school—good old CG High. Nothing is*
> *private—that HJ was pregnant when she was killed!*

Tracy sat up, quickly skimming over the rest of the passage.

Heard she missed her period and peed on one of those sticks. Didn't tell anyone, not even Kimberly. Parents are Super Religious!!

Tracy looked at the flames behind the glass in the fireplace, wondering if Roy Calloway knew of the rumors, and whether the medical examiner had checked. Her eyes shifted back to the entry.

Parents are Super Religious!!

CHAPTER 6

The following morning, Dan and Tracy awoke early. Dan took the dogs for a long run, then barricaded himself in his home office. Tracy fed and dressed Daniella and spent time with her daughter until Therese came on duty at 9:00 a.m. That was the difference between Tracy's and Dan's jobs. Dan wasn't being asked to sacrifice his career to become a father. He wasn't being asked to spend the day at home, not working. Tracy didn't regret becoming a mother, not for a moment. Giving birth to Daniella was the single greatest moment in her life. But she wanted to decide for herself what her future would hold. She'd worked hard to become a detective. She'd put up with her captain's—Johnny Nolasco's—sexist comments and attempts to force her to quit. She'd forged a path for other women detectives in the Violent Crimes Section by being the first woman and a damn good detective—instinctual and willing to work her ass off. So she didn't want Dan, or anyone else, telling her to walk away, and she didn't want her decision to be because she felt guilty leaving her daughter home, or because she had nothing in common with the twentysomethings in the PEPS group she'd attended. She wanted to make her decision on her own terms and for her own reasons.

She left two bottles of breast milk in the fridge and told Therese she was going out to run errands.

The parking lot outside the Cedar Grove Police Station had been scraped of the overnight snow. Inside the building, the female officer at the counter buzzed Tracy through the metal door without hesitation. Tracy found Roy Calloway sitting in his temporary office, talking on the telephone.

Calloway motioned for Tracy to enter and sit. He spoke into the phone for another minute, then hung up. "Sorry. Did you—"

"Was Heather Johansen pregnant?" Tracy said.

Calloway sat up, grimacing when he did. "Why are you asking?"

"Why? You're not serious."

"I am serious."

"Because it could be related to her murder."

"Are you accepting what we discussed yesterday?"

"I don't know yet. I called Seattle and I'm waiting to hear."

"Then I can't discuss the intricacies of Heather's case with you."

"Don't play games, Roy."

"I'm not playing games. I am wondering where you heard that piece of news, however."

"Sarah's diary."

"Hmm," Calloway said, revealing nothing.

"Sarah said the rumor going around school after Heather's death was that she'd been pregnant."

"Those were rumors."

"I said that. I'm asking if she was pregnant. What did the ME find?"

Calloway just sat back with the same stare he used to give them as kids, the glare that said, *I'm always around, watching you.* It had been more intimidating then, but not so much anymore.

"Come on, Roy. What did her autopsy show?"

He shook his head. "I can't violate her privacy—"

"Bullshit, Roy—"

"—or the privacy of her family," he said, raising his voice to speak over her.

"You gave the file to Kimberly Armstrong and Jason Mathews."

"They made a public records request, and Mathews had the consent of the family." He shrugged those big shoulders and again gave her that blank poker face.

Tracy sat down. Silent. Calloway shifted in his seat. She didn't. They were at a standoff.

A uniformed officer stepped into the room. "Chief," he said. When neither Calloway nor Tracy so much as looked at him, he stepped out. "Sorry."

After a long minute, Tracy said, "This is the way it's going to be?"

"This is the way it is, Tracy. I don't make the rules. I just—"

"—enforce them. I remember. You need another shtick, Roy."

"It's as applicable today as it was back then."

Another minute passed before Tracy said, "If I take this case, I learn everything."

"Absolutely."

"I mean it. No secrets this time, Roy. No bullshit. Everything."

"You have my word. You'll know everything I know."

"I'm waiting to hear back from Seattle on approval."

"All I need is your word. You can work out what you need to work out later."

"Okay then, I'll take this case."

He sat forward. "The medical examiner ran a blood test for HCG— human chorionic something—"

"Gonadotropin," Tracy said. "I just went through this."

"Then you would know better than me. The test was positive. The examiner also found an early intrauterine pregnancy—I don't know the detailed language. You can read it."

"Did the examiner say how far along Heather's pregnancy was?"

"Four to five weeks," Calloway said.

"No DNA?"

"No."

Tracy took a moment. "You talk to Finlay about it?"

"Of course."

"And?"

Calloway held out his palms. "He denied it. Finlay said he hadn't spent time with Heather since the night I went out to his folks' house and told him to knock off all the phone calls and to stop harassing her."

"Did you believe him?"

"I put the fear of God in all of you when I wanted to, in those days. Yeah, I believed him."

Calloway had a demeanor back then that matched his physical size.

"When I got the ME's report I called the hospital in Silver Spurs on a hunch," he said. "It had a record of an appointment for Heather the evening she disappeared, but no record that Heather kept it."

"That's why she was on the county road."

"That's the deduction I made."

"How did she get there, and why was she walking back to Cedar Grove?"

Calloway shrugged. "Not sure how she got there, but I operated under the assumption that she changed her mind."

"Was she seeing anyone after she broke up with Finlay?"

"If she was, nobody at school knew of it, not even Kimberly. Kimberly didn't even know Heather was pregnant."

"That seems unlikely in Cedar Grove."

"It does," Calloway agreed.

"You told her parents though, right?"

Calloway didn't answer.

"You didn't tell her parents, Roy?" The question came out raw and harsh, perhaps a lingering product of Tracy's frustration that Calloway had not been forthright about Sarah's murder.

"I asked if they knew any reason why Heather would be on the county road at night. They didn't. I didn't see the point in telling them. It was hard enough they lost their daughter, Tracy." Calloway bristled, a bit of the fire and brimstone Tracy once knew. "I didn't see the point of their losing their memory of her, not unless I could prove the pregnancy was the cause of the murder. I couldn't. We thought House killed her."

"What about when this guy Jason Mathews or Kimberly Armstrong got ahold of the file? Did they tell the Johansens?"

"I don't know."

"They've never said anything about it?"

"The Johansens? Not to me."

"I'd like to talk to them, but something like this would be better coming from you. I ruffled some feathers when I got House a new trial—"

"Ruffled some feathers? Bit of an understatement, don't you think?"

"Can you make it happen?"

Calloway picked up the telephone.

—

Before they left the police department to meet the Johansens, Calloway gave Tracy Heather Johansen's file, and Tracy took time to read the medical examiner's report. In addition to the positive blood test, the ME noted a gestational sac and a small embryo the size of a blueberry inside Heather's uterus.

After Tracy had reviewed the file, she left with Calloway, walking across the parking lot to her Subaru.

"Where you going?" Roy Calloway stood in the parking lot, putting on fur-lined leather gloves, a hat with wing flaps already pulled low to protect his ears against the biting cold.

"To my car," Tracy said.

"You don't want to take my truck? That thing even have four-wheel drive? The Johansens' road won't be plowed."

She smiled. "That *thing* is a Subaru, Chief. It's a mini-tank. That's why Dan bought it."

Calloway gave his truck a sidelong glance, like it was a pretty girl he was leaving in the corner of a dance, and walked to the passenger's side of the Subaru. He pulled open the door and considered the interior. "This thing has four-wheel drive?"

"All-wheel drive," Tracy said, already in the driver's seat and looking up at him. "Four-wheel drive all the time."

"Yeah?" He nodded his approval. "Huh." He took a moment to lower into the car, his leg giving him some trouble. Then he shut the door.

"You looking to buy a car, Roy?"

The seat belt almost didn't cross his broad chest and stomach. "Nora's been after me to get something with better gas mileage."

"Than your 1980s Suburban? A tank gets better gas mileage."

Calloway smiled. "You're a smart-ass like your father." As Tracy pulled from the lot he asked, "So Dan's on board with this, with you taking the case?"

"He said it was my decision, but reading between the lines, no he isn't exactly on board with it."

Calloway shook his head, mumbling under his breath but loud enough for Tracy to hear, "So much like your father."

They drove just ten minutes. The Johansens' dirt-and-gravel road had not been plowed, but it had only a few inches of snow. Cross-country ski tracks led to their modest one-story home. Tracy estimated the house to be fifteen hundred square feet, including the covered carport. Tendrils of lazy smoke spiraled up from the brick chimney.

"You let them know I was coming?" Tracy asked.

"I told 'em."

Tracy parked behind an older-model Ford sedan. On the other half of the carport, neatly stacked, was at least four cords of chopped wood.

As they navigated the snow-covered walk, Tracy smelled the familiar odor of burning pine. The front door pulled open before they reached the porch, and Ingrid Johansen greeted them with a tentative smile from behind a screen door. "Chief Roy," she said. Then, "Tracy."

Ingrid had aged, and not just five years, which was the last time Tracy saw her, in the gallery at the courthouse during Edmund House's retrial. She estimated Ingrid and Eric Johansen were early to mid seventies—about her parents' age if they had still been alive. Tracy's mother had liked to say that when a person hit seventy, they aged in dog's years; the transformation was that much more pronounced. Tracy had known Ingrid as a slim, attractive woman with a Norwegian accent who baked exquisite pastries for church functions. She remained attractive, though her blonde hair was now silver, her cobalt blue eyes no longer radiant and partially hidden behind thick glasses, and her fair skin marked with age spots.

"It's good to see you," Ingrid said. "How've you been?"

There was uncertainty in her voice, which was to be expected. When you'd lost a relative to a crime, you no longer believed the police stopped by for social visits. Tracy knew.

Eric Johansen stood in the small entryway, and they all made small talk as Tracy and Roy removed their winter apparel. Eric didn't look a day older than Tracy remembered him, but then, Eric had always looked old. He'd been bald in his forties and wore thick glasses. He'd put on a bit of weight, mostly around the middle, and his skin, too, was flecked with age spots. He still had the broad back, though, and the red suspenders he wore with a belt.

Eric hung the coats on an intricately carved coatrack and bench seat. Tracy recalled Eric as the skilled carpenter her father had hired to restore the woodwork inside the Mattioli mansion.

"Did you make this?" she asked, admiring the coatrack.

"I made most of the furniture in here." His voice, too, carried the lilt of a Norwegian accent, as well as pride.

"It's beautiful."

"Walnut," Eric said. "It's hard to work with, but the burl and the color doesn't require no stain. That's natural wood."

"Come in," Ingrid said. She led them to a dining room table set behind a couch and easy chair, both positioned to face a flat-screen television. "I made coffee. Would you care for a cup?"

"I might drink the pot." Calloway eased down into one of the chairs at the table. Tracy also sat, a hutch of china to her left and a window providing a view of the backyard. Snow covered the ground to the tree line at the back of the property. Ingrid poured coffee and moved back and forth from the kitchen, setting sugar and cream on the table, then a plate of fresh pastries—the smell of which evoked fond memories—and butter.

"I didn't know if you might be hungry," Ingrid said.

"Hungry or not," Calloway said, taking one of the pastries and slathering it with butter. "My waistline and my doctor are not going to be happy with me."

Tracy took a pastry, too, figuring she might as well enjoy the food she'd soon have to give up. Warm air from the fireplace made the inside temperature comfortable, though Tracy felt anything but. She anticipated this would be a difficult conversation.

"I hope we're not interrupting anything important," Calloway said, biting into his pastry and sending a shower of crumbs onto his plate.

Eric laughed. "Can't mow the lawn in the winter, and I have enough wood to last two lifetimes."

"Saw that in the carport," Calloway said.

"Do you still cross-country ski?" Tracy asked. She recalled Eric Johansen cross-country skiing down Market Street during heavy snow days to buy groceries and supplies.

"Every morning in the winter," he said. "And occasionally we snow-shoe. Our son bought us pairs for Christmas. Ingrid comes with me some mornings, though not today."

Ingrid nodded. "You remember Oystein, Tracy. He was a year or two ahead of you in school."

"I remember."

"So, have you come back to Cedar Grove?" Ingrid asked.

"We're visiting," Tracy said.

"You remember Dan O'Leary," Calloway said.

"Of course," Eric said. "He did our will for us, though we need to update it. We have four grandchildren now."

"Tracy and Dan married. They have a new daughter," Calloway said, and Tracy sensed—having worked with a partner much of her career—that this was not just chitchat. Calloway was trying to build trust.

"Really? How old?" Ingrid said, beaming.

"Just two months," Tracy said. "I got a late start."

"Show them a picture," Calloway said. Tracy pulled up one of the many on her phone and spent a moment talking about Daniella. When the subject passed, they sipped their coffee, and the unease in the room returned, as thick as the butter Calloway spread on his second pastry.

"I mentioned on the phone that Tracy might have some questions about Heather," Calloway said. "I know this is a difficult topic for both of you—"

"We don't like to talk about it," Eric said. "I'm sure you understand, Tracy, and more than most."

"I do," she said.

"The pain never leaves," Eric said. "We just bury it so we can go on."

Ingrid stared into her coffee cup.

"It was a terrible time here in Cedar Grove," Tracy said. "And I know I didn't help when I came back but . . . I had to know for certain if it was Edmund House."

"Yes, well now we have, and that man is dead and buried. May he burn in hell," Eric said. He turned to Calloway. "What are the questions?"

"You recall Jason Mathews, of course," Calloway said.

Eric nodded. "I recall," he said without warmth.

"You hired him because you had questions about what happened to Heather, just as Tracy had questions about what happened to Sarah."

Eric looked across the table at Tracy and spoke bluntly. "Tracy said she was wrong. She's satisfied Edmund House did it."

"I told you we've had doubts about Jason Mathews's death," Calloway persisted. "That we couldn't be certain it was a hunting accident."

"You told me," Eric said. "But we've put this to rest now. We can't go through it again, Chief. We've needed to move on."

"I'm curious," Tracy said, "whether Mr. Mathews ever reported back to you about anything he might have determined happened to Heather?"

"No," Eric said a little too quickly. He answered with certainty in his voice, but not his posture. His back did not touch the chair and he'd averted his eyes, looking past her, at nothing in particular. Ingrid continued to gaze into her coffee cup.

"Do you know if he spoke to anyone about Heather's file?"

"No one," Eric said.

Tracy looked to Calloway.

"You're aware that Finlay Armstrong's wife died recently," Calloway said.

"Of course," Ingrid said.

"What does this have to do with Heather?" Eric asked, looking to Tracy and cutting to the point.

Calloway sat forward. "You know that Kimberly was asking questions about Heather's death, just as Jason Mathews was asking questions."

"She came out here one afternoon to interview us," Eric said. "Kimberly and Heather grew up best friends. She said she might write a book someday—about Heather."

"Tracy would like to know what Kimberly asked you. What you talked about. What you might have told her," Calloway said.

"Why?" Eric said. "It no longer matters."

"We're still investigating Kimberly's death, Eric. We don't think the fire was an accident," Calloway said.

Eric paled. Ingrid dropped her cup onto the saucer, coffee spilling. She quickly excused herself to the kitchen and returned with a paper towel, sopping up the spill.

"Why are you here?" Eric managed. Again, he looked to Tracy.

Calloway kept his volume low and his tone compassionate. "Eric, if the fire wasn't an accident, it calls into question Jason Mathews's death as well."

"You said it was a hunting accident."

"I said it *could have been* a hunting accident, that we didn't have anything definitive to conclude otherwise."

Eric looked across the table to Tracy. "Just what are you stewing up now?" His voice hardened and his eyes shot daggers.

"Eric." Ingrid reached over and touched his arm, but Eric pulled from her grasp.

"You don't live here no more. You leave and then you come back and you stew things up. For what? What did you gain from it? What good ever came from it? It killed your father. Isn't that enough?"

"Eric!" Ingrid said. "Tracy, I'm sorry."

"No, it's okay," Tracy said.

"Tracy didn't ask to be here, Eric. I asked her to look into this," Calloway said, the gruffness returning to his voice. "I'm the one who has the questions. If you want to be angry at anyone, then start with me."

"You? Why should I be angry at you, Chief?"

"Because I'm the one stewing things up, Eric. That's my job."

"Why?"

"Because people are pointing fingers, and some of those fingers are pointing at Finlay."

"Finlay?"

"Finlay dated Heather in high school."

"We know that. Of course we know that," Ingrid said.

"And Kimberly was writing a book about Heather's death," Calloway continued.

"You think Finlay killed Heather?" Eric asked, sounding incredulous.

"I'm just saying there's a connection there, Eric. There's a connection to Finlay that we have to explore."

"That's crazy," Eric said. "Finlay was just a boy when he dated Heather."

"Yes, he was," Calloway said. "But things got heated. You remember."

"I remember," Eric said, adamant. "But you put a stop to it and that was the end of it."

"We think so too," Tracy said.

"Then why are you here?" Eric's voice rose. It sounded like a plea.

"Because there's always going to be that doubt. There's always going to be people who see that connection and wonder. Finlay shouldn't have to live with that. Not if he's innocent," Calloway said.

Eric looked like a teakettle about to boil, his face a deep red. He rocked in his chair, shaking his head. When he moved his arms to the table, his hands trembled. His wife covered them with her own.

"Eric. Tracy's just trying to help," Calloway said. "I asked her to help."

Eric started to cry. He pulled out a red handkerchief from his back pocket and blew his nose. "I'm sorry for what I said, Tracy." He wiped beneath his nose. "I'm just an old man who misses his daughter." Ingrid rubbed his forearm and used a napkin to wipe her own tears.

"I know, Mr. Johansen," Tracy said. "I know how hard this is."

"I can't look into this, Eric," Calloway said. "I don't have the kind of experience Tracy has, and I'm too close to the situation, too close to Finlay. I asked her if she'd give me a hand. She's got a baby at home. She could have said no. She could have said this was no longer her problem. But she's here, Eric, because she knows, better than anyone, what you and Ingrid have been through. She doesn't want to do it, Eric. But I asked her to do it."

"I miss my sister too," Tracy said. "My whole family is gone. And there's not a day that goes by that I don't think of them."

After a few moments, Eric Johansen let out a long breath. "What is it you wanted to know?"

Tracy glanced at Calloway, and he nodded for her to jump in. They both knew Eric Johansen had said yes, but they also knew that answer could change.

"Do you know where Heather went the night she disappeared?" Tracy asked. She didn't have to be more specific. That night was etched in all their memories.

"She told us she was spending the night at Kimberly's house," Ingrid said softly.

"How did she get there?"

"She told us she was going to walk," Eric said. "From work. She left before the storm hit. Ed Witherspoon said he let her go early. He confirmed that she did."

"Did she call you that night?"

"No," Ingrid said.

"Did Jason Mathews or Kimberly Armstrong ever suggest a reason why Heather was on the county road that night? Where she was going or where she was coming from?"

"No," Eric said decisively.

His answer caused Ingrid to flinch. She opened her mouth as if to speak but stopped herself.

"Did either of them speculate why she was out there?" Tracy tried again.

Ingrid squeezed her husband's arm. Eric looked to be struggling to hold the words in his mouth. He put his elbows on the table and brought both hands to his lips, which quivered.

When her husband didn't answer, couldn't answer, Ingrid said, "The hospital is in Silver Spurs, Tracy. Jason Mathews said she was going to the hospital."

"Did he say why?" Tracy persisted, sensing Mathews had.

Again, Ingrid glanced at her husband before redirecting her gaze to Tracy. "There was speculation, unconfirmed mind you . . . that Heather was pregnant."

It felt like someone had sucked the air out of the room. After a beat, Tracy said, "But Heather never said anything to either of you about it?"

"No," Ingrid said. "Never."

Eric removed his glasses and pressed his forehead against his hands, his shoulders shaking. After a moment, he wiped his eyes with more napkins. Then he lowered his hands and said, "She didn't do it. She never went into that hospital."

Tracy looked to Calloway, a silent statement between them that she should tread lightly. Tracy asked, "You don't know how she got there, to the hospital, do you, Eric?"

"No," he said. "We never found out."

"Had Heather dated anyone, after Finlay?" Tracy asked.

"No one," Eric said.

"She never talked about another boy? Maybe a cup of coffee or a date? Nothing at all?"

"Nothing," Ingrid said, shaking her head.

Whoever drove Heather Johansen to Silver Spurs clearly had known she was pregnant. It didn't mean the person had killed her, not necessarily. A friend could have driven her, maybe someone Heather knew, but it hadn't been Kimberly—and Kimberly had been Heather's best friend. Whoever it had been, it certainly made them a person of interest.

"How do you know she never went into the hospital that night, Eric?" Tracy asked.

"Mathews told us," Eric said. He looked to Calloway. "After he got your file. He checked the hospital for records and said she never went in; never kept that appointment."

"We had to sign some papers so he could get them," Ingrid said.

"Did Mr. Mathews tell you he'd spoken to anyone else about the possibility that Heather was pregnant?"

"No one," Eric said. "Just the two of us."

Ingrid shook her head.

"Did he say what he found in the hospital records?"

"He just said there was a record of an appointment for an abortion, but no record she kept that appointment," Ingrid was quick to add.

Inside, Tracy mulled over the fact that Jason Mathews had known Heather was pregnant. Had he brought it up to anyone in Cedar Grove where a rumor like that would spread quickly and widely? And if he had, whom had he told and whom had the rumor reached, and was that the reason for Mathews's death?

CHAPTER 7

Tracy and Calloway left the Johansens' house once again bundled in their winter clothes, but without much more information than they had arrived with. Inside the car, Tracy said, "We need to find out who Mathews might have told about Heather's pregnancy."

"Maybe he didn't," Calloway said.

"Maybe, but if he told the Johansens, he could have told others."

"You're saying he opened his big mouth," Calloway said.

"I'm saying it's possible. Maybe he was trying to fit in . . . or trying to look like a big-shot attorney with news he thought no one else in town had, not even Heather's parents."

"And that person he told was the wrong person?" Calloway said, raising his voice in question. "That's a big coincidence."

"I'm not saying it was the person who killed him. He could have told anyone, and that person could have gone home and told his wife, who went to the PTA meeting the following week and told her friends, who each told friends, until the *rumor* that a big-shot Montana attorney was saying Heather Johansen was pregnant reached the person with more at stake than even the Johansens."

"Her killer."

"Who thought he'd gotten away with it, thought that secret had been buried twenty years ago."

Calloway sighed deeply. "It's still a lot of speculation, Tracy."

"Good police work often starts as speculation."

The engine warm, she turned the defrost fan to high and shifted the car into reverse.

Calloway, as was his habit, directed Tracy to the county road—a way she could have found with her eyes closed. Tracy let him do it. She knew Calloway would always be chief of Cedar Grove and her father's friend, and to him, at least, Tracy would always be that young girl riding her bike around town.

Four miles along the county road, Calloway told her to take a right onto a paved road that was just about a mile from where they had found Heather Johansen's body. Tracy knew this side road well. She'd had a high school girlfriend who'd lived in one of the handful of houses at the end of the road. It was barely wide enough for two cars to pass on a good day, and only if they both slowed to a near stop. This day, six inches of snow had narrowed the road further.

"Good place to get lost, if that's what Mathews intended when he bought his house," Tracy said as they pitched over the ruts made by other vehicles.

"Does look that way," Calloway said. "His divorce was a bad one, apparently. According to Eric Johansen, Mathews had officially retired from the law, though he'd take on cases if the client paid cash, or traded a skill—something his ex-wife couldn't get half of."

"Nice," Tracy said, amazed at the vindictiveness of some people—especially to people they'd once professed to love. "Maybe the ex-wife shot him?" She was joking, but Calloway looked across the car at her with his eyebrows arched. "You talked to her? That's how you know the divorce was a bad one," Tracy said.

Calloway nodded. "I asked around. She had traveled to Billings the day Mathews got shot, and from what I could gather, she was glad to be rid of him, glad he left town and didn't want any more to do with him. She said he was a drinker, and not a happy drunk. I never found any evidence linking her to his shooting." Calloway pointed out the windshield. "Pull over here."

Tracy eased the Subaru from the pavement, the tires pitching as she left the asphalt and settled onto the snow. To her right, grand fir, Douglas fir, spruce, ponderosa pine, and several species of larch rose above them. She'd had a class in high school that included field trips to learn the names of what the teacher called *the most diverse tree population in Washington State*. To her left, the hillside slope was steep, with fewer trees. The temperature felt ten degrees colder beneath the thick canopy shading the road. Patches of snow on the ground and clinging to the branches looked like a fine white powder. Tracy pulled up the hood of her down jacket and moved her arms and legs to generate heat and try to keep warm. She and Calloway looked like they were performing an Irish jig.

"This is the location?" Tracy asked, each breath and spoken word emitting a white burst that lingered before dissipating.

"Just down the road," he said, leading her perhaps ten yards farther.

"Okay, let's not be coy here, Roy. It's too damn cold. Just give me the *Reader's Digest* version so we both don't freeze to death."

———

Jason Mathews felt his truck pulling to the left and heard a horn honk. He startled awake, yanking the steering wheel hard to the right—too hard. The truck crossed the adjacent lane, the tires thumping as they left the pavement. Tree limbs slapped at the windshield and along the passenger-side window. Mathews jerked the wheel to the left. The tires caught against the pavement, bounced over the lip, and the truck careened to the left. Eventually, Mathews found the center of the road.

He took a deep breath, forcing his eyes to remain open. The bartender at the Four Points Tavern had offered to call him a cab, but Mathews didn't want to spend the money. He'd been sober enough to hold his shit together to convince the bartender he could drive home, which was just a couple miles from the bar.

He'd always been good at bullshitting. That's what had made him a good lawyer, his poker face and his ability to make his opponent think he'd try a case if they didn't pay what he wanted in settlement. They usually did. Yeah, he'd been a good lawyer, and he would have kept practicing, but he wasn't going to work just to keep paying his ex-wife. Not a chance in hell, which is where she could go. He'd stashed away enough money in places she and her forensic accountants would never find. It wasn't a fortune, which was how he'd been able to hide it from her. He flew under the radar. That was his motto. Fly . . . under . . . No, that wasn't his motto. His motto was . . . What the hell was his motto?

Screw it. He didn't need a motto. And he didn't need a fortune. That was the point. He didn't need a fortune. Not here in bum-fuck Cedar Grove.

He sat up, trying to get his bearings. He needed to find the turnoff to his street. They had no signs along the county road. How the hell was anyone supposed to find a turnoff without a sign? He'd had to resort to landmarks—just past the big rock on the side of the road. That's where he turned. That was his . . . What had he been saying? Oh yeah, he didn't need a lot of money. He was good at bullshitting. Like that Norwegian carpenter—Sven or . . . Eric. That was his name. Eric was doing $2,000 to $3,000 worth of carpentry work for Mathews, and all Mathews had to do was ask around about his dead daughter. Easy money. Mathews obtained the police file and the bombshell detonated. Turned out old Eric's daughter hadn't been so squeaky clean and proper. She'd been pregnant when she died. And the police hadn't even bothered to tell Eric or his wife. Who was running things out here, Andy Taylor and Barney Fife? The look on Eric's face when Mathews told him the news could have stopped a clock. He looked like someone had slapped him and he just stopped ticking.

And then Eric told Mathews to end the investigation. Said he didn't want Mathews to look into the matter any further, that he and his wife didn't want to know anything more about their daughter's death.

Mathews had spent maybe ten hours working the file, and he'd got $5,000—no, that wasn't right . . . He'd got . . . What did he get? Screw it.

Another jolt. Another head snap. Mathews saw the boulder along the side of the road. Shit. He slammed on his brakes. The truck tires skidded on the pavement. Smoke rolled past the cab, which turned sideways in the road. Why didn't they mark the freaking turnoff? He slapped the steering wheel. Idiots!

What was he talking about . . .

He looked at the road. Oh yeah. Turn.

He eased down the narrow road, the truck cab leaning to the left. Why was he leaning to the left? The truck scraped the dirt wall. He heard something snap, a crunching sound. Mathews corrected again, back to the center of the road.

He saw something on the ground and hit the brakes.

What the hell?

Branches?

Looked like branches.

What the hell were branches doing in the middle of the road?

Was he on the road?

He stared out the windshield. Branches. Son of a bitch. In the road. Could he drive over them? Not likely. Shit.

He pushed on the driver's door. It didn't open. He pushed again, felt it nudge but not open. What the hell?

He shoved harder. The door gave a resentful creak, then a moan. He put his shoulder into it, and the door opened enough for him to get out. He stumbled but gripped the door handle to keep his balance. The entire side of his truck was dented and scraped. The side mirror was gone. Someone *must have hit him, a hit and run. Probably in the parking lot of the damn tavern. He'd have to report it to his insurance.*

He stood for a moment, uncertain. Why was he out of the truck? Then he saw the branches. Right. He let go of the door handle and stumbled to the front of the truck. He studied the branches. Definitely too many to drive over. His luck, he'd pop a tire. He'd have to move them. He bent and grabbed one of the bigger limbs, dragging it to the edge of the road. Freaking thing was heavy. He looked at the pile. Shit. This would take time. He bent and grabbed a second branch, tugging and pulling. He felt light-headed from the exertion and from bending over. He had to stop to catch his breath.

He looked up the hill on the other side of the road and winced from the rays of bright sunlight shooting through the trunks of the trees. He raised a hand to deflect the glare.

He heard a snap.

No wind though. Why would a tree branch . . .

He felt a thump.

His body pitched backward and, for the briefest of moments, he could see the sky.

Tracy watched Calloway dance from foot to foot. Every so often he'd grimace, like he'd stepped on a tack.

He shrugged. "My leg goes to sleep from the nerve damage. It's worse when it's cold like this." He pointed a gloved finger farther down the road. "We found Mathews's truck parked in the middle of the road, the engine still running. There was some brush in the road and more along the side there. It looked like he'd stopped to clear it so he could get to his house."

"Somebody put the branches in the road so he would get out of the car."

"If they did, they thought it through," Calloway said. "The branches weren't cut, which would have been easy to determine. They looked as if they'd been snapped off, and not that day."

"Somebody gathered them together and lay in wait." Tracy gave that some thought. She shoved her gloved hands deeper into the pockets of her down coat. The standing around had exacerbated the cold.

"Mathews had a blood alcohol level nearly twice the legal limit," Calloway said, "and he'd banged up the side of his truck pretty good. We had no reason to suspect an ambush since no one around here knew him well enough to hold a grudge. That's why we questioned the ex-wife."

"What about Eric Johansen?"

"Considered him as well. Eric claimed to be at home working on furniture in his carport when Mathews was shot."

"His wife confirm that?"

Calloway shook his head. "Couldn't. She was at the church. Anyway, we let people think it was a hunting accident and closed the case. We hoped that, maybe, someday something would come up. So far, nothing has."

"What time of year was it?" Tracy asked.

Calloway gave her that grin to let her know she was on the right track. "Late October."

"Deer hunting season. Who found him?"

"One of the neighbors driving in the opposite direction. She didn't see Mathews at first, just the branches and Mathews's truck. She got out, took a couple steps forward, and stopped when she saw Mathews's body partially hidden by the brush."

"Where was Mathews shot?"

"In the head."

"What caliber bullet?" Tracy asked.

"Don't know," Calloway said. "Thirty-aught-six or bigger based on the damage to his skull."

"You never found the bullet?"

Calloway shook his head. "Look around, Tracy. We searched."

"So no ballistics test," she said.

"Bullet likely would have been too mangled to be of any use," Calloway said, "based on the damage to Mathews's skull."

"And I'm guessing just about everyone in Cedar Grove and every other city around here owns a hunting rifle of that caliber."

"Including Eric Johansen."

Tracy looked up the sloped hillside. The sun had moved behind the trunk of a tree. Calloway noticed her gaze. "We climbed the hill, back when I still could. We didn't find any footprints. If someone made them, they used a branch to obscure them."

That caught Tracy's attention. Her father had taught her and Sarah that trick when they went hunting for chanterelle mushrooms. *Cover your tracks and people can't follow them to find your best mushroom locations*, he had told them.

"If he was ambushed," Tracy said, "somebody would have had to have followed him and tracked his movements, wouldn't they? They wouldn't risk the chance that one of the other property owners might encounter the branches before he arrived, would they?"

"That seems reasonable. It also wouldn't have been hard to follow Mathews. From what I could gather, Mathews spent most of his afternoons drinking at the Four Points Tavern."

"That would mean more than one person was involved."

"How so?"

"If the person couldn't risk the possibility that another property owner might stumble upon the brush before Mathews got here, then someone had to have followed Mathews to let the second person know Mathews was on his way home."

"Maybe," Calloway said. "Or the shooter could have just taken his chances. Only four homes at the end of the road, so the odds were pretty good, especially in the middle of the day when people work."

"Did you talk to people at the Four Points?"

Calloway nodded. "Not until after I got Mathews's blood-alcohol level back. It explained the damage to the side of his truck and the tire marks we found on the county road. He was pinballing from one side of the road to the other. I had an officer ask around some of the local watering holes. She learned Mathews was a frequent visitor to the Four Points."

"Bartender or any of the regulars remember him?"

"Bartender said that some days—like this one—Mathews would go in early and drink his breakfast and his lunch, then crawl home to sleep it off. Said he always offered Mathews coffee and a cab—I never bothered to find out if that was true or just ass cover. No reason to really. Anyway, he said Mathews always declined—said the drive home was just a couple miles."

"Twice the legal limit," Tracy repeated, finding it hard to believe Mathews was in any condition to drive.

"I hear you. Apparently, Mathews held his liquor well when he cared to. Bartender told my officer Mathews had been coherent and walked a straight line to the door. Again, could have just been ass cover."

"Bartender recall whether Mathews left alone or with anyone?"

"Said he always came in alone, that he'd made a few acquaintances, but nobody who would say they spent any real time with him or knew him. He wasn't the most pleasant drunk, not according to his ex-wife anyway."

"Who knew he was investigating Heather Johansen's death?"

Calloway shrugged, palms up. "As I said, the Johansens gave me a heads-up, in case Mathews needed anything, but you know this town, Tracy. If some guy nobody has ever seen comes around asking questions about a murder . . ." Calloway's voice trailed off.

"Mathews ever ask for anything?"

"Just a copy of Heather's file, which I gave him after Eric Johansen signed the paperwork. I told Mathews to knock himself out. At the time I was still convinced House had killed Heather. I told Mathews to have some discretion."

"Sounds like he didn't listen to you."

"Wouldn't be the first time."

"You talk to Finlay about the shooting?"

"You mean did Finlay have an alibi for Mathews's shooting?"

"Did he?"

Calloway shook his head. "No. Finlay was off work that day, and Kimberly was working at the newspaper."

"Finlay say what he was doing?"

"You know what he was doing. Hunting."

"With anyone?" Tracy asked, eyebrows arched in question, though she suspected the answer from Calloway's reluctant demeanor.

"Alone."

"You check his hunting rifle to see when he fired it last?"

"Yep, and it was clean. But Finlay told me up front he took it to the shooting range that week, got home, and cleaned it, as was his routine."

"So, no way to tell."

"When he last fired it? No."

"And without the bullet . . ."

"Couldn't match it to any rifle anyways."

"You said the damage to the skull was significant. Did the autopsy say anything about the likely distance the bullet traveled before it hit the target?"

"The ME estimated between a hundred and a hundred fifty yards."

That didn't help. "Anyone can make that shot with a scope, Roy. Hell, you could probably extend that distance to two-, maybe four-hundred yards and still have dozens of potential suspects around here."

"Agreed. Based on the angle of the head wound, the shot was likely taken from a rock outcropping roughly a hundred or so yards up that slope." He raised a hand to cut the glare and pointed. "Right about this time of day too."

Tracy followed his outstretched hand, shielding her eyes. "That time of year and this time of day, the shooter would have had the sun at his back, making him damn near invisible, even if Mathews had looked in that direction. The rock cropping is up there?" she said, not excited about climbing the side of the hill.

Calloway pointed again. "About one hundred to one hundred fifty yards up that slope. I'd take you, but not on this bum leg."

She handed him the car keys. "No sense both of us freezing our knockers off."

His eyes narrowed. "Knockers?"

"My Irish nanny. Never mind."

Calloway took the keys and retreated to the Subaru. Tracy walked across the road, considered a place to climb the slope, and started up. With the snow, it was hard to get her footing. Below her, she heard Calloway start the car engine. She envied him. She grabbed what foliage she could find to keep from slipping down the hill. Once she got on manageable ground and the slope flattened, she continued to the rock cropping, which was where Calloway had said—about one hundred to one hundred fifty yards up the slope. Tracy walked behind it, the sun now at her back, and climbed the rocks, sliding down several times due to the slick snow and ice. When she finally reached the top she looked down at the road, without obstruction, at her Subaru.

This had been no hunting accident.

CHAPTER 8

Tracy dropped off Calloway at the Cedar Grove Police Department—she didn't want him along when she spoke to Finlay, though she didn't tell him that. She played to Calloway's ego, saying that he remained a big presence in Cedar Grove, and not just because of his physical stature. He cast a long shadow, and never more so than the shadow he cast over his onetime protégé.

"You sure you don't want to come in for a cup of coffee and warm up before you go out there?" Calloway asked, standing outside the car and peering down at her. He had one arm on the roof, the other on the open passenger's door. "So you don't freeze your knickers."

Tracy smiled at his malaprop. "Thanks, but I want to get out there and talk to Finlay so I can get home at a reasonable hour."

He started to close the car door, then stopped. "Bring that baby of yours by the house some time. You know . . . Nora would get a kick out of seeing her."

Tracy smiled. "Tell *Nora* I'll do that," she said.

She drove from the parking lot back through town. Tracy thought Finlay might be more open to talk to a woman than to a man—his onetime boss no less; that he'd be less concerned about keeping up a strong façade and more likely to speak honestly. She'd experienced it before on the force. Her male partners on the Violent Crimes Section's A Team would get nowhere with a suspect, maybe even get a few choice swear words thrown in their faces. Tracy would ask for a chance and, before long, the man would be chatting with her like she was the only person in the world who truly understood him.

On her way to speak with Finlay, she debated stopping at the Four Points Tavern, but the chances of the bartender being the same as the one in 2013, when Mathews had been a regular customer, didn't seem likely. She'd check at some point, but now she needed to get moving so she could get home and pump.

Roy told her that, following the fire, Finlay had moved into the same motel Tracy had stayed in when she came back to Cedar Grove for the retrial of Edmund House. Roy didn't know whether or not Finlay planned to rebuild his destroyed home, or even come back to work. He said Finlay had talked of moving out of state, somewhere closer to his parents, who were currently watching his three children. He'd said the memories were, at present, too painful to contemplate staying, and until his wife's death was resolved, Finlay didn't want to subject his kids to the Cedar Grove rumor mill, which would speculate he had something to do with Kimberly's death.

Tracy could relate. She knew full well why Finlay might walk away from the only town he'd called home and a job he loved. Finlay could hardly serve Cedar Grove as its chief with speculation surrounding his wife's death, which stirred up what dust had settled over the grave of Heather Johansen, and possibly the grave of Jason Mathews as well. In a small town, what was not said could be far more isolating than the most horrible things uttered. Tracy knew. Though the town's residents had assured Tracy that her sister's death wasn't her fault, the fact that they did so meant they'd certainly contemplated it.

Tracy pulled into the motel parking lot after stopping at a drive-through burger joint. She hadn't eaten, and the greasy smell of the burgers and the French fries was intoxicating. She recognized Finlay's blue Chevy truck parked at the back of the lot adjacent to the two-story, wood-shingled motel. Tracy grabbed the carton containing the bag of food and two chocolate milkshakes, balancing it as she slid the strap of her briefcase over her shoulder. She climbed the stairs to the second story. Water trickled from the snow melt on the roof, and she could hear the drips in between the sound of semitrucks hauling on the county road.

She knocked on the door to room 12 twice, a hollow resonance. Finlay glanced at her through the adjacent window before pulling the door open. She almost didn't recognize him. He looked to have aged exponentially, far more than the five years since Tracy last saw him. Gray hair, once limited to his temples and sideburns, now dominated, and his face, once youthful, hid beneath flaccid skin. Hazel eyes, which had attracted the attention of girls in high school, now looked vacant and sad. He'd also lost significant weight, the change most obvious in his neck and shoulders—like one of those actors who'd used a weight-loss product to drop pounds far too quickly to be healthy. A black T-shirt hung loose, and his blue jeans bunched where the belt cinched tight at his waist.

"Tracy. Nice to see a familiar face." Finlay smiled, but it looked painful and reminded Tracy of the few smiles her father had managed after Sarah's disappearance and just before he'd taken his own life. She wondered if Finlay, too, had contemplated such an act in his darkest moments.

"Hey, Finlay."

Finlay stepped aside and swept his arm to the interior of his room—two queen-size beds, one half made, the other cluttered with suitcases, a laptop, and clothes. In the corner of the room was a small kitchenette with a two-burner stove and a miniature refrigerator.

"Welcome to my humble abode. I guess that's one good thing about a catastrophic fire, you don't have much left to move."

How everything could change—in just an instant, Tracy thought.

"I cleared up some space." He nodded to a round, laminated table beneath the aluminum-framed window that afforded a view of the landing and the parking lot.

Tracy set her briefcase on the dark-brown carpet and placed the bag of burgers and shakes on the table, speaking as she removed her winter coat and draped it over the back of a chair. "I thought I'd get us lunch."

Finlay raised a hand. "I'm good, but you go ahead."

"There are four burgers in this bag, Finlay. I know I'm bigger since the baby, but I'm not eating four hamburgers."

He smiled, and it brought a brief glimpse of the man Tracy had once known. "Okay."

She removed two burgers, setting one on Finlay's side of the table, along with a bag of fries and a chocolate milkshake. The room's dark wood paneling and musty smell brought her back five years. Overhead, a ceiling fan wobbled, slightly out of balance. Each rotation made a soft rumble.

"Can I offer you a cup of coffee or tea?" Finlay gestured to a pot on the Formica counter near the stove.

"I'm good with the milkshake," Tracy said, taking a seat at the table and pulling the ice cream through the straw.

Finlay poured himself a cup of coffee, black, speaking as he did. "I saw the baby announcement on Roy's desk. How old is she now?"

"Just turned two months. I guess that means she's still manageable."

"Wait until they can say no," Finlay said. "That's when the fun really starts." Though four years younger, Finlay had an earlier start to his family than Tracy. He pulled out a chair and sat across from her. "So, what brings you to Cedar Grove?" he said and sipped his coffee.

"We're remodeling."

"Uh-huh." Finlay continued to sip his coffee and ignored his burger and shake.

"How're your kids doing?" Tracy unwrapped her burger. It released the smell of cooked meat, melted cheese, and onions.

Finlay shrugged. "We're all getting by. My kids are with their grandparents. I didn't want them here, not until this is resolved."

Tracy spoke with a mouth full of burger. "Roy said you're thinking of moving away."

"Not much left for me in Cedar Grove." He sighed. "Not for any of us. But for the present Roy thinks it best if I stick around." He set his coffee on the table and sat back, hands folded in his lap. "He said you offered to help him out. I'm betting that's ass-backward. I'm betting he cornered you and asked you to help."

She took another bite of the hamburger, which tasted better than she'd expected, or she was that hungry. "Maybe a little of both."

"What is it you'd like to know, Tracy? How I refilled the can of gasoline just two days before I torched my house, or what baseball bat I used to smash in the back of my wife's head? Maybe the same bat I used to kill a former girlfriend twenty-six years ago."

Finlay said it matter-of-factly, without inflection in his voice or in his eyes.

She took another bite of the burger and wiped her hands on a napkin. Then she reached into her briefcase and set a notebook and a pen on the table. "Let's go back to the beginning. Let's talk about Heather Johansen."

"You remember," he said, getting a half grin on his face, but only for a second. "I was the disgruntled ex-boyfriend stalking her."

"I understood all that stopped after Roy had his come-to-Jesus meeting with you."

"Roy had a way of getting his point across when he took the time to actually talk to us."

"Never told me twice to not ride my bike on the sidewalk," Tracy agreed. She sipped her shake through the straw.

Finlay gave her a small nod. "He sat me down and asked me what I wanted to do with my life. I told him I thought I wanted to be a cop, like him. I'm not sure I meant it or was just scared enough to be seeking brownie points. Roy said I was eighteen. He asked me how I thought it would look on an application to the police department if I had a stalking charge on my record. Then he said if I left *that poor girl* alone, he'd help me out. I did. So did he."

"Why'd you go to the community college?"

"I think you know, but I also know you have to run me through this." He sat up, resting his forearms on the table, his hands around the mug. "I guess part of it was to avoid the shame I knew I'd feel going back to school—for how I'd treated Heather, the things I'd said. I'd made a lot of enemies, especially among the girls." He sat back, taking the mug of coffee with him, and glanced out the window. "And if I'm being honest, I think, maybe, I just didn't trust myself to leave Heather alone, and Roy had been explicit in pointing out the consequences if I didn't." He looked to Tracy and gave her a small shrug.

"But you did," she said.

"I did. Anyway, when I looked into what other options I had, I learned I could get my GED and my AA in criminal justice at the same time at the local JC." He sighed. "But getting to the question you didn't ask . . ." He looked at her across the table, not a spark of humor in his eyes. "No, I don't have an alibi for the night Heather died. Not a good enough one. Like I told Roy, I was taking a class at night in Bellingham, but the weather forecasters had indicated a big storm was coming, and the teacher knew some of us had a ways to drive to get home. He let us out early, around eight p.m. I barely made it through before they closed the county road. I didn't get home until after midnight."

"Did you see anyone else on the road?"

Another shrug, this time with a shake of the head. "A few cars. You remember they didn't plow the county road too often when it snowed hard back then?"

"No point. They couldn't keep up with it."

"Didn't have enough equipment." He sipped his coffee.

"So can I assume you didn't see Heather walking the county road alone?" She smiled again. "I have to ask."

"I know." He shook his head. "I thought about it though, when I heard what happened to her. I thought about what I would have done if I had seen her. I'd like to believe I would have stopped and offered her a ride—not that she would have likely taken it. More likely the hurt boy in me would have just driven on by. I'm not sure how I would have lived with that, given what happened. You know?"

Tracy did. She'd had to live with sending Sarah home alone on that same road. She shook that thought. "You're aware the autopsy revealed Heather was pregnant?"

"I'm aware the medical examiner said it was *probable*. But I'm betting Roy got him to add that word, seeing no further reason to hurt the Johansens."

"How'd you first find out?"

He shifted his gaze to the window and sipped at his coffee. Then he set down his mug and reengaged her. "I suppose you'll find out eventually."

She'd expected him to tell her he'd read the ME's report, but his demeanor indicated there was something more. She waited, no longer considering the food or her milkshake.

"I found out from Jason Mathews," he said.

———

Finlay Armstrong pulled alongside a Silver Spurs police vehicle parked in the Four Points Tavern parking strip.

"Sorry to bother you with this," Clay Thompson said from behind reflective sunglasses. He and Finlay had once played baseball together on a traveling AAU team.

"Not a problem, Clay. What's going on?"

Thompson pointed his thumb behind him. "The owner called 911 and asked to have a guy removed."

Finlay looked to the back of Thompson's car but didn't see anyone. "You remove him?"

Thompson shook his head. "He's fast asleep on his barstool. Owner said he passed out minutes before I arrived. He's one of yours. Lives out on Sand Point, off the county road. Figured I'd let you have all the fun."

"Thanks for that."

Thompson grinned. "Bartender doesn't want to press charges or make any waves. Says the guy is ordinarily okay, but he gets belligerent when he has one too many."

"You get a name?"

Thompson pulled a small spiral notepad from the front pocket of his shirt. "Jason Mathews. Mean anything to you?"

It did. "Yeah. Yeah, it does." Finlay didn't say Mathews was an attorney from Montana and had come into the police department asking for Heather Johansen's file and saying that the family had retained him to look into "her demise." "He's a bit pompous. Got a lot of hot air."

"According to the owner, he's become a regular. Says when he gets a couple pops in him, he gets on the subject of his ex and it ain't pretty. Thought maybe you could take him home, have a talk with him. Owner doesn't want him coming around anymore, not if he can't hold his liquor or his tongue. Says the guy's also a liability. Never lets him call him a cab. Anyway. He's in there, and he's all yours. Tell him this is his one reprieve, will you? I won't call you if it happens again. I'll throw his ass in jail." Thompson started the engine.

"I'll make it clear, Clay. And if it happens again . . . throw his ass in jail."

Thompson nodded, shifted into gear, and drove off.

Inside the dimly lit tavern, Finlay removed his sunglasses and slid the stem into the front pocket of his shirt while his eyes adjusted to the poor light. The interior wasn't much fancier than the exterior. Fans spun over the bar and half a dozen tables. He noted a pool table in the back. Finlay figured on warm days, like this, the fans kept the air moving. In the fall and winter, the fans likely helped to circulate the heat.

The bartender nodded to a man with his head on the bar. Finlay had already picked him out as the likely problem.

"Thanks for coming out," the owner said. He introduced himself as Pete Adams. "Wouldn't have necessarily bothered if it was just this, but before he passed out, he got on the subject of his ex, then women in general. I think you know what I mean."

"I get the picture."

"Appreciate it if you could drive him home, maybe have a talk with him. We get men and women in here, and we try to keep it light."

"I'll do my best."

Finlay rapped hard on the bar with his knuckles. Mathews's head sprang up as if his chair had been electrified. He looked confused.

"Mr. Mathews?"

"Who are you?" Mathews squinted.

"I'm a police officer from Cedar Grove. Can you walk?"

"Yeah, I can walk. What kind of question is that?"

"It's the kind of question a police officer asks a man who's had too much to drink."

Mathews looked more closely at Finlay's uniform.

"I'm going to ask you to slide off that stool and walk outside with me."

"Why?"

"Like I said, you drank too much. You passed out on the bar."

"There a law against that?"

Finlay suppressed a chuckle. "You're the lawyer. You tell me."

Mathews looked at Finlay as if he'd lost his train of thought. He slid off the barstool. Finlay grabbed him by the bicep to steady him, and together they walked to the door. When Finlay pushed it open, Mathews squinted and lifted a hand to block the blast of bright sunshine.

"You have sunglasses?" Finlay said, putting on his own.

"In my truck."

"Well, you're not taking your truck."

"Why not?"

"'Cause you're drunk and yes, there is a law against driving when you're intoxicated. I'm giving you a lift home and a warning that I hope will be sufficient to convince you not to do this again. Okay?"

"Okay."

"Are you going to be sick?"

"What?"

"Do you feel like you might throw up?"

"No. I'm good."

"Not sure about that," Finlay said under his breath. Then he said, "You throw up in my police car and you clean it. That's the rule. Got it?"

"Got it."

Finlay opened the back door and put his hand atop Mathews's head to prevent him from bumping it and bleeding all over the seat. "Buckle up," Finlay said.

"What about my truck?"

"You'll have to come back to get it, I guess."

A moment later Finlay backed out of the parking lot onto the surface streets. He got on the radio and provided the office with an update on the call from Silver Spurs. He told dispatch he was driving Mathews home and put the microphone back in its clip. He looked in his rearview mirror, through the grate, to make sure Mathews wasn't about to puke.

"You're the attorney for the Johansens," he said.

Mathews looked at him, as if he didn't understand. Then he said, "Was."

"Not any longer?"

Mathews shook his head.

Finlay waited.

After a beat, Mathews said, "They didn't like what I had to tell them."

"No?"

"No."

Another pause. This time Finlay had to ask. "And what did you have to tell them that they didn't like?"

"That's an attorney-client privilege," Mathews said, slurring the words.

"Okay."

They drove another few minutes. Mathews spoke without prompting. "I learned something nobody else knows."

Finlay didn't answer, thinking Mathews was one of those guys who just wanted you to think he had information. The bullshit ramblings of a drunk.

"You want to know?" Mathews said.

Finlay didn't immediately respond. He sat back in his seat. "Sure. Tell me."

"That girl. What was her name. Heidi . . . Ingrid . . ."

"Heather?"

"Yeah. That's it. Heather." Mathews looked out the window, as if he'd forgotten what he was talking about.

Finlay felt his heart skip. "What about Heather?" he asked.

Mathews looked to the rearview mirror. "Turns out she'd done the dirty deed."

Finlay felt himself flush. "Is that so?" he managed.

"Yep. Turns out she was pregnant."

Finlay stared at the rearview mirror, evaluating Mathews. The lawyer had a grin on his face, though his gaze remained unfocused. A car horn sounded. Finlay looked up. He'd drifted across the center line and quickly corrected. He took a moment to calm down. Then he asked, "How do you know that?"

"It's right there in the file," Mathews said. "The ME's report."

Finlay had never seen Heather Johansen's file. Roy Calloway kept it in his locked desk, where he kept a handful of other cases, like Sarah Crosswhite's. Roy had concluded that Edmund House had killed Heather Johansen, just as he'd killed Sarah Crosswhite.

"Did it say anything else?" Finlay asked. "The file. Was there anything else?"

Mathews shook his head left, then right. It looked so loose it might fall from his shoulders. "Nope."

"You didn't find out anything more?"

"Such as," he said, head still wobbling.

"Who the father was?"

CHAPTER 9

Finlay redirected his attention to Tracy. She tried not to show any response, but inside so many red flags were waving it could have been a parade. Tracy took each flag one at a time. "What was his response?"

"He said he didn't know." Finlay shrugged again, then grimaced. "He said he told Eric and Ingrid what was in the medical examiner's report, and they both looked like a truck had hit them, but especially Eric. I don't doubt it. They were religious people and that was their little girl."

"And they fired him?" Tracy said.

"He said they asked him to leave their house, and that was the last he worked for them, though he also told me he didn't care. He said Eric had already completed a couple thousand dollars in carpentry work. Like I said, he wasn't the most likeable guy."

"You never told Roy?"

Finlay shook his head.

"Why not?"

"You know why not. First, if it was in the ME's report, then Roy already knew, but he'd chosen not to disclose it, likely so as not to hurt the Johansens unnecessarily and second, because it was a piece of information that only the father—and possibly Heather's killer—would know."

"And then Jason Mathews got shot, and you thought it could make you a suspect again."

"I didn't want to go through what I'd already gone through with Heather's death. Roy was talking about retiring and I was set to replace him. I also figured it didn't really matter what Mathews said he knew, not to me anyway."

"Why not?"

Finlay became animated. His voice rose. "Because I didn't shoot him, Tracy. I didn't kill Heather and I didn't shoot Mathews."

"Were you worried you could have been the father?"

"Sure I was," Finlay said. "I mean, I'd kept my distance from Heather after Roy came out, but I also didn't know how far along she was in the pregnancy."

Tracy nodded. Then she said, "Why are you telling me this now, Finlay?"

"I figured if you're investigating this, you'd find out."

"How?"

"How? Roy gave you the file, didn't he?"

"No. I meant how was I going to find out that Mathews told you? Mathews is dead, and it's doubtful the Four Points Tavern is even still owned by the same guy."

Finlay shrugged. "You've read the ME's report?"

"Yes."

"And when you did, I was the first guy you thought of. I was, wasn't I?"

She nodded. "Yes."

Finlay shrugged.

"How soon after your meeting did Mathews get shot?"

"That was sometime in October that I grabbed him in the bar," he said. "After you came back to town. He got shot, during hunting season."

A month. Tracy didn't break eye contact. Neither did Finlay. "Were you aware of Heather dating anyone, after the two of you broke up?"

Finlay shook his head. "No. And I can tell you Kimberly didn't know either."

"How do you know that?"

Finlay made a face. "Because Kimberly got the file, and she asked me the same questions you're asking me. Was I the father, and who could it have been?"

"Heather didn't tell her."

"No. And Kimberly said she had no inkling of any relationship with anyone."

Tracy gave that some thought. Cedar Grove High consisted of maybe forty students per grade, fewer back when she was growing up. It was unlikely Heather hooked up with a classmate. No way to keep that quiet.

"You never heard any rumors?"

"That she was pregnant? Not until Mathews got in my car that afternoon."

"You have any theories on who the father could have been?"

He shrugged and shook his head. "Like I said, I didn't hear a thing and neither did Kimberly. Kimberly had no clue who it might have been, and I wasn't around. In fact, Kimberly was so convinced Heather would have told her—they were that close—she didn't believe it. She said she thought the ME had to have made a mistake."

"Not likely."

"I'm just telling you Kimberly's thought process."

"You had no theories?"

Finlay hesitated.

"What?"

"Nothing."

"No. Not nothing. Do you have any theories?"

"I didn't. Not until Kimberly got the file and told me the ME's report indicated Heather was only seven to eight weeks along."

"And you thought what?"

Finlay sighed again. "This is speculation."

"Understood."

Finlay sat up. "Heather was working for Ed Witherspoon at the time. I don't know if you remember, but Ed threw a Christmas party every year for his staff and his clients at his real estate office."

"I remember," Tracy said. Her father and mother also threw a Christmas Eve party, and her father said it bugged Ed that more people attended their party than his.

"I wondered, given the timing, if maybe something happened at that party, or after it. The alcohol flowed pretty freely, and it wasn't like anyone was checking IDs or anything."

"You ever share that theory with Roy?"

Finlay shook his head. "Like I said. It was speculation after Kimberly got the file. Back then we were still convinced Edmund House had killed Heather."

"What about now?"

Finlay shook his head and let out a burst of air. "I don't know anymore, Tracy. I don't know. But I'll tell you this, Heather didn't walk all that way to Silver Spurs, not on a night when everyone knew a storm was coming. I don't believe that. She wasn't dressed for it."

"You think someone gave her a ride to the hospital to get an abortion."

"And the most logical person, if it wasn't her mother or father, or Kimberly, is the baby's father. He'd be the one with reason to convince Heather to get rid of the problem by paying for an abortion."

"Then why was she walking home alone?"

"I don't know. What I do know is she didn't go through with it. The medical examiner's report confirms she didn't. Maybe whoever drove her out there got in a fight with her because she wouldn't do it, and Heather got out of the car and started walking. Or maybe the person just dropped her off at the hospital and drove off, thinking she would."

"Any evidence to support that theory?"

"The medical examiner's report, the hospital records, and the fact that Heather was on the county road, alone, with a storm bearing down on her."

"Anything else you think might be important for me to know?"

"No." Finlay sipped his coffee. Then he said, "Actually, there's something. I think Mathews was a bit of a con man."

"How so?"

"I think he worked the situation to get some free labor out of Eric Johansen."

"What makes you say that?"

"Roy tell you Mathews was reprimanded by the Montana bar for misappropriation of client funds, negligence, that sort of thing? Roy looked into it. Most of it was related to Mathews's drinking. Roy tell you he talked to the ex-wife?"

Tracy nodded.

"So then you know what I know."

"How did you find out about what Mathews was doing? You told the bartender you knew of him around town."

Finlay smiled. "It's Cedar Grove, Tracy. Everyone notices anyone they've never seen before. And I was getting paid back then to make it my business, especially after Edmund House."

"Anyone else know Mathews was looking into Heather Johansen's murder, that you're aware of?"

"Like I said, I'd assume just about everyone in Cedar Grove, but specifically, no. Specifically, just me, Roy, and the Johansens."

"Where were you the afternoon Mathews got shot?"

Armstrong nodded. "I figured you'd get there eventually. It was October, Tracy. I was where I always am on days off during deer season. The same place your dad was on his off days. I was hunting."

"Alone?"

Armstrong shrugged. "Not a lot of guys in Cedar Grove who aren't working midweek."

"Where were you hunting?"

"Just a couple miles from where they found Mathews's body." He put down his mug and again appeared to get agitated. "Let me make this simpler for you. I could have driven to the area where Roy and I think the shot was made. But I clean my rifle every time I shoot it, and after every hunt, no matter if I fire it or not. It's a habit I learned from my father. So even if I'd shot Mathews, my rifle was clean."

"Did you?"

"Did I what?"

"Shoot Mathews?"

"No," Finlay said, voice rising. "And I didn't kill Heather either . . . or my wife."

Tracy gave him a moment to cool off. Then she said, "Who knew you were hunting?"

"The only person I know for certain was Kimberly. And I could have made the estimated shot, roughly a hundred to a hundred and fifty yards, with my eyes closed."

"Did you hear a gunshot?" Tracy knew the crack of a rifle would have been heard a long distance. "When you were out hunting, did you hear anything like that?"

"If I did, I don't recall it."

"When did you hear about Mathews's death?"

"Roy came out to the house after I got home. He asked me a lot of the same questions you're asking me."

Tracy bet Roy had. She flipped a page in her notebook. "I'm sorry, Finlay. I need to ask you about Kimberly."

"I know you do."

He didn't tell her it was all right, or that he understood she was just doing her job. He didn't make it easy for her. He just sat back, like a punch-drunk fighter waiting for the next blow, no longer even bothering to raise his gloves or otherwise try to defend himself.

"You were working?"

"I was out on patrol."

"Your neighbor recalled seeing a police car in the driveway of your home."

"Alice Brentworth. Lives across the street. I went home often to eat lunch and save a little money, and I did so that day. Kimberly would sometimes meet me if she was at the *Towne Crier*, but she often worked on her stories from home and she had that day. I was home for about an hour."

"The gas can they found inside the house?"

"Mine. I filled it the prior Saturday because I drove the riding mower that day. I kept the can in the shed out back."

"Who would know that?"

He shrugged again. "I don't know, but who doesn't keep a can of gasoline in their shed? Who doesn't have a riding mower, or a gas-powered hedge trimmer, or blower?"

Growing up, Tracy recalled gas cans in their shed for precisely those reasons.

"The next question," Finlay said, "is could someone have come to my house without the neighbors seeing them?"

"Could they?"

"Drive by what's left of my home. Like a lot of homes in Cedar Grove, anyone could have parked a car a block or two away and walked through the backyard."

"Police report says there was no sign of forced entry."

"One, we didn't lock our doors when we were home. So a person could have walked in, hit Kimberly in the head, then poured the gasoline. Or, two, Kimberly could have known the person, so she wouldn't have been alarmed or on guard, at least not immediately. I think the second is the more likely."

"Why?"

"Kimberly wasn't sexually assaulted and nothing was stolen. It means the person who came that day did so for a different purpose. I believe that purpose was to kill Kimberly and destroy her research into Heather Johansen's murder."

"How far had Kimberly gotten in her investigation?"

He motioned with his finger to Tracy's notebook. "This is where you're going to want to put a star . . . or something, next to what I have to say, because it sounds unbelievable even to me."

Tracy looked at him, again uncertain.

"The answer is, I don't know. Kimberly and I didn't talk about the book, other than what had been in the ME's report."

"Never?"

Finlay shook his head. "Kimberly knew it was a sensitive subject, and even more so after she read the ME's report. She was only human, Tracy; she had the same concerns you've expressed. Could the baby have been mine? We talked that through, and she said that was another reason to write the book. To clear my name."

A tear trickled down Finlay's face and he wiped it away. Tracy wasn't sure whether the tear was born from sorrow or regret. Possibly anger. Finlay put up a hand as if to say, *so there you have it*, and Tracy knew what Finlay wasn't saying. He wasn't saying that his wife, the mother of his children, had read the medical examiner's report and that she had doubts about the man she'd married, that when Kimberly read that Heather had been pregnant, Finlay was the first name that came to mind.

"Kimberly had doubts," Tracy said.

Finlay put his index fingers to his forehead, like he had a sudden headache. "Maybe so," he said under his breath.

In the silence that followed, Tracy heard the radiator clicking and ticking and the hum of the small refrigerator, along with the thump of the overhead fan. "Finlay?"

"Hmm?" he said without considering her.

"How did you find out about the fire?"

———

Kimberly Armstrong flipped through the pages of one of the four binders on her shelf. The space heater in the corner of her office ticked and clicked, and she smelled the burned odor of the orange heating coils. Her home office had been an unpermitted addition built by the prior owners. With single-pane windows and poor insulation, the room never fully warmed in the fall and winter. Tired of being cold, she'd bought the space heater at the thrift store. Finlay hadn't been happy about it. He called the heater a fire hazard and said Kimberly had enough paper in her office to start a forest fire.

Kimberly flipped another page and continued reading. She'd been investigating Heather Johansen's death—and the subsequent death of Jason Mathews. She had made progress, even felt at times she was getting close to figuring out what had occurred, but she wasn't quite there yet. She was missing something, and lately she'd become preoccupied with a different story just as intriguing. She only went back to Heather Johansen's death when time permitted. Like today.

Mathews had been telling anyone who would listen that he had learned something explosive, something Roy Calloway had not made public. But she'd also determined that Mathews was a drunk and could have maybe just been trying to drum up business—which meant it could all just be bullshit.

Then Mathews got shot.

The police—Chief Calloway—told Kimberly, who was writing the story for the Cedar Grove Towne Crier, *that it appeared Mathews's killing had been a hunting accident. He said Mathews had picked up broken branches across the road, and a hunter, scoping the area for a deer, mistook the branches for antlers.*

That sounded like the type of bullshit Roy always tried to spoon-feed the press. The now former chief of police had become infamous for concealing the truth, and had even fabricated evidence to convict Edmund House for Sarah Crosswhite's murder.

Maybe Calloway thought Kimberly would simply play along and write the story he gave her. But certain things gnawed at her, not the least of which was no hunter had come forward to claim responsibility for "the accident." Wouldn't a person have done that?

She'd also driven to the spot where Mathews had been shot, even climbed the hillside adjacent to the road. That's when she really knew. No hunter could have mistaken the tree branches for antlers, or Mathews for a deer. And if she was correct, it meant Mathews had been ambushed—and maybe by someone trying to keep him quiet about Heather Johansen having been pregnant when she died.

She had a hunch she was on the verge of a big story, possibly a huge story. She also knew she'd have to buck her editor to get it published. Atticus Pelham was far from the courageous lawyer his parents named him after in To Kill a Mockingbird. *Pelham didn't like controversy, especially controversy involving the chief or his police department. Pelham was afraid of Roy Calloway. Kimberly wasn't. She didn't appreciate that Calloway had used her to write the story that Mathews had likely died in a hunting accident. She told Pelham she wanted to submit a public records request for both Heather Johansen's and Jason Mathews's police files. Johansen's file had been closed and was therefore available. Mathews's file should also have been closed, since Roy Calloway said he'd concluded that Mathews died in a hunting accident. When Pelham balked, concerned about potential blowback, Kimberly told him the newspaper was Cedar Grove's voice of truth. She even pulled out the famous Thomas Jefferson quote she'd learned in one of her journalism classes about liberty depending on the freedom of the press. When that didn't convince Pelham, she threatened to go to the* Bellingham Herald *with the story.*

Eventually, Pelham relented—though only to a degree. He told Kimberly she could submit a request to get copies of the police files, but he made no promises he would publish anything she wrote without it being rock-solid. Kimberly figured she'd cross that bridge when she got there.

Her determination had come at a cost, though. It had caused a rift with Finlay. He'd told her she'd put him in a difficult position, now that he was chief.

When the two files finally came into the newspaper office, three weeks later than the statute required, Kimberly expected to find redactions and missing pages. To her surprise, the files appeared to be complete. She took both home and closed the door to her office, and that's when the magnitude of what she held in her hands, the immensity of it, hit her.

The first file wasn't just any file.

The file documented the murder of her best friend, someone she'd grown up with.

Kimberly had held Heather's file like some sacred artifact of immense power. Her hands had shaken, and she had wondered if maybe she didn't want to write the story after all, didn't want to know what had happened. She had debated that question for more than an hour before she told herself that she had to go through the file, and not because of freedom of the press or Thomas Jefferson.

She had to go through it for Heather.

If Jason Mathews had been shot, and there was little doubt in her mind that he had been, then it had to be for a reason. She didn't see someone he'd maybe pissed off in the bar going that far to kill him, though maybe it could have happened that way. But she thought it more likely his shooting was because of something he'd learned in Heather's file. It was too big a coincidence to be anything else, wasn't it? In journalism school Kimberly had been taught to reject coincidences. Facts. Reporters looked for facts, not speculation and coincidences.

She'd taken a deep breath, though it had done little to quiet the flutter of butterflies in her stomach, and opened the file cover. She'd read line by line, digesting the contents slowly, feeling at times like she was somehow invading her friend's privacy. She found police reports, interviews, and photographs. She didn't look at the photographs. She wasn't mentally prepared to do that, but she'd read everything else, including the medical examiner's report. She'd never expected to find something much worse than anything she could have imagined.

But she did.

Jason Mathews had not been bullshitting.

She'd found the information he'd said he had found. She'd found the information Roy Calloway had not told Eric and Ingrid Johansen—or anyone else. She remembered feeling numb. Then she'd started to shake, and, finally, to cry.

Heather had been pregnant.

The flutter of butterflies had intensified, until Kimberly's nausea overwhelmed her. She'd pushed away from her desk, run down the hall to the bathroom, and threw up her lunch. Kneeling on the cold tile, a chill on her forehead, she'd said out loud the thought that had made her vomit.

Heather had been dating Finlay. They'd broken up. But they had dated.

And her mind filled in the other blanks. Finlay, a Cedar Grove police officer, would have had access to the medical examiner's report, wouldn't he? Finlay would have known what Jason Mathews said he'd learned from the ME's report, wouldn't he? That information alone called into question the police's conclusion that Edmund House had killed Heather, which had always lacked sufficient evidence. But now . . . now there was new evidence.

What if the baby had been Finlay's? What if that was the reason Heather had been on the county road that night? The hospital was in Silver Spurs. Could she have gone to get an abortion? And . . . and . . .

No. Stop. She had to stop.

She'd stood from her knees, catching her reflection in the bathroom mirror. She looked gray and sickly. What the hell was she thinking?

This wasn't any man. This was Finlay.

She'd been reluctant to date him because of his history with Heather, but they'd gotten past that, eventually. They dated for four years because she wanted to be sure. And she had been. She'd fallen in love with Finlay. He was a good man, a gentle man. This was her husband. The father of her children. Finlay wasn't a killer. Finlay was kind and soft-spoken.

But other thoughts flooded her, thoughts she had dismissed years before. Thoughts about what had happened when Heather ended their relationship and broke Finlay's heart. She remembered how angry he got, the things he had called Heather.

No.

She lowered her face to the sink basin and splashed it with cold water, hoping it would clear her mind. Finlay had changed. He was not the boy he'd been in high school. He'd learned from his mistake. Didn't everyone have an ex-girlfriend or ex-boyfriend who'd brought out the worst in them? That was part of growing up. Part of dating. No. Finlay had changed. He'd left Cedar Grove. He'd joined the police force. He'd learned from Roy Calloway, who'd mentored and taught him.

Which had given him full access to Heather Johansen's file.

Maybe that had been the reason for his objection to Kimberly writing the story—what Kimberly would learn from that file.

Another thought had chilled her, this time so deep her entire body shook and she had wrapped her arms across her chest.

The day Jason Mathews had been shot, Finlay had been out hunting.

She'd decided at that moment that she had no choice. She had to ask Finlay. She had to ask her husband. She couldn't live this way. She couldn't live in doubt.

When Finlay arrived home that night, Kimberly had approached him. She'd told him what she'd learned from the medical examiner's report. Finlay had listened quietly. He hadn't gotten angry. He didn't yell and scream. But she could see the pain in his face, and she knew that her questions had hurt him deeply.

"I didn't kill Heather," he'd said that day. "And I didn't kill Jason Mathews."

Kimberly had felt a great sense of relief. She told him she believed him. She told him she was going to put the story to bed, that she'd found another story to write, information in the Whatcom County building department that could be good news for all of Cedar Grove. She'd said she didn't even believe the medical examiner's report about Heather. Heather had been her best friend. She would have told Kimberly something that important. Heather would have asked Kimberly for help. So she wasn't going to believe it. She wasn't going to pursue the story.

But of course she had.

But not for Heather.

Not for Finlay.

And not for Cedar Grove.

She pursued it for herself. And for her children.

She'd pursued it because she couldn't continue to live with the doubt, not about the man she'd married, not about the man she'd shared her bed with, not about the father of her children.

She pursued it because if she had any doubt, if she thought there was even a kernel of truth that Finlay could be the brutal, calculated killer of her best friend, then how could she live another minute with him?

Kimberly heard a noise from somewhere in the house, though she couldn't immediately place it. They didn't have a dog or a cat; Kimberly was allergic. And the kids wouldn't be around this time of day.

Had Finlay come back home? They ate lunch together. Could he have forgotten something? She closed the binder, stood, and set it back on the shelf. Then she called out. "Finlay? Are you home? Did you forget something?"

No answer.

She walked from her office into the hallway, startled, and raised a hand to her chest. "You scared me." Then she said, "Wait. What . . . what are you doing here?"

And in that moment, she placed the sound she had heard—the sound of someone sliding open the glass door at the back of the house. She smelled something pungent and looked down at the floor.

"Is that our gas can?"

—

"I was on patrol," Finlay said. "It had been quiet. Just a few calls from dispatch." He paused. "Then the speaker crackled: *2b10 call received. Structural fire.*" He looked across the table at Tracy. "I remember thinking a fire at that time of year, late September, could be disastrous. The past summer had been unseasonably warm. We'd exceeded the nineties thirteen times, including five days over one hundred degrees, and the forest was dry as a bone. Worse, mountain pine beetles had decimated a large swath of the pine trees—making them rusty-brown kindling. We'd been on high alert, and for good reason. *Flames and black smoke visible,* dispatch said." Finlay said the next sentence as if speaking to himself: "*372 Bisby. Cross street Fourth Street.*"

"*Your house,*" Tracy said.

Finlay nodded. "I reached for the microphone to ask dispatch for clarification. She repeated the address. You know that feeling when you don't know what to do?"

Tracy did. She'd felt paralyzed the morning her father called to ask why the police had found her truck on the county road but not Sarah.

"I couldn't move," Finlay said. "I remember thinking that I'd warned Kimberly about the space heater in her office, that it could catch fire. That's what they thought had happened, the arson investigators—initially. Because the fire started in Kimberly's office. They thought maybe it was a bad socket, that it had popped."

Tracy listened, not interrupting.

"And then I remembered. Kimberly was home. We'd eaten lunch together." He looked again at Tracy. "And that's when I got really scared." His face pinched. He pressed his lips together until they nearly disappeared. Tracy felt her stomach grip. Finlay took a breath. A tear rolled down his cheek. "When I got there, the house was engulfed in flames and spewing black smoke. I looked for Kimberly in the crowd that had gathered across the street. I asked my neighbors. I asked anyone and everyone if they had seen her. They just kept . . ." He shut his eyes. More tears rolled down his cheeks. "They just kept shaking their heads. No one had seen her.

I looked and saw her car, her Honda, parked in the carport." He blew out a breath and took a moment. "I rushed across the lawn to the front door and tried to get past the flames. Firemen grabbed me. I don't recall my uniform catching fire or how many firemen it took to subdue me. At some point it didn't matter. They dragged me away and I stood there. I stood there, helpless, listening to those flames howling. And I knew Kimberly was inside."

Tracy waited a beat, giving Finlay a moment to compose himself. Then, in a soft voice she said, "Do you think someone could be setting you up, Finlay?"

He seemed to give her question thought, but it was clear it hadn't been the first time he'd done so. "I didn't think about it when Heather was murdered. I considered myself just a victim of circumstance. I'd dated her. I'd acted like an idiot when we broke up. When Jason Mathews died . . . I thought . . . I thought someone was trying to keep a secret, a secret that Mathews got too close to, but I didn't think it was aimed at me."

"And now?"

He lifted his gaze. "When the arson report said they'd found evidence of an accelerant, gasoline, and that they had found my gas can among the debris . . ."

"Who would want to blame you for the murders?"

"I don't know," he said.

Tracy thought again of who had known that Finlay had once stalked Heather Johansen. She thought of who knew that Jason Mathews had the police file, and the medical examiner's conclusion that Heather Johansen had been pregnant. Who knew Kimberly had made a public records request for both files?

Finlay certainly and . . .

Tracy shuddered. And Roy Calloway.

CHAPTER 10

Dan looked at the clock in the lower right corner of his computer screen—4:00 p.m.

He leaned back in his chair to see out the window, but he did not see the Subaru in the driveway. Tracy was not yet home.

Dan's day had been nonstop from the moment he had closed his office door. He'd taken just one break, to get a quick bite to eat and to check on Therese and Daniella. He'd found Therese at her easel in the family room. Her painting had become more defined since he'd last seen it. He could identify the gazebo he'd installed the prior summer over the hot tub. Dan didn't know much about painting. He thought maybe it was impressionist since Therese had painted the scene with a flurry of snow that nearly obscured the gazebo.

"She's asleep in the bassinet," Therese had said in a soft voice. "I'm using the time to paint. I hope you don't mind."

Dan didn't.

Other than that one break, Dan had not left his desk all day.

He smelled something cooking that caused his mouth to salivate, and he pushed his chair away from his desk. His Outlook pinged. The sender's email address caught his attention. Whatcom County Superior Court. Dan clicked on the email and pulled up the Notice of Decision by Judge Doug Harvey. He quickly scanned the preliminary statement of facts and looked for the word "Therefore," which preceded the actual decision on the merits.

Judge Harvey had withheld his decision on the city's motion for summary judgment, and he had given Dan thirty days to conduct discovery and to submit evidence that Cedar Grove and its officer's actions were not protected by the public duty doctrine. In other words, Harvey hadn't fully bought Dan's argument, but he was giving him a chance to put up or shut up. Judge Harvey had further ordered the City of Cedar Grove to respond to Dan's requests for production of documents, which Dan had served nearly a month earlier, and he had ordered that Cedar Grove make witnesses available for deposition.

Dan's in-box pinged again. This time the sender line showed that it was from Rav Patel. Patel inquired when Dan wished to come to his office to review the documents and attached the city's responses to Dan's interrogatories—written questions answered under oath. Patel's quick response was diametrically opposed to what Dan had anticipated—more stalling. It now appeared Patel was not going to transfer the case to outside counsel, at least not yet.

Dan hit "Reply" and requested an opportunity to review the documents the following day. After sending the email, he called his office in Seattle and spoke with Leah Battles, who said she'd read Judge Harvey's decision and was in the process of sending out deposition notices for Gary Witherspoon and members of the Cedar Grove City Council.

"Set Witherspoon's deposition last," Dan said. "After I hear everything the city council members have to say."

Dan heard a car engine and again looked out the window. Tracy drove her Subaru down the driveway and parked behind his Tahoe. She and Dan had not spoken since the prior evening, but Dan had a pretty good idea where Tracy had been.

"I'll talk to you tomorrow," he said to Battles.

He left his office and walked into the kitchen, lifting the lid on a pot and taking in the aroma of Therese's stew. Tracy pushed open the front door, straining with the weight of two storage boxes. Dan assumed they held police files.

"Let me give you a hand," he said, replacing the lid on the pot and moving to the door to help her.

"I got it." She set the boxes down on the floor. Dan shut the door. They kissed and she removed her coat and hung it on the peg. "Is Daniella up?"

"Therese took her for a walk about half an hour ago." He checked his watch. "I'm assuming they'll be back any minute."

Tracy walked to the easel and considered the painting. "This is good, isn't it?"

Dan nodded. "I was thinking of buying it and hanging it over the mantel."

"That would be a great idea," Tracy said. She paused. "Are you cooking? Smells delicious."

"Also Therese," he said. "I believe it's Irish stew."

"Comfort food. Perfect. It's starting to snow again. We can stoke the fire and relax."

Dan looked to the window and saw intermittent flakes of snow. They were both stalling. He knew where she'd been, and he had contemplated how to respond, what to say. He didn't want to escalate the situation or look like a sexist, though he'd concluded that was somewhat inevitable.

"Do I dare ask where you've been or what's in the boxes?"

"I talked to the Johansens this morning with Roy, then drove out to Silver Spurs and spoke to Finlay."

"And?"

"And I made a call to Seattle and requested permission to look into the matters."

Dan sighed. And there it was. "Okay."

"This is what I do, Dan."

"I know," he said. "You said that last night."

"I don't want this to be a problem between us," she began.

"And I understand that," he interrupted, not saying it wouldn't be.

"Let me finish."

"You don't need to."

"Dan—"

"I understand this is what you do. I also understand that you're a lot like your father, and that helping people is what gets you out of bed in the morning. I guess I just held out hope you would decide not to go back to work. That's not meant as a sexist comment. I just worry about you." He shrugged. "But this is why we have Therese . . . So you can go back to work. So . . ."

"I know you worry." She stepped to him. "And I love you for it. And I wouldn't just take any case."

"But Heather's murder reminds you of what your family went through after Sarah disappeared."

Tracy looked at the boxes. "I think someone is setting Finlay up, Dan. And whoever it is, they may have gotten away with killing three innocent people."

Dan nodded but didn't say anything.

"Just know that I'm not going to do anything stupid."

"Okay." Dan managed a thin smile, but inside he wondered how many police officers killed in the line of duty had said something similar.

CHAPTER 11

The storm that night blew through Cedar Grove like a freight train, a howling wind on which rode the clicks and clacks of tree branches banging together and snapping. It raged for most of the night, dumping more snow on the already burdened streets, and eventually subsided at 4:00 a.m. Tracy knew because she'd been up feeding Daniella—not that she'd slept much herself. She kept going over the final thought she'd had during her meeting with Finlay.

Who had enough information to have set up Finlay?

Roy Calloway.

The thought was ridiculous, she knew, but also accurate. And she'd possessed seemingly crazier thoughts, on other cases, and those thoughts, too, had proven accurate.

So she forced herself to go through the mental exercise.

Roy had certainly hidden the news that Heather Johansen had been pregnant. He'd said he'd done so to protect Eric and Ingrid, to protect their memory and the reputation of their daughter. If Tracy accepted that logic, then Roy had told the newspaper that Jason Mathews's death had likely been a hunting accident for the same reason—to deflect attention from what Mathews had learned in Heather Johansen's file. Roy knew Mathews's death had not been an accident. He'd been to the shooting site, and back then he'd even climbed the side of the hill. If he knew Mathews wasn't the victim of a hunting accident, then he had to know Mathews could have died because of what he'd learned in Heather's file. Could there have been another reason? Certainly. Mathews was apparently a bad drunk. He could have made an enemy— maybe someone from the Four Points Tavern. But that would have been a hell of a coincidence, given the timing of his death.

So was Roy's decision to keep everything quiet to protect Finlay or to set him up? Or was it just good police work—not revealing critical information to the public with the hope that when they found the killer, the killer would confirm what no one else knew? Maybe.

Tracy had gone through the facts as she nursed Daniella.

Roy knew Finlay had once been Heather's boyfriend. He knew the relationship had ended badly. He knew Finlay would be the primary suspect in Heather's death. Roy was chief in Cedar Grove, so it was not unfathomable that he also knew, through dispatch, that Finlay had picked up Jason Mathews at the Four Points Tavern that afternoon. Roy could have speculated that Mathews had told Finlay what was in the medical examiner's report—especially when Finlay never even mentioned the encounter at the bar. The latter speculation was thin, too thin to draw any real conclusions, but not too thin for Tracy to speculate further. Roy could have also made the shot that killed Mathews—with his eyes closed—and he also would have known that Finlay had taken the day off from work. Roy knew what hunters did in October, what Finlay would have done on his off day. In addition to all that, Roy knew Kimberly Armstrong had begun to investigate the deaths of Heather Johansen and Jason Mathews.

Was Roy protecting his protégé? Or was Roy protecting himself?

To believe the latter required that Tracy accept one pivotal fact. It required Tracy to believe that Roy Calloway—the man who had once ruled Cedar Grove with an iron fist—had impregnated Heather. Everything else flowed from that one event.

And that's where the theory broke down.

Tracy knew Roy, and not just as chief of police. Roy and her father had been best friends. He and Nora had been to their home dozens of times. Roy had never given Tracy any hint that he was a letch. And she'd have to believe that, wouldn't she, for the theory to work? She'd have to believe that Roy had taken advantage of an eighteen-year-old girl, possibly even raped her.

And that was something Tracy just couldn't fathom. She didn't see it. It would be like speculating that her father had slept with Heather. Some men cheated on their wives. *Once a cheater always a cheater,* her mother had once said. Some just flirted to test the waters.

Roy wasn't either of those types of men.

Tracy decided that she'd keep Roy Calloway on her suspect list, because that was good police work, but she wouldn't condemn the man. Nor would she condemn Finlay. At least not yet.

At 6:00 a.m., Tracy brought Daniella into bed with her, and they slept like the dead until nine, when her phone woke her. Andrew Laub, her lieutenant in Seattle, had approved her working the murders.

Dan had already departed—to where Tracy did not know. She hadn't heard him leave. She fed and dressed Daniella, then swaddled her in a pink blanket before handing her over to *the daytime mommy.* She thought saying the phrase might help her get used to it, and possibly diminish her guilt for leaving her baby daughter. It didn't.

By the time Tracy dressed and reached her snow-covered Subaru, she was fighting back tears. She almost went back inside the house. She almost called Roy Calloway and told him she just couldn't do it, that she was done hunting killers. Then she thought again of Daniella, and why Tracy and Dan were in Cedar Grove. Dan had initially contemplated selling his parents' home. He knew Tracy's memories of Cedar Grove were not good ones. But Tracy had convinced him to keep it. She didn't want to live her life too afraid of the memories to go home. A part of her hoped Gary Witherspoon would breathe life back into the deceased town, and that it would bloom again—maybe not the same, but alive with people who knew one another and watched out for each other, and for each other's children. She wanted that for Daniella.

She looked to the passenger seat, to the police file Roy had given her, and she thought of Heather Johansen, and of her sister Sarah, and of those dark, dark months. Cedar Grove would never be the town she'd once known, back when she'd been a child. The remodels and fresh coats of paint wouldn't cover all the shadows those two deaths had cast, the pall that had fallen over what had been a bucolic place to grow up. That was the reason Edmund House's retrial had been so painful for so many; the town did not want to go back to that dark time, when Cedar Grove started to decompose. Many wouldn't want to go back now, just when things were starting to once again brighten.

But it had been a necessity then to get to the truth. And it was a necessity to do so again now. Only the truth would bring a lasting light to the town.

Tracy needed to put Heather Johansen to rest—and Kimberly Armstrong as well—if the town were truly to survive. She felt no personal compulsion to put Jason Mathews to rest, but his death seemed to be the linchpin to solving what had happened, and if she wanted to close the book on the darkest chapter in the town's history, she had to put him to rest as well.

She backed the car down the drive and over the snow-covered streets. Traffic had compacted the accumulation of snow. She drove from town and came to a line of traffic on the county road, a change from her youth. Traffic had been nonexistent back then. The county road was the road out of Cedar Grove, and except for the long drives with Sarah and her father to compete in shooting competitions, there'd been few reasons to leave. She merged into the line of cars.

The traffic eased but remained below the posted speed limit, drivers concerned about black ice with morning temperatures in the teens. The patches of sky between the treetops allowed glimpses of winter's pale blue, without clouds, an indication that it wouldn't get much warmer throughout the day. Tracy knew this weather. It felt calm and peaceful, without even a breath of wind. It felt almost as if Cedar Grove was in the eye of a storm, the winds momentarily stilled, and the forest wrapped in a deafening silence.

Until hell broke loose again.

She checked for mile markers, but she knew her destination from memory. Everyone in Cedar Grove knew where Vern Downie's coonhounds had found Heather Johansen's frozen body. Students at Cedar Grove had placed flowers and other trinkets along the side of the road, creating a memorial. Others were just curious to see where a dead body had been abandoned. James Crosswhite had forbidden Tracy and Sarah from going. *It's no place for the curious,* he'd told them. *A young girl died there.*

She saw the turnout and gently eased from the asphalt to the side of the road, applying the brakes with a deft touch. The plows had pushed the snow to the road's edges, where it became packed, icy, and potentially a danger. Once stopped, she pulled on a knit hat, wrapped a scarf around her neck, and grabbed Heather's police file from the passenger seat. She wanted to see the place where Heather Johansen's body had been found, see if it jarred any thoughts or ideas now that she'd read the file.

One of the detectives from the Washington State Patrol Crime Scene Response Team had sketched the county road relative to the turnout, and Tracy noted that the road turned sharply to the left. The report further noted that it would have been pitch-black the evening Heather Johansen walked the road. No street lamps existed, and the dark storm clouds and the thick tree canopy would have concealed any trace of natural light. It was for this reason that the police report had initially suggested that Heather, walking the road in the dark, had been hit by a car and cracked her head on the pavement. That theory was dismissed when her autopsy revealed no other impact injuries—no bruises or abrasions—other than the blow to the head. For the same reason, the medical examiner had dismissed the possibility that Heather had been pushed from or that she'd jumped from a moving vehicle.

Tracy also didn't buy the theory that Heather had tried to walk to the hospital in Silver Spurs. She proceeded under the assumption that Heather had been driven to the hospital but refused to go in and had tried to walk home. The police report indicated what Finlay had said, that Heather was poorly outfitted for the rain and the decreasing temperatures. She had worn only a rain shell over a T-shirt and blue jeans. She would have known better if she had intended to walk.

So if the father of her baby had driven Heather to the hospital and left her, or if Heather had refused to go in and fled from the car, why didn't she hide when the car returned?

Tracy looked again at the bend in the road and wondered if the crime scene techs got it backward. Instead of focusing on what the driver might not have seen, maybe they should have focused on what Heather had not seen. On a dark night in the mountains, with a storm raging, the driver likely would have been using the car's high beams. The lights, a sharp contrast to the dark, would have blinded Heather Johansen, at least momentarily, which could have been the reason she didn't hide, giving the driver the chance to strike. That theory was supported by the medical examiner's conclusion that Heather had been moved to her final resting place after she'd suffered the blunt-force trauma to the side of her head.

The police had searched for blood along the road and on the leaves and branches of the trees leading to Heather's body but found none. The lack of blood, however, could have been due to the heavy rain and the sleet during that evening. The report also noted few shoeprints in the woods, or tire tracks along the edge of the road, but again the heavy rain, and the inattention to detail by the crime scene technicians in 1993, could have been the reason for the omission.

Tracy closed the file and stepped from her car. The cold bit at her uncovered face, and she wrapped a scarf around the lower half. She tucked the file under her arm, climbed down the embankment, and looked for a path into the woods. She ducked under or broke off low-hanging branches, getting dusted with powdery snow. With each step, the rubberized soles of her fur-lined boots sank shin deep. She trudged on until she arrived at the terraced rocks. According to the report, Heather Johansen's body had been placed on the far side of the first layer of rock, where it could not be easily seen. The careful placement, a clear attempt to hide the body, had been another significant factor in the medical examiner's conclusion that the body had been moved after the blow to the head.

Tracy stopped to catch her breath, winded from the exertion and her own lack of conditioning since having Daniella. She lowered the scarf. The puffs of steam from her mouth and nose permeated the cold air. She estimated the walk from the side of the road to be only a tenth of a mile—not an insignificant distance. The crime scene notes indicated broken tree branches and heel marks and concluded the body had been dragged to this spot, and not carried. Heather had been five foot seven and 135 pounds, certainly not an insurmountable weight for a man of average height, weight, and strength to carry, but Tracy also knew from experience reading forensic reports that a dead body is far more difficult to carry because its flaccidity makes it much more awkward to lift and much more difficult to find the center of gravity. The killer also would have been in a hurry to get the body off the road and out of sight before another car drove past, though the storm that night made that unlikely. The body had also not been buried, but rather covered in snow, leaves, and dirt. One of the crime scene technicians had raised another question. If the killer had brought a bat, why hadn't he brought a shovel?

But, again, Tracy knew from experience that the decision not to bury the body did not rule out that the killing had not been premeditated—that is, that the killer or killers failed to bring a shovel because they had not intended to kill. The ground in the North Cascades was glacial sediment—extremely hard and difficult to dig to any depth, especially at the base of a rock cropping. Tree roots would have been another complication—not to mention the killer's car would have been parked on the county road and visible should anyone pass.

Tracy heard a horn honk three times, each honk echoing in the otherwise silent woods. Odd. She unzipped her jacket and snapped free the safety strap of her holster before she backtracked to the road, stepping in the shoe imprints she'd left on the way in to ease the walk.

When she reached the road, she saw Finlay's blue truck parked behind her Subaru. Finlay leaned on the truck's hood, watching her progress. He removed his hands from his hunter-green, fur-lined police jacket and offered a bare hand, which Tracy accepted, and pulled her up the final slope to the road.

"Thought this was your car," he said. He wore a black hat with earflaps, pulled low on his forehead. He hadn't shaved, the stubble of his beard flecked with gray. "Too big a coincidence I'd find another Subaru parked here, of all places."

"What are you doing here, Finlay?" she asked.

"I was on my way back to the motel. I recognized your car from the baby seat in the back, and of course I recognized this location."

"I thought you didn't read the police report." It wasn't a question.

He smiled. "But I did live here, Tracy. We both did. Everyone who lived in Cedar Grove back then knew the significance of this place . . . and the place where they found your truck, when Sarah went missing."

Tracy couldn't dispute that. "Something you wanted to talk about?"

"No. Not really. I take it this means you received authority to take the case?"

"No, and I'm still debating it," she said.

She looked again to the bend in the road. Finlay read her mind.

"That's the direction I was coming home that night, after my class."

The statement gave Tracy pause, as did Finlay's presence at the crime scene. She wondered if Finlay's appearance at the site was more than just a coincidence. She wondered if he was stalking her movements, as he had once stalked Heather Johansen.

CHAPTER 12

Dan stepped inside the lobby of what had once been First National Bank and, years later, when he had moved back to Cedar Grove following his divorce, an assortment of random offices, including his law office. The bank teller cages remained in place, though the spaces had been converted to cubicles for various city departments and employees. Voices echoed off the red marble lobby, which included six decorative columns and was said to be worth more than gold at the time of construction. The refurbished interior glistened under the light from original, nineteenth-century bronze-and-brass basket chandeliers. The mosaic tile floor, which depicted an American eagle with an olive branch and thirteen arrows clasped in its talons, shone. Christian Mattioli had spared no expense building the bank that would hold his fortune, and Dan had to admit it felt good to see it cleaned up and alive again, teeming with people and buzzing with voices and ringing telephones.

Dan forsook the elevators and ascended the curved marble staircase with the burgundy runner and brass railing. His former office on the second floor now served as the office of the Cedar Grove city attorney, Rav Patel.

While Patel's willingness to allow Dan to review the documents so quickly had come as a surprise, Dan now thought Patel's decision to quickly produce the discovery was intended to pressure him, so Cedar Grove could refile its motion for summary judgment as soon as possible. By releasing the documents and answering the interrogatories, Patel could again argue that Dan had no evidence to prove his claim that Gary Witherspoon and the city council were not protected by the public duty doctrine and/or engaged in fraud or misrepresentation.

Dan pulled open the smoked-glass door with the words "City Attorney" stenciled in black block lettering, where once had been "The Law Office of Dan O'Leary." He stepped into the reception area. A ceiling fan with broad blades spun above the desk that had been vacant during Dan's tenancy but was now occupied by a familiar face.

"Dan O'Leary." Sunnie Witherspoon spoke his name as bright as the sunshine streaming through the arched window behind her. She rose from her chair and came around the desk to give Dan a highly unprofessional hug. "Rav told me you were coming in this morning. It's so good to see you."

"It's nice to see you too," Dan said.

Tracy and Sunnie had been childhood friends, but Dan and Sunnie had never been particularly close, and Dan's suit against Sunnie's husband, Gary, certainly didn't improve their chances of that relationship warming up. Sunnie had largely tolerated Dan as a kid because of Tracy, though she never hid her belief that Dan was an outsider. While Tracy and Sunnie grew up the daughters of a doctor and a lawyer and had lived in the finest homes in Cedar Grove, Dan's father had worked for the city, and their rambler was on the other side of the proverbial tracks.

"Tell Tracy that I'm upset with her," Sunnie said, breaking the embrace and stepping back. "I can't believe she hasn't called me. I haven't even seen the baby and she's how old now?"

"Two months," Dan said.

"Two months? Well, you tell her that I have a present, and a little advice. You know I raised four kids of my own."

"I don't think Daniella would understand," Dan said, trying and failing to make a joke.

Sunnie either didn't get it or ignored him, which she had done often when they were young.

"Someone said they saw Tracy downtown taking the baby for a walk with another woman."

"Our nanny."

"Nanny? Wait. Don't tell me Tracy's considering going back to work? She isn't, is she? Not with a new infant at home."

"She hasn't decided yet," Dan said.

Sunnie hadn't changed much since they'd been kids, at least not her personality. Sunnie could talk to a dead body for an hour before she'd notice the person wasn't breathing, and likely finish her story even after she had. Physically, she'd put on weight, like all of them, though hers had settled in her hips and lower legs. Her hair, light brown as a child, now had gold and blonde streaks. She still wore heavy makeup, including blue eye shadow marked by tiny black pinpricks made by her mascara.

"I'll catch up to her eventually," Sunnie said. "You know me. I'm like a hawk when I get my mind set on something."

"I remember," Dan said.

"Bet you didn't expect to see me here, did you? Not that I have to work. I just told Gary after the youngest of our four left the house that I couldn't spend another day without adult conversation. I was going to be a nurse. You remember?"

"I thought you wanted to be an actress or a singer," Dan said.

She waved him off. "You always were a kidder. No, I gave up my plans to stay home with the kids. Anyway, I told Gary I didn't care what

I did, but I was going to do something. My brain was mush. I'm the type of person who needs stimulation."

"I can see that," Dan said.

"You're here for the Larry Kaufman discovery, aren't you? That's the case against Gary and the city council."

"I'm here to see Rav Patel," Dan said.

Sunnie waved at him and spoke as she walked back around the desk to her chair. "Pfft . . . Don't worry about it. I know you attorneys are just doing your job. We all got to make a living, right?"

"We do," Dan said.

"So good to see you," she said again. Then she buzzed Rav Patel on the phone. A moment later the interior door opened and Patel stepped into the reception area wearing a blue shirt and tie, the sleeves rolled up to reveal a sturdy and expensive-looking watch.

"I have the documents and a copy of the interrogatory answers in my office. Would you care for a cup of coffee?" Patel asked.

"I'm good," Dan said.

"Come on in."

"You tell Tracy that I'm gunning for her. She can't hide for long in Cedar Grove," Sunnie said as Dan stepped into the interior office.

Patel closed the door behind them and looked at Dan with a tired smile before stepping past him to his desk in the octagon-shaped office Dan remembered well. Mahogany bookshelves overflowed with unused antique legal books—the same ones as when Dan had rented the office.

Patel sat beneath a ceiling fan spinning lazily and gestured to one of two chairs on the opposite side of his desk. "Have a seat."

Dan sat and crossed his legs. "I'm guessing you can no longer rent this office for fifteen dollars a month."

Patel leaned back against his cream-colored leather chair, which faced away from the curved bay window that allowed morning light to shine on half his desk. "I heard you once worked in this office."

"For about three years. I remember one of those old-fashioned radiators right over there beneath that window. Used to make a racket in the winter."

"The building's heating system was updated," Patel said.

"That must have been expensive," Dan said.

"The city received a historic preservation grant to pay for certain upgrades." Patel quickly nodded to storage boxes on a table in the corner of the office and changed the subject. "I pulled together the documents you requested. You received our interrogatory answers?"

"I was pleasantly surprised you did this so quickly."

Patel shrugged. "I had my doubts about the hearing . . . Not about the motion, but I had figured Judge Harvey would at least give you the chance to perform discovery. He's a bit of a cowboy."

"I got that impression. I thought you had me there for a while."

"It was a clever argument, going into the history of the buildings on Market Street."

"I do my best." After a pause, Dan said, "I'm surprised you're involved, Rav."

"Why is that?"

"I thought maybe you'd send the file out to the law firm in Bellingham."

"I thought about it," Patel said. "But I think this can be handled in-house." Patel sat forward and dropped his gaze to five pendulum balls ticking left and right and gently bumping into one another. The desk ornament demonstrated Newton's basic law of physics, that for every action there is an equal and opposite reaction.

"The city would like to resolve this matter so it can move forward with its plans for Market Street and the civic center."

"Cedar Grove has a civic center?" Dan said.

Patel raised his gaze and responded with a soft grin but otherwise didn't look amused. "Cedar Grove would like to have a civic center," he said. "There is discussion of closing Market Street at the end of the block and building an amphitheater to accommodate summer events, like the jazz festival this past summer. The city needs a place for people to gather."

"The only thing missing are the people." Dan smiled at Patel, who again did not look amused. "If you don't mind me saying so, the mayor and the city council have an optimistic view of the future here. Not that my client wouldn't love to have an amphitheater filled with people close to his store."

"Which brings me to your client," Patel said. He picked up a ball-point pen and tapped the tip on his desk pad. "The city would like to settle this dispute."

"I'm all ears, and if you knew me as a kid when I had a crew cut, you'd know I'm not lying when I say that."

"What would it take to resolve this matter?"

"My client wants to remain in business. He'd be willing to sell outdoor recreation equipment, if it generated sales."

"I meant, what would it take to buy him out?"

"He's not interested in being bought out."

"The city offered him ten thousand dollars. I have the authority to go higher, but we are limited by what the city council will approve."

"And what would that be?" Dan said, not interested in throwing out a number and bidding against himself.

"Would your client take fifteen thousand dollars?"

"Like I said, he isn't in it for the money. He liked having a place to go every day, getting out of the house, seeing people he knew. There is also nostalgia to consider. The company was started by his grandfather and run by his father, so there is familial sentiment."

"We could talk to the new owners and ensure that your client would be hired for at least, say, two years after the sale. I'm sure they would be interested in the goodwill your client could provide."

"I'm sure they would, but not for fifteen thousand."

"Then what would it take?"

"I've never had this discussion with my client. I honestly don't know if any amount would be enough."

"Your client is in his midseventies, and his children no longer live in Cedar Grove. He can't work forever, and his children don't appear to have any interest in running the store."

"I can't dispute that."

"And I don't think you're going to find anything that will support your theory of fraud or that Cedar Grove or any of its officers are not protected by the public duty doctrine. It was a clever argument to delay the inevitable. I think we both know that."

"Well, I guess that's why they let the horses run the races. Sometimes a horse will surprise you and win."

"Would you be willing to discuss settlement with your client and get back to me?"

"Certainly," Dan said.

Patel nodded. "I'll look forward to speaking to you, then."

"May I take those boxes?" Dan said, pointing to the boxes on the table.

"I made copies for you. The bill is inside the first box. You would have had to drive all the way to Bellingham to find a copy service large enough to do the job."

Dan smiled and stood. "Thank you for the hospitality." He looked at his watch, then to the door.

"I'll ask her to run an errand for me," Patel said, "which should give you time to get away."

CHAPTER 13

Tracy left the site where Heather Johansen's body had been found and drove back to Cedar Grove. Roy Calloway had arranged for her to have an office inside the police department. She grabbed a cup of coffee in the lunchroom, then stopped by Calloway's office and filled him in on what she'd done. She asked if Calloway had spoken with the Planned Parenthood office in Bellingham.

Calloway nodded. "Heather never contacted them."

"I was just playing a hunch. Let me ask you about the Mathews case. I read the report in the file by the officer you sent to talk to people at the Four Points Tavern, but the report was pretty bare bones—like the officer was either new and didn't have much experience, or didn't have much interest."

"She wasn't new. There just wasn't much to learn about Mathews. You know people in bars; nobody wants to say much because they don't want to get involved, especially in a death. I asked her to check and determine if Mathews had made any enemies. She didn't find anyone who would admit they knew him very well. Before you get too critical of her report, remember we weren't thinking Mathews's murder and

Heather Johansen's murder were related. So she didn't ask any questions about Mathews talking about Johansen's file."

"Did he have any enemies?"

"Not that she determined."

"She made a note to follow up again. Did anyone do that?"

"No point, back then."

Tracy actually thought that helped. It made it even more likely Mathews had been killed because of what he'd learned from the ME's report, and not by someone he'd pissed off in the bar. Still, she made a mental note to try to reconnect with the owner of the bar in 2013 and determine if Mathews ever brought up the ME's report.

Tracy left Calloway's office, and she settled in the unused office down the hall he had assigned her. She hung her winter clothing on the pegs of a rack usually reserved for tactical gear. The office looked recently vacated—the desk clear but for the computer monitor. Bookshelves were empty, but the cream-colored walls bore the nicks and scars of hung pictures, and the worn linoleum had the scuff marks from heels. Even with the door closed, Tracy could hear phones ringing and voices.

At her desk, she called home to check on Daniella.

"We're grand," Therese said. "She's in the bouncer playing with her toys and slobbering. I don't dare take her out in this cold. *It would freeze the balls off a brass monkey out there*—as my father and brothers liked to say."

Tracy laughed. "Okay."

"Seriously," Therese said. "It's like the bog in Ireland. The wet cuts through you like you're naked. What time will you be home?"

"I'm not certain," Tracy said. "Is there anything you need?"

"No worries here. This little one is getting wrecked. I'll be putting her down for her nap any minute."

Tracy wished she had an Irish translator. She assumed "wrecked" meant tired. "Anything comes up, don't hesitate to call."

"You know it."

Tracy disconnected and pulled out the Heather Johansen police file from her briefcase. She flipped to the section where Roy Calloway kept the police interviews. Over the course of the next hour she reread each one, taking notes and highlighting sentences. When finished, she flipped back to the log containing witness names and telephone numbers. About to make a call, she stopped herself and decided instead to take a drive. It was too easy to hang up a telephone, much more difficult to ignore someone in person. She'd also drive out to the Four Points Tavern—not that she expected to get much in the way of useful information, not after so many years. She'd learned from experience to dot her own i's and cross her own t's. They tended to bite you in the ass when you didn't.

—

The drive took longer than Tracy expected due to the icy roads. The sun had come out, but only briefly, and the snow that had melted had frozen again, leaving ice on the pavement. Given the short drive, Tracy just threw on her down jacket and stuffed her gloves, scarf, and hat in the pockets of her coat.

Ed Witherspoon's single-story home looked freshly shingled and smaller than Tracy remembered it—though everything looked big to a kid. It looked like Ed had built an addition on the right side, where the carport had once been, and Tracy thought she recalled Roy saying something about Ed putting in a home office. It made her wonder where Ed got the money. The front yard looked the same, though it was difficult to tell with any degree of accuracy, given the snow. Barbara Witherspoon had been a gardener in her day. For years she'd won first prize at the Cedar Grove fair and livestock auction. Tracy's mother, also a gardener, had usually been the runner-up, though her garden was four times the size and far more elaborate. Her mother had never complained about the judging. Her father hadn't been so gracious. He said the competition was rigged and repeated his mantra about Ed Witherspoon and a straight-leg pair of jeans.

Curtains covered the front windows against the cold. But someone was home, based on the smoke spiraling lazily from the brick chimney atop the roof. Ed's 1980s-era, white convertible Cadillac with cherry-red interior sat parked in the driveway. That car had been driven in more Cedar Grove fairs than Tracy could count.

Tracy rapped on the front door. Moments later, Barbara pulled it open. She hesitated, as if not seeing Tracy clearly, or not registering the face and struggling to recall how they knew one another.

"It's Tracy Crosswhite, Barbara," Tracy said.

Barbara Witherspoon fumbled momentarily, then greeted Tracy with an awkward hug. "Tracy. Yes, of course. I didn't recognize you."

"It's been a long time," Tracy said. "I've changed a bit."

"What brings you here?" Barbara asked. She folded her arms across a dark-blue turtleneck. A gold chain and crucifix dangled from her neck.

"I was hoping to talk to Ed."

"Ed?"

"Is he home?"

"He's in the back," Barbara said. "In his office. Come inside so we're not heating the neighborhood." She stepped aside to allow Tracy access. The inside felt warm and smelled of coffee and stale air. She heard the sound of a television, a game show. "Can I get you anything? I have coffee and tea. I wish you had called. I'm not prepared for guests."

The interior of the house was like the yard that Tracy remembered, everything neat and carefully groomed. "I'm fine, Barbara. Don't trouble yourself or think twice about it."

"The house is . . ."

"It's beautiful, as always, Barbara. Just like your garden."

Barbara Witherspoon smiled brightly, though her eyes had a distant, somewhat vacant glaze. She looked and sounded unsure of herself and Tracy wondered if it could be early dementia or Alzheimer's.

"You sure I can't pour you a cup of coffee?" Barbara asked.

"If I could just talk to Ed."

"Ed?" She seemed momentarily confused, then said, "Of course. He's in the back. I'll get him."

Barbara departed through a door at the back of the room, presumably to the addition. Moments later Tracy heard Ed's familiar voice booming down the hall.

"Tracy Crosswhite. I'll be damned." Ed stepped into the room looking and sounding just a little too glad to see her. "How the hell are you?" He walked across the room like he was greeting the governor and hoping to make an impression. He still had the politician's charm, though the years had not been kind to him. He'd never been heavy, but he'd always had a gut, like a man six months pregnant. His hair had thinned and was no longer of sufficient length for a comb-over. Thankfully, he'd cut the strands. He'd always had the ruddy complexion of a drinker—he'd been known to enjoy his evening cocktails—but now the ruddiness seemed more pronounced, like a bad case of rosacea.

"I'm good, Ed. How are you?"

"We're getting by, yeah." He wore khakis and a Seattle Seahawks T-shirt.

"What brings you back to Cedar Grove? You're not here to stay, are you?"

Ed didn't sound happy about that possibility. "I'm afraid not. And I'm afraid this isn't a social call, Ed," Tracy said. "It's police business. I'm helping out Roy on a matter."

The news didn't appear to have any impact on Witherspoon. "That's right. You're a cop, aren't you?"

"I'm a detective," Tracy said, playing along. Ed Witherspoon had attended every day of the Edmund House retrial in 2013. He hadn't forgotten, nor was he just remembering. Ed Witherspoon never forgot. She knew for a fact that he kept a rolodex with the names of every person he'd helped buy or sell a home or a business, as well as the names of that person's children, the person's birthday, and other pertinent information. He'd made his living in residential and commercial real estate by staying in touch with clients and would-be clients.

"I knew that. Of course. Helping Roy, huh? I knew that he'd come back while Finlay was out. Sad what happened to Kimberly. Barbara and I went to the funeral. Sad when a young person like that loses her life so tragically."

"It is," Tracy said, thinking of her sister.

"Well, come on back. I have a home office. You haven't seen it, have you?"

"I haven't," Tracy said. She turned. "Nice to see you again, Barbara."

Barbara smiled, closed mouth, but didn't otherwise respond.

Tracy followed Ed down a narrow, windowless corridor, past family pictures that hung crooked on the wall, as if someone had bumped them. She stepped down into a room that looked to be part man cave and part office. A brown leather couch and chair faced a very large flat-screen television, and there were Seahawks and Mariners pennants and pictures on the wall. The office paid homage to Ed Witherspoon, the former Cedar Grove mayor, with framed certificates and pictures of him with various people on the bookshelves. The roof had four skylights, two on each side of the ridge, that allowed light, though not a lot on this day. Most of the light came from the Tiffany lamp on Ed's desk.

"Are you still working, Ed?" Tracy asked. His expansive desk was covered in paper.

"You know me, Tracy. I can't retire. The people won't let me. And real estate is in my blood. Barbara and I left the office out on Fourth Street. You remember the building just up the street from the *Towne Crier*?"

"I do," she said.

"I built this to preserve the sanity. Mine and hers." He smiled at his joke. "I can escape here and do some work without interruption."

"What type of work are you doing, Ed?"

"Same as always—residential and commercial real estate. Cedar Grove is growing. Gary's doing a great job," he said with pride. "He's really brought in some fresh, young blood."

"I saw the changes to Market Street the other day," she offered.

"Can I say I'm proud of him?"

"Of course."

"I'm proud of him." He slapped his desk pad.

"Must be lucrative for you as well," Tracy said. "All these changes must translate into people buying and selling houses."

"Some," Ed said, not offering more.

"Are you involved in the sale of the businesses on Market Street?"

"I wish! No. No, I'm not."

Ed lowered into a hunter-green leather chair behind the partner's desk that looked big enough to land a jet fighter.

"So tell me, what's this matter you're helping Roy with? Wait a minute. Didn't you have a baby?"

"I did," Tracy said. "Two months ago. A little girl."

"I thought so." He lifted the lid on a humidor on the edge of his desk and pulled out a cigar, handing it to Tracy. "For Dan . . . or for you. I didn't mean to infer or insinuate. You got to be more careful now with all the 'Me Too' stuff."

Tracy smiled. "I'll give it to Dan," she said. "Thank you."

"So, two months. Wow. And you have time to help out Roy?"

"Working on it. Juggling a lot. Anyway, the case I was hoping to ask you about was Heather Johansen," Tracy said.

Ed's eyes went wide, but not with alarm. More like a circus showman introducing a new act that would amaze and stupefy. "Heather Johansen?" He made the sign of the cross. "I thought that poor girl was long buried and put to rest."

"Roy is just running down a few things."

"Okay. Well, listen, if there's any way I can help. I mean Eric and Ingrid, they're good people, and that was an awful time around here between what happened to Heather and your sister disappearing. God rest both their souls. I'm sorry for what you went through as well, and your family. You know some people around here didn't take too kindly to you digging up the past when you came back. It's like that old saying about some things being better off left buried."

Tracy couldn't help but notice a subtle change in Ed's tone, how he no longer sounded so glad to see her, and she wondered if there had been a message in his comment, a message intended to imply that the Heather Johansen case was better left buried.

She'd send a message too. "Heather worked for you back then, didn't she, at the real estate office?"

Ed paused, but briefly. Message delivered. "Part-time," he said, no longer so jovial. "Don't quote me on the days of the week or the hours. My memory is good but not that good. Her folks needed the money. Heather was set on going to college, and Eric was having trouble finding steady work. I paid her a dollar over minimum wage to help them out."

Tracy took out a notepad and pen and noticed Ed's gaze consider it. "How long did she work for you?"

Ed furrowed his brow and he let out a soft groan. "Wow. I don't know. And I don't imagine we'd have any of those records around anymore. Not after all this time, and the move."

"It had been a few months, though, hadn't it?"

"I think it had, but again I can't be certain. You're taxing an old man's memory."

Tracy doubted it. "Did you notice any change in Heather's demeanor during that time?"

"Change?"

Ed was still a good politician. If he didn't know how to answer a question, he responded with one. "Did Heather seem more emotional or upset about anything?"

"Such as?"

"Anything at all."

Ed scratched the back of his neck while he shook his head. "Boy. I don't know. I mean she was a high school girl." He stopped scratching and snapped his fingers. "You know I did notice a change. It was about the time of that thing with Finlay. I think you were gone by then, weren't you? Off at college? So you might not know that Finlay and Heather had been dating, and I guess Heather broke it off. From what I could gather, Finlay went a bit crazy, walked right off the pier, and it got pretty ugly. I think Roy stepped in and put a stop to it."

Witherspoon folded his hands on some papers and stared across the desk at her.

"Do you remember a specific conversation with Heather about Finlay?"

Ed grimaced, then gave her a look of concern. "Listen Tracy, I told Roy all of this way back when, but it turns out none of it mattered, not after Edmund House. I don't want to cast aspersions. Finlay's a good man here, and he's been through enough lately."

"I understand, Ed." She waited. She knew casting aspersions had been Ed's only intent.

"Okay well, yeah. Heather came into my office one night. It was not long before . . . Anyway, she came in and asked if I might give her a ride home. I asked her why and she said it was Finlay, that she was afraid of him, afraid of what he might do to her."

"Did she say whether Finlay had threatened her?"

Ed looked like a man who had a spider put down the back of his shirt. "I don't know Tracy. I mean this was high school stuff, you know boy-girl crap."

Again, Tracy waited, though not long this time.

"She said Finlay had threatened her," he said.

"Did she say how?"

Ed blew out a breath. Paused. "She said Finlay told her he'd kill her. He'd kill her if he ever caught her with another guy."

Tracy nodded. "I imagine that must have shocked you."

"Very much so."

"You told Roy, then?"

Now Ed stumbled, searching for an answer to get out of the corner he'd painted himself into. "Well, no. I mean not right away."

"Why not?"

He raised his palms. "It's like I said, Tracy. It was boy-girl stuff. High school stuff. I didn't want to be the one to condemn Finlay."

"Sounds more serious than boy-girl crap, especially given what happened."

"Wait until your daughter is older. I put three kids through high school. I know about drama."

"Did you give Heather a ride home that night?"

"No." He shook his head decisively. "I've been around long enough to know that a man does not give a good-looking young woman a ride home. There's just too much room for rumors. I had Barbara give her a ride home. She'll tell you, if she can still remember. You might have noticed Barbara's slipping a bit. She doesn't recall things, and sometimes she gets easily confused."

How convenient, Tracy thought. "Did you notice any other changes in Heather?"

"Not really, no."

"Do you recall the last time you saw her?"

"Boy, I don't Tracy."

"The police file stated you told Roy she worked for you the day she went missing."

"Well then, that's likely right. I'd go with what I said all those years ago."

"But you don't remember that day."

"Nothing more than what I might have told Roy back then."

"You didn't recall Heather behaving different in any way?"

"Again, whatever I told Roy in that report."

"She didn't say anything to you?"

"Tracy, you have the report."

"No tears you happened to notice?"

Ed Witherspoon shook his head. "Nothing I can recall, Tracy."

"How'd you find out about Heather's death?"

"Same as everyone else, I imagine. I heard that Vern's coonhounds found her. Someone told me."

"Do you recall what you did the night Heather disappeared?"

"I already answered these questions for Chief Roy, Tracy. You're not trying to trick me here are you, get me to slip up and say something different than what I told him?"

"Just asking, Ed."

"Well, I don't recall now. I think whatever I told Roy would be your best bet."

"You don't recall going out that night?"

"Again. Whatever I told Chief Roy. You wouldn't want me to guess, would you?"

"No, I wouldn't want you to do that," Tracy assured. "Anyone else working for you back then, Ed? Anyone besides you and Barbara and Heather?"

"Well, Gary of course. It's his business now. That doesn't mean no one else did, you know, maybe a couple of hours here and there during the busy season."

"Thanks for your time, Ed."

Ed Witherspoon looked surprised, then relieved the interview ended so abruptly. "Okay. Sure. No problem." Tracy stood. So did Ed. "You should consider coming back home," he said. "Gary's doing great things around here and Cedar Grove could use a good chief."

"That's Finlay's job," Tracy said.

Ed nodded but otherwise didn't respond. He walked her back down the hallway and across the living room and opened the front door. Tracy stepped out onto the covered front step and put on her jacket and her scarf.

"Real nice to see you," Ed said. "Come back again and see us any-time. We'd love to see the baby."

"Will do," Tracy said. She paused as if just recalling something. She hadn't. She'd intended to ask it in the office, but Ed had been too on guard then.

"You still throw that big Christmas Eve party?" She smiled. "That was always quite the affair."

"Not for some years now," Ed said.

"No? When was the last time?"

"I don't recall, Tracy. Listen, thanks again for stopping by. I'll let Gary know we spoke."

Tracy nodded, turned, and headed down the sidewalk, hearing the door close behind her. She recalled the last time Ed had thrown his Christmas Eve party because it was the same year her parents last threw their party. It had been 1992, the Christmas before Heather had been murdered; the Christmas before Sarah disappeared. It was, according to the ME's report, also just about the time that Heather Johansen had conceived.

CHAPTER 14

Dan called Larry Kaufman after leaving the building and told him of the city's settlement offer. Kaufman, as Dan had anticipated, rejected it.

"Is there a number you'd take to settle?" Dan asked.

"Not right now. I'm upset about how they handled things."

"Don't let your emotions dictate your actions," Dan said. "Think it over. If there's a number you'd be comfortable having me communicate back to the city, let me know. Otherwise we'll just move forward."

"They produced documents and answered the written questions?"

"Interrogatories," Dan said. "But I haven't yet had a chance to go through them. I will shortly."

"Well, why don't we wait until we find out what's in them."

"Okay," Dan said. After a few more minutes of discussion he disconnected the call.

Dan didn't have a lot of time to go through the boxes of documents, not with the press of his other cases. He hadn't expected the city to produce so much paperwork. He'd thought they'd give him the runaround, then produce a small stack. The approach Cedar Grove appeared to have chosen instead was to bury Dan under a mound of paper. If there were any golden nuggets in those boxes, Dan would have to hunt them down, but he certainly couldn't run to court and accuse Cedar Grove of stonewalling him. He would have enlisted Leah Battles to help, but he had already loaded her up with an arbitration, as well as two mediations.

Dan decided he needed to go back to Seattle. He and Battles could go through the boxes together while they attended to his other cases. Tracy and Dan had talked about this possibility before they'd moved to Cedar Grove during the remodel. Dan could sleep on the couch in his office, and the building had showers. Of course, that discussion had occurred before Tracy agreed to look into the Heather Johansen matter. Dan had expected that Tracy would be at home with Daniella. Thank God they had Therese. She'd turned out to be a godsend, not only with Daniella, but also doing the laundry and preparing dinners.

He'd even raised her salary.

Maybe Dan having to leave was a good thing, a preview of what it would be like when he and Tracy were both back at work.

On the drive back to the house, he called Tracy's cell phone, but his call went immediately to her voice mail, which meant the ringer on her phone was turned off. Her voice mail was full, which was also not uncommon. Dan shook his head. How were they to raise a child when he—or maybe Therese—couldn't even reach Tracy or at least leave a message? What if there was an emergency?

At the house Dan stuffed a duffel bag with clothes, grabbed his shaving kit, and filled his briefcase. He called Tracy's cell phone. Again, his call went to voice mail. He checked his watch. If he left now, he would be driving against traffic and could get back to Seattle in roughly two and a half hours, weather and road conditions permitting. If he waited any longer, his two-hour drive would become a three- to four-hour slog in traffic. He decided to send Tracy a text message. What more could he do?

He grabbed his duffel bag, two suits, shirts and ties, and headed out.

Therese sat at the barstool, painting, the baby monitor on the table beside her. Daniella slept in her bassinet upstairs.

"You're not moving out, are you?" Therese said, putting down her paintbrush.

Dan assumed she was joking, but he also couldn't dismiss the thought that she might have caught at least part of his and Tracy's argument the other night.

He smiled. "I have to get to my office in Seattle for a couple of days to put out a few fires."

"Put out fires? You're a fireman now," she said, returning his smile.

"All lawyers are firemen to one extent or another. Listen, I haven't been able to reach Tracy, but I sent her a text message. Will you let her know that I hope to be back in a few days, maybe the weekend. I'll be in the car for the next couple of hours if she calls."

"I'll let her know," Therese said.

"We're lucky to have you," he said. "Do you need anything?" He looked around the room. "Is there enough firewood in the box?" He set down his duffel bag and pulled open the woodbox to the side of the fireplace insert. "It's almost empty. I'll fill it for you before I leave."

"Don't be daft. You'll get sap and dust all over your clothes, and I can see for myself that you've got your knickers in a bunch already. I'm perfectly capable. Go. Take off."

"You sure?"

"I may not be a fireman, but I think I can handle stacking some wood."

"The wood is in the backyard under a tarp along the side of the shed. There's a wheelbarrow so you don't have to make multiple trips."

"I could use the exercise," Therese said. "Other than lifting Daniella, I've been a right slacker."

"Well, if you're really motivated, you can also split some of the logs back there."

"You're joking," she said. "I'd probably take off a toe."

CHAPTER 15

B y the time Tracy left Ed Witherspoon's home, the sky had turned a dark gray, and a fresh two inches of snow blanketed the ground and the hood of her car. The snow had also muted Cedar Grove in a peaceful silence. Inside her Subaru, Tracy reconsidered their conversation, as she did after each interview. Her dad would have said Witherspoon had been, well, Witherspoon—the man who never gave a straight answer. More important than understanding Witherspoon's careful avoidance of her questions, however, was figuring out why he had tried to do so.

Tracy didn't think Witherspoon's vague answers were due to the passage of years or a diminished memory. He didn't appear to have missed a beat from the man who had always been around town looking to sell a piece of real estate. Almost as often as her father called Witherspoon crooked, he'd grumbled that Ed had become mayor to promote his business and make a little money on the side. Being mayor of Cedar Grove came with a salary, one Ed had managed to modestly increase nearly every year he'd served, despite there being no increase in his duties or his responsibilities.

But Tracy wasn't buying Ed's loss of memory for another reason. She knew, as well as anyone, that you didn't forget the night a young woman who worked for you went missing and was subsequently found murdered. You'd remember that woman and that day for the rest of your life. Tracy thought of her sister Sarah every day, and nearly as often she played the "what if" game. What if Tracy had driven home with Sarah? What if her sister had stayed on the freeway and not taken the county road? What if they hadn't competed in the shooting competition that weekend? Tracy could "what if" herself silly some nights.

Ed Witherspoon saying he didn't remember certainly didn't mean Tracy could put him in the "suspect" category. To do that would require a lot more evidence, something more tangible than proving Ed Witherspoon knew Heather had been pregnant or that she had worked for him. Ed could say he'd heard the rumor, and in Cedar Grove that was plausible. However, if Tracy could prove Ed Witherspoon knew Jason Mathews had found out that kernel of truth, then Ed might become a suspect, though it certainly wouldn't be proof Ed had killed either of them.

Tracy sighed. Finding evidence would not be easy.

She checked her watch and called home to check on Daniella.

"You just missed your husband," Therese said. "He's on his way to Seattle."

"Seattle?"

"He said he sent you a text message. He tried to ring you, but you didn't answer your phone." Tracy checked her cell phone and saw that she did indeed have a text message. "He said he had things at work that couldn't wait."

Tracy pressed Dan's name and saw the text message. "Did he say when he might be back?"

"Later in the week, but more likely the weekend."

"How's everything at home?"

"It's all good. Daniella is up from her nap and we're eating. This one doesn't have a problem with her appetite. That's for sure."

"I'm going to run down a couple more things," Tracy said, figuring she might as well use the time Dan was away to get done as much as possible so they could spend time together when he got back on the weekend. "You're good for another hour?"

"Fine," Therese said. "Do what you need to do. We'll be waiting here on ya."

Tracy heard Daniella cooing in the background. It made her both happy and sad. She wanted to be there, feeding her baby girl.

"She's getting impatient," Therese said. "I think she likes the baby food."

"She's eating baby food?" Tracy asked, feeling stronger pangs of guilt. She'd tried to feed the mush to Daniella but failed miserably.

"At this age she's spitting out more than she's taking in, but that's to be expected."

Tracy felt a tear leak from the corner of her eye. "That's great," she said, though her voice caught briefly.

"I'll take a few pictures," Therese said. "And send them to you."

"I'll let you go," Tracy said.

She disconnected and pulled to the side of the road to get her emotions under control. Then she pulled up Dan's message and reread it. She knew he had a lot on his plate and that being away from the office had stressed him out—her working again certainly didn't help either. She'd miss him. It certainly wasn't her first choice for him to leave, but she knew Dan could concentrate at the office. She'd do the same in Cedar Grove and try to cover as much ground as possible. Maybe they could send Therese home for a few days, so it was just the three of them—a family.

She pulled back onto the road and drove surface streets to the county road. The snow had started to accumulate on the pavement, slowing what traffic existed and Tracy's progress. She turned south, toward Silver Spurs.

Twenty minutes later, she pulled into the Four Points Tavern parking lot beneath a darkening cloud layer, a harbinger of more snow to come. A few cars were parked in the stalls, but most were vacant.

She'd first seen the bar when she had stayed at the Evergreen Inn during Edmund House's retrial, but she'd never ventured inside. It had the cosmetic look of a dive bar, with cinder-block walls painted white and two rectangular windows, each sporting a neon sign. One advertised Budweiser, the other the Seattle Seahawks. A sheet of paper taped to the inside of the window by the door indicated some type of special on drinks and bar food on Seahawks Sundays. Tracy didn't take the time to read it before stepping inside.

—

The snowfall had become a flurry by the time Tracy exited the tavern. As she'd predicted, the bar had been sold and the new owner knew nothing about Jason Mathews. He did, however, have a phone number and address for Pete Adams, the former owner, though he said Adams and his wife sold the bar so they could spend the snow season in Arizona.

Tracy plugged the Cedar Grove address the bartender provided into her phone's GPS and, minutes later, pulled to the curb of an A-frame house. Landscaping lights illuminated a concrete walk and three steps, but the windows were dark. Tracy tried the telephone number, but her call went to a computerized message identifying the number called but not the party. She opted against leaving a message, in case the computerized voice was an indication Pete Adams was not interested in answering questions about the past, especially questions from a Seattle police detective.

She drove back to the county road. With the drop in the temperature and the snow flurry, she suspected that a fine layer of snow now covered patches of black ice. She could feel the Subaru sliding when she applied the brakes. Seeing no headlights in either direction, she rolled through the sign onto the county road in the direction of Cedar Grove.

Her cell phone rang. She hit the button on her steering wheel to answer the call.

"Hey, it's me," Dan said. "Just wanted to make sure you got my text."

"I did. Are you back in Seattle?"

"Just arrived. I need to give Leah a hand getting ready for an arbitration and a mediation. I also got answers to interrogatories and boxes of documents from Cedar Grove that I have to go through quickly."

"Better than not getting anything."

"I'll let you know. Could be a bunch of crap."

"When will you be back?"

"Probably the weekend, at least from my initial assessment of the fires burning at the moment."

"I thought maybe we could send Therese home to Seattle in one of our cars, and have a weekend together. Just the three of us."

"Sure. That sounds good. Can you take the time?"

His question had an edge to it. "I'll make time, Dan."

"Then I will also."

"I'll see you Friday afternoon. We can go back to Grandma Billie's Bistro."

"Sounds good to me. Oh, I didn't tell you I ran into Sunnie when I went to get the documents. She works for Rav Patel."

"You're kidding. Sunnie is working?"

"She said after raising kids, her brain had turned to mush. And guess what, I believe her."

"Be kind. Sunnie is just insecure."

"My guess is Gary gave Rav Patel a massive raise or browbeat him into hiring her. She said she's gunning for you and taking it personally you haven't called her."

Tracy laughed. "I'll give her a call and have coffee. That should be pain free."

"Don't count on it. She hugged me like she was lifting my wallet. I better get to it, or I'm likely to be here for weeks."

"Well then, let me entice you to hurry back, Dan O'Leary. You remember that little green lingerie?"

"I remember."

"Well it doesn't fit at the moment, so I'll be leaving it in the drawer on Friday night."

"Then I might be there Friday morning. No more. I have to focus."

Tracy laughed and disconnected. She hit the "Speaker" button again and called to let Therese know her estimated arrival. It was after five, and the standing rule was Therese received time and a half for any hours before nine or after five.

"Call Cedar Grove, home—"

She felt a jolt, hard enough that her head snapped back against the headrest, and before she realized what had happened, the car went into a spin. She saw the road in a 360-degree view once, then a second time. She fought the urge to hit the brakes and pulled the steering wheel away against the turn, skidding to a sudden stop, the car facing the wrong direction in the adjacent lane, with a curve in the road just ahead of her.

Quickly, she drove across the lane to the shoulder and took a moment to catch her breath. She assessed that she was okay. Shaken, but not hurt.

She undid her seat belt and stepped from the car to determine what had happened. She would have concluded that she'd hit black ice, but for the jolt she'd felt. She walked around the car. She hadn't gotten a flat tire. She turned on her phone light and scanned the back bumper and sides of the car. Just above the rear wheel well she saw an indentation. The paint had also been scraped, leaving a jagged line.

She looked to the road. She'd been hit.

She tried to remember if she'd seen any headlights, but she'd been making phone calls. The location of the bump indicated this had been no accident. Most vehicles are front heavy and a well-placed and unexpected tap to the back bumper will send a vehicle into a spin, rotating the car around the heaviest part of the car—the engine. Race-car drivers called it a PIT maneuver, which stood for pursuit intervention technique or precision intervention tactic, among others. Tracy had learned this, as had many law enforcement officers trained in emergency response and pursuit driving.

She looked up and down the county road covered in a blanket of snow, except for the geometric design made by her car tires. About to step onto the road to see if she might find a piece of the car that had hit her, or something unusual in the tire treads, she stopped, one thought prevailing.

Dan had gone back to Seattle.

Therese and Daniella were home, alone.

CHAPTER 16

Therese set down her paintbrush and considered the clock on the kitchen wall. It was after five. She'd expected Tracy home half an hour earlier. Under their agreement, she received time and a half for any hour or portion thereof she worked before nine or after five. Not that she'd insist on it. Mr. O'Leary had already unilaterally increased her wages, and just for doing the laundry and cooking meals. He and Tracy had been more than fair with her. She just liked it better when Tracy was home. She didn't exactly like Cedar Grove. It was fine for what it was, and likely it would be better if she were married and had a full-time job that got her out of the house. She figured that was why Tracy had decided to work. She'd heard her and Mr. O'Leary arguing about it the other night. Therese could understand Tracy's desire. It got right boring being home all day, especially when the snow was heavy and the temperature too cold to be traipsing Daniella around town in her buggy. Luckily the little lady slept a good portion of the day and, when awake, she was *as happy as Larry,* as her mother liked to say.

Therese looked to the rest of the room, to be sure things were in order when Tracy came home. The fire in the insert had burned down to red-and-orange embers, and she recalled Mr. O'Leary telling her they needed more wood from the shed. With Daniella asleep and Tracy not yet home, this was as good a time as any to fill the woodbox.

She quickly checked her spaghetti sauce simmering in the pot on the stove, using a wood spoon to taste the seasoning. Her mother had taught her that the secret to a flavorful sauce was a cup of red wine and a lot of garlic. She checked the time again, then turned down the second burner beneath the water she'd readied to cook the spaghetti. She'd wait until Tracy came home. Overcooked noodles tasted like glue.

At the front door she slipped on the pair of boots Tracy had lent her, along with her winter coat, then rethought the task at hand. The coat would likely get soiled with sap and dirt for sure. She looked through the coats hanging on the wooden dowels and found Tracy's long rain slicker.

"This will do nicely," she said.

She put it on and found a pair of leather work gloves in the pocket. Walking through the kitchen, she picked up the baby monitor from the counter and slipped it in the front pocket of the slicker so she'd be able to hear Daniella, not that she thought the little bugger would wake any time soon. She'd fill the woodbox and be back before anyone missed her.

"Right, then," she said, slipping on the gloves and pushing open the back door, the noise of which caused Rex and Sherlock to bolt from their beds to the door, where they obediently sat, anxiously waiting. Mr. O'Leary said their reaction was Pavlovian. When the dogs heard the door open, they assumed they were going out for a walk. The cat wasn't so easily fooled or interested. He remained cuddled on the couch, not about to run out in the snow.

"Well, come on then," she said to the dogs, and they both rushed out the door, bounding in the snow and biting at one another. Therese stepped out beneath the overhang. Flakes of snow tumbled from the sky. She shut the door and raised the hood on the slicker, then forged a path to the woodpile.

—

Tracy disconnected the call when Therese failed to answer her cell phone. She jumped behind the steering wheel, started the car, and hit the "Speaker" button on the car steering wheel. "Cedar Grove. Home." The home phone rang. Tracy waited. After the third ring Dan's voice came on the line. "You've reached—"

She hung up and slapped the steering wheel. "Shit."

She tried again, every few minutes, without success. She could feel the tires wanting to slide on the ice beneath the layer of snow. She had to be careful. If she drove too fast and lost control, she could end up in a ditch and be of no use to anyone.

She also watched her rearview and side mirrors, not eager for another tap to her bumper. She turned off the county road, onto surface streets, which were plowed less often. When she came upon a car, she passed it. When she came to a stop sign, she slowed and rolled through it. She kept telling herself that nothing was wrong. She kept telling herself not to let her imagination run wild.

It wasn't working.

She sped up Market Street, the stores dark, the sidewalks deserted. Cedar Grove looked as it had when she'd come home for Sarah's funeral. Drab and deserted.

She approached the lone stoplight hanging just above the refur-bished iron archway. The light turned yellow, then red. Tracy slowed behind a single waiting car, then swerved around it and into the inter-section, quickly searching for cars as she rolled through the light. Behind her she heard the driver lean on the horn.

Dan's parents' house was on the opposite side of town. Growing up, some people called it *the other side of the tracks.* Tracy didn't care about any of that at the moment. She only cared that it meant she had another two to three minutes before she'd arrive home.

She turned right on Elm and again hit the steering wheel "Speaker" button. She tried calling Therese's cell phone. No answer. She tried calling the home phone. Dan's voice picked up. She disconnected.

She turned right, drove half a block, and turned left, driving another two blocks. She turned again and found the road blocked by a downed tree. She swore, threw the car in reverse, and backtracked. She turned right at the corner to go around the block, the car fishtailing on the snow and ice.

—

Therese removed the blue plastic protecting the stacked firewood from the rain and snow and reached for the V-shaped split logs. She couldn't believe how bloody cold it was; colder even than the prior night. The gloves were work gloves, not snow gloves, and she could feel the cold in the tips of her fingers, which made grabbing the wood more difficult. She could also feel the cold seeping through her pants legs.

She dropped the log into the wheelbarrow and reached for another, loading wood until she'd filled the bed. She lifted the two wooden arms. The wheelbarrow was heavy, but she thought she could manage the weight. She just hoped she could push the cart through the snow, which had to be nearly five or six inches deep.

She pointed the wheelbarrow toward the back of the house and gave a shove. The wheel barely moved. She tried again, hoping to get some momentum. The wheel rolled half a foot and stopped, bogged down in the snow. The wood shifted, and she struggled to keep the load from toppling over. This was not going to work. Not like this.

She walked in front of the wheel and kicked at the snow, carving a trench across the lawn back to the house. By the time she'd created the path she was breathing heavily, but at least she was warm.

About to lift the wheelbarrow, she heard Daniella, a small whimper on the baby monitor. She reached into the pocket of the slicker and pulled out the receiver. She listened and heard another whimper, then silence. She'd need to hurry and get the load into the woodbox before Daniella awoke for certain.

She rocked the wheelbarrow a few times and pushed. The wheel rolled forward. She pushed harder, hoping to keep the momentum of the load, and the weight, moving forward. When she approached the back of the house, the light on the sensor over the back of the garage kicked on, illuminating her in a bright white.

———

Tracy hit the brakes, turned, felt the car skidding, corrected, and sped down the street, seeing the lights in the windows of their home. The landscaping lights outlined the driveway like an airport runway. She looked to the windows but the blinds had been lowered to keep in the heat. The car rolled to a stop. Tracy stepped out, her boot sinking in the snow. She pulled it free and quickly stomped across the lawn, almost falling on her way to the front door. She pushed on the door handle. The door was locked.

Dan had installed an electric keypad. She pressed the button to illuminate the numbers and entered the four-digit code, then pushed on the door handle a second time and barreled into the house.

"Therese?" she yelled. "Therese?"

She received no answer. She crossed the kitchen to the hallway and took the stairs two at a time, entering the door across from her bedroom. Her baby lay in the crib, awake but content. Daniella's arms and legs kicked and jerked at the sight of Tracy and she softly cooed.

Tracy lifted Daniella from the crib. "Come here. Come here," she said.

Breathing heavily, Tracy saw a light in the backyard and looked out the window. Therese stood behind a wheelbarrow filled with wood, spotted by the floodlight. She was looking up to the second story. To Daniella's window.

Tracy turned and saw the baby monitor on the changing table, then looked back to the yard. Therese wore a bright-yellow raincoat, the hood pulled up.

Tracy's raincoat.

—

Therese had pushed the wheelbarrow halfway across the lawn, making good progress when she heard someone call her name.

"Therese? Therese?"

It took a moment to realize the muffled voice had come from inside her coat pocket. She dropped the wheelbarrow handles and pulled out the baby monitor. It had sounded like Tracy. She looked to the kitchen windows but didn't see her inside. The light over the back of the house clicked off.

"Come here. Come here." Tracy's voice again came over the baby monitor. Daniella cooed.

Therese gazed up at the second story window, to Daniella's room, but it remained dark and she couldn't see inside. She spotted movement though, a ghostlike apparition in the window that made her heart skip a beat, until the apparition moved closer and she recognized Tracy.

Therese waved her hand over her head, smiling. Her movement tripped the motion sensor and the light over the back door kicked on again, bathing her and the backyard in an iridescent white light.

She heard Tracy shout through the baby monitor. This time the message was unmistakable. Odd. But unmistakable.

"Get down! Therese get down! Fall down! Fall down in the snow!"

—

Tracy moved to the window. Therese waved up at her, smiling broadly. The movement triggered the motion detector over the back door and the backyard lit up. She had a bad feeling and turned, about to put Daniella back in the bassinet, then wheeled back to the window and shouted.

"Get down! Therese get down! Fall down! Fall down in the snow!"

Therese looked up at her, confusion etched on her face.

"Fall down in the snow!"

Tracy heard the loud crack, what would sound to so many to be a tree branch snapping, overburdened by the weight of the falling snow.

But Tracy did not mistake a sound she'd heard hundreds, if not thousands of times in her life. The crack of a high-powered rifle.

She put Daniella in the bassinette and rushed down the stairs, stumbling and nearly falling. She used the bannister to regain her balance. At the first floor she cut through the kitchen and pulled open the back door. She removed her gun from its holster while crossing the yard, sinking into and slowed by the heavy snow. She took aim at the light over the back door, squeezing off a shot. The light exploded. The yard fell again into total darkness. She continued forward, like someone trying to run in waist-deep water. When she reached Therese, prone in the snow, she fell on top of her.

"Jesus, Mary, and Joseph," Therese said. "What the fuck?"

"Are you okay? Are you hit?"

"Hit?"

Therese had hesitated at Tracy's first instruction, but not the second time. The second time, she'd dropped into the snow, facedown.

"Just stay down," Tracy said.

"What the hell is going on?"

Tracy waited another thirty seconds. Daniella started to cry through the baby monitor. "I want you to get up slowly," she whispered, "and when I say *Go*, I want you to cross the lawn as fast as you can. Don't stop until you're inside. Go upstairs and get Daniella, but stay away from the windows."

Therese nodded.

"Okay," Tracy said. Her eyes scanned the fence at the back of the yard, which was up against an easement and the most likely direction from which the shot had been made.

"Go," Tracy said.

Hunched over, Therese ran to the back of the house, falling when she reached the back door. Tracy watched her get to her feet and run inside.

Tracy remained low to the ground, struggling to cross the yard. She had her gun out, her eyes searching the darkness for anything protruding over the top of the fence. At the fence she waited a beat, then rose and took aim. She saw no one on the other side. She flipped on the flashlight of her phone and shone it over the fence.

Again, she did not see anyone, but the crooked path carved in the snow indicated someone had been there, and they'd been in a hurry to leave.

CHAPTER 17

Tracy sat in the family room holding Daniella and watching Therese on the couch near the fireplace. After calling Roy Calloway, Tracy put a blanket over the window looking into the backyard, then sat Therese down, who was shaking, and started a roaring fire, hot enough for the fan to quickly kick on. She draped a blanket around her nanny's shoulders and made her tea, but Therese had barely sipped it. The room smelled of garlic from the spaghetti sauce that had been simmering on the stove. Tracy had turned the burner off, as well as the burner beneath the pot of water.

Tracy had tried to engage Therese, but each time Therese took a second to respond, usually with a question like, "What's that?" or "I'm sorry?"

Roy Calloway and a female police officer pushed open the back door, stopping to brush snow from their shoulders and stomping their boots on the mat before walking inside. A cold breeze whipped through the room before Calloway shut the door. The officer walked to the living room.

"Well, I think you're right," Calloway said, stepping into the family room.

Tracy glanced at Therese, then shook her head at Calloway. She got up and handed the baby to Therese, who seemed to find comfort holding Daniella. Tracy nodded for Roy to follow her out of the family room and into the living room, which they rarely used.

"How's she doing?" Calloway asked.

"She's scared," Tracy said. "And confused."

"Hmm. I think you're right about the path carved in the snow behind the fence. It looks fresh."

"Of course I'm right, Roy," Tracy said. She, too, remained on edge.

"You sure you heard a rifle shot?"

She gave him a look to let him know he wasn't speaking to the girl who used to ride her bike on the sidewalks. "I've shot enough rifles in my day to recognize a shot when I hear one."

He grimaced. "I doubt we're going to find a bullet, certainly not tonight anyway. We might in the morning, with better light, but given where the footprints end at the fence, from the angle of the shot, I don't think the bullet hit the house. It could have struck a tree trunk, but . . . I'll send out a couple officers in the morning and I have a call in to the Crime Scene Response Team . . ."

"Don't bother. They can't do much more now, and by morning the tracks will be filled in. I took some photographs . . ." She shook her head, not optimistic. Tracy had walked the entire crooked line from the easement to the street without finding a good bootprint. It was tough to even judge the size because the person had been kicking at the snow. "I sent what pictures I could get to a friend in Seattle, a man-tracker."

"A what?" Calloway asked.

"She's an expert in following tracks and identifying shoeprints, among other things. She might be able to tell us the make and size of the shoe. The waffle pattern indicates a snow boot of some kind."

"That eliminates pretty much no one," Calloway said. "I have two officers talking to the neighbors on the street behind the easement, asking if they saw anyone, or maybe saw a car, but most of the houses had the curtains pulled closed against the cold."

"Something else," Tracy said. "The person used the same trail to come and to go. Which means the person knew enough to try to obscure their tracks. They might have some law enforcement training."

Calloway's facial expression indicated he wasn't totally buying her conclusion. "The person could have just fled, Tracy, and the path he'd created was the path of least resistance on the way back to his car. He would have kicked at the snow because it makes running easier."

"Maybe so, but there's something else to consider." She told Roy about the tap on the drive home.

"You felt a bump?"

"Someone hit me along the back bumper."

"Did you see a car or truck, anything?"

"No. I think the car had its lights off."

"Where was this?"

"The county road."

"You're sure someone hit you, Tracy? Don't take my head off, but black ice accumulates under the surface of the snow—"

"I know that, Roy, but black ice doesn't leave a dent and scratch the paint above my rear tire well. Take a look when you leave. It was a PIT move, or close to it."

"A what?"

"It's called half a dozen names. The importance here is that the maneuver is taught at any emergency response and pursuit driving course." Tracy shrugged. "I think it's worth considering."

Calloway had a look of concern etched across his face, letting Tracy know he'd connected her dots. "I've known Finlay a long time, Tracy. He's a good man. And right now he's suffering."

"He seems to be Roy, but at some point, you can no longer ignore the evidence."

"I don't see it, Tracy."

"I think you should look into whether Finlay ever took an emergency response driving course." She also wondered if Roy ever had, though she wasn't about to ask.

"Okay." Roy looked down the hall to the kitchen. "What are you going to do about the young lady?"

"I was hoping one of your officers could drive her back to Seattle."

"We can do that. It'll be slowgoing with the snow, but we can get through."

"Not sure how I'm going to pursue this any further. Not sure I can without her to watch Daniella."

"Whoa, Tracy. You're done. This was a bad idea from the start. You got a little girl to think of, a family now."

"I know," she said. "But you have a family, too, Roy. Every officer you have on staff has a family." Tracy, too, looked down the hall. "I'm always going to have a family now, Roy. That's what pisses me off. Someone took a shot at me, or who they thought was me. But they didn't just shoot at me. They shot at my entire family."

"Don't make it personal, Tracy."

"They made it personal, Roy. My daughter was asleep upstairs."

"That's exactly what I mean, Tracy. You got your father's temper."

"Don't—"

He raised his voice and his hand. "You need to calm down, okay? Just calm down." He turned and took several steps toward the kitchen, then turned back. "Think about it. We'll talk in the morning. All I'm saying is you can't do this for personal reasons."

"You did, Roy. When Sarah disappeared."

Calloway looked wounded. Her words had stabbed him. It wasn't the first time. She also had her father's tongue. "I'm sorry, Roy."

"Don't be." He shook his head. "You're right. I did make it personal, Tracy. And you saw how that worked out. I got a lot of regret about what happened. You don't want that regret—or worse."

———

Tracy shut the front door, applied the deadbolt, and set the alarm. Therese, to her credit, had initially refused Tracy's suggestion to return to Seattle, but she was just being brave for Tracy's sake. Therese was afraid to stay. She cried when she left. "I truly love that little one," she said. "And working for you and Mr. O'Leary."

Tracy pulled back the blinds covering the front window. The Cedar Grove police officer sat in her patrol car across the street. It would be a long night in the cold for her. It would be an even longer night for Tracy.

She crossed to the stairs, noticing Therese's painting on the easel. The palette, paint tubes, and brushes, however, were no longer on the scrap of plywood.

Therese had left the painting.

Daniella fussed through the baby monitor. Tracy checked her watch. Her daughter's regular feeding time. *Top her off,* Therese had liked to say. *And you'll both have a long sleep.*

Tracy started up the stairs, stopped halfway, then went back down and checked that she'd bolted the front door. She crossed to the kitchen table and her holster draped over a chair. She took the gun with her upstairs and set it on the changing table in the nursery. She lifted Daniella from the crib. "Are you hungry?" she asked and checked Daniella's diaper. She laid her daughter on the changing table, unwrapping and pulling free her diaper. "We'll get you changed. Then I'll feed you and change you again. I'm sure." She said the last part through tears that blurred her vision, and made the job more difficult. She cleaned Daniella, slathered her bottom with a cream to prevent diaper rash, and put on a fresh diaper. She swaddled Daniella in her blanket and held her little girl close.

"Come on, little one." The tears streamed down Tracy's face, and she felt powerless to stop them.

She sat in the rocking chair, cradling her daughter, weeping. A deep pain gripped her stomach, like the pain that had gripped her when she'd learned Sarah had not come home, all those years ago.

Daniella fussed. Hungry.

Tracy lowered her daughter to her breast, then set her head back against the headrest, gently rocking. She'd held herself together in front of Roy and the other officer, but now she had no one to impress and the tears flowed. She took several deep breaths, struggling to control her emotions. *Hormones.* She again considered the tap to her bumper and the rifle shot. Therese had been wearing Tracy's yellow raincoat, with the hood up.

She tried to dismiss these thoughts, but each time she tried to plug one hole, the thoughts swept through another.

She shut her eyes and started to sing a song she hadn't heard in years, one her mother used to sing to her and to Sarah when they'd been sick or upset; a song her mother said their grandmother used to sing to *her*. Her mother would cradle Tracy's head to her chest, humming and softly singing the words. Though Tracy hadn't thought of the song in years, the words came as if she'd just heard them.

She hummed at first, softly, gently rocking.

"Too-ra-loo-ra-loo-ral. Too-ra-loo-ra-li. Too-ra-loo-ral. Hush now, don't you cry." She struggled through her tears. "Too-ra-loo-ra-loo-ral. Too-ra-loo-ra-li. Too-ra-loo-ra-loo-ral. That's an Irish lullaby."

CHAPTER 18

Eventually, Daniella fell fast asleep in Tracy's arms. Tracy would not sleep.

She set her daughter in her bassinet, placed the baby monitor beside her, and picked up her gun. On her way out of the room she shut the door, though not entirely. She walked across the hall to her bedroom and found Rex and Sherlock waiting for her. They could go in and out through the electric dog door at the back of the house. She was glad to have them. She thought of Therese, what she'd said the night Dan and Tracy went out to dinner.

I'd like to see someone try to get in. It wouldn't be much of a row with the two of them at my side.

Tracy rubbed them both about the head. They seemed to sense her unease and their duty. "You two will keep a close eye on me and Daniella, won't you?"

Rex whined and lowered to the floor. Sherlock remained attentive.

Tracy looked out the window. The police car also remained parked across the street.

She stepped into the bathroom, Sherlock following her. She considered her face in the mirror, her eyes red and swollen. She had never been a crier, not since her sister had disappeared. She'd shed all her tears during those horrible days, believing that nothing she ever experienced in her life would again hurt so deeply.

She'd been wrong.

The pain she'd felt tonight, not for herself, not even for Therese, but for her daughter, for Daniella, was gut-wrenching. What kind of a world had she brought her little girl into? What kind of a world where young women could so easily fall prey to evil? She inhaled deeply and blew out a breath, then lowered her head and splashed cool water on her face, drying it on a towel.

She gripped the edge of the sink and looked again at her reflection.

What kind of a world would it be if no one resolved those cases? If no one put those girls to rest? If no one provided the families with answers?

She would not raise her daughter in such a world. Not if she could help it. She'd put Heather Johansen and Kimberly Armstrong to rest, and Roy Calloway would not stop her. She'd put them to rest because no one else would.

Because she cared.

Because she could.

Every cop she knew had a family. Every cop put his or her ass in danger every day, knowing it could be the last day he or she saw their family. Tracy could relate to all of them. Was she scared?

More than ever, but more for Daniella than herself.

Could she quit? Dan made enough money for her not to work. She could go home and be a housewife and mom.

She'd had this debate since Daniella's birth. It didn't seem right to quit because she could afford to, while so many couldn't. She wasn't built that way. Roy was correct. She was built like her father. She didn't back away from a challenge, and she wouldn't be scared into hiding.

It would require greater precaution, like the police officer stationed in front of the house.

Her cell phone rang in the bedroom. She walked to her dresser and picked it up.

Dan.

She contemplated what she would say to him. What could she possibly say that would not cause him to worry about her and Daniella?

"Nothing," she whispered.

For the first time in their relationship, Tracy pressed the button and rejected the call. She sat on the edge of the bed. What could she say? She would not lie, but she did not want to alarm him.

She sent him a text message.

Putting Daniella to sleep. Both safe and sound. The dogs are guarding us close. Will call tomorrow.

♡

Dan responded.

Love you too. Sleep well. Couch here is lumpy. Wish I was with my two girls.

Tracy replied:

☺

She set the phone down and stared out the dormer window, seeing stars in the sky. She thought of what Roy had said, that he was having a hard time believing it could be Finlay. She, too, had a hard time believing Finlay killed his wife, but she was having a more difficult time not believing it. Coincidences were rare in law enforcement, and those that existed were usually discovered after hours of hard work by a dedicated police detective doing her job.

Coincidence my ass, Vic Fazzio, one of her Violent Crimes Section partners liked to tell everyone. *And I got the biggest ass around here.*

Her phone rang again.

Tracy leaned over, expecting to see Dan's name, knowing she could not avoid the conversation. He was owed an explanation. She steeled herself.

Instead of Dan's name, she saw "Vic Fazzio." She smiled. *Coincidence my ass.* She answered the call.

"Vic."

"Tracy," he said in that deep, gravelly voice.

"Hi Tracy," Vera said.

"That was Vera," Faz said.

"Hi Vera," Tracy said.

"It isn't too late to call, is it?" Vera said.

Tracy checked the clock on the bedside table: 9:42.

"It's not too late," Faz said to his wife. "I told you it's not late. Tracy's a night owl. She used to do graveyard standing on her head."

Vera ignored her husband. "It's not too late, is it Tracy?"

"It's not too late," Tracy said.

"How's our goddaughter?" Faz asked. Faz and Vera had one son, Antonio, who was getting married the next summer. They had no grandchildren yet and treated Daniella as their own.

Tracy struggled to control her emotions. She swallowed her words. "She's good. She's . . . she's sleeping."

"Hey, you okay?" Faz asked.

"Yeah. I'm . . ."

"Hey, Tracy. This is Faz. We've known each other a long time. What's wrong?"

It came out in a burst. She didn't want it to. She didn't want to sound emotional or hormonal, like she didn't have things under control. But she couldn't hold it in. Faz was a work colleague, but he and Vera had also become part of the family Tracy longed for. It was the reason she'd asked them to be Daniella's godparents.

"When did this happen?" Faz asked.

"Tonight," Tracy said. "But we're good. We're safe. We have an officer out front watching the house, and the two dogs are inside with us."

"Yeah, well screw that. Vera and I are coming up."

"No, Faz. That's not necessary."

"You let me worry about what's necessary. Vera can take the time from Antonio's restaurant. That's no problem. And I'm not scheduled to return to Violent Crimes now for another month. The fuckin'—"

"Don't swear," Vera said.

"The freaking doctors still won't clear me because I'm still getting these headaches."

Faz had sustained his injuries during a brutal beating while investigating a gang killing. He'd been off work two months. The external injuries, the cuts and bruises, had healed, but Tracy knew the internal scars took longer. No salve could soothe those injuries. No stitch could suture those wounds. There was only time. And even time couldn't heal the deepest wounds. Those you just lived with, the best that you could.

"You're okay, though, right?" Tracy asked.

"Yeah, I'm okay. I'm fine," Faz said. "I'm like a bull. You can stab me, but I'm still moving forward. We're coming. And that's the end of it."

Tracy wanted to tell them no. She wanted to tell them she was fine, but a part of her wanted them there, because she would feel safe, and because she'd again have the flexibility to do what she needed to do.

She was her father's daughter. She couldn't let this case go. She didn't want to escalate the violence. She wanted to end it. She wanted that part of her that felt safe and secure when her mother sang to her to be for her daughter. She wanted Daniella to know that her mother would never allow any harm to come to her.

So much like your father, she heard Roy Calloway say in her thoughts.

"I'll wait up," she said.

CHAPTER 19

D an heard the latch to his office door click and lifted his head from the pillow on his couch, momentarily disoriented.

"I thought I saw your car out there," Leah Battles said. She eyed his duffel bag on the floor and his suits and shirts hanging behind his door. "Your wife kick you out? Or are you this desperate to get a good night's sleep with the new baby?"

Battles had been a JAG lawyer, defense counsel assigned to Naval Base Kitsap in Bremerton. Tracy met her on a drug case she'd investigated and had liked Battles's attitude. When the case resolved, Battles told Tracy she was looking for something in the private sector, after she completed her duty. Dan had been looking for help. He didn't want a raw attorney straight out of law school whom he had to supervise, which would have been more work for him. He wanted someone who was . . . well, battle-tested, had trial experience, and was not afraid to handle difficult cases. He hired Battles and assigned her the white-collar criminal cases his reputation attracted. He wanted to segue out of criminal law and civil litigation, not that there was anything civil about it, and focus his practice on business matters, which weren't as tied to a court calendar and gave him more control of his schedule, and hopefully more time with Tracy and Daniella.

Dan swung his legs from the couch to the floor and sat up, twisting his neck to loosen a kink from sleeping on the throw pillow. "Hard to get stuff done," he said. "Thought I'd give you a hand with that upcoming arbitration."

"Settled it yesterday afternoon," Battles said. She gave him a narrow grin and shoulder shrug.

The case had been contentious, the opposing counsel from a large Seattle law firm. "How did you manage that? I thought we were millions apart."

"I took Lombardi's deposition and kicked him in the nuts . . . sorry." She wasn't. The law was not the only thing Battles had picked up in the Navy. "I beat him up pretty good. After the deposition he found that religion he'd been missing."

"What did we pay?"

"Fifty thousand. Same amount we offered a year and a half ago, before he spent five hundred thousand on legal fees."

Dan got up from the couch and stretched his back. "Client must be happy."

"Offered to take me out to dinner. We settled for drinks. His eyes roamed too much for my taste." Battles was five foot six, with dark hair, a dark complexion, and a figure sculpted from years of Krav Maga training, self-defense popularized by the Israeli secret service. Battles was physically fit, which attracted men. She could also kick their ass if they got out of line.

Dan continued to stretch the sleep from his joints. "We still have the Benedetti mediation or did you settle that as well?"

"You expect a lot in a few days, don't you?"

"I never know what to expect from you."

"The mediation is set for next week, which is why I'm in at this ungodly hour."

Dan looked at the clock on the wall of his office. It was ten minutes before six.

Battles continued, "The Wentworth mediation, however, was put over until next month at the defense attorney's request. He wants to conduct limited discovery."

"Speaking of discovery."

"Yeah, yeah. I knew you didn't come back just to be altruistic. I went through the interrogatory answers you emailed me last night after my Krav Maga class. Every one of those Market Street businesses was sold to an LLC. I looked up the officers through the Secretary of State's Office and compiled a list of the names, but the only phone numbers listed are the business numbers. The calls go to voice mail."

"All of them?"

"All of them."

"Probably because the businesses are still under construction and not yet open. What about a designated agent for service of process?"

Battles grinned. "That's where it gets more interesting. Each business lists the same agent for service of process, an attorney in Bellingham."

Dan thought he'd misheard her. "Each business lists the same attorney?"

Battles nodded. "I have the name and address. I tried calling yesterday but got voice mail. I decided it best not to leave a message." Battles shrugged. "Told you it was interesting. He filed all the formation papers so I'm assuming he also prepared them."

"For every business?"

"Maybe he was offering a special."

Dan wondered.

Battles moved to the door. "I'll put on the coffee."

"Thanks," Dan said. "I'm going to grab a shower before I get started."

Half an hour later, with a cup of coffee in hand, Dan went through the city's answers to his interrogatories, as well as the formation papers

Battles had printed out from the Secretary of State's Office. It was as she had described. Each business was a limited liability company, which was common for individuals seeking to protect their personal assets when starting a business. What was not common was for each LLC to list the same person as the agent for service of process. That agent was a lawyer from Bellingham, Washington, named Zack Metzger.

Many of the people in Cedar Grove were unsophisticated when it came to the law, and the businesses had all been sold at roughly the same time. Dan thought it was at least possible the new owners might ask one another for a referral to a lawyer. Setting up an LLC was not difficult, and Metzger could have offered a discount for each referral, as Battles suggested.

Still, something didn't seem right.

Dan called Metzger's phone number, but he, too, got a voice mail message, not a receptionist or even a call center. Dan left a message and asked for a return phone call, but he did not indicate the purpose for his call. He continued through the boxes of documents produced by Rav Patel, finding most of them relevant to the requests he'd made, but not particularly enlightening. He went through each of the contracts Cedar Grove had entered into, first to purchase the buildings from the existing owners, and then for the subsequent sale of the buildings to the LLCs.

He had the names of the members of each limited liability company as well as each LLC's address and telephone number on Market Street, but not the members' addresses or telephone numbers.

—

Daniella woke Tracy after just a few hours of fitful sleep. Tracy nursed her and changed her. All the while she smelled the aroma of coffee brewing—and bacon. When she brought Daniella downstairs, Vera immediately got up from the table and took the baby.

"There she is," Vera said. "There's my angel."

Faz stood at the stove flipping bacon, a frying pan on another burner and a bowl of scrambled eggs ready to be cooked. He had a red-and-white checked towel draped over his shoulder, and his reading glasses rested on the tip of his nose. He looked like an enormous fry cook in some greasy-spoon diner.

Rex and Sherlock had taken an immediate liking to Faz—or to the smell of the bacon. They sat in the kitchen staring up at him with an expectant look.

Tracy knew neither Vera nor Faz had slept much. They didn't arrive at the house until after one o'clock in the morning. Thankfully, the weather had held and there had been no additional snow. The three of them had stayed up another hour before Vera convinced them all to go to bed and start again in the morning.

Vera sat at the kitchen table talking to Daniella, nursing coffee, and eating toast with some of Dan's homemade jam. Faz peeled out a copy of the sports section and handed Tracy the rest of the newspaper. "Nearly froze to death just walking to the mailbox to get the paper," he said from behind bloodshot eyes. His face looked splotchy, and a couple of scars remained visible from the beating he had endured, but otherwise he looked like the same old Faz—a bodyguard you'd expect to find in one of the *Godfather* movies.

Tracy had no doubt Faz had nearly frozen, given his traditional attire—slacks, a loose-fitting bowling shirt, and leather loafers the snow would destroy before he reached the end of the driveway. Dan had an extra pair of boots that would likely fit, but she hoped Faz had at least brought a warm coat. At six foot four and more than 250 pounds, there was no hope he'd fit in one of Dan's.

"How'd you sleep?" Vera asked Tracy.

"Not great. How about you? Was the bed big enough?" Faz and Vera had slept in the queen-size bed in the guest room, which had been Therese's room.

"It was fine," Vera said.

"Fine for you," Faz said. "You're a twig. Me? I felt like a sardine."

"You snored like one," Vera said. "The bed was fine, Tracy. Have some coffee and breakfast."

Tracy reached for the pot. "Decaffeinated?"

"Of course," Vera said. "You can't have caffeine when you're breastfeeding."

"Yeah, well I may look like I can breastfeed, but I ain't," Faz said. "So where do I find the caffeinated coffee. Otherwise I'm going to be asleep at the table."

After eating breakfast, Vera excused herself to put Daniella down for her morning nap. Tracy brought a plate of food to the officer in the car watching the house, then joined Faz at the kitchen table.

"Fill me in," Faz said. "What's going on?"

For the next half hour, Tracy went through the evidence and what she had determined concerning the three murders. She also told Faz about the love tap to the rear of her car on the drive home.

"The shot was intended for you?"

"She was wearing my jacket and she had the hood up."

"Might not be a cop then," Faz said. "I agree that the evidence would indicate it's . . . what did you say his name was, Fenway?"

"Finlay. Finlay Armstrong."

"But a cop would also know that killing another cop would bring down the wrath of God on this place. This town would be crawling with detectives."

"That's a good point," Tracy said. "I hadn't thought of that."

"You also said someone could be setting up this guy, Finlay?"

"I think we have to at least consider it."

"Tell me why."

"Something Finlay said regarding the timing of Heather Johansen's pregnancy. The ME concluded that Heather would have conceived right around the holidays, 1992. Neither her parents nor her best friend at the time, Kimberly Robinson, had any knowledge that Heather was dating anyone, even casually."

"Could have been a one-night stand, some teenage party," Faz said.

"Maybe, but unlikely. This is Cedar Grove, Faz. There are only forty kids per grade in the high school. Everyone knows everyone and everyone's business. It seems unlikely Heather would have had a boyfriend, or hooked up with someone and her best friend didn't know. It's possible. I'm not dismissing it. Not entirely."

"What was Fenway's take on it?"

"Heather worked for Ed Witherspoon, and Ed threw a Christmas Eve party every year."

"Fenway thinks this Heather person went to the party and got laid?"

"The timing is right, according to the ME's report. Without much else, I think it's worth exploring."

"You said you talked to Ed Witherspoon about it."

"I did."

"What did he have to say?"

"He was squirrely. He acted like he couldn't remember."

"That's a long time ago. It's possible he doesn't. You also can't remember something that didn't happen."

"I don't think he was having a memory problem, Faz. You don't forget the night that a young girl who works for you is murdered. I don't care how many years pass. Ed claimed he couldn't remember that either."

"So maybe he's a liar, but does he strike you as a killer? Let me rephrase that. Does he strike you as a guy who would bash in a girl's skull?" His eyebrows raised. "I mean to shoot someone with a gun in anger is one thing. To hit a girl with something like a baseball bat . . . That sounds like rage to me, Tracy."

"I agree. And to answer your question, I don't know. We all have a dark side. You told me that once before."

"Yeah, we do."

"So maybe there was more to it. Let's assume that's how Heather got pregnant. What if she put the screws to him, told him she wasn't getting an abortion, and she was going to have the baby. Maybe he snapped."

"Maybe, but then why the other two murders?"

"What if someone else who got the ME's report did the same kind of speculating that Finlay did—figured out it was right around the holidays, Ed had a regular holiday party, and Heather just so happened to attend that year."

"Like who?"

"I was thinking the lawyer, Jason Mathews. We know he had the file, so we know he knew Heather was pregnant."

"And he confronts this guy Witherspoon with the information? It's thin."

"I know. But is it too far-fetched not to at least consider?"

"Okay, so then we have this guy Fenway's wife. What was her name?"

"Kimberly."

"You think maybe she figured it out too?"

"She also got the file, so she also knew. She, too, could have looked into the timing. She was a reporter. Maybe she started asking around about the pregnancy and word got back to the wrong person."

Faz sipped his coffee, then ran a meaty hand over his tired face. "Maybe. But where do we go from here?"

"I'm thinking we go back to where I started, this time with a different set of questions and without Roy Calloway present."

"The girl's parents?"

Tracy nodded.

"You want me to come with you?"

"I do. Having you present will let them know I'm serious about resolving their daughter's death."

"Okay. Let me go to the bathroom. This coffee has got me percolating."

"TMI, Faz. By the way, what size shoe do you wear?"

"Twelve. Why?"

"Because those leather loafers won't last in the snow," she said.

Faz excused himself and Tracy cleared the table. The front doorbell rang, which was rare, and it set off Sherlock and Rex barking. Tracy looked out one of the side panels, swore under her breath, and pulled open the door.

The female police officer who'd been watching the house stood on the porch beside Sunnie Witherspoon.

"Tracy," Sunnie said, looking and sounding alarmed. "Will you please tell this officer that we are friends?"

"It's okay," Tracy said to the officer. "Thank you for checking."

The officer nodded and went back down the walk to her car. Sunnie looked warily at Rex and Sherlock.

"Hang on," Tracy said. "Let me put the dogs outside so they don't wake the baby." Tracy closed the door, Sunnie still outside.

She put the two dogs in the laundry room at the back of the house. Excited, they bolted out the electric dog door into the yard, jostling and playing in the snow.

When Tracy reopened the front door, Sunnie stepped in quickly and lowered her voice like she was part of a grand conspiracy.

"I heard about what happened last night. Are you all right?"

"I'm fine. How did you hear about it?"

"Gary called me on my way in to work."

"How did Gary find out?"

"He's the mayor, Tracy. And this is Cedar Grove. Don't you remember what it was like when you came back for that trial? Someone shot through your front window and the whole town knew about it before the bullet stopped traveling. Are you sure you're okay?"

"I'm fine," Tracy said.

Sunnie's eyes roamed the interior of the house and she quickly changed subjects. "This was Dan's parents' home?"

"Just the foundation and the back bedrooms."

"So quaint and homey," she said, removing her gloves as she walked into the kitchen.

Tracy followed her. "Anyway, I'm fine, Sunnie."

"Oh, I'd love a cup of coffee," Sunnie said, looking to the pot. "You have time, don't you? For an old friend."

Tracy smiled. "Of course. Hang on a second." She grabbed a mug from a cabinet in the kitchen, picked up the caffeinated coffee Faz had made, rethought that decision, and poured Sunnie decaffeinated. "Here you go." She handed Sunnie the cup.

"So, tell me what happened?" Sunnie said.

"We don't really know, Sunnie."

"Oh posh. I heard someone took a shot at you. You think it could be Parker House? Isn't he the one who shot Dan's dog the last time? He always was a crazy bastard, living up on that hill alone. You think maybe he still holds a grudge, because of his nephew?"

"I don't think so, Sunnie."

"Then who? Everyone in town loved you. Loved your whole family."

"The town's changed," Tracy said. "A lot of new faces."

"Is it because of Dan? Because of that lawsuit he filed against Gary? The town loves Gary, Tracy. I can't walk down Market Street without five people stopping to tell me what a great job Gary is doing. Don't get me wrong, it's flattering, but sometimes I just want to get to where I'm going."

Tracy was sure Sunnie loved all the attention. "I don't think it has to do with Gary," she said.

"What could it be then?" Sunnie sipped her coffee, then again lowered her voice. "I did hear you were asking questions about Kimberly Armstrong's death. A rumor is floating around town that you're back because Roy needs outside help to avoid the appearance of a conflict of interest."

"I wouldn't know, Sunnie," Tracy said.

Sunnie looked hurt. She set down her coffee and picked up her gloves. "I understand. I get it."

Tracy felt bad. She always felt bad, at least once a day when she and Sunnie had been friends. "Listen, Sunnie, you know I can't talk about police business, okay? I'm not hiding anything. I just can't talk about it."

Sunnie nodded. Then she smiled. "I don't really care. I figured it had something to do with Kimberly Armstrong. What a tragedy. Everybody in town was just sick about it. I heard the fire was from a heater Kimberly kept in the office, that she'd maybe forgot to unplug it. Finlay must have been crushed. Who wouldn't be, right? I mean if they lost a spouse like that? But then Roy came back as chief, and Finlay is still out . . . The rumor now is it wasn't the heater, and Kimberly didn't die from smoke inhalation, that the fire was just a cover-up."

"It's a sad situation," Tracy said.

"You know Finlay dated Heather Johansen, right? You remember that poor girl. Everyone thought Edmund House killed her, but now . . . Well, it makes you wonder, doesn't it? You'd gone to college by then and weren't around, but I was still here."

"Sarah told me what happened," Tracy managed to say.

"So you know Finlay got pretty upset when Heather broke up with him. A lot of people thought he had something to do with her death . . . And now Kimberly . . . You have to admit, there's some sense to it."

Tracy didn't respond. Inside, however, she was thinking about how Sunnie's gossip only confirmed that the Cedar Grove rumor mill remained active.

"Tracy?" Faz walked into the kitchen, stopping when he saw Sunnie. "Oh, hey. Sorry. I didn't know you had company."

Sunnie set down her coffee and stood from the table. She stuck out a hand. "Sunnie Witherspoon. I was Tracy's best friend growing up."

"Vic Fazzio," Faz said. "Tracy and me—"

"Vic is Daniella's godfather," Tracy said, not wanting to give Sunnie any more gossip. "He and his wife came up to see their goddaughter. We were just about to head out. I'm going to show Vic Cedar Grove."

"Take him down Market Street," Sunnie said, perking up again. "It's changed so much. Dan told me at the office that you have a nanny. You are living the good life." Sunnie smiled and turned her attention to Faz. "I had four children, and I was lucky if my husband would spring for a babysitter once a month so we could go out."

Tracy smiled. "Vic and I should get going, while Daniella's sleeping."

Sunnie picked up her gloves and put them on as she walked to the front door. "I know that feeling. You got to strike while the iron is hot." She slid on her coat and scarf and leaned forward to give Tracy a hug and an air kiss on each cheek.

"Mwah," she said. "Thanks for the coffee. Gary and I still want to have you and Dan for dinner. We have that big house out near where you used to live. You remember my parents' home?"

"Of course," Tracy said.

"I inherited it. It needed a lot of work. But I told Gary I was not going to live another day in that one-story shack we raised the kids in."

Tracy pulled open the door. "Dan had to go back to Seattle to handle some of his cases. I'm not sure when he'll be back in Cedar Grove, but we'll get together when we can."

Sunnie held out a hand to Faz. "Nice meeting you. Tell Tracy to take you down Market Street. There's a coffee shop with pastries called The Daily Perk. It's cute. A good place to get out of the cold." Sunnie stepped onto the porch, speaking over her shoulder. "Talk to Dan," she said, as she stepped down the pavers back toward her Mercedes.

Tracy quickly shut the door.

"God save the freaking queen; what the bloody hell was that?" Faz said.

Tracy let out a sigh, as if exhausted. She leaned her forehead against the closed door. "Grade school friend."

"She could melt all that snow out there by herself. Just strap her to the front of the car and let her start talking. What did she want?"

"Gossip." Tracy looked out the side panel as the white Mercedes drove down the block. "She's been that way since I can remember. If Sunnie doesn't know everything going on she gets offended, which confirms that the Cedar Grove rumor mill is as I remembered it."

She turned to Faz. "And that supports the theory that Mathews and Kimberly Armstrong could have been killed for what they learned in that file and didn't keep to themselves."

Faz crossed himself. "Let's get out of here before she comes back and blows the house down."

CHAPTER 20

Tracy decided not to call ahead to let the Johansens know she was again stopping by. She parked in the driveway, which had been cleared, and pushed out of the car. Faz met her at the hood. He looked like he was walking in slow-motion wearing Dan's snow boots.

"God almighty. How the hell do you people walk in these things? I feel like an astronaut walking on the moon." The boots were half a size too small, but they were better than ruining a good pair of leather shoes.

Tracy looked to the Johansens' front door. "I'm not sure what to expect," she said. "Eric Johansen is guarded and protective of his daughter. He might choose not to talk to me."

"Knock on the door and let's find out before we freeze to death."

Tracy rapped on the door and, after a moment, Eric pulled it open. He looked surprised to see her, and really surprised when he saw Faz. "Tracy?"

"Hi, Eric. I wonder if we can talk again."

Eric again looked at Faz. "What about?"

"Something has come up. This is detective Vic Fazzio from Seattle."

"Seattle?"

"He's also here to give me and Roy a hand."

Eric nodded to Faz. Then he asked, "Chief Calloway isn't with you?"

"He had some other matters to take care of this morning."

"I don't doubt he did," Eric said. "I went downtown this morning, Tracy. Took my cross-country skis to the pharmacy to get Ingrid's blood pressure medication. There's a lot of talk going around town about you. Someone said you'd been shot at last night."

Tracy gave him a tight-lipped smile. "You know how rumors are here in Cedar Grove, Eric. It could have just been the wind. We lost a few branches around the house."

Eric looked uncertain. "I'm busy this morning. I have—"

"How far did you cross-country ski?" Faz asked. "That has to be what, five miles from here?"

"Six and a half."

Faz whistled to let Johansen know he was impressed. "Thirteen miles round-trip? That's a lot of work."

"I've done more," Eric said. "Twice as much."

"We had a cross-country course back in New Jersey when I was a boy. I know I don't look like it now, but I could do the eleven-mile loop faster than anyone in my age group. I used to love it, too, the way it makes you feel. That furnace starts burning inside and it spreads to your limbs. What type of skis are you using?"

"Rossignol," Eric said, sounding more interested.

"That's a good ski," Faz said. "I used Salomon back in the day. I'll bet they've come a long way since then though."

"Would you like to see them?"

"If it's not too much trouble," Faz said.

"I keep them in the closet."

Eric stepped back to allow them inside and shut the door. He turned for the closet near the coatrack. Tracy looked to Faz, who smiled. She doubted Faz had ever strapped on a pair of cross-country skis in his life. But she doubted more that he'd ever had a door slammed in his face.

Inside, Faz and Eric went over the finer nuances of cross-country skiing. If Faz was making it up, he was doing a hell of a job. Eric told Ingrid to make coffee and put out pastries. After several more minutes, he looked to Tracy with a much brighter smile. "You said you had something more to talk about?"

"I do, Eric. And I'll try my best not to take up too much of your time."

Eric said, "No worries. I've already got my workout in." He smiled at Faz and led them to the dining room table. The four of them sat. Orchestral music played softly in the background. Beside the La-Z-Boy chair, an open newspaper rested on the side table, a stack of unopened papers and magazines on the floor. Outside the windows, bright sunshine made the snow on the lawn glisten as if it were a blanket of thousands of tiny diamonds.

Tracy made small talk as Ingrid put coffee and pastries on the table. Faz, never bashful, helped himself to both. Tracy eased her way into the reason for her visit. "I was wondering, Eric, if the lawyer you hired, Jason Mathews, said anything more about what he'd found in the police file."

"More?" Eric asked.

"Did he discuss the medical examiner's report?"

Eric stiffened. "Why do you want to go back there, Tracy?"

"I don't, Eric. Not if we don't have to. But I'm curious if Mathews said anything that struck you as inappropriate."

"Something that might have got him shot," Faz said. "If I can speak to you straight up, man-to-man."

Eric looked to Faz. After a beat, he ran his thumbs under his suspenders and said, "We didn't care for Mr. Mathews."

"Is that why you fired him, Eric, because of what he'd told you about Heather possibly being pregnant?"

"Not for what he told us. But we didn't want him going and spreading unconfirmed rumors about Heather all over town."

"And you thought he was going to do that, spread rumors?"

"He told us he was going to do that." Eric looked to Ingrid for confirmation, and she nodded.

Tracy glanced at Faz. This was new. "What did he say?" she asked Eric.

"Mathews said that a bit of information such as that could shake some trees."

"Shake some trees? Did he say what he meant by that?"

"He said it was an attorney's tool. He'd talk to some people and make it seem like he knew more than he did, more than what was in the report."

"Like the name of the father?"

Eric raised his hand and shook his head. "She wasn't pregnant, Tracy. That was purely speculation."

"I'm just trying to understand what Mathews might have said."

"He said he had a theory." Eric looked to Ingrid. He was starting to get worked up. His lower lip quivered again.

Ingrid spoke for her husband. "Mr. Mathews said that *if* Heather had been seven or eight weeks pregnant then the . . . the conception . . . would have been around the holidays. He wanted to know if Heather had gone to any holiday parties around that time."

Bingo, Tracy thought.

Faz blew out a held breath. "I'm sorry," he said.

"Do you have a daughter, Mr. Fazzio?" Eric asked. He pressed his lips together and held back tears.

"No, Eric. I don't. But I'm going to have a daughter-in-law soon and granddaughters someday, and I'm godfather to Tracy's little girl. I can only imagine how hard this must be for you."

Eric gave a curt nod. "We appreciate that. We do."

"Were there any Christmas parties you recall, Eric?" Faz asked. "A party that Heather attended?"

"There were always Christmas parties in Cedar Grove back then. You of all people should know that, Tracy. Your parents threw the best one. Ingrid and I never missed it."

"They loved that party," Tracy said, smiling. "Was Heather with you that year?"

Eric shook his head. "She had a work obligation. You know Ed Witherspoon also threw a party."

"Did he? I'm not sure I knew that," Tracy said, though of course she did.

"Ingrid and I attended both that year. We felt it right since Ed gave Heather a job."

"Which party did you go to first?" Tracy asked.

"We went to Ed's first," Eric said. "To get it out of the way." He smiled. "Your father had the better food and drink."

"Eric," Ingrid said. "It wasn't a contest." She directed her comments to Tracy. "Ed had given Heather a job and we were grateful to him for having done so."

"I see," Tracy said. "So Heather went to Ed's party?"

"She did. She thought it important that we all go."

"Did she leave Ed's party with you to come to our house?"

"No," Eric said. "She said she'd better stay."

Tracy felt butterflies and tried to control her questions. "Do you know how she got home that night from the party?" Tracy asked.

"She didn't say. So you see, Tracy. That's a dead end. And we told that to Mr. Mathews."

Tracy nodded. "Well, I needed to ask, Eric. And you've both been gracious with your time."

"Are you in town long, Mr. Fazzio?" Eric pushed back his chair and stood. "If you like, I could take you cross-country skiing. I know a loop that goes around the lake. It's just about eleven miles, and I have another set of skis."

"I'm a few pastries past my skiing days, I'm afraid."

"Well, you let me know. The offer stands."

The two men exchanged handshakes and Tracy said her good-byes. When she and Faz got inside the Subaru, Tracy asked, "Have you ever been on a pair of cross-country skis, Faz?"

"You'd have a better chance of getting a polar bear on a pair of skis."

"Where did you learn all that information about cross-country skiing?"

"That part was true. My uncle got me and my cousin summer jobs working at his club. Over the winter holidays, the golf course was a cross-country track. We waxed the skis and rented equipment. In the spring and summer, we worked in the clubhouse and drove the refreshment truck on the golf course." He nodded. "Looks like you were right about the Christmas Eve party. Heather was there."

Tracy nodded. "And about a possible reason Jason Mathews might have got shot."

"Guy like that, who's willing to tell the parents of a dead girl . . . I'm betting by *shake some trees* he meant make a buck from the information. That sounds like someone willing to put the screws to some people," Faz said.

"I agree. I also doubt he'd stop just because the father told him to." She sat back. "So the burning questions are: Who gave Heather a ride home from the party that night? And who did Jason Mathews talk to about her being pregnant?"

"What about your cop? Fenway?"

"Finlay? He definitely talked to Mathews, he told me that, but he'd pretty much left Cedar Grove when Heather was murdered."

"What do you mean left?"

Tracy explained it to him.

"Okay, that was February. What about December? Could he have got her pregnant?"

"I don't recall him being at my parents' party, but that was a long time ago and we weren't close. I doubt he would have been welcome at Ed Witherspoon's, not with Heather there."

"He could have waited outside the party for her and convinced her to let him give her a ride home."

"Maybe," Tracy said. "But if she didn't have a car, wouldn't she have left the party with the person who drove her home?"

"Could she have walked?"

"Maybe, but this was December, and it was Christmas Eve."

"True," Faz said. "But don't cut Fenway loose just yet. From what you're telling me, he still crosses the most t's and dots the most i's."

Tracy thought so too.

CHAPTER 21

With Leah having settled the arbitration and one of Dan's mediations kicked over for a month, she didn't need Dan's help. There was little reason for him to stay in Seattle.

"I don't want you hovering over me like a mother hawk," she'd said, when they discussed the second mediation.

Dan's workload had lightened considerably, but he had no doubt his dance card would fill up again, and quickly—it always did. That's what made being a lawyer stressful. Some attorney would file an unexpected motion or send a pithy letter with a pithy demand and Dan would have to respond. Lawyers learned early in their careers to put the lull between the storms to good use. For Dan, that good use was spending quality time with Tracy and Daniella. Fail at that, and there would be real consequences.

"Go back to Cedar Grove," Battles had told him when he walked into her office and asked how he could help lighten her load. "Hell, if you don't, I might. You're making me nervous."

Dan smiled. "Okay, I know when I'm not wanted."

"Surprise your wife," Battles said as Dan stepped to her office door. "Bring her flowers."

"Bring her flowers?"

Battles curled the corner of her mouth, and Dan knew sarcasm was about to fly. "You probably said or did something stupid, like leaving her up in the mountains in a snowstorm with a two-month-old."

Dan chuckled. "Touché."

He'd pick up flowers.

He left two suits and laundered shirts and ties in his office, packed his briefcase, and grabbed his duffel. "Help me get these boxes back in my car?" he asked Battles, referring to the Cedar Grove documents.

"Anything more of interest?" Battles asked. She picked up two of the boxes without much effort.

"They're responsive, for the most part. The formation papers list the members of the various LLCs, but I haven't been able to locate any of them, so I'm guessing they aren't local. That raises additional questions, like why outside investors would choose to invest in a place like Cedar Grove."

Battles stepped onto the elevator when it arrived. "Those small towns are changing. I read about it in an article in the *Times*. With the population in Seattle exploding and housing getting prohibitively expensive, more and more people are moving farther out, and looking for places to escape to on the weekends. Those mountain towns are becoming weekend destinations."

"Camano Island perhaps, or even La Conner, but Cedar Grove is still a pretty far drive."

"From Seattle sure, but not from Bellingham, or Everett, both of which are also growing," Battles said.

The elevator opened on the ground floor, and Dan followed Battles off. They stepped outside into bright sunshine but cool temperatures. Dan used his fob to open the back of his Chevy Tahoe. The wind gusted, whipping low-lying gray rain clouds across the sky. Dan slid his boxes into the back of the car and Battles pushed in the final two.

Dan pulled open the driver's door. "Call me if you need anything."

"I won't," Battles said.

Dan got in the Tahoe and started the engine. Battles mimed for him to lower the window. When he did, she said. "Flowers."

—

Dan made good time getting out of Seattle, but he hit traffic south of Everett that slowed his progress. He wanted to make it home before it started to snow, which the meteorologists were again predicting. He listened to an audiobook, a habit to help pass the time on long commutes. The only problem was, if his mind wandered to one of his cases, as it had throughout this drive, he could lose twenty minutes of the book's plot.

Once outside Everett, traffic picked up again, and Dan hoped he could make up some of the time he'd lost. He'd decided not to call Tracy; he'd rather surprise her.

"Flowers," he said out loud.

Mindful of Battles's suggestion, he exited the freeway and drove into Bellingham. Soot-colored piles of snow had been pushed to the curbs. Snow wasn't unheard of in Bellingham, but it also was not the norm. Just south of the Canadian border, the city was built around Bellingham Bay. The Olympic Mountains to the southwest and the Cascades to the east offered protection from severe storms. Most months produced moderate temperatures and less rainfall than Seattle. Like Cedar Grove, Bellingham had been a gold-rush town of prospectors, immigrants, and investors. It morphed into a coal town when the latter was discovered in abundance, as well as a cannery town, given its access to and from Alaska's rich fishing waters.

The architecture reflected the city's blue-collar heritage—low-rise, stout brick and stone buildings alongside more modern structures. The population had grown to more than 100,000.

Dan pulled to the curb and used his cell phone to hunt for a flower store, but again his mind wandered, this time to the documents in the back of his car—specifically the formation papers for each LLC completed by the law offices of Zack Metzger. Metzger had not returned Dan's phone call.

Dan pulled up the number and called again. His call went to voice mail one more time. He decided against leaving another message. He used his phone to search for Metzger's law office. When he found the address, he plugged it into his GPS and learned he was just five minutes away. He checked his watch. Unless Metzger kept banker's hours, he just might be in. And if he wasn't, Dan had only lost a few minutes of commute time.

About to pull from the curb, Dan had another thought. He typed "attorney Zack Metzger" into the phone's search engine and located the lawyer's biography. Using the dates provided, Dan calculated Metzger to be roughly forty-nine years old. He had been practicing law for sixteen years, which meant the law had not been his first profession. Reading further, he learned Metzger had graduated from a law school in Washington not associated with one of its universities. Dan had never heard of the school, but in Washington, graduation from an unaccredited law school did not prevent a person from practicing law—if they could pass the bar exam. Metzger's resume indicated a nine-year lapse between his law school graduation and his being sworn in as a lawyer, which often meant the person had failed the Washington State bar exam. In this instance, maybe as many as nine times.

Dan followed the GPS's directions to an address on Meridian Street. He double-checked the listing because, from what he could tell, the address was for an Asian market. He parallel parked and got out. Wind gusted, bringing chilled temperatures as he crossed the street to the market. He looked for an address but didn't see one. He did find a glass door to the right of the market's storefront windows. When he pulled it open, bells rattled against the glass—a metallic ping. He climbed a narrow staircase that looked off-kilter, like an earthquake had twisted it. It smelled of mildew.

At the landing he encountered a closed door with a yellow sticky note: *Across the Street. O'Halloran's.*

The note was dated November nineteenth. Dan doubted the sticky note could have remained on the door for three months, which meant either Metzger was out of business or O'Halloran's had a daily happy hour and Metzger recycled the note.

He descended the stairs and leaned into the door, struggling to push it open against another gust of wind. Outside, he looked up and down a sidewalk of leafless trees and saw a sign projecting off the side of a red-brick building with green shamrocks and a leprechaun. Had to be the place.

Up close, O'Halloran's green door looked to have been painted— badly. The chipped paint revealed an assortment of different colors. Dan pushed on it and stepped into an interior as dark as dusk. He took a moment to allow his eyes to adjust. The bar smelled like his fraternity— fried food and beer. To call it a hole-in-the-wall would have oversold the hole. It was more like a crack in the hole-in-the-wall, no more than perhaps two hundred square feet. Three men sat at barstools. Two men stood at the corner, drinking and talking. None of them resembled Zack Metzger's picture from the Internet. Dan shifted his focus to a handful of tables littered with empty beer bottles, glasses, and plastic food baskets.

Zack Metzger sat at a table near the back. The open legal file in front of him gave him away. He had his head down, intent on whatever he was reading. Dan saw an orange basket with a half-eaten hamburger, some fries, and a wad of ketchup.

"Mr. Metzger?"

Metzger looked up. "Yeah? Who are you?" He had curly salt-and-pepper hair that appeared to be thinning, and a five-o'clock shadow. He wore a shirt and tie, the knot lowered and the top button of his collar open.

Dan stuck out a hand. "Dan O'Leary."

Metzger gave Dan's hand a perfunctory shake. His hand was soft and small, and he wore a woven gold bracelet on his wrist. Initially his face gave no indication he recognized Dan's name, but then he said, "O'Leary?" He quickly fingered through a stack of pink slips on the table and pulled one out. "Thought I recognized that name." He held up the slip. "Sorry. My receptionist's handwriting is the shits. I can't read a Goddamn word I wrote except for your name." He grinned briefly, crumpled the slip, and tossed it at a can three feet away, missing. "What can I help you with?"

"Can I sit?" Dan said, gesturing to a chair.

"Free country. Pull out a chair. Is this a criminal matter or civil?"

Dan smiled. "I'm an attorney from Seattle."

"An attorney? Shit, they ought to strike up the band. I doubt they've ever had two attorneys in here at the same time."

A woman in blue jeans, a sleeveless pink top, and a face that shouted *tough living* appeared at the table. "You want something?" she asked Dan.

Dan looked at Metzger's glass with a caramel-colored liquid and melting ice. He wondered how many drinks Metzger had polished off. "Can I buy you a drink?"

"Sure. Coke."

Dan suppressed a smile. "Make it two."

One of the bar patrons walked to a jukebox and slipped in quarters, studying the selections. Metzger asked, "So what brings you all the way up to Bellingham, Mr. O'Leary?"

"It's Dan."

"Sure. Dan."

"I have a practice in Seattle, but I grew up in Cedar Grove, and I recently took on a case there."

"Yeah? Am I on the opposite side?"

"No. Not exactly. I represent the former owner of Kaufman's Mercantile Store on Market Street."

"Market Street I know. Kaufman's I've never heard of."

The waitress returned with the two drinks. "It's three fifty." She wasn't going to provide a check or let Dan pay when done. Dan reached for his wallet.

"Put it on my tab," Metzger said. "As long as we're not on competing sides."

"We're not," Dan said. A country music song played on the jukebox, and the man who'd made the selection retreated to his barstool. "Thanks for the drink." Dan sipped his Coke and set the glass down. "I'm suing the city, the mayor, and the city council."

"Tell me you need local counsel and it's going to be lucrative," Metzger said.

"At the moment I'm handling it on my own."

"Too bad."

"How well do you know Cedar Grove?"

"Never been, but I did do some work for some businesses up there. They're redoing the downtown."

"You did the formation papers for the businesses. That's the reason for my call."

"It must be something important for you to track me down here."

"I'm on my way to Cedar Grove. I stopped at your office and saw the note."

"If you had gone in, you'd know why I'm here. What do you want to know?"

"How did you get all the businesses to hire you? The LLCs all identify different members so I'm assuming they are all different entities, but maybe I'm wrong?"

"No, you're right. It was like manna from heaven. I did the first one—a pastry shop—and next thing I know I got a call about a second, then a third."

"The pastry shop referred you."

"I don't know."

"Did you ever ask?"

"And look a gift horse in the mouth? I don't think so. I was happy for the work."

"You didn't ask who had referred you?"

"I know who referred the businesses to me. The city."

"The city? You remember a name?"

"No, but . . ." Metzger sat back, his face narrowing and inquisitive. "Maybe you better tell me what your case is about—so I'm not shooting myself in the foot."

Dan did. "I'm trying to find the members of the limited liability companies so I can talk to them, ask them what the mayor and the city represented to them. Seems a bit neat and tidy that every new business came to the same attorney. Not that I really care."

"I don't recall the names, but the files are in my office. Make me a deal. If you depose any of those other business owners, you give them my card, tell them I'm available."

"Sure," Dan said. Not that he would.

"Okay." Metzger waved for the check. "Let's go to my office. You think this place is small? Just wait."

Metzger hadn't exaggerated. His office was the size of a storage room. Dan was lucky he wasn't claustrophobic. "Now you see why I get out to the bar or the coffee shop. You're probably wondering why I bother to stay here? I'll tell you why. I pay two hundred bucks a month in rent and I have six kids. Two go to Western and three are in private high schools. The youngest is at a private grammar school. I go to bed thinking tuition and wake up thinking tuition." Metzger looked at a cluttered desk and an equally cluttered credenza behind it. He moved to the window ledge above an accordion radiator and pulled up a stack of legal files.

"Here they are." He transferred them to his desk, atop a pile of open legal books and documents, and flipped open the first file, scanning the pages. "Here. I knew it was a funny name."

He turned the file so Dan wasn't reading the name on the message slip upside down.

Sunnie Witherspoon.

CHAPTER 22

Tracy disconnected the call and lowered her cell phone. "No answer," she said. After leaving the Johansens, they tried calling Pete Adams, the former owner of the Four Points Tavern, where Jason Mathews had hung out.

"How far away is this Silver Spoons place?" Faz asked.

"Silver Spurs," Tracy said. "About fifteen minutes."

"Drive by. Give me the guy's name again. I'll make some calls, see if we can get someone to check property records in the Phoenix area."

Tracy drove the county road to Silver Spurs. The wind had picked up, a harbinger of the predicted storm. When she pulled up to the home belonging to Pete Adams, she found it dark, as she had the previous day.

"Thanks," Faz said into his phone. He'd called Kinsington Rowe, another of the Violent Crimes A Team. "Yeah I'm doing good. Hoping to be back as soon as they clear me. Will do." He disconnected the call and handed Tracy a slip of paper. "Pete Adams bought himself a house forty minutes outside of Scottsdale."

"You get a phone number?" Tracy asked.

"Not listed. I'm thinking maybe it better if we pay this guy a visit, see what he has to say."

"That's going to be a little problem," she said. "Unless we want Daniella to starve to death."

Faz frowned. "Yeah, I see what you mean. Okay. I'll go."

"What? No. That's not what I wanted. I can't ask you to do that, Faz."

"Arizona in February? Yeah, that's tough duty. Seventy-degree weather, but I'll suffer my way through it. You think I could take Dan's golf clubs with me?"

Tracy smiled. She knew Faz didn't want to travel to Arizona any more than she did. "I'll ask the chief in Cedar Grove. See if he can spare anyone."

"Seriously, Tracy. Me and warm weather go together. This up here, the snow, I don't know how you deal with it."

"You grew up in New Jersey, Faz."

"Yes, but that was eighty pounds ago. I could walk across the snow back then like Jesus crossing the water. Now I sink up to my waist."

She laughed. "Let me call Seattle and see if I can get the cost authorized. They're being tightfisted. You good if we make one more stop before heading back home?"

Faz looked out the window. "I think that's all the weather is going to allow us."

Twenty minutes later, Tracy turned off of the county road and weaved her way through Cedar Grove to the burned-out remains of what had been Finlay Armstrong's home. Portions of the house still stood, the charred remnants a sharp contrast to the white snow. Finlay's blue Chevy truck was parked in the driveway, Finlay sitting in the driver's seat. Tracy pulled alongside the truck. Finlay looked over at her and shook his head. Then he wiped his eyes.

Tracy and Faz stepped out, as did Finlay. They met at the hood of his Chevy. Finlay wore jeans and a stained Carhartt jacket. He'd pulled a Mariners baseball hat low on his head.

"Hey, Tracy."

Tracy made the introductions, and Finlay and Faz removed their hands from their coat pockets long enough to shake.

"What are you doing here?" Tracy asked.

Finlay shrugged. "I don't know. I couldn't sit in the motel. I'm going stir-crazy, Tracy."

"I'm sorry."

"I'm sorry about your wife," Faz said. "I lost a home in a fire once. Feels like you lost your past."

"That's exactly what it feels like." Finlay spoke to Tracy. "What are you doing here?"

"Just thought I'd look around. I hadn't come by yet."

"You getting any closer to figuring all this out?"

She gave him a tight-lipped shake of the head.

"I heard someone took a shot at you last night, that the police were at your house."

"Where'd you hear it?"

"I was in the pharmacy. The doctor has me on antidepressants. Some of the people were talking about it. Is it true?"

Again, Tracy didn't answer.

Finlay sighed. "Yeah. I know. I was just leaving." He got into his truck and backed from the driveway into the street, leaving without so much as a wave.

"That is one messed-up individual," Faz said.

Tracy looked at him. "Did you lose a house to a fire?"

"We did," Faz said. "Vera and I were just starting out. We'd rented a house in Green Lake. Faulty wiring. Luckily we both worked and we didn't have much back then to lose. Still, it's devastating. Fire destroys your past, all the photo albums. You can't get that back. It's like you never existed."

Tracy hadn't asked Roy Calloway if Finlay listed photo albums among his possessions lost. Insurance companies often made decisions on whether fires were intentionally set based upon whether the couple had saved the photo albums or the family pets.

"So what are we doing here besides freezing?" Faz asked.

Tracy started across the lawn. The lack of snow that day and the cold temperatures had frozen the top layer, and it crunched under their weight. "According to the police report, the neighbor across the street saw Finlay's police vehicle parked in the driveway between noon and one fifteen the day of the fire."

"Finlay acknowledge that to be the case?"

"He did. He said he went home to have lunch. The neighbor is like a one-woman watch program. She did not recall seeing any other cars in the driveway, other than Kimberly's Toyota, the rest of the afternoon."

"Did she see Kimberly after Finlay left?"

"No."

"Any other visitors?"

"No one that she saw."

"Maybe because no one came."

"Finlay thinks the killer came through the back of the house so as not to be seen. I want to see if that was possible. Come on." Tracy led Faz around to the back of the charred home. She did not see a fence, just the tree line. She crossed the snow-covered lawn and they entered the trees, exiting on the road one block over. "I think Finlay might be right. The killer could have driven here and walked through the trees." She looked up the block to where the houses ended. "He could have parked his car up there, where it wouldn't be seen, and used the trees for cover."

"Sounds like somebody who knew the area and thought it out ahead of time."

"It does," Tracy said. "Just like the person who walked the easement to my backyard fence."

"I assume the police canvased this area, talked to the neighbors back here, asked if they saw anyone?"

"They did. No one saw anyone."

"Didn't see anyone, or didn't see anyone who didn't belong? The two are not the same. People get used to seeing someone around, they don't even think about it."

"They didn't see anyone." She shook her head. "At least that's what the police reports say. I'm not sure where to go from here, Faz."

"Maybe we should talk to them again, see if anything jars their memories."

"Maybe."

He looked about. "Hey, it's not a bad first day, though. We've done worse. Let's go home, get out of this cold. You can feed the kid and we can talk it out, find out what you learned and discuss possible places to go from here. And we can call the office and see about getting me travel to Phoenix."

CHAPTER 23

Dan drove from Bellingham, east on the Mount Baker Highway, and from the looks of the darkening sky, just one step ahead of the predicted storm. The wind had picked up, gusting hard enough to make the car shudder. A light snow started to fall, one that would become heavier as the temperature dropped. He didn't bother to restart the audiobook. He knew he'd have enough trouble concentrating on driving with all the questions swirling in his head.

Dan had reviewed the formation papers with Zack Metzger. The papers identified the LLC members, two in each instance, but provided no addresses or telephone numbers. Metzger said he'd never met the individuals, that Sunnie Witherspoon had been his only source of contact with the buyers of the businesses. Metzger said he'd never been asked to review any subsequent agreements between Cedar Grove and the LLCs he'd formed, which meant the buyers either acted without an attorney, or they'd hired a different attorney. But that raised other questions. If they had an attorney, why had they hired Metzger at all? If they didn't have an attorney, why not just let Metzger also review the contract? Did they even need an attorney? According to Larry Kaufman,

Dan's client, and according to the City of Cedar Grove's answers to Dan's interrogatories, Cedar Grove had sold the businesses to the new owners for just one dollar, though the purchasers were responsible for bringing each of the buildings up to code. Gary Witherspoon had been quoted in the *Towne Crier* as saying the deals were good for both sides. Cedar Grove got an interested party, and the purchasers were able to put the money they otherwise would have spent on the purchase to fix the building code violations and, in the process, help rejuvenate Market Street.

Sunnie worked for Rav Patel, so perhaps it made some sense that she would be the person shepherding the documents between the parties. Patel would have acted on behalf of Cedar Grove. It would have been a conflict of interest for him to communicate directly with the other parties, though he could have spoken to Metzger. Metzger, however, did not recall the name. Dan had reviewed the contracts produced by Cedar Grove at his office before leaving. They had been signed by members of the various LLCs, but he found no letters from attorneys acting on the purchaser's behalf.

Again, that seemed odd.

Dan contemplated sending another round of discovery to Patel asking for the LLC members' home phone numbers and addresses, but he didn't have time to wait thirty days before the new hearing date. Still, it didn't hurt to ask.

Just before the turnoff for the county road, Dan pulled into a gas station to fill the Tahoe's tank. He pulled out his cell phone and called Rav Patel. Sunnie Witherspoon answered. Ordinarily, Dan would have rather stuck pins in his eyes than get into a protracted conversation with Sunnie, but in this instance, and under these circumstances, he had a different agenda.

"Hi, Sunnie. It's Dan O'Leary."

"Dan O'Leary," she said in her chipper voice. "I'm sorry, Dan, but Rav isn't in. He had a meeting outside of the office. Don't ask me where, though. He never tells me a thing."

"Maybe you can help me, Sunnie. I'm trying to find the telephone numbers and addresses for the individuals who bought the businesses on Market Street. It was part of the discovery I sent over to Rav."

"I'm afraid this is all flying over the top of my head, Dan. Can I have Rav give you a call tomorrow?"

Dan decided to push her, let her know how much he knew, figuring Sunnie would tell Patel, and it would be less likely Patel would give Dan some bullshit answer, which he really didn't have time for. If Sunnie was acting as the city's liaison, she certainly had the purchasers' phone numbers and/or addresses. The gas pump clicked off, and Dan got out of the car and removed it as he continued the conversation.

"You can, Sunnie, but let me be more specific. I just left Zack Metzger's law office in Bellingham. I believe you know Mr. Metzger."

For once, Sunnie didn't respond.

"Mr. Metzger, as you know, acted as the attorney who set up the limited liability companies for each of the purchasers. That struck me as odd, each purchaser using the same lawyer."

"I do know him, and I do know the purchasers all used him, Dan," Sunnie said, which surprised him.

"You do?"

"Sure. One of the purchasers needed an attorney, don't ask me which one, and asked Rav for a referral. Rav gave me that job. I didn't know an attorney, not in Cedar Grove, but I found Mr. Metzger online. I assume he must have been pleased and referred the others, or some such similar thing."

"Yeah, it could have happened like that," Dan said. He slid behind the steering wheel and started the engine. "Except Mr. Metzger said he never met or spoke to any of the purchasers. He said everything came from you, that you acted as a liaison between each purchaser and Cedar Grove."

Again, Sunnie didn't immediately respond.

"Sunnie? Did we get disconnected?"

"No, I'm still here. I'm afraid Mr. Metzger gave me far more responsibility than was reality, Dan. If that were the case I'd have to ask Rav for a raise, wouldn't I?"

Dan put the Tahoe in gear and drove from the station to the county road, waiting for traffic to clear. "What I'm interested in, if you were . . . shuttling the paperwork back and forth, is the addresses and phone numbers for each of the purchasers. I'm assuming, given Judge Harvey's order that the parties cooperate, that the city would be willing to provide that information?"

"You know I can't make that decision, Dan. It has to come through Rav."

"Okay. Well, it was worth a try."

"You wouldn't be trying to take advantage of our friendship, would you Dan?"

"Of course not." Dan merged onto the county road. "Will you tell Rav the information I need and tell him that I'm hoping the city will voluntarily provide it?"

"I'll do that, Dan."

"I appreciate it. And only because Judge Harvey has us all on such a short leash, will you also tell Rav that unless I hear affirmatively from him by noon tomorrow, I'll have to seek to compel the information, ex parte."

"Rav's in court in Bellingham tomorrow morning, Dan."

"Then he won't have to travel far. Ex parte papers are heard at three o'clock. I'll need time to get my papers filed and provide Rav with notice though. So if you could get me an answer in the morning, I'd appreciate it."

"I'll let him know, Dan."

"Thanks. Oh, and Sunnie?"

"Yes."

"Will you also tell him that, if I have to compel the information, I'm going to also ask that the court allow me to take your deposition? Will you tell him that? Sunnie?"

Dan heard a dial tone. He didn't think it was the storm. A broad smile spread across his face. How could anyone not love this job?

―

Tracy entered the kitchen. Faz sat at one of the barstools at the counter watching Vera on the other side, cooking at the stove.

"Vera, I told you no working after five," Tracy said, coming into the kitchen. She'd been upstairs caring for Daniella, whom Vera said had been "as good as gold" all day. The baby spent some time on her stomach and could now lift her head. They'd also gone for a walk, with the police officer.

"Working?" Vera said. "I'm cooking, Tracy. This is my passion."

"Just the same. Sit down and have a glass of wine."

"I'm enjoying my wine right here." She lifted a glass.

"I'd help you out, Tracy," Faz said, "but honestly, how do you think I got this fat?"

"Besides," Vera said. "This is good sauce. Did you make it?"

"No. It was the Irish nanny."

"Irish?" Vera's eyebrows arched in question. "She knew what she was doing. I'm just adding a little more red wine and another clove of garlic. Vic says the two of you have a few things to discuss before we eat. The sauce needs to simmer a few more minutes so you two go ahead and do what you need to do."

"Come on, Tracy, have a seat," Faz said. "We'll go over what we know so we don't have to do it over dinner."

Tracy filled a glass with ice water and sat on an adjacent barstool. She took out her notepad and flipped to a clean page. "Okay, we know, based on the ME's report that Heather Johansen was seven to eight weeks pregnant when she was killed, which means she conceived around Christmas. We know Heather attended Ed Witherspoon's Christmas Eve party. We know her parents also attended that party but left early to attend my parents' party. We know Heather opted to stay, thinking it would be good for her possible future employment."

Tracy sipped her water and set her glass down on the counter before continuing.

"We know Heather didn't have her own car and would have needed a ride home that night, but the Johansens said they don't know how she got home, and Ed didn't remember either."

"We're speculating that the driver is the person who got Heather pregnant, though we don't know that," Faz said. "Heather could have got pregnant some other time and place than the Christmas party."

"Okay, that's my cue to go read," Vera said, citing her third passion after cooking and gardening. "This needs to simmer for another fifteen minutes." She grabbed a paperback off the counter and took it into the family room.

"Heather could have," Tracy said to Faz. "Except Heather's best friend and the Johansens had no knowledge Heather was dating anyone after Finlay."

"Could have been a one-night stand. What do they call it now? A hookup?"

"It could have been, though Cedar Grove is small and, as you've quickly learned, it's hard to keep a secret in this town. Let's play this out," Tracy said, tapping her pen on the words "possible drivers" she'd written in her notepad. "Who are the possible drivers, if it wasn't Barbara?"

"Ed Witherspoon," Faz said.

"And his son, Gary," Tracy said.

"Write down the former boyfriend if we're listing possibilities," Faz said. "Fenway. Maybe he was still stalking that girl and sweet-talked her into letting him drive her home."

Tracy wrote Finlay's name.

"Anyone else?" Faz asked.

"I'd have to think about it for a bit, try to remember who Ed and Barbara were close to in town and would have attended the party." She paused and looked at the magnetic calendar on the wall.

"What?" Faz said.

"I was just thinking that it was about this time that Heather died. She died two days from now, twenty-six years ago."

"Shame when a young person dies," Faz said.

Tracy took a breath and continued. "Okay let's keep going," she said, and she went over what they already knew or suspected, writing everything down.

They discussed Eric's comment that Mathews suggested they use the information on Heather's pregnancy to flush out the father. Then Tracy said, "We know Mathews tried to make a buck off of this and talked about it," she said.

"Speculation at this point," Faz said, pointing to her notepad.

"Not entirely. We know he told Finlay."

"That's true. But we don't know he tried to make a buck from it."

"No, but if he told Finlay, we can assume he told others."

"That bring us to this Kimberly person?" Faz said. "Fenway's wife."

"Okay. Here we're speculating that when Kimberly Armstrong learned Heather was pregnant, she did the math, and concluded Heather got pregnant around the holidays. She might have even speculated, as we're doing, that Heather got pregnant at Ed Witherspoon's party."

"Okay, but was this Kimberly the type to try to blackmail anyone?" Faz said.

"No, she wasn't. But she could have told someone what she suspected."

"Seems to me that's the key—who Kimberly told. We start there. I know you don't think so, Tracy, but who is a wife most likely to tell?"

From the living room couch Vera said, "Her husband, the cop."

Faz looked at Tracy and shrugged.

Rex and Sherlock barked and sat up from their dog beds, startling everyone.

"Jesus, Mary, and Joseph," Vera said. "You don't need an alarm on this house."

"Rex, Sherlock. Shh!" Tracy scolded. "Don't wake the baby."

The two dogs barked again and moved quickly around the back of the couch to the door. Tracy was about to shush them again when she heard what had made them bark. It wasn't the wind or the creaking of the tree branches outside the house. It was the sound of a car engine. She looked to the windows and saw the headlights of a car pulling into the driveway.

She moved to the door and used her leg to push Rex and Sherlock back, then ordered them to sit. The two dogs sat. "Now stay. Both of you. Stay."

"I should try that with you," Vera said to Faz.

"You say it like that and it might work," Faz said.

Tracy pulled open the door. She recognized the Tahoe through the flakes of falling snow and her stomach gave an anxious twitch. Dan had come back early. Tracy hadn't told Dan about Therese. She hadn't yet told him what had happened. She'd kept it from him because she'd been afraid of what he might say, how he might react, what he might do. It didn't make it right. It was just human nature.

Another thought came to her, one so clear she turned and looked to Faz, about to speak out loud when Sherlock bolted out the door, Rex following, distracting her.

Dan greeted the dogs, but his attention quickly turned to the female police officer who had exited her car and approached him. The two had a brief conversation, and Dan turned and looked to the door, to Tracy. After another minute, he and the dogs came up the paver stones, his path partially lit by the landscape lights.

Tracy felt sick to her stomach, the way she'd felt during the first months of her pregnancy. Dan stopped outside the door and stomped his boots on the welcome mat. "What's going on? Why is there a police car parked outside our house? Why did she want to know who I was and what business I had here?"

Tracy stepped to the side so Dan could enter. He stopped in the entry. "Vera. Faz." He looked to Tracy, even more uncertain. He looked to the easel with the unfinished painting, then to the kitchen.

"Where's Therese?" he asked.

CHAPTER 24

Dan shut the door to their bedroom, but not before Rex and Sherlock hurried inside the room. They sat up in the glow of the dresser lamp, as if expecting a show. Tracy instructed their Alexa to turn on music, hoping the noise would help to drown out their voices.

"When were you going to tell me?" Dan said.

Tracy shook her head. "I should have told you right away, Dan. I don't have a good reason for not telling you."

"Why didn't you?"

She sighed. "I could say that I know how busy you are, how much work you have, and I didn't want you to worry . . ."

"But that's not the reason, is it?"

She shook her head softly. "No. It isn't."

He leaned against the bed frame. "What is it you thought I would say?"

Tracy shrugged. "That I couldn't be a detective and a mother, that your initial concerns had proven to be accurate, that I was putting my life in jeopardy, and it would be our daughter who paid the price because of my stubbornness."

Dan lowered his eyes. "And me."

"And you," Tracy said. "Am I right?"

Dan looked up at her. "Yeah, probably."

He looked upset, but not angry. His reaction confused her, then concerned her. Multiple thoughts flooded her. Was he going to tell her he couldn't live this way? Was he going to tell her it was over? Had he gone to Seattle to see a doctor and had cancer but didn't know how to tell her? That he was having an affair?

"I'm sorry, Dan. I'm sorry I put our family at risk. I—"

"No, Tracy. I'm sorry."

She studied him, trying to read him. "I don't understand. Why are you sorry?"

"I'm sorry that I wasn't here, that I left you and Daniella."

For a moment she just stared at him. Then she said, "You said you left because you had work. I understand—"

"No. That wasn't the reason." He took a breath and ran a hand through his hair. Again, her thoughts ran wild. "I did have a lot of work, and I did need to be in Seattle, but that isn't the reason I left."

Her stomach churned. "It isn't?" she asked, tentative.

"No, it isn't. I left in part because I was upset that you didn't listen to me and took the case."

"I did listen. I—"

He raised a hand. "I know, and I'm sorry, Tracy. Leah said something to me and it hit home. I should have been here. I should have never left you and the baby in the middle of a snowstorm. I let my pride and ego get in the way. My first responsibility is to the two of you and I failed you, but it won't happen again. I won't let my pride or my ego come before my responsibility to us again. I won't do that to you or to Daniella. That was a promise I made to myself when you were pregnant, why I hired Leah."

She didn't know what to say. She had expected Dan to be upset at her. She'd expected him to tell her she had to choose between work and being a mother, that he'd leave if she couldn't put him first. And in that moment, she realized why she had made that assumption. That had been what Ben, her first husband, had said to her all those years ago, when she'd been chasing Sarah's killer. Ben had told her he couldn't be her second priority—and wouldn't. He had forced Tracy's hand. Then he left. She'd never seen or heard from him again.

"I should have told you, Dan. It was wrong to keep it from you."

He nodded. "It was. But you couldn't tell me, and I'm sorry that you felt like you couldn't."

"That has nothing to do with you, Dan."

"It does. You had a right to expect more from me. I'm sorry that I didn't behave in a way that made you feel like you could tell me, whatever the underlying reason, which I suspect carries over from Sarah's murder and your first marriage."

Tracy nodded. "It does, but please stop blaming yourself. It's not helping. We both could have handled things differently. We both have something to be sorry about."

"Agreed."

She fell forward into his arms. "You understand why I can't let this go, why I have to finish this?"

"I understand it's who you are."

She pulled away, looking him in the eyes. "But do you understand that this isn't about me? I'm not doing this because of Sarah. This is about Heather and Kimberly and all the women out there who will lose their lives to some psychopath. Maybe I'm overstating it, but I don't want that kind of a world or that kind of Cedar Grove for Daniella. Someone is out there, Dan. Someone who I think has killed three people."

He sighed. "I know, but I wish you hadn't told me that."

"I'm sorry. But Roy has a police officer watching the house 24-7. And he or Faz will be with me wherever I go."

"Well . . ." He shrugged. "I don't like it, but this is what I signed on for when I married a detective, and I know you've put up with an incredible amount of bullshit from your captain to do this job. I'm not going to be the one to tell you not to do it, or to issue any ultimatums. But as your husband, I'm asking you to please be careful. Let Roy help you."

"I've thought about it, too, and if you want, you can take Daniella home with you. Therese might come back as long as we're not here, or I know Vera would watch her."

Dan smiled. "I'm not exactly equipped to feed her," he said.

"We can wean her to a formula. We're trying already."

"How's that going?"

Tracy shrugged.

Dan shook his head. "I'm not going to leave you or Daniella, Tracy. That's why I came back."

"I know. And I don't want you to leave me, or Daniella," she said.

"I'm serious, Tracy. I want you to be careful. I don't know what I'd do if I lost you. My life hasn't exactly been as I expected, but all my disappointments faded when I met you."

"For me too." She embraced him. Held him tight. She'd never deserve him, she knew, and she'd never again assume to know what he was thinking.

"Is Therese okay?" Dan asked when they broke their embrace.

"She's pretty shook up, but not physically hurt. She wanted to stay, but I thought it best to send her home with one of Roy's officers."

"You called Faz?" he asked.

"No. He called me just after it happened, when I was still pretty upset. It just kind of poured out of me. Next thing I knew, he and Vera were here. Vera's been watching Daniella, and Faz has been watching me."

Dan smiled. "Sounds like Faz. I'm glad. Come on, we better get out there before they think one of us killed the other."

"I found out some things," Tracy said.

"So did I." He quickly told her of his meeting with Zack Metzger and about Sunnie Witherspoon referring the LLC members. "She was either doing Rav Patel's bidding or Gary's bidding. Maybe both, given how close those two are. I think someone is making a buck from all this. I just don't know how or who yet. But I can smell it. This is about money. It almost always is. We can talk later. Let's go eat Vera's spaghetti. It smells great."

"Actually, Therese made the sauce."

"Therese? Really? Damn we're going to have to get that Irish girl back."

CHAPTER 25

J ust past midnight, Daniella fussed, and Tracy got up to check on her, thinking perhaps she had a dirty diaper. She had just fed Daniella and couldn't imagine she could be hungry already. When Tracy went into the nursery, Daniella had gone back to sleep, but someone was awake downstairs; she saw a light on in the kitchen. She grabbed her robe from the back of her bedroom door and put it on as she went down the stairs. She could still detect the faint odor of Therese's spaghetti sauce and Vera's garlic bread.

Faz sat at the kitchen table, reading on his Kindle, and looked up at Tracy over his half-lens reading glasses. "Hey. I didn't wake you, did I?" he said.

"No, I was up with Daniella. Can't sleep?"

Faz groaned. "I've never been a good sleeper. It got a little more pronounced when Vera got diagnosed with breast cancer."

Tracy sat in the chair beside him. "But she's okay, right?"

Faz set his Kindle on the table, along with his glasses. "Yeah, yeah. She's good. Everything came back negative her last checkup. So now we wait another few months and check again. Five years we do that. Seems like forever."

"Is that why you can't sleep?"

Faz shrugged. "Contemplating one's mortality or the mortality of someone we love isn't conducive to getting a lot of sleep."

"No, I guess it isn't," Tracy said.

"I got a few years on you. Both my parents are gone. I'm next man up, you know?"

"I know," Tracy said. "I lost my whole family, too, remember?"

"Geez, I'm sorry, Tracy. I didn't mean to sound like I was lecturing you."

"Don't worry about it. If I'm being honest, I wasn't going to get much sleep tonight either."

"What's bothering you?" Faz asked.

"This case."

"You got to find a way to leave the job at the office."

"Normally I can. I lock my cases in a mental box, and they stay there until I'm back at work. In theory anyway. It doesn't always work."

Faz gave her a tight-lipped smile. "But you've never had a kid to think about before now. Am I right?"

Beneath the rough exterior Faz liked to project, especially to suspects—the New Jersey Italian who looked and sounded like he'd just as soon bust your kneecaps—was a teddy bear, a man Tracy had found to be quite wise.

"I've been there, Tracy, though I'm not putting you and me in the same position. In my position, there was never any question Vera would stay home with Antonio and I'd work. She worries about me, especially after what happened recently, but as I've said to you before, worrying is a part of loving." He raised his palms. "She loves me. So, she worries about me. Me? I never worried so much for myself as I did for Vera and Antonio. I figured if it was my time, it was my time. Antonio's grown now, and he's in a good place with a good job and a good wife-to-be."

Tracy sighed. "I'm worried I'm not going to be here for Daniella," she said. "The other night scared me, Faz. What could have happened scared me."

"Sure it did," Faz said. "It would have scared anybody."

"Even you?" She smiled.

"Probably twice as much. Look, we didn't choose to sell shoes or to be lawyers. There are days we're going to put our asses on the line. It comes with the job. My uncle gave me that bit of advice back in New Jersey. He said that was the scary part of the job, but it was also the part that got him out of bed every morning for thirty-five years. Don't get me wrong; I can do without guys like Little Jimmy doing a tap dance on my face, but I love the job. So you got to ask yourself. Do you love the job enough to put up with the bullshit?"

Tracy nodded. "I'm assuming you don't have that answer for me."

Faz shook his head. "Nobody does. Seems to me you put up with a lot of bullshit already, though, and you're still here."

She nodded. She'd probably have that debate with herself for many days. "I thought of something tonight, when Dan came home."

"That when you gave me that look?"

"You noticed it."

"I tell Del it's that look you get when you get hit with lightning."

"Never knew that."

"What was it this time?"

"I thought about the reason why I didn't tell Dan what had happened the other night."

"You were protecting him. You didn't want him to worry."

"That would have been a better answer, but to be completely honest, I wasn't sure what his response would be, and I was afraid he'd make me choose, tell me that I had to quit. So I didn't say anything."

"Sometimes it's easier if we don't tell our spouses everything."

"True. But it's also human nature, isn't it?"

"Absolutely. We try to protect those we love."

"So that got me thinking about Kimberly Armstrong, about the research she'd done and what she might have found. And I was thinking, maybe she didn't tell her husband what she'd found out."

"Because she found out he did it?"

"No, because she knew it would hurt him. She was trying to protect him."

"I'm not following."

"She'd hurt him if she let him know she had doubts, about him, about whether he was guilty. I was having a hard time believing they wouldn't talk about something as important as that, but I guess now I can understand why maybe they wouldn't have. She didn't want to hurt him. She wanted to protect him."

"Yeah, I guess I can buy that," Faz said. "Then again, she might have found out that he did it, Tracy."

"Here's where I'm going with this. Let's assume Kimberly figured what Jason Mathews figured out, what Finlay suspected and told me."

"That Heather might have become pregnant at a Christmas party?"

"Right. But Kimberly couldn't tell Finlay her research without potentially looking like she was doubting him. If we accept that premise, then who could she tell? A piece of information like that, even unconfirmed, would be hard for her to hold inside. But she couldn't tell Finlay, so who could she tell? Kimberly was a reporter. Who does a reporter talk to?"

Faz got that gleam in his eye. "Her editor."

Tracy nodded.

"But if she told her editor, wouldn't he . . ."

"Say something? Publish a story?" She shook her head. "Not necessarily. I know Atticus Pelham."

"Atticus?" Faz said not hiding his sarcasm. "Like in *To Kill a Mockingbird*?"

"His parents were big fans."

"That's no reason to punish the kid."

She smiled. "Atticus doesn't like to publish anything controversial. Finlay said that's exactly what Atticus told Kimberly when she said she wanted to look into Heather Johansen's murder. Apparently, he agreed to let her look into it, but he was making no promises he'd publish what she wrote."

"What else do you know about this guy Atticus?"

"What do you mean?"

"How old is he? Could he have been at the same party?"

"No. No, he isn't from Cedar Grove. He came here maybe twenty years ago, well after 1993."

Faz shrugged. "It can't hurt to ask, I guess. You'll have to have that big police chief go with you. You comfortable with that?"

Before they'd gone to bed, Seattle had authorized Faz's trip to Phoenix to talk to Pete Adams, the former owner of the Four Points Tavern, and Faz had made a reservation for a morning flight from the airport in Bellingham.

"I've known Roy Calloway my whole life. I might not always agree with what he does or how he does it, but I know he has other people's best interests at heart. Do me another favor?" she asked.

"Sure."

She left the table and came back with a sheet of paper.

"What's this?" Faz asked.

"These are the people who bought the businesses here in Cedar Grove. Dan is trying to find them. I know we aren't supposed to use police resources for a civil matter . . ."

"But you feel guilty for not telling him what happened, and you want to make it up to him?"

She smiled and stood. "Don't let anyone ever tell you that you don't have good intuition, Faz."

"I've been married thirty years."

She gripped his forearm. "Thanks, Faz. I mean it. Thanks for everything."

"Hey, we're family now. This is what we do."

She smiled. It had been a long time since she'd heard those words. "I'm going back to bed. Mornings come early around here."

Faz picked up his Kindle. "Tell me about it."

CHAPTER 26

Dan threw the Tahoe into four-wheel drive and drove Faz over snow-covered roads to the airport in Bellingham, an hour-and-ten-minute drive. Faz had offered to drive himself, but Dan rejected that idea after looking over the tires on Faz's car. They weren't bad, but they weren't as good as the snow tires Dan put on his Tahoe in the winter, and Faz hadn't had a lot of recent experience driving on mountain snow and ice. Besides, Vera might need their car to get out of the house and keep from going stir-crazy.

Faz looked at the stone-and-wood exterior of the lone airport building. "I've seen REI stores in Seattle bigger than this." He grabbed his small duffel—he'd packed a change of clothes, uncertain how long it would take him to find Pete Adams—and pushed from the car.

"Thanks for everything, Faz." The two shook hands, cold air seeping into the Tahoe through the open door. "Tracy and I both appreciate what you and Vera have done."

"It's like I told Tracy last night, Dan," Faz said, steam rising with each word. "We're family now. This is what family does. Thanks for the ride. Tell Tracy I'll keep her posted."

Dan thought about Faz's comment of being family as he pulled away from the building and drove back in the direction of Cedar Grove. The words no doubt had brought comfort to Tracy. She'd lost her entire family, as had Dan, though her loss had been far more violent and at a much younger age. Tracy had been the princess of Cedar Grove, her father a respected doctor, her mother well-connected to the community, and she and Sarah the two town darlings gaining fame on the shooting circuit. The next day Sarah had disappeared, and the fairy tale vanished. It never came back. The tale only got worse.

Dan thought about the day they'd found Sarah's body, twenty years after she'd gone missing, and what that day must have been like for Tracy. Her mother and father were dead by then. She had no one to lean on; she hadn't had anyone for years. Sarah had been buried just days before hydroelectric dams went on line, damming the river and creating a lake that covered the site where Edmund House had buried Sarah's body. They didn't find the body until they took down the dam as part of an environmental movement to restore the natural habitat of salmon, and the lake waters once again receded.

They took the dams down and the water receded.

Dan sat up. The thought came to him like a bolt of lightning. "The water receded back to its original dimensions," Dan whispered to himself. Could it be that simple? He thought again of *all* the businesses on Market Street suddenly being bought out by the City of Cedar Grove. Why? People rarely did anything for nothing. Was Gary Witherspoon simply motivated to revitalize an old town and take advantage of Cedar Grove's natural resources, as he'd proclaimed? Was he trying to impress his father by one-upping him?

Or was he making a buck, somehow?

Someone is trying to make a buck.

What motivates people?

"Greed," Dan said.

Before the dams went on line, the area above the river had been slated to be developed into a mountain resort. A development company had come into Cedar Grove with plans to build golf courses, a clubhouse, a pool, and dozens of homes. People had said the resort would transform Cedar Grove, that real estate would skyrocket and the businesses would flourish, but it never happened. It had all gone underwater, literally, when the hydroelectric dams went on line.

Could the property be up for development? Could that be why new owners would take a chance on new businesses?

Dan considered how far he'd driven. Could he even find the road that had been cut to what, at the time, had been the site for the Cascadia Resort? He recalled the road being between Silver Spurs and Cedar Grove. Figuring he had nothing to lose by playing a hunch, Dan checked his rearview mirror—traffic on the county road was virtually nonexistent with the snow overnight—and slowed. He crept along, with one eye searching for the turnoff. It had never been marked, but he and Tracy had gone up the road in 2013 so Dan could see where Sarah had been buried, and he understood that hunters still used the road to gain access into the backcountry.

He drove another tenth of a mile, then another, and a third. Just as he started to think he'd gone too far and to contemplate doubling back, he spotted what appeared to be the road between a stand of trees. The entrance had been partially obscured by the snow, pushed to the edge of the road by the snowplow.

Dan dropped the transmission into low, and he took a left. He bounced over the lip of frozen snow and kept up his speed. The snow felt compacted, though a good four inches had fallen overnight, and another twelve inches the prior week. There was no reason he knew of for anyone to have been recently driving the road. Hunting season was still months away.

When the road flattened, Dan stopped, threw the SUV into park, and stepped down from the cab, sinking up to his ankles. He walked to the front of the Tahoe and used his hands to brush away the snow. Beneath the top layer he saw what looked to be two ruts, tire tracks, embedded in the snow.

Someone had come up here, and recently.

Dan climbed back into his Tahoe and drove on, the SUV bumping and pitching over the terrain. Another quarter mile and the road came to a dead end. Twenty yards ahead, just to his right, he saw the top of a concrete post protruding from the snow, what had been the entrance to the Cascadia Resort. The developer had once had an office here—a construction trailer. Inside that trailer, a sales representative showed interested parties pictures of the various models of the homes, the club, and of the golf courses. Dan didn't see any recent activity—no construction equipment or trucks. No new logging of trees. No tire tracks. The place looked like he recalled it when he and Tracy came up the road to gain access to where Sarah's body had been found. Trees had been cleared to make room for the office. Twenty years had not changed its appearance much.

Dan slipped out of the car, pulled on his coat and gloves, and walked forward, sinking with each step, nearly to the tops of his Sorels. He felt the cold on his uncovered head and face. His glasses fogged. He removed them, clipping a stem to a button on his shirt, then zipped closed the jacket. He trudged to the concrete post and stopped, trying to remember the layout, where the office trailer had been.

He spent the next twenty minutes walking in a circle, kicking at the snow, increasing the diameter with each revolution, searching for signs of recent development activity, like survey stakes buried in the snow. Steam escaped his lips and nostrils, and he soon felt himself perspiring beneath his jacket. He leaned against a tree to catch his breath. This was futile. Even if survey stakes had been driven into the ground, he'd never find them, not with this much snow. He'd have to think of something else. He could call the company that had planned to develop Cascadia, but he doubted it still existed after all these years. He recalled articles about the company filing for bankruptcy after Cascadia failed. Dan wished he'd thought of this possibility while he was still in Bellingham. He could have gone into the Whatcom County building department and looked to see if there had been any pre-development papers filed or any pre-application meetings.

Shit. He'd have to drive back. But first, he needed to pee. He'd drunk a cup of coffee on the way to the airport.

He stepped to the side of a tree, unzipped his fly, and let loose a steady stream. As he did, he looked toward the tree ahead of him and noticed a silver tab nailed into the bark. The tab was the width of a gum wrapper and half an inch in length. He turned his head and looked at the tree on his left and saw a similar metal tag. Quickly zipping up, he opened his jacket and removed his glasses. The warm lenses immediately fogged when they encountered the cold air. He used his shirt to clear them and slipped them on. The tab had a number pressed into it. Dan had seen tabs like this before, when he'd sought to remodel his parents' home. Whatcom County had required that he have all the trees on his parents' property surveyed by an arborist, so the county could be certain Dan didn't clear cut the lot, thereby ruining the ecosystem by increasing the carbon dioxide levels in the atmosphere, destroying the ozone layer, and setting off cataclysmic events dooming all humanity to higher temperatures and certain skin cancer.

Not that he was bitter about having to spend the money on a regulation that, up until that point, he had never heard of.

Anyway, that regulation had not existed twenty-five years ago, when the Cascadia site was first considered for development. It had only come into existence in the intervening years, when ecologists had become much more aggressive about protecting the environment, which had been the reason for the removal of the hydroelectric dams in the first place—to restore the salmon's wild habitat.

So the tree tabs had to be recent. Dan moved to the next tree. It, too, had been tagged. In the next five minutes he'd found fifteen more trees, all over eight inches in diameter, some well over.

"Son of a bitch," he said, a smile spreading on his freezing face.

CHAPTER 27

Tracy fed Daniella and gave the baby a bath in the stainless steel sink. Then she dressed her, fed her again, and put her down for her morning nap.

"I shouldn't be long," she said to Vera.

"Take your time," Vera said. "This one is an angel compared to my Antonio. He was colicky for the first six months. If he was awake, he was screaming."

"I'll try not to be long," Tracy said again.

Vera smiled. "Tracy, I've been a cop's wife for twenty-nine years, and married to a detective for more than twenty. I know how it is. You have to follow leads, and sometimes those leads direct you to other leads, and you end up working long hours. We'll be fine. Especially with the police officer outside watching us, and the two dogs inside."

Tracy's first stop was the police station. She spent fifteen minutes filling in Roy Calloway and telling him what she wanted to do. Then they jumped into her Subaru for the short ride over to the *Towne Crier*'s offices on Fourth Street, an old miner's cabin the town had designated as a historical landmark before Tracy was born.

"You learn anything more on the shooter at my house the other night?" Tracy asked.

Calloway rubbed at stubble on his chin. "No. The neighbors don't recall hearing a thing with the storm raging—not even the shot from the rifle. What about those pictures you sent down to have taken a look at by the . . . What did you call her?"

"Man-tracker. I talked to her this morning. She didn't have anything definitive but said from the photos I sent, the tracks were made by an L.L.Bean snow boot, a men's size nine or ten."

"That's not that big," Calloway said.

"Not for someone your size, maybe, but a size ten is pretty common. If she could have measured the depth of the indentations, she could have estimated the weight of the person who'd made them."

"So, not much help," Calloway said.

"Not much," Tracy agreed.

She parked on Fourth Street, two short blocks west of Market Street. The old building, wood logs with mortar oozing from the cracks between them, looked to be open for business. The hours were posted, but that meant little in Cedar Grove. People usually came to work and went home when convenient.

"You want to handle this, right?" Calloway said.

"Yeah, I do."

"And I'm here to keep Dan happy?"

"No. You're here because you can still intimidate simply by being present," she said, feeding his ego. Calloway didn't respond, but Tracy saw the corner of his mouth inch up as he stepped from her car.

She stomped the snow from her boots on the welcome mat and pushed open the door to the log cabin. Inside, she approached a rack of back issues of the *Towne Crier*. Behind a counter was a series of desks with computer terminals and several filing cabinets. Two women pecked on their keyboards. On a counter to Tracy's left she saw a sink, a half-filled coffeepot, which she could smell, mugs, and packets of sweeteners and powdered milk. A refrigerator rested under the counter. A memory struck her. She'd been in the building after Sarah's disappearance—in the summer of 1993. Those days had mostly become a blur, but she recalled accompanying her father to this office. He'd brought the editor recent photos of Sarah for a front-page article about her disappearance. The paper had also used the photo to make fliers, which Tracy helped her father and a team of people tack up all around Cedar Grove, Silver Spurs, and outlying towns. Tracy recalled the sharp smell of ink on that visit. Now the office smelled like an antique store, a thick, oppressive must. She noticed two offices behind sliding glass doors at the back of the building. The doors looked to have been a recent addition. Atticus Pelham sat behind a desk in one of the offices, talking on the telephone.

"Chief Calloway." One of the two women looked up from her desk when Roy followed Tracy into the room. "What brings you here?" She glanced at Tracy as if uncertain whether she might bite.

"Margaret, this is Tracy Crosswhite. She's a Seattle homicide detective. I don't believe you ever met."

The woman came around the back of her desk and approached the counter. She wore a white short-sleeve sweater and blue stretch pants. She didn't look, or sound, happy to meet her. "No," she said, "we haven't. But we wrote a few articles back in 2013 about the retrial in Whatcom County."

"That's right," Calloway said. "You did."

Margaret turned her attention from Tracy to Calloway. "What brings you here today?"

"We'd like a moment of Atticus's time."

She glanced over her shoulder at the glass office. "He's busy this morning. Been on the phone since he got in."

"It's important," Calloway said, not bothering to elaborate, yet making it clear he did not need to.

Margaret nodded. "I'll let him know you're here."

Tracy watched the woman slide open the glass door and lean into Pelham's office. Pelham removed the phone from his ear and covered the mouthpiece, holding it down by his chest. After a few seconds he turned his head and looked out into the newsroom, at Calloway and Tracy. He gave Margaret a nod, said something, and put the phone back to his ear.

Margaret returned. "He's finishing up a conversation. You want coffee?"

Calloway shook his head. "Had a cup this morning but thank you."

She gestured to a couple of chairs against the wall. "Make yourself comfortable."

Calloway nodded but made no movement toward the chairs. He wasn't used to being kept waiting in Cedar Grove and didn't expect to be now. He wanted Atticus to see him standing in the newsroom.

They didn't wait long. Atticus hung up and pushed away from his desk. He slid back the glass door and approached, though with an uncertain smile. Perhaps five foot six with a full head of red hair and only flecks of gray, Pelham stood about a foot shorter than Calloway and four inches shorter than Tracy. He wore a short-sleeve white shirt, black slacks, and black tennis shoes. Just before reaching them, he used the ball of his thumb to push his glasses onto the bridge of his nose.

"Chief Calloway." Pelham extended a hand. "What brings you here?"

Calloway introduced Tracy.

"I remember when you came to town," Pelham said. "When was that?"

"It was 2013," Margaret said from her terminal.

"We sold a lot of papers covering the retrial of your sister's killer."

"Tracy is helping me out on a couple of matters, Atticus. She has questions she'd like to ask you."

"Finlay?" Pelham said.

"I told her you'd be happy to sit down and give us half an hour of your time."

Pelham looked to Calloway, perhaps picking up on the fact that Calloway wasn't asking for his time; he was telling him.

"Sure. Sure, I can do that." He looked about the cramped room. "Let's do it in my office. It'll be crowded but private."

"We don't mind," Tracy said.

Pelham grabbed a chair from behind one of the vacant desks and wheeled it into his office, which reminded Tracy of the small interview room they used at the Justice Center to question suspects. The interview room was intended to be crowded and uncomfortable.

Pelham positioned the extra chair next to another and made his way around the edge of his desk. They all sat. "So what can I help you with?"

Tracy started to speak, but Pelham's desk phone interrupted her.

"Sorry," Pelham said. "Hang on a second." He pressed buttons on his phone. "It will go straight to voice mail now. Okay. So what is it you wanted to know?"

"I have some questions about Kimberly Armstrong."

"Tragic," Pelham said. "Really tragic. Just a horrible tragedy. Kimberly was like family here. We still haven't recovered emotionally or logistically. Kimberly wrote a lot of our news stories as well as a weekly column. We've been scrambling."

"I also understood Kimberly wrote longer pieces, pieces that involved more research," Tracy said.

"On occasion," Pelham said. "But we're not really that kind of newspaper. We don't do a lot of the hard-hitting news. We mostly cover local stuff, businesses opening, the jazz festival, all the new updates to Market Street. People in town who do something interesting. City council meetings are about as hard-hitting as we get."

"But Kimberly did, on occasion, propose other, maybe more con-troversial stories?" Tracy asked.

Pelham tried to smile, but it looked like a grimace. He picked up a paper clip from his desk blotter and sat back, fidgeting with it. "We had a few debates on that end," he said.

"What stories did you debate?"

"It really wasn't a debate," he said, backtracking. "Kimberly would bring something up and I'd tell her we didn't run those kinds of pieces."

"Did she push you?"

Now Pelham smiled. His hands continued to work the paper clip. "She tried. I'd say, *Kimberly, when your name is on this door, you can make those decisions. Until then, that's my responsibility.*"

Tracy decided to take a different tack to get Pelham to relax. "You own the newspaper?"

"I do."

"Do you rely on advertising dollars?"

"As do most of the newspapers in small towns still giving it a go. It's tough. We're thinking of going completely digital, but then people say they still like to have an actual paper in their hands. So we've compromised."

Tracy thought of the papers in the rack at the front of the building. "How often do you publish a hard copy of the paper?"

"Once every two weeks. We have an online presence—a locals' blog, gardening tips, and police or fire news. We call it 'What's New' around Cedar Grove. We update daily."

Pelham relaxed into the familiar as Tracy continued to ask him about the paper. He put down the paper clip. "Were those the types of articles you meant when you said Kimberly worked on news stories?" Tracy asked. "Local events."

"No. Kimberly mostly did straight news. She covered the mayor's office and the city council. She wrote about the budget every year."

"She covered Gary Witherspoon's office?"

"That was one of her responsibilities, yes."

Tracy thought that interesting. "Did you ever get a call from Gary, perhaps about one of the stories Kimberly was working on?"

Pelham picked up the paper clip—a definite tell that he was uncomfortable with a question. "Not that I recall, no."

"Didn't you and Kimberly have an argument about a story she wanted to write about Heather Johansen's murder?"

Pelham blanched and struggled to recover. "Not an argument . . . a discussion perhaps. But that isn't anything Gary called me about."

"No?"

"No. And it wasn't really an argument," he said, again backtracking. "She wanted to pursue it, and I told her she could do what she wanted with her free time, but I made no promises we would publish an article."

"But she *was* working on a story," Tracy said.

"She could have been."

"You didn't have any discussions about it?"

"Not that I recall. Not really, no."

"Did she talk to anyone here in the office about it?"

"Not that I'm aware of."

Dead end, Tracy thought. Not what she had been expecting. "Any other stories she was working on that you had a disagreement about?"

Pelham smiled, but his fingers had unbent the paper clip, and he spun it between his thumb and index finger, like helicopter blades. "Editors and reporters always argue about such things, like what we cut from their stories. It's all part of the game."

"What game is that?" Tracy asked.

"The newspaper game."

"So what else did you and Kimberly discuss, as part of the newspaper game?"

Pelham looked and sounded flustered. "I can't recall anything specifically . . . It was just in general terms."

"What did you discuss in general terms?"

"I just used that as a term . . . I didn't—" He looked to Calloway like a player looked to a sideline coach when he wanted to come out of a game.

"Atticus," Calloway said in that deep, authoritative voice that sounded like the school principal talking to a student. "I asked Tracy to give me a hand while Finlay is out. It sounds to me from this seat that you're dancing around her questions like a young man attending his first high school prom—awkward and self-conscious. Now settle down and get to the point. We need to know what it was Kimberly might have been working on."

"Can I ask a question, Chief?" Pelham said.

"Sure."

"What's this about? We all were told Kimberly died in a house fire. Are you saying she didn't?"

For a reporter, Pelham's question was not specifically phrased, and Tracy noticed Calloway dance around it. "No, I'm not saying she didn't. She definitely died in a house fire."

"Then what's the reason for all the questions?"

"I can't tell you that at the moment, Mr. Pelham," Tracy said. "But I'd be happy to sit down with you when I can, one-on-one, just the two of us." Pelham didn't look satisfied. "Was Kimberly working on the murder of Heather Johansen?" Tracy asked.

"Like I said, she brought it up and we argued about it, but I never heard about it again, except for Kimberly telling me that she hadn't gotten very far."

"So then you did discuss it?"

Pelham looked like a man on the edge of a cliff struggling to find something to hold on to. "No. Well in that respect, yes."

"What was said?"

"Okay." He set down the paper clip and let out a sigh. Then he raised his hands. "You're making more out of this than it was." He looked to Calloway as if seeking another lifeline. Roy didn't provide one. Pelham sighed. "Kimberly gave me some indication that she'd read the police file and that the medical examiner's report indicated Heather Johansen had been pregnant. I'm sure I'm not telling you anything you don't know, Chief. She speculated that maybe it was the father of the child who killed Heather. Now listen, Roy, you know me and you know that I wasn't about to go running off printing some story like that without something firm to back it up. Not with Eric and Ingrid still alive. Not after what they'd been through."

"I know you, Atticus," Calloway said.

"Did Kimberly say she wanted the paper to run the story?" Tracy asked.

"No. That's just my point. Kimberly dismissed the report."

"The medical examiner's report?" Tracy asked, confused.

"Yes."

"Did she say why?"

"She said that she had been Heather's best friend in high school, and that she would have known if Heather had been pregnant, that Heather would have told her."

The answer gave Tracy pause. It sounded like something Kimberly might say. It also sounded like a woman trying to talk herself out of pursuing a story. Was it too painful to go down that path? Was Kimberly worried that she'd discover the baby's father had been Finlay, or could have been? It raised another question as well. If Kimberly had put the story on the back burner, then what story had she been working on?

"Any other stories she was working on that you know of?" Tracy asked.

Pelham pulled at the skin beneath his chin. "Okay, listen . . . I don't want to be starting any unsubstantiated rumors."

"God forbid," Calloway said.

"Kimberly came in one afternoon and said she thought there was more to the redevelopment of Market Street than Gary and the city council were letting on."

Red flags waved inside Tracy's head. Dan had just said essentially the same thing. "Did she say what she meant by *more to it?*"

"Not entirely."

"What did she say?" Calloway interjected.

"She said that it *appeared*, and I'm emphasizing that word . . . It *appeared* that perhaps someone had pulled a permit at the building department in Bellingham to develop the property above Cedar Grove."

"The Cascadia property?" Tracy asked.

"That's what she said. I wasn't here back when it was originally going to be developed, so I don't know for certain, but that's what Kimberly said."

Tracy glanced at Calloway. A redevelopment of Cascadia, perhaps to put in the mountain resort planned twenty-five years ago, would dramatically increase the value of the businesses on Market Street, not to mention the homes in Cedar Grove. It could explain what Dan had been ruminating on from the start of his case—why people might be willing to invest money to renovate buildings and start businesses in a city in which just about every business had failed. This was not the information she had expected this morning, but it made sense.

"Did she say why she suspected someone took out a permit to develop the land?" Tracy asked.

"It sounded to me like innuendo and speculation," Pelham said.

"What did she say, Atticus?" Calloway said.

"Kimberly wondered why someone would remodel a business that had failed, and I said because Gary was working to change the culture. He was trying to emphasize Cedar Grove's access to outdoor recreation and to bring in tourists."

A vibrant business community would also mean more businesses looking to advertise, and that meant more money for Atticus Pelham and the *Towne Crier*. Tracy didn't see Atticus letting such a possibility go without exploring it further.

"Had Kimberly done research to confirm her suspicions?"

Pelham shrugged. "I don't know. She just told me she thought the property was going to be developed."

"She didn't say how she knew that?"

"She didn't say she knew it. She said she *thought* that might be the case."

"Did she say why she thought that might be the case?" Tracy asked. She could do this all day if she had to.

"Not to me she didn't."

"Did she say anything else?"

"No. Not to me."

"To anyone you knew?" Tracy asked.

"It's possible. I mean, Kimberly was a talker." He shifted his gaze to Calloway. "You know that, Roy. Once Kimberly got to talking, she just kept on going . . . like that battery commercial."

Tracy had a hunch and decided to play it. "What about you, Mr. Pelham?"

Pelham started to fidget with the paper clip again. Tracy lowered her gaze to his hands and he set it down. Then he asked in a hesitant voice. "What about me?"

"Did you talk to anyone about what Kimberly thought was going on with the redevelopment?"

"Well, of course I did. That's my job."

"What's your job?"

"The news."

"I thought straight news was Kimberly's job?"

"It was, but I mean I'm the ultimate arbiter."

"Who did you talk to about it, Atticus?" Calloway asked.

"I might have brought it up one afternoon when I was having a drink with Gary."

"Gary Witherspoon?" Tracy said. She glanced at Calloway.

"Yes," Pelham said.

"You told him that Kimberly suspected about the Cascadia property maybe being developed?"

"I asked if he had any knowledge of it."

"What did he say?"

"He said he didn't know anything about it, but if it was true, he'd sure like to know, because it could mean big things for Cedar Grove. He said something like that could really accelerate all his plans for the downtown. Then again, he said that if something like that was happening, he would have known about it."

"When was this conversation?" Calloway asked.

"It was in the summer."

"When in the summer?"

"It was at the jazz festival. The night of the jazz festival."

Calloway looked to Tracy. That had been at the end of August. Kimberly Armstrong had died in September.

CHAPTER 28

Faz exited the rental car lot and headed east on the Loop 202 South Mountain Freeway to the 101, where he'd head north for approximately forty-five minutes. The entire drive was just under an hour. Pete Adams's snowbird house was at the foothills of the Tonto National Forest, in a place called Rio Verde.

"Rio Verde? No kidding?" Faz had said to the woman behind the counter using a highlighter to mark his map.

"No kidding."

"Well yippee-ki-yay."

If Adams wanted a place the polar opposite of Silver Spoons, or whatever the hell the name of the town, he'd found it. The farther Faz drove, the fewer the trees, except for cacti, if cacti were technically even trees. He didn't know. When he left Bellingham, the temperature was in the low forties. The temperature here was a balmy seventy-seven degrees. Faz started sweating the moment he exited the airport, and he didn't stop until he was inside the air-conditioned rental car. If he stayed in the sun too long down here, he'd melt.

After approximately twenty miles on the 101, his GPS pinged. The woman's voice, a British accent—because he liked the way the accent sounded—advised him to take the North Pima Road exit. "Jolly good," he replied.

He followed North Pima Road for nearly seven miles. After that, he turned left and right as instructed, driving past adobe-style homes a rust-brown color that blended with the landscape. Some homes had walls with gates. They looked to be decent in size, built on lots well spaced from neighbors. The landscaping consisted of rocks, pebbles, and everything in between, plus cacti and a few flowering plants Faz couldn't begin to name.

Another fifteen minutes and he pulled into a driveway as instructed by his GPS. An adobe wall, about six feet in height, surrounded the property, with an iron gate across the driveway. Not bad for a guy who'd owned a bar most of his life. Then again, Faz figured real estate prices in the desert were nothing like in Seattle, given that the temperature in the summer had to consistently hit 115 degrees. He figured Adams bought the house for a song.

Something like AC/DC's "Highway to Hell."

He punched a button on an intercom embedded in the wall and looked through the gaps in the gate to the windows of the house. Through them he saw a glistening pool in the backyard, but no people. He pressed the button a second time but got no answer. He'd called the telephone number for Pete Adams before he'd left Bellingham, to ensure Adams hadn't left on some vacation—then again why would he? Sun, mild temperatures. This *was* a vacation. A woman had answered but said Pete wasn't home. Faz said he'd call back.

He looked up and down the barren landscape. If he waited in the sun, he really could melt. He decided to drive to the nearest town, park his butt in an air-conditioned restaurant, and call Adams a little later.

Dan pulled into the parking lot for the Whatcom County assessor's department on Grand Avenue in Bellingham. He felt like a yo-yo—driving to Bellingham, back to Cedar Grove, then back again to Bellingham—but he also believed he was on the verge of uncovering something important, something that could potentially break wide-open Larry Kaufman's suit against the city.

He met with a young woman from the assessor's office named Celia Reed, told her he was hoping to obtain the parcel number for a certain piece of property, and gave her a description of the property's location. Reed tapped her keyboard for a few minutes, then told Dan the property he'd described actually comprised three separate parcels with three unique lot numbers. Not busy, Reed showed Dan how to use the parcel viewer to pinpoint the parcel numbers. After doing so, she then tapped into the tax assessor's site and read from the computer screen while Dan scribbled down notes.

"Between 1984 and 1993 the parcels were owned by the Cascadia Redevelopment Corporation. The land was condemned by the State of Washington in 1993."

"It was flooded," Dan said. "The state allowed the installation of hydroelectric dams on the river and it flooded that area."

"That was before my time," Reed said.

"Unfortunately, not mine," Dan said, smiling. "Anything else?"

Reed ran her finger across the screen. "In 2014 the three parcels were purchased by a limited liability company, Cedar Grove Development LLC."

Dan listened, his mind churning. "What other information can I get on the property or the purchaser?"

The woman sent Dan to the county planner's office on Northwest Drive. Once there, he used the parcel numbers to determine there had not yet been any pre-development meetings or pre-development applications filed for the three parcels. There was also not yet a report filed of the topographical survey, though Dan was certain one had been done to map the significant trees on the parcels. The lack of information made sense—if someone was trying to keep redevelopment quiet, at least until after Cedar Grove had purchased all the businesses on Market Street for next to nothing. Dan didn't expect the topographical survey, or any reports of pre-development meetings, to be filed until after the stores on Market Street were up and running. He also suspected he now knew the reason for the city's eagerness to settle Larry Kaufman's lawsuit. If news of a development leaked, the value of Kaufman's business would skyrocket.

Dan drove back to the assessor's office and asked Celia Reed if there were any available computers. He wanted to access the Washington Secretary of State's Office.

"You want to look up Cedar Grove Development LLC?" she asked. Dan did.

Reed tapped the keys of her keyboard and turned her screen so Dan could see the information she had retrieved. It was as he expected. Of particular note was the limited liability company's designated agent.

—

Just after 1:30 p.m., Faz called the number for Pete Adams from the restaurant he'd found and got a live female voice. He asked for "Pete."

"He's just getting off the golf course and is on his way home. Who's this?"

"It's the club," Faz said. "Looks like he left some golf balls in the cart this afternoon. We'll run them over to the house."

"I can call—"

"No problem, ma'am." Faz disconnected the call. There was probably little reason for subterfuge, but Faz hadn't come all this way to get a phone hung up on him, not without the chance to make a first impression in person.

He drove back to the house and pulled up to the intercom. Behind the iron slats of the fence he now saw two parked cars. The gate pulled apart and he drove over cobblestones, parking beside the two vehicles. As he stepped out, he put on sunglasses to combat a blinding sun. A man came out from the front door and walked toward him. He looked to be early seventies, with a thin build, silver hair, and a reddish tan on his arms. He wore golf shorts and a collared shirt and gave Faz a curious look. "Are you from the club?"

"I'm actually a Seattle detective, Mr. Adams. I'm here because I'd like to ask you some questions."

"What about?"

"The years you owned the Four Points Tavern in Silver Spoons."

"Silver Spurs?"

"Yeah, that's the one."

"That's a little broad. I owned it for thirty years. What about it? I sold the Four Points several years ago. I'm retired."

"I can see that, and let me assure you this has nothing to do with anything you did or didn't do. We're trying to run down some things in a couple of cold cases."

"The attorney? What was his name? Mathew something."

"Jason Mathews?"

"That's the one." He gave Faz an inquisitive look. "You came all this way? Why didn't you just call? Why'd you make up the excuse that you'd found my golf balls?"

"Call it paranoia. A detective's curse."

Adams smiled, mildly amused. "What is it you wanted to know?"

"Would you mind if we went indoors, someplace air-conditioned? I'm not exactly built for the heat the way you are. I'm sweating just standing here, and the top of my head feels like it caught fire."

Adams smiled. "Sure, come on in. I'll get you an iced tea."

When Dan pulled into his driveway, the police car remained parked across the street. He had spoken to Tracy on his drive home, after his second meeting with Zack Metzger, this time to discuss Metzger's formation of Cedar Grove Development LLC.

Inside the house, Dan handed Tracy the documents Celia Reed had printed for him at the Bellingham building department.

"This is the story Kimberly Armstrong was working on at the time she was killed," Tracy said, reviewing the documents. "Her editor didn't know how far she'd gotten in her research, but she told him the land was going to be redeveloped. If she knew that much, she knew someone bought the Cascadia property from the state."

"And Sunnie was the contact person with the attorney in Bellingham who became the agent for service of process."

"It has to be Gary," Tracy said. "Cedar Grove Development has to be his company."

"My first guess is it's Ed's. Ed always liked to make a buck, and development would dramatically increase home and business values in Cedar Grove. If it's not Ed's, then it could belong to Gary and Rav Patel. I don't think Patel came to Cedar Grove because he was getting a pay raise."

"How could they set up a company and expect to get away with it?"

"Because they didn't think anyone would bother to investigate. They didn't expect Kimberly to pursue it, nor did they expect any of the Market Street owners to turn down what amounted to free money. When Larry Kaufman balked at their offer, it threw a wrench in their plans, but again, they probably doubted he would go so far as to hire an attorney who would look up the other companies. They likely figured they could just increase their offer and he'd take it and go quietly."

"Those companies are going to be worth a small fortune if a resort goes in, Dan."

"I think so, too, and they've already started the process with the topographical survey, but they haven't done anything further, at least nothing they've filed. I think they're waiting until they've got all the business matters settled before they move forward. Did you hear back on the addresses and phone numbers of the members of those LLCs?" Dan asked.

Faz had asked Kins to try to run down the information. "Not yet, no," Tracy said.

Dan paced, as he always did when thinking through information. "I'm betting these companies were bought by Witherspoon's relatives or fraternity brothers, people with enough money to do the repairs and keep things quiet. Or Ed and Gary could have taken out loans, created each of the LLCs, and are playing with the banks' money until the development goes in. Individually the loans wouldn't be that significant a financial burden. It's sort of like the Cedar Grove of old—they're mining for gold, but this time they've assured themselves of a strike. The improved condition of Cedar Grove with viable businesses makes the redevelopment a lot more lucrative, and vice versa."

Tracy nodded, but didn't respond.

Dan knew that look. "Something else bothering you?"

"I don't disagree with anything you've said, but I'm having a hard time believing someone would kill Kimberly over this."

"It's a lot of money, Tracy. And you said the editor told you he mentioned to Gary what Kimberly had found out."

"Thought she'd found out."

"Do you think this editor has any interest in this?" Dan asked.

"No. Nothing beyond the newspaper. He and Gary are close, given their positions in town. I'm sure he mentioned it in passing to Gary because the redevelopment of Cascadia would be a boon for the city . . . for both of them actually. Improved business would mean increased advertising revenue. But if you met Atticus Pelham you'd understand why I don't think he's involved. That's what I started to say. I've done this for a long time now, Dan. To shoot someone can be an instantaneous bad decision. But to beat someone—a police officer's wife—is indicative the killing was motivated by something besides money. And what about Heather Johansen's death, and Jason Mathews's? How do they fit into all this?"

"Their deaths might not be related to Kimberly's death."

"Heather was also beaten to death, and Kimberly was also asking about her death."

"You said her editor told you Kimberly had backed off that story."

"He did. He said that after Kimberly read the ME's report disclosing that Heather was pregnant, she told Pelham she didn't believe it, that she and Heather had been best friends and Heather would have told her. But I wonder if she backed off for another reason."

"She didn't want to know the father?"

"Maybe it scared her to think that the father could have been Finlay."

"I still can't see how the two deaths could be related," Dan said. "In 1993 the hydroelectric dams were going in. The property was worthless. There's no way Ed or Gary or anyone else could have foreseen this happening now."

"I'm not saying Heather was killed because of some scheme related to the redevelopment. I'm just saying the manner of death, both women bludgeoned, is too similar to dismiss as unrelated."

"Maybe," Dan said. "But how are you going to prove they're related?"

"I don't know."

"I'm working on an idea. It came to me on the drive home. I'm not sure it will work, but if it does, it could help both of us," Dan said. "And I just may have a hard-ass judge willing to accommodate me."

CHAPTER 29

Faz stepped to sliding glass doors and looked out onto a small back-yard with a kidney-shaped pool and several trees, the branches weighed down by lemons or grapefruit.

"What do you do with all the lemons?" Faz asked.

Adams handed him an iced tea. "Make lemonade, lemon marma-lade, all kinds of things. You want to take some with you? I have more than I can use."

"I don't think I'd get them on the plane."

They sat on red leather furniture. The floor was tile and the décor southwest. "You said some things have been called into question about Jason Mathews's death. I understood that was a hunting accident."

"That's what's been called into question," Faz said. "We understand he was a regular at your tavern."

"For a while. You do know Cedar Grove sent over an officer after Mathews's death to find out if Mathews made any enemies in the bar, right?"

"Had he?"

"Not that I knew of."

"What did you know of him?"

"Not a lot. He'd come in and keep mostly to himself, unless he drank too much. Then he could get loud and offensive."

"In what way?"

"His ex was usually the target of his comments. Let me ask you something. Outside, you said this had to do with two cases. What's the second case?"

"Young girl who disappeared along the county road in 1993. They found her body partially buried in the snow."

"Thought that might be it."

"Why's that?"

"Because he wasn't exactly discreet about it."

"Who? About what exactly?"

"Mathews. I recall he was doing some work for the family of that girl or at least said he was."

"You remember anything more?"

"I remember him saying he'd learned something, something the police didn't report. Probably just bullshit. He was that kind of guy."

"Did he say what that was?"

"If he did, I don't remember. That had to be five or six years ago now."

"What about somebody else in the bar, someone he may have spoken with, a drinking buddy?"

"Nobody regular. Like I said, he wasn't liked much. I had to call the police on him once when he wouldn't stop bitching about his ex-wife. He was using some pretty crude language to describe her."

"When was that?"

"When I called the police? I don't know."

"Can you relate it to the time he died? That was in October 2013."

"I can't; I'm sorry. I imagine the police likely have a report."

"That would be the Silver Spurs police?" Faz said.

"I called Silver Spurs, but they called Cedar Grove since that's where Mathews lived. I guess they figured he was their problem and if anyone was going to have to drive him home, it might as well be them. He was pretty drunk. Passed out on the bar."

"You recall the name of the officer who came out to get him?"

"Sure. It was Finlay Armstrong. He later became the chief in Cedar Grove."

Tracy had told Faz something similar, but he hoped remembering the incident might spur something else in Adams's memory. "You sure?"

"Positive. Finlay came into the bar and escorted Mathews outside."

"You talk to him? I mean Finlay."

"Nothing beyond just *There he is*, you know."

"You said this guy Mathews had a loose tongue. Did he ever talk about the young woman or what he was doing for the family? Anything at all?"

"Not to me, but yeah, he likely did, though I couldn't say to who in particular. He was one of those guys. He talked like he was a big shot."

"I'll bet you became a pretty good judge of character owning a bar all those years," Faz said, looking to feed Adams's ego and keep him talking.

"I wasn't bad. Got tired of it, though. That's why I sold it."

"Can you recall anything Mathews said about the girl?"

"I'm sorry. I just remember him saying the parents hired him and that maybe the guy they thought killed her didn't do it. Something like that. Best that I can remember anyway. I think he was just lonely and trying to get people to pay attention to him."

"And he never hinted at the information he'd uncovered?"

"Never did," Adams said.

"And no one else in the bar who Mathews seemed to have a connection with? No one who he might have talked to about it in more detail?" Faz asked, trying again.

Adams shook his head. "Like I said, nobody in there cared too much for him. I'm sorry, I wish I could offer more."

"What about anything unusual or out of the ordinary? You recall anything like that?"

"Well, there was something. I'm not sure if it means much but . . ."

Faz, at this point, would take anything. "What was that?"

"Someone came into the bar one night, and he and Mathews sat at a table in the back talking."

"Did you know this person?"

"Oh yeah," Adams said with a smile.

"From Silver Spurs?"

"No. He was from Cedar Grove."

———

Jason Mathews sat at the table at the back of the Four Points Tavern, the table farthest away from the pool table and the shuffleboard, where he could expect a little privacy. He had a business negotiation to conduct. The Johansens might not want to profit from their daughter's death, but Mathews saw no reason why he shouldn't. He suspected the Johansens would sing a different tune when he told them he knew who was behind their daughter's death. And if they didn't? That really wasn't Mathews's problem. More money for him.

He sipped his vodka tonic. He wasn't sure how many he'd had, enough to calm his nerves and get him in the right frame of mind. He'd even dressed the part, putting on one of the three suits he'd kept from his days practicing law in Montana. The others he'd either outgrown or worn out. He gave those to a local Goodwill before he'd left Montana. Good riddance.

The door to the bar pushed open and his visitor stepped in, stopping to allow his eyes to adjust to the dreary illumination provided mostly by neon lights glowing in the windows and mounted on the wall behind the bar.

The visitor looked like he was about to approach the bar. Mathews pushed back his chair and stood, giving the man a nod. They hadn't formally met, though Mathews had made enough noise around Cedar Grove that he had a hard time believing the guy didn't know what he looked like. The fact that he had come to the bar meant he knew exactly who Mathews was, which was a good sign. It told Mathews he was on the right track.

Mathews thrust his hand across the table when the man approached. "Mr. Witherspoon. I'm Jason Mathews."

Ed Witherspoon ignored the hand, pulled out a wooden chair across from Mathews, and sat. A woman approached and tossed a coaster on the table. On it was the head of a deer, a four-point buck. "Whiskey. Jim Beam or Wild Turkey, on the rocks," Witherspoon said.

"Another vodka tonic," Mathews said. Then he, too, sat.

"You said you had information I'd want to hear. I'm all ears," Witherspoon said. He sat back, smiling, trying to look cocky.

"Don't you want your drink first? I think you might."

"Look. I know who you are, and I know what you're doing. I know everything about everyone in Cedar Grove. So let's cut the bullshit and cut to the chase. Why am I here?"

"If you know everything, maybe I should be asking you that question," Mathews said, thinking it a clever retort.

"Are you drunk, Mr. Mathews? Did I get called out of my house in the dark by a drunk?"

"Would you have come?"

"No, I would not have."

"And yet, here you sit, Mr. Mayor. Why is that?"

"I'm no longer the mayor, and I'm here because you said you had information on the death of Heather Johansen I'd like to hear."

"She must have meant a lot to you to get you out of that warm house of yours."

"She worked for me."

"Is that all?" Mathews grinned.

"What exactly is this, Mr. Mathews?" Witherspoon said. "I'm tired of playing games."

The cocktail waitress brought their drinks. Mathews raised a hand and waved off Witherspoon, though he hadn't reached for his wallet. "This is on me." After the waitress departed, Mathews said, "So we've established that Heather worked for you."

"I told you that."

"I believe she continued to work for you all the way up until her demise in February 1993, did she not?" "Demise" was a good word. He liked that. A lot more subtle than "death."

"Again, I told you she worked for me."

Mathews rocked in his seat. "I've heard rumors around town that you throw one heck of a Christmas party, or you did, back then."

"We threw a holiday party at the office for our employees and our clients."

"I assume Heather was there that night then, given that she worked for you."

"I told you she was an employee. The party was for employees. What year are you talking about?"

"December 1992."

"I don't know. If she was working for me then, I assume she came to the party. So what?"

"Her parents were there?"

"Again, I assume they were. A lot of people come and go. It's an open house. I do my best, but I can't and don't entertain everyone. Can we get on with this?"

Mathews put up a hand. "Hold on. Hold on. Don't be impatient. The Johansens said they left your party to go to another party that night."

"I wouldn't know."

"They said Heather stayed," Mathews said.

"She might have. I don't know."

"Oh, you know she did, Mayor. You know very well she did."

"A lot of people came to that party back then. And it was a different time."

"By that I assume you mean there was a lot of drinking?"

"People weren't as informed as they are now about drinking and driving."

"I think people are people, same then as they are now."

"What do you mean by that?"

"I mean a young girl drinks too much at a party . . . She can be easy pickings, can't she?"

Witherspoon did not verbally answer but his Adam's apple looked like a bobber on a lake when a bass strikes.

Mathews continued. "And here Heather was drunk and alone. Stuck without a ride home."

Witherspoon leaned forward and lowered his voice, but not his intensity. "Are you accusing me of something, Mr. Mathews? Because I was home with my wife. You can ask her. She'll vouch for my whereabouts that night. We told all of this to the police. You can ask them. Beyond all that, you can go—"

"Oh, I'm sure Barbara would verify it. And I know that big police chief already asked you that question. It was in his report. But that was before the bombshell broke."

"The bombshell?" Witherspoon sipped his drink but Mathews thought it was to give his lips and hands something to do, besides shake.

"You know the bombshell. After all, you said you know everything about everyone in your town. I'm sure you knew about Heather, didn't you?"

"What is it you want, Mathews? Is this some poor attempt at blackmailing me?"

"Blackmail? Why that would only be appropriate if I was talking to a guilty man, wouldn't it?"

Witherspoon fumbled. "You just seemed to be going in that direction."

"I'm going in that direction, Mayor Witherspoon, but I don't consider it blackmail."

"I told you; I'm no longer the mayor. And if this isn't blackmail, what is it?"

"Restitution, sir. Restitution."

———

Faz sat back against Adams's leather couch. He felt sweat dripping from his armpits though the climate-controlled temperature kept the house cool.

"Did you tell the police officer about this meeting in the bar between Mathews and Ed Witherspoon?"

"Didn't really think about it. She asked if Mathews had any enemies in the bar. It didn't really register on my radar back then."

"I take it you never talked to the mayor? Never asked him the purpose of him meeting with Mathews?"

"I really didn't know him, being from Silver Spurs. I just figured maybe he and Mathews knew one another."

"But your impression from the conversation that night . . . changed?"

"I guess. Maybe. I didn't know their relationship. All I know is what I saw. The mayor didn't look happy to be there, and the longer he stayed the more unhappy he looked. It wasn't unfriendly. I mean there was no yelling or anything like that, but when the mayor left the bar he looked . . . well, pretty upset."

"What about Mathews?"

"My recollection is Mathews stayed for a while, nursing his drink. I also recall he looked . . . smug."

"Smug?"

Adams struggled for a better description. "He looked like the cat who'd just swallowed the canary."

CHAPTER 30

The following night, Faz returned to Cedar Grove. They all sat at the kitchen table—Dan and Tracy, Faz and Vera, and Roy Calloway. Vera had cooked dinner—ravioli in a cream sauce, and a pork loin that was almost too heavenly for Tracy to describe. They'd listened to music, opened a couple bottles of Syrah, and took time to enjoy dinner, putting work aside for the moment. By the time they'd finished eating, Daniella had fallen back to sleep. Tracy took her upstairs to her bassinet, bringing the baby monitor downstairs to the kitchen table. Vera cleared plates and glasses and started to load the dishwasher.

"I'll do that, Vera," Tracy said. "The cook gets to sit."

"Not tonight. I know you all have a lot to discuss, and I don't like to know too many of the details of Vic's work. It just makes me nervous. You go do what you have to do."

"Then just leave the dishes and I'll do it later."

"Don't be silly. This keeps me busy. I'll listen to music and drink my wine. Go on."

When Tracy returned, Faz, Dan, and Roy Calloway were already talking. She brought a glass of ice water with her and looked at Faz, who was already telling Calloway about Arizona. "This guy Pete Adams owned the Four Points Tavern in Silver Spurs. He said the attorney came into the bar just about every day."

"Jason Mathews?" Calloway asked.

"Yeah. He said Mathews didn't have any friends in the bar, that he was a talker, a self-promoter type. He said when Mathews got drunk he could get obnoxious and belligerent about his ex, that he used colorful language that I will not repeat here in the presence of ladies."

"Thank you," Vera said from the kitchen.

Faz continued. "I think Tracy told you about the time Mathews passed out on his barstool and Adams called the local police, but they figured Mathews was a Cedar Grove problem and called you. And who shows up but your guy Fenway."

Calloway gave Tracy a puzzled look. Tracy said, "Finlay told me about it when I spoke to him. He didn't try to hide it. He said when he drove Mathews home, Mathews told him he'd learned from the ME's report that Heather Johansen had been pregnant."

"Why didn't Finlay tell me?" Calloway asked.

"Because Finlay knew he'd been a suspect in Heather's death, and news of the pregnancy would only have made him more suspect. Then Mathews got shot . . ."

"I get it," Calloway said.

"Especially when you knew Finlay had been out hunting that day and without any alibi."

"It looks like Mathews also followed through on what he told the Johansens," Faz said. "Based on what Adams told me, anyway."

"What do you mean he followed through? On what? To who?" Calloway asked.

"Adams said Mathews was in the bar one night wearing a suit and in walked the mayor, Ed Witherspoon."

Calloway again glanced at Tracy before returning his attention to Faz. "Did this guy Adams hear their conversation?"

"No, but he said they talked for about fifteen minutes, the mayor didn't look happy to be there, and he looked even more unhappy when he left. He said Mathews, on the other hand, looked like the cat that ate the canary."

"When was this?" Calloway asked.

"Just a couple weeks before someone used Mathews as a deer."

"But we don't know what they talked about?" Calloway said.

"Adams couldn't hear them," Faz said.

"But let's assume they talked about Heather Johansen's pregnancy and how close that occurred to the date of Ed's Christmas Eve party," Tracy said to Calloway.

"That's a big jump," Calloway said.

"Not that big," Tracy said. "Mathews clearly knew Heather worked for Ed, and it's a fact that Heather had been at Ed's Christmas party that year. When he got the ME's report, Mathews easily could have done the math. In fact, he told the Johansens that he could use the pregnancy information to *shake some trees*. So what if he did? What if his meeting with Ed was to shake a tree and see what fell?" She rested her forearms on the table, the cork to the wine bottle in her fingertips. "And, Ed didn't tell me about the meeting when he and I talked."

"Did you ask Ed about Mathews?" Calloway asked.

"No," Tracy said. "But I asked him about Heather. He could have told me."

"Maybe he didn't bring it up because that isn't what he and Mathews talked about," Calloway said.

"Or maybe he didn't bring it up because it is," Tracy said. "At the very least, we have a link between Heather Johansen, Jason Mathews, and Kimberly Armstrong."

"Ed Witherspoon," Dan and Tracy said together.

"What's the link between Ed and Kimberly? Atticus Pelham?" Calloway asked.

"Seems logical Gary would have told Ed what Atticus said Kimberly had learned about Cedar Grove Development."

"It's not evidence that the murders are related," Calloway said.

Tracy set down the cork and stood. She walked to the drawer in the hall, the one that Dan had specially built and labeled "Tracy's junk drawer." The drawer was her place to throw things. She grabbed a pen and her notepad and brought both back to the table.

"Let's go through this chronologically." She drew a line down the sheet of paper and wrote *1992* on the left. She spoke as she wrote the facts on the right. "Heather Johansen was working for Ed Witherspoon. Heather attended Ed's Christmas Eve party that year with her parents. Heather stayed when her parents left the party to attend my father's party. Heather was killed February 6, 1993. Her body is found in the woods along the county road. An autopsy reveals she's been beaten to death. An ME's report, that you requested"—she looked to Roy Calloway—"reveals Heather was seven to eight weeks pregnant.

"We also know Heather had an appointment at the hospital in Silver Spurs," Tracy continued.

"An appointment she never kept," Calloway said.

"Right. We can assume someone drove her," Tracy said.

"We've never confirmed that," Calloway said.

"Heather grew up here, Roy," Tracy said. "She knew how cold it can get in February, and she knew what it meant when meteorologists warned of an incoming storm. She also knew how far it was to Silver Spurs. She never would have tried to walk, not wearing the clothes she had on and not in those conditions. She would have asked Kimberly to give her a ride, but Kimberly said she never knew. The fact that Kimberly did not know means someone else gave Heather a ride."

"This guy Ed Witherspoon is my choice." Faz tapped his finger on the table.

"Let's move on for the moment," Tracy said.

"In 2013 I got Edmund House a new trial. That got the Johansens thinking that House didn't kill their daughter."

"So they hire Mathews," Faz said.

Tracy nodded. "Mathews gets your police file and he learns Heather was pregnant. The Johansens fire Mathews."

"To protect Heather's reputation," Calloway said.

"Which was easier than accepting that she was pregnant and contemplating an abortion," Tracy said.

"But this guy Mathews, he doesn't see it that way. He sees it as an opportunity," Faz said. "So he blackmails . . . or tries to blackmail Ed Witherspoon, who Mathews thinks is the father, and therefore maybe Heather Johansen's killer. And Mathews ends up dead." He shrugged. "Seems like we can tie all of this together with Ed Witherspoon."

"We can't prove what Mathews and Ed Witherspoon discussed," Calloway said.

"What else could it have been?" Faz said.

"I'm just saying we can't prove it," Calloway said.

"Roy's right," Dan said. "We can certainly presume that's what they talked about, but we can't prove it."

"Let's keep moving forward," Tracy said again. She scribbled *2018* in the left-hand column. "Time passes. Kimberly Armstrong is a reporter for the *Towne Crier*. She's also married to Finlay, who is Cedar Grove's chief of police. Kimberly, we learn, is pursuing two stories, one against her editor's wishes. First, she has the Heather Johansen police file and also learns Heather was pregnant. According to Atticus Pelham, Kimberly dismissed that because Heather never told her. I can buy that as an explanation Kimberly would give for not pursuing the story further, but I don't think that's the actual reason. I think she feared the possibility of learning that Finlay was the father."

"I think so too," Calloway said.

"So Kimberly turns her attention to a second story, this of the possible development of the Cascadia resort by a company called Cedar

Grove Development LLC. We know from Atticus Pelham that Kimberly learned this, but we don't know the extent of the research she'd gathered because of the fire."

"Maybe that's worth asking Finlay about. Maybe she discussed that story with him," Calloway said.

"Maybe," Tracy said. "But let's assume Kimberly unwittingly walked into a time bomb when she pursued that story."

"Atticus said he talked to Gary about it," Calloway said. "And Gary could have told Ed."

"That's one scenario," Tracy said. "Another is Kimberly might have found what Dan found, that Sunnie was the contact person for the attorney who formed the limited liability companies."

"You think she called the town gossip asking about the development?" Faz asked.

"Seems the logical thing for a reporter to do," Calloway said.

"And it's also logical that if Kimberly called Sunnie, Sunnie would have told Gary, and Gary would have told Ed," Tracy said.

"Yeah, but given how much that woman talks, she might have told everyone," Faz said. "Which doesn't help us narrow down the killer."

"But we are back to Ed again," Tracy said. "It's a reasonable assumption he knew what Kimberly knew."

"I don't know," Calloway said. "I don't see Ed killing Kimberly over a potential business deal."

"Word gets out of a development going in, and all those businesses on Market Street are suddenly worth a lot more money," Dan said. "They engaged in fraud and misrepresentation to get those businesses for next to nothing."

"Maybe," Tracy said. "But I'm having the same problem as Roy, especially because Kimberly and Heather were both beaten to death, which usually is indicative of a crime of passion, or rage, not a crime involving money."

"Maybe somebody wanted both deaths to look like rage," Faz said. Everyone at the table shifted their attention to him. "I mean, who was the early suspect in Heather Johansen's death?"

"Finlay," Calloway said.

Faz nodded. "So, what if Heather's killer, after the fact mind you, knows Finlay was the prime suspect, and deliberately makes Kimberly's death look like a crime of passion, or rage, so people will think it was Finlay. You know, to throw you off."

"I'm not following," Calloway said.

"I'm saying what if, as this Mathews character starts kicking up the dust on Heather's death, and then Kimberly starts to kick up that dust even more, the killer does his best to make Kimberly's death look like a crime of passion, a crime of rage, so you all will relate it back to Heather's death—for which Finlay was the prime suspect—and not consider that her death really had to do with the possible development and the value of those businesses."

"So how does Mathews fit in all this? How does he relate to the redevelopment?" Calloway asked.

"He doesn't," Tracy said. "But the killer could have known Finlay is a hunter and an excellent shot. So he picks a day he knows Finlay is hunting. Everything is done to make it look like the same person who killed Heather killed Mathews and Kimberly."

"That's a twenty-year conspiracy," Calloway said.

"Twenty-six," Dan said.

"He might not have thought it out, not everything in advance," Tracy said.

"He was making it up as he went?" Faz said.

"To some extent, possibly."

"It's thin," Calloway said. "You won't get far in court with what you got, and it's not going to compel someone that smart to admit to anything."

"Certainly not to any criminal acts," Dan said.

"Tell them what you told me earlier," Tracy said to Dan.

He leaned into the table. "What if I can get witnesses in court, including Gary and Atticus. What if they think I'm asking them about the civil action, and that I don't know anything about Cedar Grove Development or any links between the three murders?"

"How are you going to get them into court?" Calloway asked.

"I'm talking about at the rehearing of Cedar Grove's motion for summary judgment. I've been thinking about this for several days, how I could do it. I did a little research. I can make a request to Judge Harvey that I be allowed to put on live testimony to oppose the motion for summary judgment."

"You can do that?" Calloway asked.

"Can I? Technically yes. Will Judge Harvey allow it? I don't know." Dan sat back. "I saw it done once before, when I was practicing in Boston. I was on the opposite side. It was a conspiracy case, so the allegations were broad, and the parties didn't get along. The judge allowed it. I can get ahold of Leah and ask her to give me a hand with the research. Judge Harvey is a cowboy. He might go for it."

"How long will it take to find out?" Calloway asked.

"I can file the motion requesting live testimony at the end of the week and give six days' notice. Cedar Grove would file an opposition and Judge Harvey would decide within two weeks. If he grants the motion, we can be in front of him before the end of the month."

"I'm not sure we can stay that long, Tracy," Faz said.

"That's okay," Tracy said. "Dan and I talked this through." She looked to Calloway. "We can use the Cedar Grove rumor mill to spread the news that you're closing both the Heather Johansen and the Kimberly Armstrong investigations."

Calloway nodded, understanding where Tracy was headed. "And I'll reinstate Finlay to make it look like I've closed those files."

"The killer or killers will think they've dodged another bullet," Tracy said. "You're going to have to call off the officer outside my house as well."

"I don't agree to that," Dan said.

"Nor do I," Calloway said.

"If we're going to sell this, then we have to do it. Besides, if the killer thinks he dodged a bullet, there's no reason he would come after me."

"All right, but I'll have one of my officers make frequent drive-bys, and I'll give you a cell number to call if anything happens. You agree to let her know if you're going out and where you're going so she can be around, sniffing the air."

"And me and Vera will come back when you get the hearing," Faz said.

"*If* I get the hearing," Dan said.

Faz's cell phone rang. He put on his glasses and checked caller ID. "Kins," he said to Tracy, referring to Kinsington Rowe. "Kins, I got you on speaker. I assume you're calling about that list of names I sent over."

Tracy jumped in. "Is this the list of addresses and telephone numbers of the members of the LLCs buying the businesses on Market Street?"

"It is. But I got some questions," Kins said. "And I need some clarification because as it is, something isn't adding up."

"What do you mean?" Tracy asked.

As Kins explained the difficulty he was having, Dan looked to Tracy, and she could see the wheels spinning inside his head. Tracy thanked Kins, and Faz disconnected the call.

"Holy shit," Calloway said.

"Now what?" Tracy asked.

"I'm going to have to rethink the people I call to testify, and in what order," Dan said. He looked to Calloway and to Faz. "But I think I'm going to need to call the two of you last, if Judge Harvey even lets me get that far."

CHAPTER 31

Over the course of the next few days, Faz and Vera returned to Seattle; Dan holed up in his office, on the phone with Leah; and Roy Calloway began the process of stoking the Cedar Grove rumor mill. Calloway reinstated Finlay Armstrong and removed the officer stationed in front of Dan's house. Finlay expressed reluctance to return, but Calloway convinced him he was needed, if only until they found a replacement. Tracy stayed home with Daniella and ventured around town as if everything was fine. She wore a gun, however, hidden under the winter clothing, and dared anyone to outdraw her. It didn't take long before people in Cedar Grove started talking about the police department closing the Kimberly Armstrong investigation and Finlay's return to work.

On a cold Saturday morning, the anniversary of Heather's murder, Tracy bundled Daniella in her stroller and went to the cemetery. There she found a Presbyterian minister with Eric and Ingrid Johansen, as well as Heather's brother Oystein and his wife and three children.

"Tracy," Eric said, surprised to see her. "It's so nice of you to come."

"I'm sorry for your loss, Eric. I hope I'm not intruding."

"Of course not." He welcomed Tracy and she reintroduced herself to Oystein and to his family. "They say it gets easier with time," Eric Johansen said, viewing his daughter's headstone, "but I haven't found that to be true. You just find another way to exist. But I guess I don't have to tell you that either."

"I understand," Tracy said.

"Is this your little one?" Ingrid bent down to look into the buggy.

"This is Daniella."

The family fussed over the baby for a few minutes, then got to the ceremony, which was short, given the cold, but handled nicely. When it ended, the Johansens invited Tracy to lunch, which was also their tradition. She politely declined, knowing it was not her place. She took Daniella instead to a different section of the cemetery, where her parents and her sister, Sarah, were buried. The tombstone included Sarah's and her father's cowboy names: "Doc Crosswhite" and "The Kid."

Tracy faced the stroller so Daniella could view the tombstone, not that she could see much of anything. She was bundled so tightly she could hardly move.

Tracy knelt and picked at some of the longer strands of grass along the edge of the tombstone, tidying. "Mom, Dad, Sarah," Tracy said. "This is your granddaughter and your niece, Daniella. We've come home to Cedar Grove to visit. Dan kept his parents' house and we're hoping this can be a place of good memories for Daniella, as it once was for all of us. I want her to know where her parents grew up, and where her grandparents and her aunt Sarah lived and are buried."

She took a breath, feeling the cold in her lungs. "I don't know what kind of mother I'm going to be. Mom, I wish I had you here to give me some instruction. And Dad, I wish you were here to teach Daniella how to shoot." Tracy looked at Sarah's name. "I hope she's going to be a lot like you, Sarah. I hope she's a fighter who doesn't take crap from anyone. I know I used to say that you drove me crazy, but those were some of the best moments of my life. You would have taken on the world when you thought you were right, and I always admired you for your conviction. I miss you all . . . more now than ever before. I think Eric Johansen is right. I don't think I'll ever get over your deaths, but I hope I can find that other way to exist. I do promise you this. Daniella will get to know you all."

—

When Tracy returned home from the cemetery, Dan came out of his office to greet her. "We filed the motion this morning. Get ready for some fireworks."

"How do you feel about it?"

He shrugged. "We fashioned an argument under Civil Rule 56, which was the basis of Judge Harvey's decision to stay his ruling on the motion for summary judgment. Under section 'f,' the judge is given broad powers to make a just order. Leah also found language in Civil Rule 43, supported by a Washington appellate court case, which provides that the judge may direct that a matter be heard wholly or partially on oral testimony, and in Whatcom County, a judge has the authority to modify or suspend any civil rule to prevent a failure of justice. I argued that calling witnesses to the witness stand, in open court, and placing them under oath, is the only way to ensure honesty and to expedite the resolution of this matter. I hope that appeals to Harvey's desire to get a result."

"Do you think Rav Patel will bring in the law firm from Bellingham?" Tracy asked.

"He's going to have to. I've listed him as a witness. He prepared all the contracts for the new businesses. That will be another battle, I'm sure, but I don't want Patel acting as counsel if he is involved in this. He might see where I'm headed faster than a hired gun out of Bellingham, and I'm going to need as much lead time as possible to stay out in front. If I can get Calloway and Faz on the witness stand, we have a chance.

If not, I'll lose, and you'll have to think up some other way to find evidence to prove what happened."

Days later, Rav Patel filed his withdrawal, and the firm in Bellingham appeared on behalf of Cedar Grove. It filed an opposition to the motion for live testimony. Six days later, Judge Doug Harvey granted Dan's motion to solicit live testimony and set a Civil Rule 56(f) hearing on the motion for summary judgment.

"Brass balls," Dan said when he read Harvey's order. He'd won the motion. Now he had to get the witnesses subpoenaed to appear in court. He had to present them to the court in a way that didn't look like he was trying a criminal matter, at least until, and if, he put Calloway and Faz on the stand. He was certain Judge Harvey, while curious, did not suffer fools.

And Dan had no intention of becoming one.

CHAPTER 32

Two weeks later, Dan tried to temper his butterflies as he stood beside Larry Kaufman at counsel table in Whatcom County Superior Court. Together they watched Judge Doug Harvey enter his courtroom in his flowing black robe and ascend to his seat behind the raised bench. To Dan's left, on the other side of the lectern, Lynn Milne, a name partner at the law firm Hogan, Milne, and Peek, stood alongside two associates. Milne had filed pleadings requesting to continue the summary judgment hearing for a month, arguing she needed more time to become familiar with the case. Dan replied that this hearing was on Cedar Grove's motion for summary judgment. If Milne wasn't prepared to defend it, Cedar Grove shouldn't have filed it. He argued that if Cedar Grove dismissed the motion, Milne would have all the time in the world to prepare for the hearing. It was a challenge he hoped Milne would not accept.

She didn't.

Dan had amended his complaint to include a cause of action for civil conspiracy. Simply stated, he argued that either two or more people acted together to achieve an unlawful objective, or acted to achieve a

lawful objective by criminal means. Washington was a notice pleading state and simply required Larry Kaufman to provide notice of his
claims. He did not have to provide specifics. The civil conspiracy allega-
tion broadened the scope of his complaint, and Dan would rely heavily
on that breadth to justify his questions at the hearing. He had no doubt
Milne would object that his questions were not relevant, but he hoped
the new cause of action, and Judge Harvey's curiosity, would compel
the jurist to give Dan some leeway.

Harvey had given Milne a one-week continuance to respond to
the amended complaint and to the motion. She and her associates filed
more than fifty pages of pleadings and documents, raising new affirma-
tive defenses and highlighting the civil conspiracy cause of action—as
Dan had hoped. Milne would have a hard time objecting that Dan's
questions were not relevant when she'd spent so much time in her
papers refuting the conspiracy claim.

Dan filed a short, two-page reply, arguing that while Milne's arguments were relevant, they were not persuasive. Despite his posturing,
he was far from certain he had the better legal argument. He certainly
didn't have much authority to support his right to put on oral testimony, but Leah Battles's research had revealed something that wouldn't
be found in case law or statutes. She'd learned that Judge Harvey had
once been a battle-tested litigator with a reputation for pushing the
judicial envelope—not just citing law but creating it. He had a dozen
appellate court cases with his name attached to them.

Harvey positioned the files on his desk, his silver hair accentuated
beneath the bright fluorescent lights. The oak paneling and furniture
gave the modern courtroom a softer feel than the battered older court-
rooms in Seattle, but it remained a place of gladiators.

Before Harvey had the chance to look up from his papers, Milne
spoke. "Your Honor, Lynn Milne on behalf of Cedar Grove." Milne
wore a navy-blue skirt and jacket with a square cut that accentuated an
athletic build—broad shoulders and a thin waist. She had short brown

hair she habitually folded behind her ears. "The defense objects to the plaintiff seeking to elicit live testimony at this hearing. We offered to make the individuals whom counsel subpoenaed available for deposition and he declined."

Harvey spoke without looking up, now intently reading a legal pleading. "Does your verbal objection here in court have any authority other than the authority already cited in your fifty-plus pages of briefing?"

"It does not, Your Honor. We believe—"

Harvey removed his glasses and glanced at Milne's side of the courtroom with his piercing blue eyes. "So you are assuming I did not read your brief?"

"No, Your Honor—"

"Then you're assuming I read your brief but I am not competent to have deduced the arguments made therein?"

"No, Your Honor. We merely—"

"You merely want to reiterate the arguments you've already raised in your brief to preserve your right to appeal should this hearing result in an unfavorable decision."

Milne looked stumped. Dan didn't utter a sound.

"Your objections are noted and denied. They are preserved for appeal should your client decide to take that route." Harvey put his glasses back on and turned to Dan. "Mr. O'Leary, this is your show. Let's get to it."

"Very well, Your Honor. The plaintiff calls Rav Patel."

The bailiff stepped into the hallway and held the door open. Rav Patel entered in a mud-brown suit and a frown as he made his way to the witness stand. Attorneys were often the worst witnesses, believing their place to be on the other side of the podium, asking, not answering questions. After the clerk swore Patel to tell the truth, the Cedar Grove city attorney sat.

Dan quickly established that Patel had been the city attorney for Cedar Grove since 2013, when Gary Witherspoon became mayor, and that Patel and Witherspoon had a long history dating back to college.

"You were in the same fraternity, Tau Kappa Epsilon?"

"We were, yes."

Sensing Harvey wanted him to move quickly, Dan jumped to the matter at hand. "In the course of your position as city attorney, did you have occasion to prepare purchase and sale agreements on behalf of the City of Cedar Grove?"

"Yes," Patel said, continuing with succinct answers.

"Did you prepare the purchase and sale agreement for Cedar Grove's purchase of the Hutchins' Theater?"

"Yes."

Dan marked the exhibit and entered it into evidence, then displayed it on his laptop, which projected the document on the courtroom's computer monitors. Patel looked at the document and authenticated it. Dan went through the contracts for the purchase of the other seven businesses on Market Street. Patel affirmed he had drafted each agreement on the city's behalf.

"And when you say the city, who do you mean to be your client?"

"The city acts through its mayor and city council members," Patel said.

"Mayor Gary Witherspoon?" Dan asked.

"And the city council members, yes."

"Did you also prepare the agreements to sell those Market Street businesses to private owners?"

"Yes."

Dan marked each of those agreements and Patel authenticated them. He directed Patel to the agreement selling the Hutchins' Theater to a new owner, Barry Sewell.

"Did Mr. Sewell have legal counsel in his purchase of the Hutchins' Theater?"

"I don't know."

"Did you deal with an attorney working on Mr. Sewell's behalf?"

Patel squirmed a bit. "No."

"You worked with Mr. Sewell directly?"

"I did not speak to him, if that is what you mean."

"Did you meet with him?"

"No."

"How did you communicate with him?" Dan asked.

"My secretary obtained his email address and emailed the agreement. He signed that agreement and sent it back."

"And who is your secretary?"

"Sunnie Witherspoon."

"Is she related to the mayor?"

"Sunnie is Gary Witherspoon's wife."

"I see." Dan noticed Judge Harvey's eyebrows furrow. "And did Barry Sewell make any changes to the purchase and sale agreement?"

"No."

Dan went through the other agreements Patel had drafted to sell the other businesses and got the same responses—Patel never met nor communicated with anyone but Sunnie Witherspoon. Each agreement was sent by Sunnie to the new owners, and they returned them signed and without changes.

"Were you surprised not one of these people made any changes?"

"No," Patel said. He sounded convinced.

"Why not?"

"Because they bought the businesses for one dollar. Cedar Grove sold each for that nominal amount so the new owners could use their money to bring the buildings up to the current building codes."

"It was a heck of a deal," Dan said.

Patel shrugged. "I suppose it was."

Dan thanked Patel and sat. Milne did not bother to ask Patel any questions, and Judge Harvey excused him. When Patel descended from the witness chair, he moved to a pew in the gallery on Cedar Grove's side of the courtroom.

"Mr. O'Leary, call your next witness," Judge Harvey said.

"The plaintiff calls attorney Zack Metzger."

If Patel was alarmed to hear Metzger's name, he did a good job hiding his concern. Metzger entered the courtroom and bounded to the stand as if in a great hurry to finish testifying so he could get on to matters that made tuition money. He wore a maroon jacket with a knit tie that looked like someone had cut it off at his belt buckle. He'd pulled down the knot and unbuttoned the collar of his white shirt.

Again, Dan established Metzger's credentials. Then he asked, "Were you ever asked to create limited liability companies for individuals seeking to buy businesses in Cedar Grove?"

"Yes."

"Did you form a limited liability company on behalf of Barry Sewell to buy the Hutchins' Theater?"

"I did."

Dan had the formation papers creating the limited liability company marked and entered into evidence on the computer monitors. Again, Milne did not object. Dan suspected she was just trying to catch up.

"Did you speak to Barry Sewell about creating the limited liability company on his behalf?"

"No. It's like I told you when we met," Metzger said, "I received the paperwork from a secretary at the City of Cedar Grove."

"And do you remember that secretary's name?"

"I didn't, but I looked it up for you when we went back to my office. Her name is Sunnie Witherspoon. She works in the city attorney's office. At least that's what she told me."

Again, Harvey's reaction was subtle. He sat back, rocking his chair.

"And was all of your contact with Sunnie Witherspoon?"

"It was, but it wasn't much. She sent me the names of the members in each of the LLCs I was creating. She said the members asked for an attorney to assist in that process."

"Did Ms. Witherspoon say how she got your name?"

"She didn't."

"Where did you send all the formation papers after you prepared them?"

"I sent them back to her. She said she would forward them to the business owners. I kept copies in my office."

Dan put another exhibit on his computer monitor. "If I asked you about these other seven limited liability companies you created, would your answers be the same? That is, was all of your contact with Sunnie Witherspoon, a secretary with the Cedar Grove City Attorney?"

"My answers would be the same."

"You never actually met any of these individuals who became members of the LLCs you created?"

"I did not."

"And you didn't talk to them on the phone?"

"I did not."

Dan got Milne to stipulate to the admission of the Secretary of State papers establishing the other limited liability companies. Then he placed a blown-up exhibit on a courtroom easel with the name of each limited liability company, and below the company name, the names of each of the individual members of each corporation. He wanted those names before Judge Harvey throughout the hearing.

Dan stepped to the side of the podium, where he could watch Rav Patel. "Did you also create the limited liability company for Cedar Grove Development LLC?"

Again, Patel did not react. Milne simply looked confused, flipping through documents in a binder, searching for the company name.

Metzger confirmed he created the Cedar Grove Development LLC, but again said he never personally met with any of the company members.

"How did you communicate?" Dan asked.

"Everything was done over the Internet," Metzger said.

"Did Ms. Witherspoon get involved?"

"No."

Dan put another blown-up document on an easel, this one from the Secretary of State's Office listing the individual members of the Cedar Grove Development LLC.

Again, Milne did not question Metzger. Dan expected Metzger to leave as if shot from a cannon, but the attorney slid into a pew on Dan's side of the courtroom. He, too, looked curious as to where Dan's argument was headed.

Judge Harvey sat forward, intently gazing at the exhibit boards. The names of each company's individual members, researched by Tracy's partner, Kinsington Rowe, would have greater significance later in the hearing.

"Call your next witness," Judge Harvey said.

"Your Honor, the plaintiff calls Atticus Pelham."

Pelham entered the courtroom dressed in the same black slacks and a dark-blue down jacket. He removed the jacket, revealing a short-sleeve white shirt. After the clerk swore him in, Dan established Pelham's position as editor of the *Cedar Grove Towne Crier*.

"Mr. Pelham—"

"You can call me Atticus, Dan. Everyone does."

Judge Harvey sat forward. "This is an official hearing, Mr. Pelham, not a chance meeting at a coffee shop. You understand that, don't you?"

"Oh, yes sir. I do."

"Then let's stick with last names, or you can call the attorneys 'counselor.'"

Dan paced, though not far from the lectern. "Mr. Pelham, you've owned the *Towne Crier* for twenty years, am I right?"

"Little more than twenty, but yeah, that's about right."

"And how does the *Towne Crier* sustain itself? How do you earn a salary and pay your employees?"

"Well, some months I don't take a salary."

"And the other months?"

"We charge for the paper, a buck fifty, but really our main source of income is from advertising."

"And who advertises in the *Towne Crier*?"

"Some individuals, but mostly businesses."

"Do the businesses in Cedar Grove advertise in your newspaper?"

Milne stood, maybe just to let the court know she was alive. "Objection, Your Honor, but I don't see the relevance of this line of inquiry."

"Overruled. I'll allow it. Mr. O'Leary, keep it tight, please."

"Yes, Your Honor. Do the businesses in Cedar Grove advertise in your newspaper, Mr. Pelham?"

"Some do, but we haven't had a lot."

"Do you know why not?"

"The businesses on Market Street weren't making any money. Most had closed. Only the pharmacy, Kaufman's hardware store, the Chinese restaurant, and The Daily Perk were still in business. They supported the paper, but they didn't have money for advertising."

"Has that changed, recently?"

"It has. We started getting advertising dollars from the new businesses opening on Market Street—mostly announcing they would be open soon, that sort of thing."

"Did you have a reporter covering the new businesses opening on Market Street in Cedar Grove?"

Pelham started to answer, then looked like he swallowed a word. He cleared his throat. "Yes, I did."

"Who was that reporter?"

"Kimberly Armstrong."

"And did Kimberly Armstrong determine any change in the circumstances of Cedar Grove that might explain why people would buy failing businesses on Market Street and begin to advertise?"

"I know she was pursuing a theory she had."

"A theory for an article for the newspaper?"

"Well, I hadn't agreed to publish it, but yes."

Dan nodded. "And what was her theory?"

Milne quickly stood. "Objection, Your Honor. Hearsay. Mr. O'Leary should call Kimberly Armstrong to testify as to what she did and what she believed."

"Mr. O'Leary?" Harvey asked.

Dan nearly thanked Milne for the opening. "Your Honor, I'm sorry. I should have established that Kimberly Armstrong is dead. She died in a house fire in Cedar Grove."

"Continue."

"You said Kimberly had a theory, Mr. Pelham?" Dan asked again.

"Kimberly believed the property in the hills above Cedar Grove was going to be developed again."

"Was it developed before?"

Pelham explained the history of the site. "Kimberly said the presence of this new Cedar Grove Development company indicated the land was going to be developed into a resort, like Cascadia, and this was why new owners were willing to take the chance on new businesses in Cedar Grove."

Dan addressed Pelham. "Was Kimberly Armstrong successful in reaching the individuals who were members of Cedar Grove Development to ask them questions?"

"Not that I'm aware of."

"How about any of these new owners of the businesses on Market Street?" Dan said, gesturing to the list on the exhibit. "Did she tell you she talked to the individuals who were members of these LLCs?"

"No, she didn't tell me she had."

"Let me ask you, Mr. Pelham, as the editor of the *Towne Crier* for more than twenty years, and someone with a lot of experience in advertising revenue, in your opinion would the new businesses on Market Street be worth more money with a new development like the Cascadia resort built above Cedar Grove?"

Milne shot to her feet. "Objection—relevance. Also Mr. Pelham is not an expert on valuing businesses, so the question goes beyond his personal knowledge."

Harvey's eyes narrowed. "I'll allow it. The court will take into account that Mr. Pelham is not an expert at valuing businesses."

Pelham looked confused.

"You can answer the question," Dan said.

"I don't know about the value of those businesses, but I can tell you they'd have more money for advertising with a Cascadia-type resort. Heck, that's just common sense. Those businesses would have a couple thousand people coming to the development and into town on weekends and during vacations and holidays, and those people spend money."

"To your knowledge, did Kimberly Armstrong ever determine how far along the Cedar Grove Development company was in developing a new resort?"

"Not to my knowledge."

"When did Kimberly die?"

"Not long after she told me about the new developer."

Dan paused to give that information due weight. Then he said, "Did you ever speak to anyone, besides Kimberly, about the possible redevelopment?"

"No," Pelham said.

"Did you ever talk to Cedar Grove's mayor, Gary Witherspoon?"

"Oh that. Yes, I did, but just in passing. Gary told me he knew nothing about it."

Milne again shot to her feet. "Move to strike. Hearsay."

"Sustained," Harvey said.

Dan didn't care. The information was out. Dan thanked Pelham and sat. Milne took the opportunity to establish that Pelham had no expertise in valuing businesses. Then she, too, sat. Her tactic appeared to be the less said, the better.

Dan also knew that he had not yet hurt her case, and he would have to do so, or they would all get tossed out.

CHAPTER 33

Tracy felt like the proverbial cat on the hot tin roof waiting at home with Vera and Daniella while the hearing went forward at the Whatcom County Superior Court, but they all had agreed that her attendance would be a bad idea.

"They can't see this as a criminal matter," Dan had said that night at the kitchen table. "If they do, they'll object, and I won't get the chance to put on Roy, let alone Faz. I suspect Judge Harvey, no matter how curious he might be, will draw the line somewhere."

Calloway agreed. "If you're in the gallery, they're going to know you aren't just a spectator watching her husband. Your reputation as a homicide detective precedes you."

They were right, Tracy knew, but rationalizing didn't make waiting at home any easier. She'd asked Roy to call and provide her with updates, but Dan didn't want Roy or Faz waiting in the hall with the other witnesses, for the same reason he didn't want Tracy there. He told the two men to wait at a coffee shop in Bellingham. He would phone or text them when the time for them to testify approached.

"Let's go for a walk," Vera said, getting up from the couch. "It's supposed to snow again this afternoon. Let's get Daniella outside while the weather is cooperating."

"I think I better stay," Tracy said. "I won't be much company as it is, and I want to be available in case Dan or Roy has a question or needs anything." Tracy had the three criminal files open on the kitchen table.

"Are you sure?" Vera said, entering the room in her winter clothing. "Fresh air clears the mind. It's always worked for me."

"I'll get out in the back for a bit, but I want to stay close to the files."

"Okay," Vera said. "You need anything while I'm out?"

Tracy didn't.

"Find something to do with your time so you don't go stir-crazy."

"Too late," Tracy said.

—

After lunch, Dan called Celia Reed to the witness stand, the woman who had assisted him at the Whatcom County building department. Dan quickly established Reed's credentials, and she testified as to the history of the three parcels, including the sale of the property from the State of Washington to the Cedar Grove Development company. Dan put up a court exhibit with the three parcels of land outlined on a map. He established there had not yet been any pre-application meetings to discuss development of these three parcels, and he had not been able to locate any topographical surveys.

"So Whatcom County isn't aware of any development activity to indicate these three parcels of property are going to be developed?"

"There is nothing in our files."

Again, Milne did not ask any questions.

After Reed, Dan called upon a real estate and construction expert he'd used in his other cases, and with whom he'd met during the weeks before the hearing date. William Peters had expertise in commercial and residential real estate, as well as in the development of property. Tall and lanky, Peters had played college basketball before entering the workforce. He approached the witness stand in a gait like he could still step onto a court and play the game.

After establishing Peters's credentials, Dan asked, "Are you familiar with the necessary steps to the development of a piece of property?"

Peters was, and he proceeded to outline those steps.

"Did I ask you to determine if there had been any development activity for these three parcels of land?" Dan used a pen as a pointer and roughly circled the three tracts on the exhibit board propped on an easel.

Milne stood. "Your Honor, I believe we're getting far afield here."

"Is there an objection, Counsel?" Harvey asked.

"Relevance, Your Honor."

"Mr. O'Leary, we do seem to be veering off course here."

This was where Dan had expected to get the relevance objections, and he had a ready response he hoped would persuade Judge Harvey to grant him leeway and hoist Milne by her own petard. "Your Honor, conspiracies are by their very nature difficult to prove because they are done surreptitiously. Counsel filed more than fifty pages of pleadings on that very topic. I fail to see how she can now argue the cause of action is not relevant."

Harvey nodded and Dan thought he saw a thin smile. "You did overwhelm my staff, Counselor," he said to Milne. "I'll allow the questions, Mr. O'Leary, but I want to see a connection—soon."

"Did you do anything to determine if the property was in a stage of pre-development?" Dan asked Peters.

"Yes. I drove out to the site of those three parcels on the exhibit, and I noted that the trees had been surveyed."

"What does that mean?"

"In many counties in Puget Sound, trees that are eight inches or more in diameter five feet above the ground cannot be removed without a permit."

"How do you know the trees on those three parcels had been surveyed if there was nothing in the building department files?"

"The trees that met the requirements I just described had silver tags about the width of a gum wrapper tacked to their trunks."

"Do you know by whom?"

"Not from the tags. There is just a number."

"Did you try to determine who put the tags on the trees?"

"I called the number for the Cedar Grove Development company."

"Did you speak to anyone?"

"No. I got a message machine."

"Did you do anything else?"

"I looked online for arborists in the area who perform topographical surveys. I found three."

"Did one of the three do a topographical survey on these three properties?"

"Yes. The Bellingham Tree Company. I called and spoke to the president of the company, Carol Gilmore, and she confirmed they performed the topographical survey last summer."

"Did she say for whom they performed the survey?"

"She didn't." Peters corrected himself. "I guess I should say she wouldn't?"

"What do you mean she wouldn't?"

"Some developers want to keep a project quiet, for any number of reasons."

"In your experience, as an expert, what are some reasons a developer would not want the public to know it was developing a site?"

Milne stood and objected. "This is pure speculation, Your Honor."

"He's an expert. He can speculate," Harvey said. "I'll allow it. But, Mr. O'Leary, are we getting to the point any time soon?"

"We are, Your Honor."

"I hope so."

Dan repeated his question.

"When word of a development gets out, the land around the development increases in value. The developer will often seek to purchase that additional land to expand a project, if popular, in later years. You can also get blowback from environmental groups who don't want the land developed. Those organizations can tie up a project in courts for years. Developers like to get as much done as quietly as possible so that when the development becomes public knowledge, they are ready to counter any negative publicity with details of the resort, models, and amenities, that sort of thing."

"What else did I ask you to do?"

"I was asked to determine the value of the businesses on Market Street at present, and the value if a development project were to go in, a resort."

"How did you do the valuation?"

"I used three comparable pieces of property with characteristics similar to Cedar Grove." For the next twenty minutes, Peters identified the other resorts and how he'd calculated the value of the businesses before the resorts went in, and the value of those businesses after the resorts had been constructed. He discussed the unique aspects of each resort, and the unique aspects of the Cedar Grove area.

"And taking all of that into consideration, what did you find with regard to the value of the businesses on Market Street in Cedar Grove?"

"The value of those businesses should increase significantly, as will the value of homes."

"Can you put a percentage on it?"

"Not to any degree, but the three comparable properties I've mentioned should be a good comparison."

After half an hour of cross-examination by Milne, Peters was dismissed.

"Call your next witness, Mr. O'Leary."

Dan called Gary Witherspoon. Witherspoon entered the courtroom looking nervous, but not overly concerned, that is until he saw the blowups of the companies and the names of the individual members of the LLCs. Then he paled.

Dan quickly established Witherspoon's position as mayor. He looked the part in a suit and tie. As a young man, Witherspoon had dishwater-blond hair that nearly touched his shoulders, like a surfer. Most of that hair was now gone, and what remained had significantly receded.

"As mayor, you've been involved in a dedicated plan to redevelop Market Street. Is that a fair assessment on my part?"

"Yes, that's fair," Witherspoon said, his eyes darting again to one of the exhibits.

"Can you explain to the court how you are achieving that?"

"A lot of ways." Witherspoon sipped from a glass of water. "My first order of business was to move the city government into the First National Bank building, which has historic significance and is on Market Street near the merchants. I felt it was important to hear what they had to say so we could decide collectively what we needed to do to rebuild the city."

"What did you do next?"

"I went after grants and federal loans to revitalize our downtown and improve our image. We're rebuilding around Cedar Grove's unique heritage and attributes." Witherspoon was giving a sales pitch, and Dan was happy to let him give it. "Cedar Grove needed a lively civic center that would attract college-educated millennials with entrepreneurial ambition. You fill a city with young talent, and people and their money will follow. We're about to begin a streetscape project, adding trees, patterned brickwork sidewalks, and pedestrian lighting. And we're in the process of refurbishing the façades of the Market Street buildings with state funds. It isn't costing Cedar Grove citizens a penny."

"Mr. Witherspoon, why would these new owners invest money in businesses that had failed for decades?"

"Because we're selling the businesses for a dollar. That allows the new owners to put their money into modernizing the building. We've also begun a comprehensive marketing campaign emphasizing Cedar Grove's proximity to the mountains, and to lakes and rivers. We're emphasizing outdoor activities like rafting and fishing, hiking, biking, and cross-country and downhill skiing. People who come to Cedar Grove for these activities will need a place to eat and drink. They'll need prescriptions filled and maybe pay to see a movie."

Time to get to the point. "Are you aware of the limited liability company Cedar Grove Development LLC?"

"I am not."

"Did you have a conversation with Atticus Pelham regarding the potential revitalization of the Cascadia resort?"

Witherspoon backtracked. "Oh yes. Atticus brought up the subject of a potential new developer last summer at the jazz festival. He didn't use a name."

"What did he tell you?"

"He said Kimberly Armstrong learned that someone had bought the old Cascadia property—a developer. I told Atticus I hadn't heard any such thing, but I'd certainly welcome it."

"Did you try to determine if Kimberly had been accurate?"

"I didn't, no."

"You didn't call the Whatcom County building department?"

"I didn't."

"As mayor trying to revitalize the downtown and bring in new businesses, wouldn't that have been an important piece of information to sell Cedar Grove to new business investors?"

"I guess, but . . . well, I've been pretty busy," Witherspoon said, looking and sounding less than convincing.

"Did you speak to any of the new business owners on Market Street?"

"Not personally, no."

"You never welcomed them to Cedar Grove?"

"The buildings are still undergoing building code repairs. There will be plenty of time to welcome the new owners when they're up and running."

Dan went through each business and each individual member. Witherspoon denied knowing or speaking to any of them. "Did you ever talk with your wife about these new owners?"

"She told me she'd helped with the paperwork and the contracts, that sort of thing."

"Did you ever tell my client that he had to perform expensive repairs to his building?"

"I didn't, no."

"Did you have a building inspector tell him that?"

"He may have sent him a letter. I'm not sure."

"You don't know?"

"I don't know."

Dan got what he wanted from Witherspoon and released him. Milne asked no questions.

As Witherspoon stepped down from the witness stand, Dan lit the first firework. "Plaintiffs call Roy Calloway."

Witherspoon spun on his heels and looked to Dan.

Lynn Milne stood. "Objection."

CHAPTER 34

Tracy stood outside the shower, thinking hot water might soothe her nerves. When he'd remodeled, Dan installed a steam shower in the master bath, with jet sprays at various heights along the back wall, and a bench seat. He'd also outfitted the bathroom with high-end speakers, telling Tracy that he equated a steam to something close to a heavenly experience. Tracy didn't share his enthusiasm. She didn't particularly like hot water. She'd never been one of those people who could just sit in a sauna or a hot tub. It seemed like a waste of time. With Daniella now in the picture, Tracy didn't like to linger where she couldn't hear her daughter, even when Dan or Therese were present. Normally, she was in and out of the shower in minutes.

With Vera taking Daniella on a walk, and the stress of the weeks manifesting in her neck and shoulders, Tracy decided to give the steam another chance. At the moment, she had nothing but time while Dan went forward with the hearing in Bellingham. She hadn't heard from him, which she assumed was good news.

She set her phone on the sink counter, streamed the music to the high-end speakers, and chose Dan's classical music station. She lowered the volume, and stepped into the shower. For the next twenty minutes, she let the pulsating streams of hot water massage her muscles and help her to relax. She shut off the water, wrapped herself in one of the luxury spa towels Dan had bought to further accentuate the experience, and cleared a streak on the mirror above the sink.

The image staring back looked tired, dark circles prominent beneath both eyes, and her crow's-feet seemingly more pronounced. Maybe being a mother and a homicide detective was too much. Maybe she was burning the candle at both ends and not doing a very good job of either. Maybe her place was at home with her daughter. Maybe she should reconsider the life she had once dreamed of, as a little girl, a life raising her children and becoming involved in Daniella's school and activities and taking carloads of kids on field trips. She smiled at the irony of her thoughts. She couldn't even take a twenty-minute steam without thinking of something better to do with her time. Now she was contemplating spending hours at home just being a mom.

"You'd make yourself crazy," she said to the image in the mirror.

She wasn't built that way. The dream, like most dreams, had been at a time before Tracy truly knew herself and what made her tick. Roy Calloway was right. She was a lot like her father and becoming more like him every year—a compulsive overachiever, a person who liked her work and liked helping others, and someone who hated injustice.

A lot of women had children and careers. She'd be one of them.

She lifted a cream from her counter and rubbed it into her face, then used another on her arms and her legs. She went into her bedroom. The doorbell rang, which caused the dogs to bark.

Vera?

She looked at the clock on the dresser. Only thirty minutes had passed since Vera had left on a walk with Daniella. Tracy looked to the window. It wasn't snowing. Thirty minutes seemed a short time for Vera to be gone, and why would she have used the doorbell?

The bell rang a second time. The dogs continued to sound the alarm.

Tracy pulled on sweatpants and a sweatshirt and hurried down the hall. The doorbell rang a third time.

"Hang on," Tracy called out. "Rex, Sherlock. Go basket." She clapped her hands. The two dogs dutifully went back to their beds, though they remained upright, intent on viewing this visitor.

When Tracy reached the door, she looked out the side windowpane. She did not see her Subaru in the driveway, which Vera had driven so she didn't have to transfer the car seat. Confused, she pulled open the door.

"I figured if you were not going to come to me, I was going to come to you," Sunnie Witherspoon said, hands on her hips, a purse dangling from her right forearm and a bag in her other hand. "Tracy Crosswhite, have you been avoiding me?"

CHAPTER 35

M ilne had the eager look Rex and Sherlock got each time Dan mentioned the word "walk." She nearly pranced to the lectern, and she clearly had been waiting for this opportunity to pounce. Dan wondered if her prior deer-in-headlights look had been just an act.

"Your Honor," Milne said, "we've been here all morning and we've listened to testimony on the value of property, on a supposed developer in the foothills above Cedar Grove, and speculation that the businesses in Cedar Grove will increase in value. None of this amounts to a city acting in a private business transaction, or of a conspiracy. To the contrary, the city's purchase of dying businesses and its resale of those same businesses to persons willing to make a go of it, even persons who could reap the benefit of a potential redevelopment, will be a win for all of Cedar Grove, which is exactly what the mayor and the city council are supposed to do—act in the best interests of the citizenry. Mr. O'Leary hasn't proven private business dealings; he's proven the appropriate application of the public duty doctrine. Now he's called to the stand the former Cedar Grove chief of police, for what purpose I do not know, but I fail to see how this witness can add to any argument that the city engaged in a private transaction."

Harvey looked to Dan. This was the objection Dan expected. He had known all along Calloway would be the tipping point he needed to get past, and he couldn't count on Harvey's curiosity being the weight that caused it to tip in his favor.

"Your Honor, we've established that the City of Cedar Grove was buying and selling properties, which is not a traditional city action. We have proven that a limited liability company called Cedar Grove Development has purchased and started the process of developing a resort above Cedar Grove that could make those businesses, including my client's business, worth a lot more than the city paid for them. But beyond that, as I've said, conspiracies are not done in the open, they are done in a room with the doors closed and the drapes pulled tightly shut."

"Yes, but to get past a motion for summary judgment, you need to pull back the drape and let in some sunlight, Counselor. I agree with Ms. Milne. It's still pretty dark in the room."

Dan persisted. "What we have shown so far is that Cedar Grove bought back the businesses for next to nothing and sold them to entities that stand to reap a substantial profit either running the business or selling it—if and when the mountain resort is developed."

"So what? That's a benefit to the new owners, a smart business move on their part."

"But if the mayor and the city council knew of the resort when they bought back the businesses and didn't tell the prior owners, that's a different scenario."

"The city is under no obligation to tell the former owners of a potential development, which might never occur," Milne said. "The former owners had an obligation to determine the value of the businesses they sold. If they did not, that's their fault. I don't see how this testimony dictates against application of the public duty doctrine."

"I'm sorry, Mr. O'Leary, but I gave you a lot of rope—" Harvey started.

"Your Honor, the court has been patient, I agree. But as I said, if a conspiracy was easy to prove, there would be no conspiracy. I will represent to the court that we are getting close to the end, and when I get there I won't have to explain what we can prove to you or to opposing counsel. I intend to hit you over the head with it like Moe from The Three Stooges. It will be very clear. I have just two more witnesses, after which, we'll submit the matter to the court's discretion."

Harvey smiled. "I grew up watching The Three Stooges, Counselor." It was clear Harvey was debating which way to lean. If he did not allow Calloway and Faz to testify, then Larry Kaufman would lose. More than that, Tracy and Calloway might never determine who had killed Heather Johansen, Jason Mathews, and Kimberly Armstrong, if it had been the same person.

"I'll give you a little more leash, but don't make me look like Joe DeRita. I want to be one of the relevant Stooge brothers."

Dan stifled a sigh of relief. "I won't do that, Judge."

Milne shook her head and sat.

Calloway took the stand dressed in civilian clothing. Dan quickly went through his background and got to the point. "Did you investigate the death of Kimberly Armstrong?"

"I did. I called Seattle and ordered the investigation by an arson specialist."

"You thought the fire that killed Kimberly Armstrong was deliberately set?"

"I knew the fire was deliberately set. We located a gas can and could smell gasoline in the burned-out remains of the house. The house also went up like a pile of straw, with black smoke billowing hundreds of feet in the air, indicating an accelerant. I wanted to confirm my suspicion."

Dan introduced the arson investigator's report. Milne objected on the grounds of relevance, but Harvey admitted it. "Did you initiate any further investigation?"

"I called in a medical examiner from Seattle to do the autopsy of Kimberly Armstrong because I suspected she did not die from the fire."

"What did the medical examiner determine?"

"The medical examiner determined that Kimberly Armstrong died from blunt-force trauma to the back of the skull before the fire was set. The fire was set to cover the evidence of her murder."

With those two sentences it felt as if someone had sucked the air out of the room. Dan looked at Harvey, who was no longer reading or taking notes. He was staring at Chief Calloway.

"Chief Calloway, did you find any notes or binders of materials regarding any stories that Kimberly Armstrong was working on at the time she was murdered?" Dan asked.

"No. The arson investigator said the fire was started in Kimberly's home office, that the office had been doused with gasoline, and her husband said that all of Kimberly's research, including her computer, went up in smoke."

"Did you attempt to determine what articles Kimberly Armstrong was pursuing at the time she was murdered?"

"I spoke to her editor, Atticus Pelham, of the *Towne Crier*, and I learned that Kimberly had been investigating an entity that had purchased the three parcels of property shown on that map over there. A company called Cedar Grove Development."

Dan waited, though only a beat, but in that brief second you could hear people behind him murmuring. Then he said, "Chief Calloway, you said you suspected that Kimberly Armstrong didn't die in the fire even before you received the arson and medical examiner reports. Why did you suspect that?"

"Objection," Milne said.

"Overruled," Harvey said before Milne had even fully risen from her chair. "Continue Chief Calloway."

"Because I knew Kimberly was also investigating the murder of a young woman in 1993, Heather Johansen. Kimberly had obtained our police file on that investigation, and she had been gathering reports on Johansen's murder and asking a lot of questions of people around town."

"And did you think Kimberly Armstrong's murder was somehow related to her investigation of Heather Johansen's death?"

"I did."

"Why?"

"Because what Kimberly Armstrong learned from the police file was that Heather Johansen had been pregnant at the time of her death. We'd never disclosed that information. We also didn't disclose that, in the medical examiner's opinion, Heather Johansen became pregnant around the Christmas holiday. In addition, Heather, like Kimberly, was killed by a blow to the back of her head from a blunt-force object. So I was operating under an assumption that whoever had murdered Heather might have also murdered Kimberly Armstrong to keep her from investigating Heather's murder."

Milne stood, this time looking exasperated. "We are way off course here. You told counsel to stay on course and he has taken a left turn to nowhere."

"Overruled," Harvey said quietly, without even looking in Milne's direction. "Continue."

"Chief Calloway, who was your primary suspect in the deaths of Heather Johansen and Kimberly Armstrong?"

"The primary suspect in Heather Johansen's murder was Heather's former high school boyfriend, Finlay Armstrong. The primary suspect in Kimberly Armstrong's murder was Kimberly's husband, my deputy, Finlay Armstrong."

CHAPTER 36

Tracy hadn't been avoiding Sunnie, not entirely, but spending time with her while Dan sued Gary for fraud and conspiracy would have been more than a little uncomfortable, and even more so now that they suspected Gary and Ed in matters far worse than fraud.

"Sunnie. Hi," was all she could manage.

"Well, are you going to invite me in or make me stand out here and freeze to death in the snow? I picked us up some lunch. Nothing special—sandwiches and drinks."

"Sorry. Yes, come in, please." Tracy stepped back and allowed Sunnie into the house, closing the door and shutting out the wind. The dogs came forward, barking and sniffing. Sunnie looked uncomfortable. "Hang on. Let me lock them in the back." Tracy walked to the rear of the house. The two dogs once again shot out the dog door into the snow, playing. Tracy shut the laundry room door.

When she returned to the family room, Sunnie remained standing in the entryway. "I think it's high time I saw that little girl of yours. I've heard she's cute as a button."

"I've been busy, Sunnie. I thought it best to call after Dan's case resolved."

Sunnie waved the thought away. "Forget about that case. Gary says it will get resolved soon, maybe today."

"Today?" Tracy asked, playing dumb.

"Gary got a subpoena to appear in Whatcom County Superior Court this morning. He said it was for the business suit with Larry Kaufman. Didn't Dan tell you?"

Tracy shrugged and did her best to deflect her knowledge. "Dan mentioned a hearing but he didn't say anything about subpoenaing Gary."

"That doesn't involve *us* anyway," Sunnie said. "We've been friends since we were old enough to walk. I told Gary that up front, when he said Dan was representing Larry Kaufman. I said, *Gary, I don't want to hear about that case. That's between you and Dan. Don't you let it ruin my friendship with Tracy.* Business is business, but friendships last a lifetime." She gave Tracy a hug.

"Come on in," Tracy said, leading Sunnie into the kitchen and family room.

"I still can't believe this was Dan's parents' house. Well, it's cute. Very homey," Sunnie said, as if describing a dollhouse. "It's nice that Dan kept it small."

Tracy bit her tongue. "Well there's only the three of us, and it will be a vacation home."

"Speaking of which," Sunnie said, looking about. "Where is the little angel?"

Tracy noticed Sunnie's gaze lingering on the police files open on the kitchen table. "She's out with her godmother getting some sun."

"Oh, that is a shame." Sunnie walked to the kitchen table and looked at the files. "Are you working? You haven't retired yet?"

Tracy crossed to the table and casually closed the files. "Let me get these out of the way," she said. "And we'll eat." The last thing Tracy wanted was for Sunnie to leave and tell her husband and father-in-law Tracy was still looking into the murders of Heather Johansen, Jason Mathews, and Kimberly Armstrong.

"Is that the Heather Johansen case? Ed said you asked him questions about it. He said you were working with Chief Roy on it. I hope I'm not out of place here, Tracy, but why would you want to dredge that up again, especially after what happened in that retrial. I think some things are just better left buried."

"I think you're right," Tracy said. "I guess that's why Roy shut it down—a dead end."

Sunnie set her purse and grocery bag on the table and shrugged the jacket from her shoulders, draping it over the back of a chair while Tracy moved the files out of the room. "At least you have help with the baby. I had four under the age of ten—"

"I recall," Tracy said from the living room.

"Gary never would have sprung for a nanny—not that I can even think of a nanny in Cedar Grove. The best I got was a babysitter once a month so we could go to a show, or have an early dinner," Sunnie said, repeating her conversation from several weeks earlier.

"Sounds like things are changing for you, though," Tracy said as she reentered the room.

"How's that?" Sunnie asked.

"You said you bought your parents' home, which was beautiful."

Sunnie didn't sound happy. "I inherited that. Gary didn't spend a dime. He wanted to sell it. I told him, *No way*. I knew that was my one chance to get a nice home. But it was dated by the time my mother finally died. I had to gut all the bathrooms and the kitchen . . . You'll have to come out so I can show you everything I've done. It's all new and bright. We put in skylights and larger windows."

Tracy remembered the Witherspoons' home to have been a lot like her parents' home, a Victorian-era structure with historic charm and significance. Her father spent years restoring the Mattioli mansion to its original luster. Gutting it would have been a four-letter word to him.

"We couldn't very well entertain in that old home, not with Gary being the mayor and all," Sunnie continued. "It would have been embarrassing." Sunnie paused to catch her breath. An awkward pause followed.

"Aren't you going to offer me coffee? It smells delicious," Sunnie said.

"Sure. Of course. I'm sorry, Sunnie. I just stepped out of the shower when I heard the doorbell. I didn't even think about it." Tracy walked behind the stove, opening a cabinet and removing a mug.

"Gary has so many meetings now, we needed a home that reflected his position here in town," Sunnie continued, making it sound as though Gary had become state governor, exaggerating as she had always done.

Tracy filled the cup with the coffee Vera made. "Sugar or cream?"

"I'll take it as it is." Sunnie accepted the cup and sipped her coffee. "This is good. Look at you, being all domestic." She sat in a chair at the table. "So funny to hear you talking about being a mom."

"Why?" Tracy moved to the opposite side of the table and sat across from her.

"I guess maybe I just got used to you being a homicide detective, and now . . . Being a mom was all you ever wanted when we were growing up. Remember? You wanted to teach chemistry at the high school, have three kids, and live right here in Cedar Grove next door to your sister."

"Plans change."

"Tell me about it. I was the one with plans."

"You wanted to move to Los Angeles and become an actress, or to Nashville to pursue a country music career."

Sunnie sipped her coffee, then said, "I guess all our plans changed."

Tracy bristled at the comparison of Sunnie's "career change" to hers. Tracy's life had been turned upside down when a psychopath killed her sister and her family imploded. Her husband walked out on her, her father killed himself, and her mother became a recluse. Tracy had been left alone. Sunnie got pregnant straight out of high school, and not after she got married, which was just what her family tried to get everyone to believe, then she had four children before she was thirty.

"I guess so," Tracy said, not seeing a point in dredging up the past.

"You and Dan are happy?"

"Very," Tracy said.

"That's another one I never saw coming. You were so different growing up. You were kind of the 'it' girl in high school."

"I don't think there was an 'it' girl at Cedar Grove High," Tracy said.

"Please. You were student body president, played volleyball and soccer, and you and your sister were two of the best shooters in the state. Do you still compete in the shooting competitions?"

"Not with Daniella so young. I don't really have time. But I'd like to teach her, when she's older. I think it's empowering for a young girl to be able to take care of herself."

"Empowering," Sunnie said softly. "You sound like your father. You remember he tried to teach me."

"I remember. You were a pretty good shot."

"Never like you or Sarah though. I could never beat you."

"You had other things on your mind with all those singing and acting lessons."

Sunnie smiled, but she didn't look happy. She sipped her coffee and looked to the window, as if expecting someone, then set down the mug. "You know there never were any singing or acting lessons," she said, her voice subdued for a change.

Tracy had suspected as much, and very early on, but she knew it would be more hurtful to call Sunnie on the lie. Sarah, on the other hand, had never cared much for Sunnie, and voiced often her disbelief.

"What?" Tracy said, trying to look and sound surprised. "What about all those auditions—and all those commercials?"

"There were no auditions . . . or commercials." Sunnie shrugged. "My mom drove down to Bellingham on the weekends to care for her parents when they were elderly. I just made up that stuff because it was more exciting. I wanted people to think I was off on exotic adventures, like you and Sarah."

"You didn't have to make anything up, Sunnie."

Sunnie gave Tracy that same defeated grin. "Do you know how hard it was to be friends with you?"

"What?"

"To always be the afterthought?"

"That's not true, Sunnie."

"Of course it's true. Everyone knew you and Sarah. You were Doc Crosswhite's daughters. You were the pistol-shooting champs. People used to see you and Sarah downtown, and they'd light up and ask you all kinds of questions about the last competition, and I'd just be standing there, the third wheel, looking like an idiot. I was always your third wheel."

Tracy dismissed it, to be polite, but she knew there was some truth to what Sunnie said. People in town would stop her and Sarah outside the pharmacy or Hutchins' Theater to talk about the most recent competitions, and to congratulate them on their success. Dan couldn't have cared less about the attention. He went inside the store and did his own thing. Sunnie, though, clearly had been bothered. Tracy recalled her as a young girl, standing on the sidewalk, as if waiting for the person to direct their inquiries to her. They never did. That was about the time Sunnie started talking about her acting and singing lessons, and about the auditions in Bellingham. By the time they reached high school, Sunnie had moved to another group of friends, and she and Tracy drifted apart. They'd remained cordial to one another, but Tracy imagined Sunnie had moved on because she'd fallen into a spiderweb of lies and had become more and more entangled, until she couldn't get herself free.

That thought, the spider's web, caused Tracy to turn to where she'd placed the three files on the table, though she was not completely certain why. She turned back to Sunnie. She wanted to say something. She wanted to tell Sunnie she was sorry if she had done anything to make Sunnie feel dismissed, but she also didn't want to look like she pitied her. That, she knew, would be a greater slap in the face, one Sunnie would not tolerate well. A knock on the door saved her from saying anything.

"Let me see who that is," she said, standing from the table and moving to the door. She hoped it was Vera and Daniella.

She pulled the door open. Finlay Armstrong stood on the porch, dressed in his khaki police uniform and bulky green coat.

"Finlay?" Tracy said, wondering if Finlay had been sent to watch her. She played coy. "What are you doing here?"

CHAPTER 37

Dan put his hands behind his back, speaking softly but deliberately. "Do you still believe the two murders are related, Chief Calloway?"

"I do."

"Is Finlay Armstrong still your primary suspect in either murder?"

"No."

"Why not?"

"I believe the person who killed Kimberly Armstrong did so to prevent her from making public the information she had learned about the potential redevelopment of a resort in the mountains above Cedar Grove, a resort that would stand to make that person very wealthy if it succeeded."

"Do you have any suspects?"

Calloway pointed. "The people who formed Cedar Grove Development."

Dan had pushed this envelope about as far as possible. Faz would be the witness to ignite the biggest and most explosive fireworks. He thanked Calloway and sat. Lynn Milne didn't even attempt to cross-examine

Calloway. She looked like she had walked in halfway through a meeting and had no idea what was happening. Before she could voice any objection, Dan quickly called his final witness, Vic Fazzio.

Faz walked into the courtroom looking like an Italian gumba about to stand trial for capping someone in a car. He wore loafers, cream-colored slacks, a navy-blue sport coat, a white shirt, and a blue tie with red horizontal stripes. When he stepped onto the witness dais, he dwarfed the courtroom clerk who swore him in.

Faz sat and looked up at Judge Harvey. "Good afternoon, Your Honor."

"Mr. Fazzio," Harvey said.

Faz turned his attention to Dan and they quickly dispensed with the preliminaries. "You work in the Seattle Violent Crimes Section?"

"I do."

"Could you tell the court what you're doing in Cedar Grove?"

"Sure. I'm freezing." Faz got a chuckle out of Harvey and those in the gallery. "Actually I came up here because Tracy Crosswhite, one of my partners in the Violent Crimes Section, needed help with cases she was investigating."

"Which cases?"

"The murders of Heather Johansen and Kimberly Armstrong."

For the next ten minutes Faz explained the seeming connection between those two cases, as well as the connection to Jason Mathews. Then he said, "As part of my investigation, I traveled to Scottsdale, Arizona, and met with the former bartender of the Four Points Tavern."

"What did you learn?"

"I learned that two weeks before Jason Mathews was shot, Mathews had a meeting in the tavern with Ed Witherspoon, the former Cedar Grove mayor."

Dan glanced to the gallery where Gary Witherspoon sat, still pale and now looking scared. Roy Calloway had taken a seat at the end of the same row, closest to the door.

"What else did you learn in the course of your investigation?"

"I learned that December 24, 1992, Ed Witherspoon threw a Christmas Eve party attended by Heather Johansen, and that either he, or someone at that party, drove Heather home that night. I also learned that the medical examiner's report concluded that Heather Johansen was pregnant when murdered, and the date of her conception coincided with the date of the Christmas Eve party, or very close to it."

Milne stood. "Your honor the defense would like a standing relevancy objection to Detective Fazzio's testimony."

"Denied," Harvey said. "A conspiracy is the perpetration of acts for criminal purposes. His testimony is, therefore, relevant."

Capitalizing on that statement, Dan was about to ask the question everyone had waited for. "Detective Fazzio, what is the relevance of your investigation to a business dispute in Cedar Grove between my client, Larry Kaufman, and the City of Cedar Grove?"

"The relevance is: Kimberly Armstrong was investigating the potential development of Cedar Grove by the recently formed Cedar Grove Development company, as well as all of the businesses that were being bought and sold in Cedar Grove, and that put her life at risk."

"And why would that put her life at risk?"

"Because the whole thing is a scam."

Milne shot from her chair. "Objection, Your Honor. Move to strike. There is no foundation that this witness has any basis for such a statement. It's an improper opinion, and I reiterate, it's not relevant to the reason we are here."

"Sustained," Harvey said. "But I think the reason we all came here today went out the window about two witnesses ago, didn't it, Mr. O'Leary?"

"I can lay a foundation, Your Honor."

"I'm hoping you can, because I don't have hearings like this . . . well, ever. And I'd hate to throw all this evidence out."

Dan looked to Faz. "How do you know that the transactions involving the businesses on Market Street in Cedar Grove are a scam?"

"Because I looked into the names of every person you have listed on those exhibits, Exhibits 3 and 4."

Dan walked to Exhibit 3 and pointed to the list of the limited liability companies that had been formed to purchase the businesses in downtown Cedar Grove, which included the names of the members of each company. "You looked up the members of each of these limited liability companies? And what did you learn?"

"I learned that all those people are dead."

Dan waited. You could have heard a pin drop inside the courtroom. Then he said, "You're telling this court that each of the individuals named as a member of each of these limited liability companies is dead?"

"That's exactly what I'm saying."

"What else did you learn in your investigation?"

"I learned that every one of those people, at one time or another over several decades, had either purchased or sold a home in one of the cities outside of Cedar Grove, which explained how the person or persons who fraudulently formed those companies had those individuals' social security numbers, bank accounts, even their signatures, which could therefore be forged."

"And did those people have a real estate agent?"

"Ed Witherspoon," Faz said.

Milne didn't even bother to object. She turned and looked to Rav Patel as if to ask, *What the hell have you got me into?* Patel, however, was staring at Gary Witherspoon, who sat as if frozen in his seat.

"The companies doing business in Cedar Grove are just shells," Faz continued. "So is the Cedar Grove Development company. In my opinion, it's all one big conspiracy to make someone or some people very rich."

CHAPTER 38

Finlay looked at Tracy, clearly perplexed by her question asking him what he was doing at her home. "What do you mean?"

Outside, it had started to snow. Tracy looked past Finlay, then up the street, hoping Vera and Daniella were on their way home. "Come inside," she said, not wanting to let out the warmth in the room.

Finlay removed his hat and stepped inside the house. He turned toward the kitchen table. "Hey, Sunnie."

"Hi, Finlay."

Tracy shut the door, expecting Finlay to tell her why he was there, though he appeared self-conscious with Sunnie in the room. When Finlay said nothing, Tracy sensed something wrong. "What's up?" she asked.

Finlay looked even more perplexed. "I don't know."

Tracy shook her head. "I have no idea."

Finlay looked to Sunnie, who sipped her coffee, then directed his gaze back to Tracy. "I got a call from dispatch. She said you called and asked that I come here ASAP."

Tracy shook her head. "Why would I have called dispatch? I would have just called your cell—"

And in that instant, that moment Tracy had experienced just before the doorbell had rung, when the dogs barked and her train of thought had been interrupted, came rushing back to her—the reason Tracy had looked to where the files had been on the kitchen table. She had thought specifically of the Heather Johansen file, and that spiderweb she'd imagined, the one that Sunnie had spun as a young girl from a simple lie, until that web had entangled her so tight she saw no way out of it.

Her thoughts came quickly now. Ed Witherspoon would not have been in any condition to drive Heather home from the Christmas Eve party. He always drank too much. Barbara might have driven her, but Ed wouldn't have asked Barbara. He would have asked someone else, readily available, to do it. He would have asked his son, Gary.

Tracy turned toward the kitchen table. Sunnie stood, no longer holding a coffee mug. She held a revolver.

CHAPTER 39

A fter Dan dismissed Vic Fazzio, Judge Harvey stroked his chin as if to rub away the sting of a boxer's punch, a blow he hadn't expected, but that had nevertheless impressed him. The courtroom remained eerily quiet.

"Mr. O'Leary?"

"Plaintiffs rest, Your Honor," Dan said with all earnestness.

Harvey chuckled and sat back, staring at Dan. After a beat he said, "I don't know exactly what went on here today, but I do know it was about a lot more than a business deal gone bad. I'm not sure I appreciate you using my courtroom for whatever purpose you used it . . . But I will say it was a hell of a lot more entertaining than my usual calendar." He paused again, choosing his words carefully. "I also realize that three people are dead, and I don't find that at all entertaining."

"No, Your Honor. Neither do I."

"I'm not exactly sure where you're going to go from here, but I suspect you do." He looked out at the gallery. "And I suspect that goes for you also Chief Calloway, and for you Mr. Fazzio." He paused, then he said, "As for the defendant's motion for summary judgment, which is the only matter before me this morning, it is denied. The court finds there exist questions of fact as to whether or not the City of Cedar Grove, acting through its officers, engaged in fraudulent acts constituting a civil conspiracy . . . and possibly a lot more than that. We are adjourned." He rapped his gavel and quickly left the bench.

Dan closed his binder and slipped it inside his briefcase. He turned to Larry Kaufman, who had sat stoic through the entire hearing, but was no doubt confused. "I know I owe you an explanation. Come into the hallway and I'll try to explain."

———

Roy stood from his pew as Dan and Larry Kaufman walked past him and into the hallway. Dan would no doubt talk to Kaufman, then head home. Roy and Vic Fazzio would talk to Gary. This was a criminal matter now, and it was time to find out what Gary knew. If he would talk. Witherspoon remained seated in the gallery. Roy put a hand on Gary's shoulder. Witherspoon flinched but did not look up. He knew who the hand belonged to.

"We need to talk," Roy said.

Gary stood and they made their way out of the courtroom. In the hallway, Roy gestured to an empty room and followed Gary inside.

Roy shut the door. He imagined the room was used to sequester jurors during a trial since he saw no phone, no reading material, just a table and chairs and four beige walls. Since Gary was a suspect, Roy intended to read him his rights. He'd been burned before for not doing so, when he'd brought in Edmund House to question him about Sarah Crosswhite's disappearance. Roy sat across from Gary, took out his phone, hit "Record," and put it on the table.

"Before we get started, Gary, I have to read you your rights." Gary did not protest.

"You have the right to remain silent. Anything you say can and will be used against you in a court of law. You have the right to an attorney. If you cannot afford an attorney, one will be provided for you. Do you understand the rights I have just read to you? With these rights in mind, do you wish to speak to me?"

"I don't know."

"Do you understand your rights I just read to you?"

"Yes, I understand them."

"Do you wish to speak to me?"

Gary looked pale. He didn't immediately speak. He looked as though he was struggling to catch his breath. He lowered the knot of his tie and unbuttoned the collar of his shirt. Then he lowered his head and his gaze to the floor as if he might pass out—or throw up. Roy slid a garbage can closer to Gary's side of the table.

Just before Roy was about to speak, Gary lifted his gaze. "What did she tell you?" he asked.

"Who?" Roy said.

"Sunnie. What did Sunnie tell you?"

Uncertain, Roy said, "Why don't we start with the Cedar Grove Development company? We know the LLC members are dead. We also know they were at one time your father's clients, and you had access to those names. We also know that the members of the new LLCs in Cedar Grove are dead, and they, too, were at one time your father's clients, and that you also had access to those names. Who gave Sunnie that information, you or Ed?"

Gary shook his head and closed his eyes.

Roy said, "This will be a lot better if you tell the truth, Gary."

Gary looked up, crying. Then he chuckled. "The truth? I don't even know the truth anymore, Chief. I haven't known the truth for twenty-five years."

"Start with my first question. Who gave Sunnie the information to pass on to the attorney in Bellingham?"

"I didn't give her any of that information. Neither did my father."

"This will be harder if you lie, Gary."

"I know." He looked down at the table again. Roy thought this was the moment Gary would ask for an attorney.

"I've been lying for years, Roy," Gary said. "That's how this all got started, because of one lie."

"Then tell me about that one lie. Start with that," Roy said, still uncertain what was to come, but following Gary's lead.

Gary blew out a held breath. "I was the person who drove Heather home from my father's Christmas Eve party at the real estate office. She had drunk too much and so had he. My father always drank too much at that party. My mother didn't like to stay out late on Christmas Eve. I don't think she liked to see him when he drank that much. Sunnie drove my mother home in our car. I drove my father's car. I drove him home with Heather in the backseat. I don't know why Sunnie just didn't drive Heather home. I'd had my share of drinks that night also. It's not an excuse, I know, but . . ." He sat back and looked to be struggling to breathe.

Roy patiently waited.

"We had sex in the car," Gary said. "She was pretty drunk. She was really drunk actually."

"Passed out?"

Gary shrugged. "I don't know."

"And then eight weeks later . . . ," Roy said.

Gary nodded. "Heather came to me at work crying. She said she'd taken one of those pregnancy tests and it was positive. I should have told Sunnie right then . . . I should have told her what I'd done. But I didn't. I told Heather she needed to be sure. I told her she needed to get checked at the hospital in Silver Spurs. I told her I would take her. I told her that if they confirmed it, she'd have to get an abortion. I said I'd pay for it. I told her I'd drive her to the hospital and stay with her."

"What was her response?"

"She said she'd go. She said she was scared, but she'd go. That night, after work, I drove her to the hospital. She was quiet. She didn't say a word in the car. When we arrived at the hospital, she got out. She told me she didn't need me to go in with her. Something didn't seem right, so I waited. She didn't go in. I got out of the car and I told her she had no choice. I told her that I couldn't provide for her and a baby. I was married. I had two kids. And Sunnie was pregnant, again. We were struggling financially."

"What happened, Gary. What did you do?" Roy asked.

"What did I do? I left Heather at the hospital."

"You left her there?" Roy said.

He shrugged. "I thought she'd go in on her own. I knew it wasn't the right thing to do, but I . . ." He let his voice trail. He looked like he might get sick.

Roy pushed the garbage can closer.

Gary took several deep breaths. He sat up. "When I got home, Sunnie asked me what was wrong, and at that point I didn't see a choice. I told her. Sunnie seemed remarkably calm. She said she knew Heather. She said she would talk to her. She said she'd convince her to get an abortion. I told her that I'd tried, that I'd just come from the hospital and Heather had backed out. I told her I'd left her at the hospital. That was when Sunnie got upset. She called me an idiot. She said that if Heather called someone for a ride home, she'd have to tell the person what had happened, why she was in Silver Spurs. She said that type of news would get around Cedar Grove like wildfire and it would make her a laughing stock—the pregnant wife with two kids and a husband who was out fucking high school girls. She stormed out the front door. I heard her start the car." Gary shook his head. The tears were stronger now, almost too much for him to talk. "I didn't know she'd kill her, Roy. I never thought that Sunnie intended to kill her."

Roy was sure the tears were real. But he wasn't sure the story was true. He was trying to think through the evidence, the three cases, but the information was coming quickly. He needed time. Could Sunnie have killed Heather Johansen? Could she have dragged her body into the woods? Atticus had told Gary about the development. Gary would have told Sunnie.

What the hell happened in his town?

The door to the room opened. Vic Fazzio stepped in. He looked at Gary Witherspoon, who had tears streaming down his face. Then he looked at Roy. "I can't get ahold of Tracy. She isn't answering her phone. I called Vera. She's out with the baby. She said she left Tracy at home, alone."

CHAPTER 40

S unnie smiled, but Tracy had seen that smile before, and it had always had a sad quality to it, a smile of resignation, like when she'd been a kid. "Do you recognize this pistol, Tracy? It was once yours. Your father gave it to me when he was teaching me to shoot. You remember?"

"I remember, Sunnie," Tracy said.

"Only you, your dad, and your sister would know that bit of information. And now you, Finlay."

"Put down the gun, Sunnie," Finlay said firmly. "What the hell are you doing?"

"Shut up, Finlay," Sunnie said. "And speaking of guns. I want you to very slowly take off that gun belt and put it on the counter. You try to snap off that safety and I'll put a bullet between your eyes. And if you don't think I can do it, you just ask Tracy here. I learned from the best. Doc Crosswhite taught me well, didn't he, Tracy?"

Finlay looked at Tracy, who nodded. "Do it, Finlay." What Tracy needed now more than anything was time.

Finlay seemed tentative, uncertain.

"Do it, Finlay," Tracy said again.

Sunnie pulled back the hammer on the pistol. "It really doesn't matter to me if I kill you now, or I wait," Sunnie said.

"Take it easy, Sunnie," Tracy said. She needed to keep Sunnie talking, which had never been hard to do under ordinary circumstances.

Sunnie directed the gun at Tracy. "Take it easy?" She shook her head. "That is so like you. So like your father to project calmness and strength." She redirected her aim at Armstrong. "Finlay, if you don't lay that gun on the counter I'll shoot you where you stand. And this time, I won't have to burn down the house to cover it up."

Finlay had removed his gun, but he hesitated when he heard what Sunnie had said.

"You killed Kimberly?"

"Kimberly killed herself," Sunnie said. "Now put down the Goddamn gun."

———

Sunnie stood in Kimberly Armstrong's hallway. Kimberly looked down at the gas can on the floor, then back up at Sunnie. "Wait. What . . . what are you doing here?"

Sunnie raised the baseball bat.

Kimberly backpedaled, a look of terror filled her eyes. She turned and stumbled. Sunnie delivered the first blow—to the back of the head. It made a hollow, sickening sound. The blow knocked Kimberly to the floor, but she continued to move, to crawl on hands and knees. Sunnie stepped over her and raised the bat overhead, swinging it like an ax. She hit Kimberly a second time, and then a third.

Breathing heavily from the exertion, she set down the bat. She still had work to do. She picked up Kimberly by her arms, dragging her across the carpet to the office. She kicked aside the swivel chair behind the desk and pulled Kimberly across the plastic pad, leaving a streak of blood. It didn't matter. No one would see it.

Kimberly's files were on the shelf, one on her desk. The Heather Johansen police file. "So close," she said to Kimberly.

Hurrying to the living room, she picked up the can of gas, the one she had found in the shed two weeks earlier when she'd snuck along the easement to Finlay's backyard. She knew Finlay would have gasoline. He had a ride mower and a gas hedge trimmer.

But she had to be certain. She had worked too hard for too long to make a stupid mistake now.

———

Tracy watched Finlay place the gun on the kitchen counter. She turned to Sunnie. "Why Kimberly?" she asked.

"Because Kimberly couldn't leave well enough alone," Sunnie said. "She kept looking into Heather's death, and then she started asking questions about Cedar Grove Development. Atticus told Gary." Sunnie scoffed. "She worked for the *Towne Crier*. Who did she think she was, Bob Woodward?"

"You're Cedar Grove Development," Tracy said.

"I'm a lot of things, Tracy. I'm also the pastry chef, the delicatessen, and soon to be the mercantile store."

"You got the people's names from Ed's files."

"I wasn't sure how much you knew."

"Why?" Tracy said. "Why did you do it?"

"I had to keep both Ed and Gary on a tight leash to be sure they kept their mouths shut about Heather. I used those names because it would look like I was just doing what Ed and Gary told me, the dumb little secretary." She shrugged and smiled. The smile faded.

"I'd put everything I owned into Cedar Grove Development. I mortgaged the house and used every penny my parents had left me to buy up the businesses. I wasn't going to be left behind. Not again. Not this time, Tracy. I wasn't going to be the one stuck in Cedar Grove with nothing to show for it. I was going to get everything I deserved. Everything I had dreamed of."

"You killed Kimberly." Finlay said the words as if still trying to understand.

"But that's not how it's going to look," Sunnie said. "It's going to look like you killed Kimberly and Heather Johansen."

And Tracy realized what Sunnie intended to do.

"I didn't kill Heather," Finlay said.

"You always were an idiot," Sunnie said.

—

Sunnie watched Heather Johansen step onto the edge of the pavement and wave her arm overhead. In that instance, Sunnie thought of hitting the gas and just running the little bitch over, making her the victim of a tragic hit-and-run. But she'd seen the damage a deer could do to a car, and she figured a human could do the same, even one as skinny as Heather.

Even a dent would be a problem. How would she explain that?

Sunnie braked and heard the pads squeal from the accumulated water, the tires struggling to grip the wet pavement. The headlights dipped momentarily, then corrected. Heather walked forward, then abruptly stopped. She looked like someone had just spoiled a surprise. She looked dejected and defeated.

She had not been expecting Sunnie.

Maybe Gary . . . or a stranger, but not Sunnie.

Surprise!

But not a surprise to Sunnie. She'd seen the way Gary looked at Heather when she visited the real estate office. She recognized the desire in his eyes because he'd once looked at her that same way, before she'd gotten pregnant and put on forty pounds. She'd told him she was on the pill; she thought it would be different, if they had a child together. She thought Gary would love her—as much as she loved him.

But he didn't even want to marry her.

He'd said the child wasn't his. He'd said Sunnie had been sleeping around with other guys. He'd said Sunnie should get an abortion. He said a lot of things, hurtful things—until Sunnie got her father involved. Ed and Gary didn't realize the power Sunnie's father held in Cedar Grove. They didn't realize the type of lawyer he could be when someone screwed with his family, especially with his daughter.

Her father had a talk with Ed and Barbara. He'd made Gary's choice clear. Either Gary married his daughter, and cared for her the way she deserved, or he'd sue them all and take everything from them in the form of child support. Since Gary didn't have shit, that meant Ed's real estate business.

Sunnie and Gary married a week after high school graduation, and Gary went to work for his father. She thought Gary would learn to love her, but he never had.

And now this betrayal, with this little bitch.

Sunnie pushed open the driver's door. Heather threw back her shoulders, seemingly defiant.

"Heather?" Sunnie said as if this were just a chance encounter. "What the hell are you doing? You're going to freeze to death out here."

Heather seemed to relax, if only for a moment. She raised her voice to speak above the wind. "I need a ride to the Crosswhites' house."

"The Crosswhites?"

"Will you take me?"

"Why do you want to go to the Crosswhites'?"

"I just need to figure some things out. Please, will you take me?"

"What things?" Sunnie asked.

Heather started around the hood of the car, to the passenger's side. "It doesn't matter. It's personal. Can you please just take me there?"

Now the surprise. "You need to let this go, Heather. This was an accident. A mistake."

Heather stopped walking. She turned to Sunnie.

"You need to think of the lives you're ruining, including your own," Sunnie said to her.

"I am," she said. "One life in particular."

"No. You're just being stubborn . . . and emotional. I'll drive you to the hospital in Silver Spurs. We can all just move on."

"No. I'm not going back there. I'm going to Doc Crosswhite's house. If you won't take me, I'll walk."

She started past the car, down the road. Sunnie yelled at her, her voice faint.

Defiant little bitch! "Get in the car, Heather! You want to ruin your life that's your business, but you have no right to ruin mine!"

Heather stopped, turned, snow falling onto her face. She wiped the flakes away. Then she turned and started walking again. "Just go!" she shouted over her shoulder. "Leave me alone!"

Sunnie felt her rage spreading from her chest to her limbs, making her muscles tight. She knew Heather wouldn't do the smart thing. She knew it when she got in the car. Heather didn't care about humiliating Sunnie in front of all of Cedar Grove. But Sunnie would not be humiliated.

Heather picked up her pace, starting to run. Sunnie would never catch her on foot. She ran back to the car, climbed behind the wheel, and punched the accelerator. The car lurched forward. She hit the brakes to keep from driving off the edge of the pavement into the mud and made a U-turn, the engine squealing. The tires struggled to gain traction on the wet pavement.

As she approached, Heather glanced over her shoulder and jumped from the road, falling momentarily, then struggling to get to her feet.

Sunnie drove past her and hit the brakes, turning the wheel to use the car to cut off Heather's escape. She grabbed Gary's baseball bat from the backseat and flung open the door. The dome light briefly illuminated the interior, then extinguished when she slammed the door shut.

Heather shouted something over her shoulder and continued walking. Sunnie could no longer hear what she'd said. The only sound came from deep within her, a guttural foreign sound. She raised the baseball bat and started to run.

Heather turned, then raised a hand against the glare of the car's lights. She stumbled, off-balance. Sunnie swung the bat as if to chop down on a thick block of wood and heard the hollow impact with Heather's skull. The blow drove Heather to her knees where she wobbled for an instant, then fell backward, her head hitting the pavement. She lay there, eyes open, staring up into the falling snow.

Sunnie stepped over her.

And raised the bat a second time.

CHAPTER 41

Roy stepped into the courthouse hallway, shutting the door to the room behind him. He gave Vic Fazzio an abbreviated version of what Gary Witherspoon had told him so far.

"You believe him?" Faz asked.

"I don't know. Maybe not fully. I'll tell you more later," Roy said. "Right now, get ahold of Dan. Find out how far out he is from Cedar Grove."

Faz pulled out his cell phone and stepped down the hall to make the call.

Roy looked at his watch, considering the time it would take for Dan to drive home. He'd still be too far from Cedar Grove. He pulled out his cell and called his police department. He asked for Finlay Armstrong. The secretary said Finlay was out of the office. Roy disconnected and tried Finlay's cell phone, but he got no answer. His frustration mounting, he again called the police station and instructed dispatch to get a car out to Dan O'Leary's house. "Tell them to move."

Roy disconnected and stepped back into the room. He looked at Gary Witherspoon, turned on the recorder, and again put it on the table. He didn't have to ask a question. Gary started talking.

"I didn't have a choice," Gary said, pleading now. "Sunnie said if I told anyone she'd say I killed Heather. She'd tell you I got Heather pregnant, that I'd raped her, and that when Heather came to me, I killed her to cover it up. She even kept the baseball bat she'd used hidden someplace, so I couldn't clean it. She said you wouldn't believe me if I said it was Sunnie. She said no one would believe my story, that it would sound like the desperate words of a man trying to hide his crimes."

"Why should I believe you?" Roy asked, as he sat. "How do I know you're not lying to me now?"

"Because you know me and you know my father, so you know neither of us has the kind of money to buy out the businesses in Cedar Grove, and to restart the Cascadia development."

"Sunnie did that?"

Gary nodded. "It was the money she inherited from her parents. She hired the lawyer in Bellingham to do the work. It was why she asked for the job with Rav Patel, to make it look like the contracts were coming from the city attorney's office. When I learned what she was doing and told her to stop, she just laughed at me. She said she'd tell you she was just doing what I told her to do. She said no one would believe she was doing it on her own. I found out she'd used the names of my father's former clients. She had access to his files. She said I could either go along with it, and I'd look like the hero who saved Cedar Grove, or she'd blame everything on me and my father, and she had the evidence to make her allegations stick."

Roy didn't know what to believe at this point. But he didn't like the fact that neither Finlay nor Tracy were answering their phones.

Sunnie shrugged her shoulders in response to Tracy's question. "Heather wouldn't listen to reason. I tried to get her to listen to reason. It didn't have to end that way, not for any of us. But I wasn't going to go back to Cedar Grove humiliated, and I wasn't going to be blamed, not for doing what Gary didn't have the balls to do."

Keep talking, Sunnie, Tracy thought. The longer Sunnie talked, the better her chance of figuring out a way to get the pistol. She didn't think it likely she could reach the Sunnie she'd once known, the insecure young girl. Sunnie had resented Tracy, and for many years. That kind of resentment festered like an untreated wound, poisoning the body and the mind. She held out little hope she could talk Sunnie into putting the gun down, not after so many years of lies and killings to cover those lies. The girl she had known growing up, the one she had seen nearly every day of her life, was gone. The person standing now in her kitchen was troubled—paranoid and narcissistic. Sick. She didn't know the woman in her kitchen. Still, she had to try, if only to buy time. Whatever Tracy was going to do, she'd have to do it before Vera and Daniella returned home. She would not put either of them in danger.

"I realized something else though, that night," Sunnie continued.

"What night?" Tracy asked.

"The night Heather died. I realized that Gary could no longer control me. He could no longer tell me what to do. Neither could Ed. Do you have any idea what it was like living with a man who doesn't love you? No, of course you don't. You got Dan. Mr. Optimism. Is he still that way? Still the good guy paying you compliments?"

"We all have problems, Sunnie. It's part of marriage."

"Does he call you fat and ugly when he gets drunk?"

"I'm sorry," Tracy said.

Sunnie waved off Tracy's apology. "What would you know about it? You were always so perfect. You were always so pretty, your figure so . . . His father was worse," she said, changing thoughts without a pause. "After my father died, I lost the hammer that I had held over them both while he was alive. I lost the threat. I got the hammer back, though. I told Gary if he ever mistreated me again, I'd tell Roy about Heather, and he'd believe me. Gary didn't think I would. He didn't think I had it in me. Then I killed the attorney." She smiled. "He no longer questioned whether I had it in me, and he no longer questioned who Roy would believe."

"You set the branches in the road."

"It would have been easy for someone of your talents, but I'd done some practicing. I'd gone to the range."

Sunnie looked to Finlay. "I never meant to involve you, Finlay, but, really, that was your own fault. You were the one stalking Heather. You were the jilted boy who couldn't get past his high school crush. I thought you were going to be arrested, but then Edmund House did us all a favor when he kidnapped your sister," she said, turning back to Tracy. "He became the convenient suspect in Heather's death. I suspect Roy knew otherwise, but without DNA, how could he prove it?"

"Why did you kill Jason Mathews?" Tracy asked. *Keep her talking. Keep talking, Sunnie.*

"That was your fault."

Tracy decided to push her. "Tell me how it was my fault." Tracy suspected she knew Sunnie's reasoning, but as long as she kept her talking, she had a chance. She glanced at the gun on the counter, unsure she could get to it, and not before Sunnie pulled the trigger. She looked for something to throw, anything.

"If you hadn't come back to Cedar Grove to prove Edmund House was innocent, the Johansens never would have got it in their heads that House didn't kill their daughter. They never would have hired Mathews to look into it, and everything would have gone on as it had."

"Except Mathews met with Ed at the Four Points Tavern in Silver Spurs," Tracy said.

"How did you know that?" Sunnie looked paranoid. "Who told you that? Ed? Did Ed tell you that?"

"Am I right?"

Sunnie scoffed. "It was always so important for you to be right. You were all so damned competitive, you and your sister. Even your father. Yes, it was because of that meeting. Ed didn't know any of this until Mathews opened his big mouth. Ed came to our house that night and confronted Gary. He wanted to know if it was true, if Gary got Heather pregnant. He wanted to know if Gary killed her."

"And you saw another opportunity."

"Not at first. At first, I was scared, but as the days passed, I realized this was my chance to have power over both Gary *and* Ed. So I kept an eye on Mathews. I learned his drinking habits, which wasn't difficult. He practically lived at the Four Points. Then I watched you, Finlay. I watched you and I waited for a day you went out hunting. I went home, grabbed my deer rifle, and waited until Mathews left the bar. He was so drunk I thought he might crash before he got to the branches I'd placed in the road. I drove up the backside of the property using the fire access trail. You remember the fire trail, Tracy. We used to take that road up to the lake when we were kids."

"I remember," Tracy said.

"I knew I could make the shot. After all, I was trained by Cedar Grove's very best."

"You asked me how I knew about Jason Mathews blackmailing Ed," Tracy said. "I knew because we spoke to the bartender. He recalled that meeting. We also know all about Cedar Grove Development and the use of Ed's former clients' names as members in the LLCs you set up. Dan's putting on that case in a courtroom right now, Sunnie. This is over. It's time to end this."

"I did my homework, Tracy. I'm not the idiot you think I am."

"I never thought you were an idiot, Sunnie."

"Then you should know that I know what Dan is doing in Whatcom County." She shrugged. "But it doesn't matter. They'll think Ed and Gary set up the fake LLCs. It's why I chose his former clients to be members. Ed always was a greedy son of a bitch and Gary was always a willing minion. Roy will know that. He isn't going to accept any argument that it was the poor little housewife that put this all together. And I'll play that part, wounded at what my husband and my father-in-law tried to do to me, how they cheated me out of my inheritance."

"You can't explain us," Finlay said. "Ed and Gary aren't here."

"I don't have to. Right now, Ed and Gary are guilty of fraud, not murder. The prime suspect in the deaths of Heather Johansen, Jason Mathews, and your wife is still you, Finlay. Or have you really not yet figured out why I invited you to this party. You thought Tracy was getting too close to those answers, that she had pieced this all together, that she had concluded you were the killer. So you stalked her . . . That's something that will be easy enough for Roy to believe, and you waited until she was alone. You came here to kill her, but you forgot one thing. You forgot that Tracy was always fast with a gun and she, too, managed to get off a shot. It wasn't fast enough to save her, but it was fast enough to kill you.

"Everyone will believe that, won't they Tracy? They'll be talking about how fast you and your sister always were with a pistol, at your funeral."

CHAPTER 42

D an's cell phone rang, a 206 area code, but not a number he recognized. It was not Tracy and it wasn't Leah Battles. "Hello?"

"Hey, Dan, it's Vic Fazzio."

"Is Gary Witherspoon talking?"

"Yeah, he is. He's in with Calloway. I'm not sure of all the details but he's telling a story I don't think any of us predicted."

"What do you mean?"

"Calloway said that Gary's put the blame on Sunnie."

"Sunnie? That's ridiculous."

"Maybe not. Gary admits he got Heather Johansen pregnant, and he admits that he drove her out to the hospital to get an abortion, but he said that was the end of it. He said Heather refused to go through with it and he left her there. He said Sunnie was the one who went back, that he never thought Sunnie would kill her. He said Sunnie told him if he ever said a word, she'd tell Calloway the truth about him getting Heather pregnant, and she'd say Gary killed Heather because she had refused to get the abortion."

"He's lying, Faz. Sunnie isn't sophisticated enough to put this all together."

"I don't know about that. I just know that Roy told me to get ahold of you. Tracy isn't answering her phone."

Dan felt a sickness rapidly spreading.

"I called Vera," Faz continued. "She said Tracy wanted to stay at home, in case one of us called with a question about one of the files."

"Where's Vera?"

"She took Daniella for a walk. She's heading home now."

"No," Dan said. "Call Vera back. Tell her not to go home. Tell her not to take Daniella home."

"Okay. Okay. I'll call her back."

"Did you call Finlay?"

"Roy handled that."

"You call Vera."

"I'll call Vera."

Dan hung up quickly and tried Tracy's number. She didn't answer. He called the police station and asked for Finlay. They said he wasn't available. Dan said it was an emergency. That he needed to reach Finlay, at Roy Calloway's instructions. The woman said she'd call Finlay and have him call Dan.

Dan spit out his cell number, then hung up. He tried calling Tracy again. She didn't answer. He looked at his watch. He was still half an hour from Cedar Grove.

As he waited for Finlay to call back, he thought about everything that had happened and tried to reconcile it with the story Gary Witherspoon was apparently telling, that Sunnie had killed Heather Johansen.

Dan knew Sunnie. Yeah, she made shit up but . . .

Could Sunnie have killed Heather Johansen and held it over Gary's head all these years?

He thought again of the meeting between Jason Mathews and Ed Witherspoon. Ed would have confronted his son, because Ed would have known that Gary had driven Heather home from the party. And if Ed had confronted Gary, then Sunnie would have also known.

Gary wasn't a hunter. The thought came to him like a bolt out of the blue.

Gary didn't know the butt end of a rifle from the barrel. He could not have made the shot that killed Jason Mathews.

But Doc Crosswhite trained Sunnie to shoot.

A hundred yards? With a scope?

That would have been no problem for Sunnie.

"Oh my God," Dan said, and he pressed down on the accelerator.

Tracy struggled to keep her thoughts straight. She'd kept Sunnie talking for minutes, but sensed she was not about to talk much longer. "You haven't thought this through Sunnie."

"Please, educate me, Tracy. You always were smarter than me."

"Once Dan proves the limited liability companies are shams, Gary and Ed are going to sing. And they're going to sing the same song, that this was all your idea. It was your money. They're going to plead poor. Then they're going to sing about Heather Johansen, about how you were the person who killed her."

Sunnie smiled. "Who will believe them, Tracy?"

"I do. And so will others. Heather's killing has always bothered me. And so did the killing of Kimberly Armstrong. I told Roy about it. Roy knows."

"Knows what?"

"Kimberly Armstrong's killing wasn't a burglary or an assault and she didn't die in the fire. That killing was an act of rage, just like

Heather's killing was an act of rage. To beat someone with a bat is an act of rage, Sunnie."

Sunnie smiled. "So Ed and Gary sing, and they say it's my money. So what? I'm just a dumb high school graduate." She deliberately raised her voice an octave. "Your Honor, I had no idea what my husband and my father-in-law were doing. My husband handles all our finances. And as for the phone calls to the attorney in Bellingham, I was just following my husband's instructions. He told me to send the names to the attorney in Bellingham and ask him to set up the limited liability companies. I had no idea what my husband intended to do with them. And I had no idea my husband killed Heather all those years ago. My God. I've been living all these years with a killer. Why Tracy Crosswhite said the murder was an act of rage, and I guess I can see that now—the rage of a man about to lose everything because a young girl carrying his child wouldn't get an abortion. I've seen the same kind of rage directed toward me." Sunnie smiled.

"The weather," Tracy said, thinking quickly, but in control.

"You mean the snow?"

"You'll leave your footprints in the snow."

"I put a pair of Gary's snow boots outside your door before I knocked, Tracy. They're men's, size 10—the same boots I wore when I snuck up to your back fence and took a shot at you." Sunnie looked to the clock on the wall. "Time for me to go."

Finlay Armstrong started to laugh, a sound so out of place Tracy didn't initially recognize it. It wasn't a nervous giggle or the anxious laugh of a man realizing he is about to die. This was an ironic laugh, the laugh of someone who knew something nobody else in the room knew, and he was amazed they hadn't thought of it.

"What are you laughing at?" Sunnie said.

"I'm laughing at you, Sunnie. I'm laughing because you were always such a poor judge of people."

"We'll see about that. I'd say I've judged everyone spot-on. So instead of laughing maybe you should take the time to pray."

Finlay smiled. "For what?" he asked. "That's what you still don't get."

"What?"

"Who am I going to pray for, Sunnie? You killed my wife, my soulmate. You took my reason to live."

"Finlay, don't," Tracy said, recognizing what Finlay intended.

"You made one mistake, Sunnie."

"Did I?"

"You underestimated how far a desperate man will go . . . when he has nothing to lose."

Finlay shoved Tracy to the ground and rushed Sunnie. The pistol in Sunnie's hand exploded as Finlay hit her, his momentum and weight shoving her backward into the wall. For a moment he had a hold of Sunnie's hand grasping the gun, but then he tilted to his right, stumbled a couple steps, and fell to the ground, knocking over one of the barstools at the kitchen counter. Blood stained the front of his uniform near his stomach.

Sunnie, distracted, glanced down at him, then quickly redirected her aim at Tracy.

"Don't," Tracy said. She held Finlay's Glock.

"Tracy Crossdraw," Sunnie said. "You always were fast."

Tracy kept her voice calm. "Put down the gun. We can get you help."

Sunnie smiled. "Remember what your dad always used to say?"

Tracy had no idea what Sunnie referred to. "Put the gun down, Sunnie, and you and I can talk. I'm sure we can talk about this, and I'm sure we can get you help. I'll testify for you."

"You don't remember, do you?"

Tracy wondered if she could hit Sunnie in the shoulder of the arm holding the gun. Wound her. But Sunnie had remembered all of her training. She held the gun in front of her, her arms creating a pyramid, the gun at the apex. "What did he say, Sunnie? What did my dad say?"

"He used to say, *to be the best you have to beat the best.*"

"No, Sunnie. Not like this. It doesn't have to be like this."

Outside the window Tracy heard the sirens of approaching police vehicles. Sunnie heard them too. She turned her head to the sound, though only for a moment. She never lowered her weapon.

She looked again to Tracy and gave her that tired smile of resignation and of defeat. It was the same smile the little girl had given to the people of Cedar Grove when they'd ignored her and treated her like she was invisible. Sad. It was just so sad.

"I never could beat you," Sunnie said.

"Don't," Tracy said, her finger on the trigger. "Sunnie! Don't make me do it!"

Sunnie smiled. "Why Tracy Crossdraw, I wouldn't think of giving you the satisfaction of beating me again."

Tracy suddenly understood what Sunnie meant, what she intended to do, but in that moment of thought, Sunnie had already turned the gun, pointed the barrel at her temple, and pulled the trigger.

CHAPTER 43

Dan pulled into the driveway. His anxiety and stress had spiked when he drove down the block and saw several Cedar Grove police cars and a Whatcom County ambulance. He left the Tahoe's motor running and the driver's door open and high-stepped through the snow, nearly falling, plowing toward the front door in the trampled path created by others. Two police officers stopped his approach.

"This is my house. Where's my wife?" he said, panicked.

Tracy stepped out the front door. "It's okay," she said to the officers. "It's okay. He's my husband."

They let Dan past. He wrapped his hands around Tracy, holding her. "Are you okay?"

"I'm fine. The ambulance is for Finlay. She shot Finlay."

"Sunnie?" Dan said.

"She shot herself, Dan." She fought to hold back tears. "After everything she did, I still can't help but feel sorry for her, can't help but think of that girl I grew up with."

Dan held her. "I'm sorry, Tracy." He was breathing heavily, having trouble catching his breath. After a moment, he released her and stepped back, taking several deep breaths and blowing them out. He bent over, hands on his knees, and he vomited. She saw the depth of his pain, what she had done to him, and it nearly buckled her knees. My God. How could she do this to a man who loved her so much?

"Are you okay?" she asked.

After another moment, Dan stood. Still breathing heavily. "I think so."

"How did you know?" Tracy asked.

"Faz called. Gary is apparently telling Roy everything. At first, I thought it was a lie, but the more I listened . . . The murders of Heather Johansen, and Jason Mathews. It all started to make sense. And the more it did, the more I worried something was going to happen to you."

"She thought no one would believe him," Tracy said. "She thought no one would believe Gary."

Dan nodded. "She was always an accomplished liar, even as a kid." He shook his head. "You sure you're okay?"

"I'm fine but Vera and the baby are on their way home. Meet them outside the house. I don't want Vera to see any of this."

"Faz got ahold of Vera and told her to stay at The Daily Perk. I'm going to call her there."

Tracy heard a noise and turned. The paramedics carried a gurney out of the house. Finlay lay on it, an IV tube in his arm. He was awake, and as he passed he reached out and grabbed her arm. He looked like he wanted to say something, but then he dropped his hand. "It's going to be all right, Finlay," Tracy said. "You have to believe me when I tell you, it's going to be okay. It takes time. You won't heal, never completely, but it will get better with time."

Finlay didn't respond. A tear rolled from the corner of his eye and along the side of the mask covering his nose and mouth. He dropped his gaze as the paramedics continued past her.

Several hours later, after the paramedics and forensic team had departed, after the throw rug in the dining room had been removed and the tile floor cleaned with an antiseptic, Tracy sat at the kitchen table with Dan and Faz. They sipped cups of coffee and listened to Roy Calloway, who had come from the police station. Vera, not wanting to know, had gone upstairs to care for Daniella.

"What happened to my town, Tracy? What happened to our town?"

"I don't know, Roy."

"It feels like the devil walked here in 1993 and spread evil. So much evil. Edmund House. Sarah's disappearance. Your father's death. Heather Johansen. Sunnie. How can there have been so much evil in one small town?"

"I don't know, Roy."

They sat in silence.

"Did Gary give a written statement?" Tracy asked.

Calloway nodded. "Not Ed though. Ed asked for an attorney."

"He'll talk," Tracy said.

"I don't know," Calloway said. "He always was a righteous bastard."

"He won't have a choice," Tracy said. "Not with Gary talking. Ed will try to find a way out, and Sunnie's death might be that way. He'll do what he's always done. He'll say whatever he thinks will protect him."

"You're probably right," Calloway said. "Your dad liked to say something similar about Ed."

"*So crooked he couldn't put on a straight pair of jeans,*" Tracy said.

"That's it," Roy said, briefly smiling.

"How's Finlay?" Dan asked.

"Still too early to tell," Roy said. "The bullet passed through without damaging any vital organs. He's likely going to lose his spleen, but the doctors think he'll be all right, physically."

"What are you going to do while he's out?" Tracy said.

"I don't know. Nora pitched a fit last time I stepped in. And I'm not sure I want to stay any longer." He looked to Tracy. "I don't suppose—"

"No," Tracy said. "I'm not interested, Roy. Absolutely not."

Calloway shrugged and stood from the table. "Well, then, I guess as chief it's my responsibility to let Eric and Ingrid know what happened before the Cedar Grove rumor mill gets cranked up. They deserve to hear this from me."

Tracy looked to Dan. "Go," Dan said. "I know you want to. I'll take care of Daniella."

"That's all right," she said, thinking of Dan throwing up in the front yard, of the pain she'd already put him through. "I'd rather be here."

"Go," he said again. "You need to do this. You need to put this to bed. Finish what you started. I know it's important to you."

Tracy looked to Roy, who'd moved to the door, waiting for her. "Tell the Johansens I'll stop by some time tomorrow and pay my respects," she said. "Right now, I'm going to go upstairs and be a mom. I need to be with my family. I need to see my daughter. I need to sing her to sleep, the way my mother used to sing me to sleep."

EPILOGUE

Tracy opened the car door with her eyes shut and reached for Dan's hand.

"Keep 'em closed," Dan said.

"I will."

She was glad to be away from Cedar Grove. The time they'd stayed had begun to wear on her. The town gossip machine had been working on overdrive since news of Sunnie's death and Gary's and Ed Witherspoon's arrests as accessories after the fact for aiding and abetting Sunnie's crimes. Tracy had largely barricaded herself inside her home, going to town only when necessary and feigning ignorance when asked about what had happened. She'd used the time to read books she always wanted to read, everything she could get her hands on that would help take her mind off of Sunnie and what she'd done. Mostly, she spent time with her daughter, witnessed her eat food and roll over on the bed. Little things, but things she'd never forget.

She, Dan, and Roy had spent several days with the Whatcom County prosecuting attorney in Bellingham, providing him with the evidence they had accumulated, and putting him in touch with witnesses. Rav Patel had resigned his position as city attorney, though it appeared he knew nothing about the criminal actions. Patel's actions in the civil case remained under review by the prosecuting attorney and the bar association.

Larry Kaufman's civil action remained pending, and the former owners of the other businesses had joined his lawsuit, alleging fraud. It would be an uphill battle, and likely a hollow victory. Because there was no longer a company intent on developing a mountain retreat, the businesses were again not worth much. It was possible another company would step in, but when was anybody's guess.

Gary Witherspoon had resigned as mayor. His cooperation with the prosecuting attorney would help his case, but probably not enough to keep him from doing some jail time. Tracy couldn't help but feel for him. He was a father with four children. Ever the good son, Gary was doing his best to absolve his father of any wrongdoing. Whether he succeeded or not would be up to the prosecuting attorney.

Tracy had spent time with the Johansens, who seemed both relieved and troubled. They were relieved to finally know the truth about what had happened to their daughter, but the new information had dredged up a dark and painful period in their lives.

"It's like Heather has died all over again," Eric told Tracy.

She knew the feeling. When they discovered Sarah's remains twenty years after her disappearance, it felt to Tracy like those terrible days had returned, and she grieved for her sister all over again.

All construction on Market Street ceased, and the downtown had become a ghost town again. Tracy couldn't help but feel nostalgic when she went to the pharmacy, or when she and Dan went out to dinner. It would have felt good to see the downtown alive again with new businesses and a new theater. It would have been nice to see people on the street. Maybe it would happen, someday. She hoped so. For Daniella's sake.

"No peeking," Dan said as he guided Tracy out of the Tahoe.

"I'm not peeking. I can't see a thing."

He grabbed her arm and led her away from the car. "Okay come this way." She felt disoriented. She knew she was home in Redmond, but Dan didn't want her to see the house until he was ready. He wanted it to be a surprise. She'd closed her eyes as they drove down the driveway. Tracy heard the dogs barking and running around the yard.

"You have Daniella?" she asked.

"She's here in her car seat," Dan said, positioning Tracy's shoulders. "A couple more steps. All right, stop. Are you sure you're ready?"

"Dan!"

"Okay. Open your eyes."

Tracy couldn't speak at first. She didn't even recognize what had been their three-room cottage. She knew the architect and builders had saved only the foundation so they could call it a remodel and not a new home. It had to do with permits and building codes. Tracy had left that to Dan, deciding she wanted to spend what time she had remaining of her maternity leave with Daniella.

"You like it?" Dan asked.

The outside of the house looked like a country farmhouse, a pale-yellow color with white trim and a wraparound porch with a wide front staircase. It all sat on a foundation with a brick façade. The landscaping had not yet been done, just dirt and brown grass.

"Tracy?"

"Oh my God, Dan. It's beautiful," she said. "It's so beautiful."

"You think you can see yourself living here?"

She smiled. "As long as you're here, Dan O'Leary, and Daniella." She looked to the car seat in which Daniella slept.

"It's not done," Dan said. "I had them finish the kitchen and the family room so we could get back in. And Daniella's room, so she isn't breathing in any construction dust."

"It'll be fine."

Dan picked up the car seat and they walked up the steps to the porch. A white swing hung from chains in an alcove to the right of the front door. To the left sat three rocking chairs. On the other end of the porch was a table with four chairs. "I thought we could eat outside on nice days," Dan said.

"I can see Daniella swinging on that porch someday. Who knows, maybe with a man just like her daddy," Tracy said.

"Let's get her out of diapers before I have to start thinking about that," he said. "Although I did position the swing so we can watch it from the family room."

Tracy laughed. "You're as big a worrier as I am, Dan O'Leary."

"Bigger," Dan said. "Much bigger." He got to the front door, put the car seat on the porch, then fumbled with his pockets.

"What's the matter?" Tracy said.

"I forgot my keys," he said. "Hang on." He reached out and knocked on the door.

"What are you doing?" she asked.

The door swung inward. "I was wondering what you were doing out there," Therese said. "You were gabbing so much I thought you were going to just describe the house to her. Don't you know a picture is worth a thousand words?"

"Therese?" Tracy said, smiling.

Therese gave Tracy a hug.

"You're back?" Tracy asked.

"Well, I should hope so. We couldn't leave this little one at home with just anyone when the daytime mommy goes to work now could we?" Therese looked at Dan and winked. "And who wouldn't want to live in a home like this? Come see for yourself." She stepped to the side so Tracy could enter.

The floors were dark hardwood. "Teak?" she asked, looking down at the floor and recognizing the wood.

"Like your home growing up in Cedar Grove," Dan said.

To her left was a two-level staircase leading upstairs. It also resembled the staircase in her childhood home. Straight ahead was the kitchen and to her right the family room. Hanging above the fireplace mantel was the painting Therese had been working on of the gazebo in the snowstorm.

"You finished it," Tracy said.

Therese smiled. "No, ma'am. My mother likes to say *a house isn't a home until a family moves in*. Now that you're finally here, I'd say you finished it." She took the car seat from Dan. "I'll put Ms. Daniella down in her bassinet while you give Tracy the tour."

Therese took the car seat and walked up the stairs.

"What do you think?" Dan asked.

Tracy wiped a tear. "I think I'm home, Dan. I think we both finally made it home."

ACKNOWLEDGMENTS

There are moments in life that we never forget, some good and some not so good. I was in the airport at Johannesburg, South Africa, with my wife, preparing for the long flight home after a three-week safari when I received an email from a friend. She asked if I had heard the news. Those words can inspire fear or joy. I sensed dread. She wrote to me that Scott Tompkins, of the King County Sheriff's Office, had died. He was just forty-eight. I read the message and felt that awful sensation of disbelief and sadness. I'd had dinner with Scott and his fiancée, Jennifer Southworth, not more than a month prior. He looked happy and healthy. Scott had died unexpectedly, of a heart attack. I cried in the airport that day. Life can be so unfair.

Scott Tompkins changed my life and the lives of my family members in 2013 when I called to ask him questions for a book I was writing about a female Seattle detective named Tracy Crosswhite. Scott never hesitated. He sat down with me for two hours to answer my questions.

Then he said, "You need to meet my girlfriend, Jennifer—she's a Seattle homicide detective." I nearly fell off my chair. Could a writer ask for anything better? A person to help make my character authentic and human. I never could have written *My Sister's Grave* or these next Tracy Crosswhite novels without Scott and Jennifer. Scott was always so giving of his time, even when he didn't have it. Beyond that, he was a good guy whose company I enjoyed. He was always upbeat, despite the difficult job he had, and was always a lot of fun to be around.

I remember sitting down with him to go over an idea I had for a subsequent novel. Scott listened closely, then said, "Forget all that. Here's what you should do. You should put a body in a crab pot." He then went on to describe for me a true story of a victim whose boyfriend had killed her and put her in a crab pot. It was gruesome, and the perfect idea for what would become *The Trapped Girl*, one of my best-selling novels.

I attended Scott's funeral, and it seemed surreal to think he was gone. If you've never been to a police funeral, it is immensely moving. I cried many tears that day for Scott, for Jen, and for everyone else he left behind who loved him—and there were many. I didn't know what to say to Jen after the ceremony. What can you say? I told her how sorry I was and I told her I would pray for her, that God would provide strength and understanding.

I knew that day I wanted to dedicate this novel to Scott, and for that reason I also decided that I would bring Tracy Crosswhite back home, to Cedar Grove, to where the series began, when I first met Scott. It seemed only fitting.

Thank you, Scott. I hope, in some small way, this novel, dedicated to you, will let you live on, forever.

Thanks to Meg Ruley, Rebecca Scherer, and the team at the Jane Rotrosen Agency. They are literary agents extraordinaire. They have supported me all over the world, and we've had fun together in New York,

Seattle, Paris, and Oslo. I'm thinking an Italian book festival should be next on the list.

Thank you to Thomas & Mercer, and to Amazon Publishing. This is the tenth book I've written for them, and they have made each one better with their edits and suggestions. They have sold and promoted me and my novels all over the world, and I have had the pleasure of meeting the Amazon Publishing teams from the UK, Ireland, France, Germany, Italy, and Spain. These are hard-working people who somehow make hard work a lot of fun. What they do best is promote and sell my novels, and for that I am so very grateful.

Thanks to Sarah Shaw, author relations. Thanks to Sean Baker, head of production; Laura Barrett, production manager; and Oisin O'Malley, art director. It's getting redundant for me to keep saying I love the covers and the titles of each of my novels, but I do. I am always astounded at the ways you take care of me. Thanks to Dennelle Catlett, Amazon Publishing PR, for all the work promoting me and my novels. Dennelle is always there, always available when I call or send an email with a need or a request. She actively promotes me and makes my travel easy. Thanks to the marketing team, Gabrielle Guarnero, Laura Costantino, and Kyla Pigoni, for all their dedicated work and new ideas to help me build an author platform. I hope they never stop asking me, because they make each new idea a great experience. Thanks to publisher Mikyla Bruder; associate publisher Galen Maynard; and Amazon Publishing vice president, Jeff Belle, for creating a team dedicated to their jobs and allowing me to be a part of it.

Special thanks to Thomas & Mercer's editorial director, Gracie Doyle. Gracie and I collaborated on each new novel, kicking around ideas and news articles and ultimately the next great Tracy adventure. We have a lot of fun coming up with the ideas, then working to make them as strong as possible.

Thank you to Charlotte Herscher, developmental editor. This is book eleven together, and she pushes me to never settle for mediocrity.

Thanks to Scott Calamar, copyeditor, who I desperately need. Grammar has never been my strength, so there is usually a lot to do.

Thanks to Tami Taylor, who runs my website, creates my newsletters, and creates some of my foreign-language book covers. Thanks to Pam Binder and the Pacific Northwest Writers Association for their support. Thanks to Seattle7Writers, a nonprofit collective of Pacific Northwest authors who foster and support the written word.

Thanks to all of you tireless readers, for finding my novels and for your incredible support of my work all over the world. Hearing from readers is a blessing, and I enjoy each email.

Thanks to my mother and father for a wonderful childhood and for teaching me to reach for the stars, then to work my butt off to get them. I couldn't think of two better role models.

Thank you to my wife, Cristina, for all her love and support, and thanks to my two children, Joe and Catherine, who have started to read my novels, which makes me so proud.

I couldn't do this without all of you, nor would I want to.

ABOUT THE AUTHOR

Robert Dugoni is the critically acclaimed *New York Times, Wall Street Journal*, and Amazon bestselling author of the Tracy Crosswhite series, which has sold more than four million books worldwide. He is also the author of the bestselling David Sloane series; The Charles Jenkins series, including *The Eighth Sister*; the stand-alone novels *The 7th Canon, Damage Control*, and *The Extraordinary Life of Sam Hell*, for which he won an *AudioFile* Earphones Award for the narration; and the nonfiction exposé *The Cyanide Canary*, a *Washington Post* best book of the year. He is the recipient of the Nancy Pearl Book Award for fiction and the Friends of Mystery Spotted Owl award for best novel set in the Pacific Northwest. He is a two-time finalist for the International Thriller Award, the Harper Lee Prize for Legal Fiction, the Silver Falchion Award for mystery, and the Mystery Writers of America Edgar Award. His books are sold in more than twenty-five countries and have been translated into more than two dozen languages. Visit his website at www.robertdugoni.com.